Praise for Ben Bova

"Bova proves himself equal to the task of
showing how adversity can temper character in
unforeseen ways."
—*The New York Times*

"Bova gets better and better, combining
plausible science with increasingly
complex fiction."
—*Daily News* (Los Angeles)

"[Bova's] excellence at combining
hard science with believable characters
and an attention-grabbing plot makes him
one of the genre's most accessible and
entertaining storytellers."
—*Library Journal*

apes and

angels

BEN BOVA

A TOM DOHERTY ASSOCIATES BOOK
NEW YORK

This is a work of fiction. All of the characters, organizations, and events portrayed in this novel are either products of the author's imagination or are used fictitiously.

APES AND ANGELS

Copyright © 2016 by Ben Bova

A Tor Book
Published by Tom Doherty Associates
175 Fifth Avenue
New York, NY 10010

www.tor-forge.com

Tor® is a registered trademark of Macmillan Publishing Group, LLC.

ISBN 978-0-7653-7953-5

Our books may be purchased in bulk for promotional, educational, or business use. Please contact your local bookseller or the Macmillan Corporate and Premium Sales Department at 1-800-221-7945, extension 5442, or by e-mail at MacmillanSpecialMarkets@macmillan.com.

First Edition: November 2016
First Mass Market Edition: October 2017

Printed in the United States of America

0 9 8 7 6 5 4 3 2 1

To christi and Joe Hucks, with thanks
for their many kindnesses

We may prefer to think of ourselves as fallen angels, but in reality we are rising apes.

—*Desmond Morris*

apes and angels

the death wave

Humankind headed out to the stars not for conquest, nor exploration, nor even for curiosity.

Humans went to the stars in a desperate crusade to save intelligent life wherever they found it.

A wave of death was spreading through the Milky Way galaxy, an expanding sphere of lethal gamma radiation that had erupted from the galaxy's core twenty-eight thousand years ago and now was approaching Earth's vicinity at the speed of light. Every world it touched was wiped clean of all life.

Guided by the ancient intelligent machines called the Predecessors, men and women from Earth sought out those precious, rare worlds that harbored intelligent species, determined to protect them from the death wave, to save them from the doom that was hurtling toward them at the speed of light.

Star Flight

All star flights are one-way voyages.

The stars that beckon to us at night are mind-numbingly distant. Even traveling at nearly the speed of light, it takes decades, centuries to reach just the nearest of them. Then, when the star rovers come back home to Earth, more decades, centuries will have elapsed. The returning travelers will be strangers on the world of their birth.

Some humans accepted that inescapable fate. Some men and women willingly boarded the starships and journeyed into the unknown, driven by personal demons that outweighed all other consequences. Some were among humanity's best and brightest. Some were fleeing into the future willingly. The psychotechnicians who examined and tested them realized that in some cases, the difference between genius and madness was too slim to separate.

Mithra

++

++

The star was called by humans Mithra, after an ancient Persian deity of light and the upper air. In the religion of Zoroaster, Mithra became an attendant of Ahura Mazda, the god of light and goodness.

Mithra was a red dwarf star, less than a tenth of the brightness of the Sun. Some two hundred light-years from Earth, the star was accompanied by six planets, four of them bloated gas giants the size of Jupiter and larger, two others smaller, rocky worlds—like Earth.

Mithra Alpha, the planet orbiting closest to the star, was a "hot Jupiter": a gas giant world slightly larger than our own solar system's biggest planet, and orbiting so close to its star that its "year" was a mere twelve Earth days long. Covered with gaudy striped clouds, it bore a planet-wide ocean beneath the cloud deck, populated by a complex biosphere including tentacled octopus-like creatures that filled their world-girdling ocean with sounds.

Communication?

Intelligence?

The next two planets—Beta and Gamma—swung 'round their red dwarf star in forty-year-long, highly elliptical orbits that nearly intersected when they were at their closest approach to the star. Both were small, rocky, Earthlike worlds. Mithra Beta appeared to be lifeless, but Gamma, the outer of the two, bore a thin skin of atmosphere, small seas of liquid water—and life.

Intelligent life.

Preindustrial, little more than paleolithic creatures living in scattered villages, they were totally unaware that the death wave was hurtling toward them.

Mithra's three outermost worlds orbited far from the "Goldilocks" zone where water could be liquid. They were frozen iceballs; lifeless, sterile, silent, and aloof.

Like all the life-bearing planets in the Milky Way galaxy, the Mithra system was threatened by the expanding wave of intense gamma radiation that would kill everything, scrub those planets down to barren, smoking ruins.

If the star-traveling humans didn't save them.

In all the hundreds of billions of planets in the milky way, nothing was so rare as intelligence. Intelligent species seldom arose, and often destroyed themselves before they could give rise to practically immortal intelligent machines.

The ancient machine intelligences of the Predecessors recognized the threat that the death wave posed, and had striven for millennia to save as many intelligent species as they could reach. The Predecessors enlisted the help of Earth's humankind in their ongoing race against the death wave. In return, they gave the humans the shielding that would protect Earth and the rest of the solar system from inevitable catastrophe. And the knowledge to build ships to span the light-years between the stars.

Humankind rose to the challenge and sent expeditions to the worlds nearby where intelligent species lived, preindustrial civilizations that were blithely unaware of the doom rushing toward them at the speed of light.

Starship *Odysseus* was one of those missions. It was a lenticular-shaped vessel, propelled by dark energy and capable of reaching relativistic velocity, close to the speed of light.

Its crew and passengers slept the centuries that it took to reach Mithra, their bodies frozen into deepsleep and their memories downloaded into the ship's master computer, then uploaded back into their brains once they were thawed and revived.

Now they faced the task of saving a world, and the intelligent creatures who lived on it.

Odysseus's technical staff were a strangely youthful group, picked with meticulous care for their star mission. Nearly all of them were alone in the world, orphans or loners who had no families, no loved ones to keep them from leaving the Earth they knew, hardly any people they cared for or who cared for them.

They flew off to save a world from annihilation, knowing that they would never return to the world of their birth, not caring that when—if—they returned, it would be to an Earth that was more than four hundred years changed from the planet they had left.

bOOk OnE

++

++

Discoveries are often made by not following instructions, by going off the main
road, by trying the untried.

—Frank Tyger

Adrian Kosoff stood at the rail of the balcony circling the starship's main auditorium, smiling like a genial paterfamilias at the young men and women down on the main floor celebrating their arrival at Mithra's planet Gamma.

There were almost twelve hundred scientists and engineers on the expedition's technical staff: mostly young, mostly recent graduates from the best schools on Earth, all of them volunteers for this star mission, all of them aware that they had exiled themselves from their homes and everything they knew back on Earth, all of them happy to have completed the two-hundred-light-year voyage successfully. After two years of training on Earth and two hundred years sleeping away the distance to Mithra, they had arrived at last at their destination.

Kosoff was a burly figure of a man, thick torso and limbs, his bearded face square and blunt-featured, his eyes a piercing blue, his thick mop of mahogany-dark hair and bristling beard showing streaks of gray that he refused to alter with rejuvenation treatments.

"We've made the trip here to the Mithra system successfully," he said to the men and women looking up to him, his amplified voice booming godlike across the auditorium. "No human being has ever traveled so far from Earth. This night we celebrate our safe arrival. Tomorrow we begin the task of saving the intelligent creatures of planet Gamma from the death wave."

They applauded. They cheered. Then they started their celebration, mixing and swirling across the auditorium floor. Music sounded. Some couples began to dance. Others headed for the makeshift bars that had been set up along one side of the cavernous room. Laughter and the sounds of conversations filled the air.

The key leaders among the technical staff were almost all former students of Kosoff's or students of his graduates. Kosoff thought of himself as the respected—even revered—leader of this scientific expedition. Head of the family. He knew that some of the younger echelons thought of him as a beneficent dictator, even an enlightened tyrant. So be it, he told himself.

Satisfied that the celebration was well and truly launched, Kosoff turned from the railing and went to the table where the ship's captain was sitting behind a collection of bottles and glasses.

Kosoff sat across the table from Rampalji Desai, captain of *Odysseus*. Nominally, Desai was Kosoff's superior, but the two men had formed a friendly partnership: Kosoff ran the technical staff, Desai ran the starship. Conflicts between them were nonexistent, so far. Of course, like all the humans aboard *Odysseus,* they had both slept the two centuries of the voyage in cryonic suspended animation.

Desai was actually several centimeters taller than Kosoff, but so lean and quiet in demeanor that he gave the impression of being the smaller man. Dark of skin and hair, his eyes were large and liquid, nearly feminine, and his voice was almost always hushed—but when he had to, he could roar out a command that made everyone on the bridge jump to comply.

Now, leaning slightly across the bottles and glasses scattered on the round table that separated the two of them, Desai pointed to the partying throng below and said in his soft, almost lyrical voice:

"They seem to be enjoying themselves."

"Why not?" said Kosoff. "They've arrived safely, thanks to you and your crew." Nodding toward the wall screen that showed the lushly green planet they orbited, he added, "Tomorrow they begin the task of saving the natives of the planet. Tonight, it's eat, drink, and be merry."

"I think perhaps they are happy that their memory uploads were successful."

Kosoff waved a hand airily. "I'm not so sure they're celebrating the uploads. There are plenty of memories that I'd rather have done without."

Desai smiled, gleaming white teeth against his glistening dark skin. "Ah, but you have led a vigorous life. Very vigorous, from what I've heard." Gesturing at the gyrating crowd below, he went on, "They are mere children, they don't have any regrets that they want to forget."

"Not yet," said Kosoff, dead serious.

Desai merely sighed.

brad macdaniels leaned his lanky frame against the makeshift bar that had been set up on the auditorium's floor and sipped at his lime juice.

He was an impressive figure, just a fraction of a centimeter over two meters tall, slender as a laser beam, his unruly dirty-blond hair flopping across his brow, his pale green eyes watching his fellow passengers enjoying themselves.

The youngest member of the anthropology team, Brad had the reputation of being a loner, but in truth he longed to be in the midst of the festivities—he simply didn't know how to do it without making a liar of himself.

The French among the scientists called him *"deux metres"*; the others, "Beanpole" and "Skyhook" and less gentle nicknames. Brad accepted their ribbing with a slow smile and a patient shrug, but inwardly he stung from their attempts to humiliate him.

Born and raised at the Tithonium Chasma scientific base on Mars, Brad had never been to Earth until he volunteered for a star mission. He had survived the avalanche disaster that had wiped out half the base on Mars, including both his parents and his younger brother. He had cremated his family, then helped rebuild the base and gone on to win a doctorate in anthropology for himself. He had volunteered for the star mission, knowing that he would be leaving everything he had known behind him, forever.

Good riddance, he told himself.

He kept his hurts to himself; he bore a scar that he never showed, an inner wound that bled every day, every night, every minute. If they knew, he told himself, it would kill me. They would all hate me.

So he stood leaning against the bar, alone in the middle of the swirling, dancing, laughing throng.

"Hey, Skyhook, why so glum?"

It was Larry Untermeyer, a fellow anthropologist, short and a little pudgy, with a lopsided grin on his round face.

"C'mon, Brad, join the party, for Chrissakes. You look like a flickin' totem pole."

Larry gripped Brad's wrist and towed him out among the dancers. "God knows we're not gonna be partying like this for a *looong* time," Larry shouted over the din of the music and the crowd. "So enjoy yourself."

And he left Brad standing amidst the dancers. Brad could sense people eying him, a solitary beanpole poking up in the middle of the crowd. For several agonizingly long moments Brad just stood there, trying to think of what he should be doing.

Then a dark-haired, good-looking young woman glided up to him and held out both her hands. With a smile she asked, "Like to dance?"

Brad made himself smile back at her and took her hands in his. She was tiny, not even up to his shoulder. Brad recognized the game. His erstwhile buddies had talked the woman into getting Brad to dance. They thought it would be funny to see the Skyhook stumbling across the floor with a tiny partner.

Brad took her firmly in his arms and stepped out in rhythm to the blaring music. He felt a trifle awkward but, calling up the memory of his school-day dance lessons, he quickly caught the beat. Just don't step on her feet, he warned himself.

Craning her neck to look up at him, she said, "My name's Felicia Portman. Biology."

Brad saw that she was really pretty. Gray eyes, deep and sparkling. Trim figure. "I'm—"

"Brad MacDaniels, I know," Felicia said. "Anthropology."

"Right." And Brad realized that they all must know the beanpole that stuck up above everybody's head.

The song ended and she led him out of the crowd of dancers, toward the tables arranged along the side wall of the auditorium. Felicia pointed a manicured finger to a table that was already half filled.

"Some of my bio teammates," she said.

Brad followed her and folded himself into a chair beside her as she introduced the others. A robot trundled up and took their drink orders.

"Lime juice?" asked one of the other guys.

Brad nodded. "I'm sort of allergic to alcohol."

"Allergies can be fixed," said one of the others.

"It's not an allergy, really," Brad said, trying to keep his face from showing the embarrassment he felt. "Not in the medical sense."

"Ah . . . a psychological problem."

"Sort of."

Felicia changed the subject. "What's an anthropologist doing on this mission? Why do we have an anthro team, anyway?"

"Yeah. They stuck you people on board the same day we left Earth orbit. Like you were a last-minute idea."

"Besides, the creatures down on the planet aren't human. What's an anthropologist going to do with them?"

Brad answered, "We're not here to study the aliens. We're here to study you."

"Us?"

"What do you mean?"

"The people here on this ship form a compact group

isolated from other human societies," Brad explained. "It's an ideal laboratory to study the evolution of a unique society. All of the star missions have anthropology teams with them."

"I'll be damned."

"I don't know if I like being the subject of a study."

"Well, you are," said Brad, "whether you like it or not."

The looks on their faces around the table ranged from curious amusement to downright hostility.

Brad said, "We're only a small team: twelve people. I'm the juniormost."

"We'd all better be on our best behavior," Felicia said with a grin.

Several of them laughed and the tension eased away.

As the party finally wound down, Brad walked Felicia to her quarters, squeezed her hand gently as he said goodnight, then left her at her door and went along the curving corridors until he found his own compartment.

He stripped and slid into bed, the only light in the room coming from the wall screen, which showed the planet they were orbiting: green from pole to pole, except for some grayish wrinkles of mountains and a few glittering seas here and there.

Hands clasped behind his head, Brad dreaded the inevitable sleep and the inescapable dream that it brought. He recalled the poem that was never far from his consciousness:

They cannot scare me with their empty spaces
Between stars—on stars where no human race is.
I have it in me so much nearer home
To scare myself with my own desert places.

Brad saw Professor Kosoff a few paces ahead of him, striding purposefully along the corridor, a sturdy, compact bear of a man, marching as if he were leading a parade.

He caught up with the staff's director in two long-legged strides.

"Good morning, sir," said Brad.

Kosoff seemed almost startled. He looked up at Brad, frowning slightly. Then, "Ahh, MacDaniels, isn't it? Anthropology."

Implanted communicator, Brad figured. Instant link with the ship's master computer.

"Yes, sir," he answered. "I've been assigned to sit in on the planetology team's meeting this morning."

Kosoff broke into a slightly malicious grin. "Studying the tribe in its native habitat, eh?"

"That's what anthropologists do, sir."

"Fine. Fine," Kosoff said airily. "I've decided to attend their meeting myself."

For two months the scientific staff had been studying the planet and its inhabitants—remotely. Surveillance satellites had been established in orbit around both Mithra Alpha and Gamma. The satellites were loaded with sensors that measured the alien worlds' atmospheres, Alpha's all-encompassing ocean, Gamma's globe-spanning forests, and particularly the primitive villages that dotted Gamma's landscape.

The life forms in the planet-wide ocean of Mithra Alpha showed no obvious signs of intelligence, although they seemed to communicate among themselves, like the whales of Earth. *Odysseus*'s scientists concentrated their attention on Mithra Gamma.

Only the leaders of the planetology team were present for this meeting, yet there were more than two dozen men and women filing into the conference room. Brad watched them from the door as they took their seats at the long, polished conference table. They assembled themselves in what seemed like a random, unhierarchical pattern, except for the department chief, who sat himself at the head of the table, of course.

What are the relationships among these people? Brad asked himself. What's their pecking order?

He saw that Kosoff casually pulled out a chair for himself halfway down the table, next to an attractive blonde. But all eyes shifted from the department head to Kosoff as he sat down.

There was one nonhuman member of the conference: the ship's master computer. It contained all the data that had been amassed so far. The holographic displays along the walls of the room all bore the same computer-generated human face, bland-looking and inoffensive. It had been drawn by the ship's psychologists to be as attractive as possible to the multiracial staff: golden tawny skin, slightly almond cast to the eyes, high cheekbones, downy hair of sandy brown. And smiling, always smiling, so that the humans it worked with and for would find it friendly no matter what it reported.

Brad almost smiled back at it as he took a chair near the foot of the table.

The chairman—Dr. Olav Pedersen, a dour-looking lean and pale Scandinavian—called the meeting to order. Then he said, in his slightly nasal voice:

"The master computer has analyzed the orbital data

we have obtained so far, and has some very interesting—even disturbing—conclusions to share with us."

Without preamble, the synthesized face of the master computer said flatly, "This planetary system is unstable."

One of the women halfway down the table challenged, "How could an intelligent species arise on a planet that has an unstable orbit? It takes billions of years for intelligence to develop." Brad noticed that she looked at Kosoff as she spoke.

The master computer's avatar replied blandly, "The system was not always unstable. Some incident altered the orbits of the planets Beta and Gamma into unstable elliptical paths and pushed Mithra Alpha into its current star-hugging orbit. Very likely there were other planets in the system that were either ejected into interstellar space by the incident, or perhaps pushed into the star itself."

"An incident, you say," Kosoff said to the face on the wall screen. "How did it happen? And when?"

The computer's avatar replied, "Insufficient data. It is clear that something has disrupted the planets' orbits, probably slightly more than a hundred thousand Earth years ago. But what that something was is unknown at this time."

One of the younger men asked, "Will the system break up, Emcee?"

"Emcee?" Kosoff asked.

Looking slightly embarrassed, the young man said, "Master Computer: Emcee. It sort of humanizes it, a little."

Kosoff smiled at him. "Yes, I suppose it does."

Brad nodded to himself and thought, He's trying to go a step farther. The psychologists drew a human face for the computer; he's given it a name. Makes it easier to work with the machine, apparently.

Fodder for his notes and, eventually, the report he would write.

Emcee resumed, "Planet Gamma is now approaching its perihelion—"

"The closest it gets to its star," Kosoff interjected.

Unperturbed, Emcee continued, "Once it passes its perihelion it will begin its long swing away from Mithra. Conditions on the planet's surface will become colder, even frigid."

"Will the aliens be able to survive their winter?" the department chief asked.

"They apparently have, in the past."

But Kosoff said, "We'd better get our work done quickly, before conditions on the planet's surface become too difficult for us."

"That would be a wise course to take," said the master computer.

Dr. Pedersen asked, "Is it really necessary to make contact with the natives? Why can't we plant the energy screen devices in uninhabited locations around the planet and leave the aliens undisturbed?"

Kosoff shook his head vigorously. "To come two hundred light-years to a planet inhabited by intelligent aliens and not make contact with them? Unthinkable!"

A woman with thickly curled brick-red hair, sitting across the table from Kosoff, objected, "But the shock of contact could harm them. That's what the psych team believes."

"That's a risk we'll have to take," Kosoff replied, his eyes fixed on her. "We are *not* going to throw away this opportunity."

A man sitting at Pedersen's right said, "Besides, suppose we plant the energy screen generators and leave without contacting them. And they discover the equipment. And try to tinker with it. They could blow up half a continent, for god's sake."

"Not very likely," said the man next to him.

"But possible."

"We could put the generators in orbit around the planet, instead of on its surface."

"That's possible," Pedersen agreed.

Kosoff said, "Anthropologists have built up protocols about contacting isolated tribes on Earth, like the hunter-gatherers discovered back in the twentieth century."

"That was nearly two hundred years before we left Earth," Pedersen objected.

"Yes, but the protocols make sense, even today," Kosoff responded. "They found that, in some cases, contact is less harmful to a primitive society than leaving those people isolated."

"In any event," the redhead said, "contact is a very delicate matter."

"Agreed," said Kosoff. "But we *are* going to make contact."

brad sat alone in the main cafeteria, as usual,
munching on a slightly overdone soyburger.

Something disrupted this planetary system, he repeated
to himself for about the fortieth time. Planet Gamma is
heading for a deep freeze. According to Emcee the planet's
been following this orbit for at least a hundred thousand
years, so the aliens must be able to survive their long
winter.

But, based on the orbital data they had calculated, Gamma's glacial winter lasts almost forty Earth years. How
can the aliens survive that, with the primitive technology
they've shown?

Then a new thought struck him: Maybe they have only
a primitive technology because every time they get started
developing a higher one, the damned winter closes in on
them and everything freezes.

Interesting, he thought. Let's see what the biologists have
to say about that.

The biology team meeting that afternoon was superficially like the planetology meeting: same conference room,
same shuffling, seemingly random seating selection. Once
again Kosoff sat in on the meeting and, again, he chose
a chair halfway down the table, next to an attractive young
woman.

And again everyone's attention focused on Kosoff,
rather than the department head.

There was one other difference, Brad saw. Felicia

Portman was at this meeting, looking petite and altogether lovely among the other biologists. She recognized Brad down at the end of the table and smiled brightly at him. He grinned back at her.

He had seen Felicia, of course, now and then during the two months since they'd first met. But always with other people around: a casual group, usually biologists. Although they had shared a few meals together with her teammates, Brad had not asked her for a date.

Abruptly, Kosoff got up from the chair in which he'd seated himself and went around the table to take the chair next to her.

Before Brad could even think of what to do, the department's chairwoman called the meeting to order. Dr. Ursula Steiner was a handsome woman, regally tall, with splendid yellow hair coiled atop her head like a crown of gold. Do you have to be blond to be a department head? Brad wondered.

Again, Emcee began the meeting with a summary of what the remote sensors had learned of the intelligent natives of planet Gamma.

The sensors—palm-sized and disguised to resemble ordinary rocks—had been strewn near several of the villages that dotted the green fields and rolling hills of the planet. Since the natives appeared to be diurnal creatures, the "rocks" had been delivered by nearly silent helium-filled airships at night. None of the aliens seemed to have noticed them.

The three-dimensional wall display showed one of the aliens: bipedal, tall, and willowy slim. Its skin was pale, blotched with irregular blue spots. No clothing at all. No obvious sexual organs.

Its head rose above its shoulders like a bullet-shaped protuberance. No discernable mouth. Large staring eyes on the sides of the head; they moved with a persistent back-and-forth twisting of the head, apparently scanning their surroundings constantly. A vertical slit between the eyes appeared to be a nostril.

"Predators?" asked one of the biologists.

"None identified, as yet," answered Emcee's voice.

Apparently they were warm-blooded, apparently hermaphroditic. Two arms, consisting of intertwined muscular tentacles that could separate or wrap themselves together, at will. The ends of the writhing, twisting strands served much like fingers when they were brought together.

"While various noninvasive scans have produced a rough picture of the creatures' innards, further details can only be obtained by direct examination of several individuals," said the computer's synthesized face from the wall screens.

"We'll have to go down to the surface and pick up a few of them," the chairwoman said, looking at Kosoff.

"Eventually," Kosoff replied.

"They are omnivorous," Emcee reported.

"I don't see a mouth in its head."

"It has a mouth in its abdomen. Observe."

The image on the screen flickered as it jumped ahead; now it showed one of the aliens crouching near a flowering shrub at the base of a tall tree. It froze into immobility.

"Hunting behavior," said Emcee. "Note the fingerlike extremities."

The alien's arm flexed the ends of its muscular strands, which twitched like boneless fingers. In its other arm it gripped a short, pointed stick.

Faster than the humans' eyes could follow, the alien's arm flashed into the shrubbery and spitted a writhing, screeching animal the size of a small reptile. A mouth in the lower section of its torso opened wide, showing wet red tissue inside, fringed with writhing, coiling, wormlike appendages. The alien stuffed its shrieking prey inside and the mouth snapped shut, cutting off the screams of the doomed animal.

"Yuck!" said a disgusted woman across the table from Kosoff. Brad felt his own stomach turn uneasily while moans and gagging gasps filled the conference room.

Dr. Steiner rapped her knuckles on the table. "Come on, now. We're professional biologists, not children at a freak show."

"It looks pretty freakish," one of the younger men said—weakly.

They spent the next hour discussing what data the remote sensors had amassed about the natives' physiology.

"What about their social organization?" Brad heard himself ask.

Dr. Steiner looked surprised, but quickly answered, "We've concentrated on their physical structure and basic biochemistry. Studies of their social behavior are scheduled for later."

Kosoff said, "They seem to have established villages for themselves."

"Yes, built of dried mud bricks," said the chairwoman. "Like adobe."

"And they have farms on the outskirts of their villages."

Kosoff asked, "Any signs of conflict between villages?"

"None that we've detected," replied Steiner. "They seem comparatively peaceful, noncompetitive. Of course, the villages are fairly well separated. Contacts between them must be comparatively rare."

"They're hermaphroditic," said Felicia Portman. "That removes a major source of conflict."

"I suppose we'll have to go down and take a few of them up here to the ship for detailed physical examination."

Brad asked, "Do we have the means to do that without letting them know that we're here?"

Dr. Steiner scowled down the table at him. "If we want them to remain ignorant of our presence, I suppose we'll have to sacrifice any specimens we bring up here for examination."

"Can't be helped," said one of the men halfway down the table.

"But that would be murder," Felicia objected. "I mean, after all, they're intelligent creatures."

"Can't be helped," the department head echoed, looking squarely at Kosoff.

Kosoff shrugged his heavy shoulders. "This is a decision we don't have to make today. Perhaps not for several weeks."

"I agree," said Steiner. Shifting her gaze to Brad, she went on, "No need for further discussion. Meeting adjourned."

Brad saw the hostility in her face. I should keep my big mouth shut, he told himself as all the others pushed themselves up from their chairs and headed for the door. I'm an observer here, a guest. They resent my sticking my nose into their business.

But Felicia came up to him, a questioning smile on her lips.

"Are you going to join the bio team?" she asked teasingly.

Brad got up from his chair like a carpenter's ruler unfolding. Embarrassed, he muttered, "I didn't mean to interfere—"

Kosoff came up to them as the department head swept by and shot an annoyed glare at Brad.

"For an anthropologist," Kosoff said, "you don't seem to be able to sit back and observe without interfering with the subject of your study."

Brad felt his cheeks redden. "I just thought that—"

But Kosoff had already turned his attention to Felicia. "I wonder if you'd like to have dinner with me tonight, Dr. Portman?"

And he reached for her hand.

A look halfway between surprise and alarm flashed across Felicia's face.

Before she could reply to Kosoff, Brad said, "Um, I've already invited Felicia to dinner."

Looking relieved, she said to Kosoff, "Perhaps some other time, Professor."

Brad gripped her arm lightly and the two of them headed for the door, leaving Kosoff standing there. Brad could feel the heat of the older man's anger, like the glow of red-hot lava spilling from a volcano.

"Thanks," Felicia whispered to him as they reached the door.

Brad nodded. Terrific afternoon, he thought. I've made enemies of the head of the biology department and the director of the scientific staff. Great.

Yet he asked, half afraid of the answer, "You'll have dinner with me?"

Grinning, Felicia replied, "I'll have to. Otherwise the professor will know you lied about it."

Brad suddenly felt buoyant, realizing that he was going to have dinner with the best-looking biologist on the ship.

dinner

The starship *odysseus* had been designed to make life as agreeable as possible for the voyagers who would travel two hundred light-years from Earth. Each living compartment was furnished comfortably—within the constraints of budget and the psychotechnicians' estimation of the difference between comfort and extravagance.

There were three dining areas on the ship, plus a cafeteria big enough to handle roughly half the ship's complement at a sitting. Robot servers were unfailingly polite and efficient. Hydroponics farms provided fresh vegetables and fruits, biovats produced high-quality meats from cell samples that were cultured and grown continuously, and seafood was bred in the artificial stream that meandered through the ship's middle.

The most lavish of the dining rooms had been dubbed the Crystal Palace in a naming contest carried out before the ship's human travelers entered cryonic sleep.

Now, as Brad escorted Felicia into the dining room, he saw how appropriate the name was. Crystal chandeliers—donated by a consortium of European jewelers—hung from the high ceiling, and crystal candlestick holders decorated every one of the damask-covered tables. Even the stubby flat-topped robots that buzzed between the tables each bore a fresh flower in a crystal vase.

"It's all so beautiful," Felicia said as the human maitre d' led them to a table for two along the far bulkhead. She was wearing a V-necked golden blouse and a knee-length skirt of deep brown. Brad felt distinctly shabby in his usual slacks and turtleneck.

He admitted, "It's a lot fancier than any restaurant I could afford back Earthside."

As they took the chairs the robots proffered, Felicia said, "I thought you've never been to Earth."

Brad felt a pulse of alarm. *She's read my dossier!*

"Only for the final stage of our training," he replied. "In Kazakhstan."

"It must have been difficult for you," Felicia said, her face etched with concern, "with the higher gravity and all."

Brad nodded. "I had to wear an exoskeleton suit until my body adapted to a full *g*. I still get back pains now and then."

"Even though we're at half Earth-normal gravity?"

He nodded and changed the subject. "So where are you from?"

Once Felicia started talking there was no stopping her. Brad happily listened right through the appetizers and their main courses, glad that he didn't have to say anything more than the occasional "Really," as Felicia spoke warmly of her childhood in Oregon and her family.

But then her tone changed and her face grew somber. "Then my parents divorced. I was twelve. It was a blow."

"You didn't know . . . ?"

With a sad shake of her head, Felicia replied, "I thought they were happy together. They kept their quarrels from me until the very end."

"That's sad," Brad sympathized.

"It hurt," she said softly. "It still hurts. You wonder if maybe it was your fault, maybe you made them unhappy."

Brad reached across the table and took her hand in his. "It wasn't your fault. Couldn't be."

"I don't know."

"Couldn't have been your fault," Brad insisted.

Felicia tried to smile. "Strange. I've never told anybody on the ship about the divorce. It hurt too much." Her smile brightened. "But I told you. We're practically strangers and I told you."

Suddenly feeling uncomfortable, Brad tried to think of some way to change the subject. "Have you ever been married?" he blurted, as their serving robot trundled up to their table with two orders of tiramisu on its flat top.

"Almost," she said, her smile dimming again, "but it didn't work out."

Smart move, Brad chided himself. You picked a great subject to lighten the mood. He wondered if the failed romance led to Felicia's joining the star-voyaging volunteers. Or did she leave Earth because of her parents' divorce?

"And you?" she was asking. "Have you been married?"

"Almost," he echoed.

"What happened?"

"She walked out on me. I guess I wasn't enough of a party animal for her."

"On Mars?"

"Tithonium Chasma."

Felicia's tentative smile disappeared completely. "That must have hurt."

"Yeah," he said tightly.

"Your whole family died in that avalanche?"

"Father, mother, and kid brother."

"How terrible for you."

"Yeah," he repeated.

Trying to brighten up, Felicia said, "Well, that's all in the past. We're here now, and we've got an important job to do."

Brad nodded agreement. Glad to be on easier ground,

he asked, "Felicia, you're a biologist. Do you think it could be possible to bring a couple of the natives up here to the ship and then return them to their villages without their being aware of it?"

"We'd have to keep them sedated the whole time. Otherwise it would be a tremendous emotional shock to them. They wouldn't know what to make of us."

"Maybe they'd think we're gods, and they've been transported to heaven."

Shaking her head, "Where the gods open them up to see what's inside them?"

"We'd have to keep them sedated, like you said."

"I suppose so. Dr. Steiner doesn't seem to be happy with the idea, though."

"She'd rather kill them once she's through with them," Brad grumbled.

Strangely, Felicia's smile came back. "The difference between biology and anthropology," she said. "She sees her subjects as animal specimens, you see them as equivalent to humans."

"They're intelligent."

"Do they have souls?" Felicia asked, almost jokingly.

Brad answered, "If they do, Steiner won't find them on her dissecting table."

More seriously, Felicia wondered, "Do we have souls?"

"We have intelligence, that's what a soul really is: the smarts to recognize the difference between right and wrong."

"You think?"

"Yes, I do. Don't you?"

She shrugged her slim shoulders. "I'm not sure. I know it's an old, ancient concept, the soul. But maybe it's something more than intelligence, some divine spark . . ."

Brad countered, "Look, those intelligent machines that the New Earth people call their Predecessors—do you think they have souls?"

"Machines?" She seemed startled by the thought. "No, they can't have souls. They're not alive, not the way we are."

"But they have an ethical sense. They built New Earth—built an entire planet—and populated it with humanlike creatures, just like us. And why? To get us to help them reach other intelligent species that're going to be wiped out by the death wave unless we can save them."

"And here we are," Felicia said, "two hundred light-years from Earth, trying to save a world."

"A world that hosts intelligent creatures."

"Yes."

"And Steiner wouldn't blink at killing a few of them, so she can study their innards."

"It's not right, is it?"

Brad felt his guts clenching. "I didn't come all this way to commit murder."

Felicia stared at him for a long, silent moment. Then she asked, "Why did you come all this way, Brad?"

He started to answer, held himself back. At last he murmured, "To save an intelligent species from the death wave."

But he knew that wasn't the truth. Not all of the truth, at least. He had come to Mithra to save his own soul.

Dinner finished, Brad and Felicia left the crystal palace. He saw that they would have to pass a table filled with department heads, and Adrian Kosoff, who was cheerily telling a longish joke as they approached.

"Oh, oh," Brad muttered.

Felicia took his hand in hers and said, "Pay them no attention."

Kosoff hit his punchline and the whole table erupted in raucous laughter. Brad hoped that Kosoff wouldn't notice them, but he thought he saw, out of the corner of his eye, Kosoff's face abruptly turn from laughter to smoldering anger as he and Felicia passed by.

"He's sore at me," Brad said as they reached the restaurant's door.

"He's sore at *us*," Felicia corrected.

They walked hand in hand to the moving stairs, then down two levels to the area where their living quarters were, Brad feeling as if they were being watched every step of the way.

When they reached Felicia's door, she said, "I'm pretty sure that I have some lime juice in the fridge."

Brad hesitated, but only for a moment. Kosoff can see the surveillance camera footage, he knew. All the passageways are scanned constantly. But not the living quarters, they're private.

Yet he heard himself say, "It's a little late. Thanks for having dinner with me. I hope we can do it again."

Felicia seemed neither surprised nor hurt. Releasing Brad's hand, she merely said, "Sure, anytime."

Impulsively, Brad leaned down and kissed her. Felicia's lips felt warm and soft.

"Goodnight," she whispered.

Feeling awkward and stupid, Brad mumbled, "Night."

Then he turned away and started down the passageway. He heard Felicia's door slide open and, a moment later, click shut again.

And he realized he was heading the wrong way. Hoping she wouldn't see him go past, he put his head down and resolutely marched to his own quarters.

The phone woke him. Casting a bleary eye at its screen, Brad saw that it was 0645 hours, and his caller was the head of the anthropology department, not Felicia.

The black, heavy-browed face of the chief of the anthropology team filled the phone's screen. James Littlejohn was an Australian Aborigine: short, slightly potbellied, but nimble both in body and mind.

"Sleeping the day away, Bradford, my boy?"

Brad told his phone, "Audio only," then rose to a sitting position, the sheet slipping from his shoulders onto the floor.

"I'm awake, sir."

Littlejohn smiled maliciously. "A strenuous night, eh?"

"Nossir, nothing like that."

"According to Professor Kosoff you had a very romantic dinner with a lovely little biologist."

"I, uh, had dinner, yes."

"You must have impressed Kosoff. He called me at the crack of dawn."

Dawn, on the ship, was 0600 hours, when the internal lighting system went into its daytime mode.

"About me?"

"Yes. He tells me that you brought up a good point at the bio team meeting yesterday."

"I did?"

Littlejohn barely suppressed the grin that was trying to curve his thick lips. "He thinks so. Come over to my quarters and we'll have breakfast over it."

"I'll be there in half an hour, sir."

Littlejohn's eyes flicked away from the phone camera for an instant. Then he said, "Take your time, no hurry. I'll see you here in forty-five minutes."

Littlejohn seemed amused. He was always an agile sort; Brad often pictured him as a black leprechaun, grinning as he hopped across the Australian outback.

This morning, in his quarters, he appeared to be even more sprightly than usual. The chief of the anthropology department, amused beyond words at the antics of the people he was studying.

"You seem to have made quite an impression on Professor Kosoff," Littlejohn said to Brad as he gestured to the bar that separated the sitting room from his tiny kitchen.

Pulling out one of the stools at the bar, Brad replied, "I think he's sore at me."

"Really?"

Littlejohn's quarters were superficially identical to Brad's and almost everyone else's on the ship. A sitting room, bedroom, efficient little kitchen, and a lavatory. But the Aborigine had filled his sitting room with items from home: family photos, a holographic image of a kangaroo standing in the corner beside the sofa, a stuffed dingo snarling at the world, and a sagging little potted dwarf tree that looked close to death.

Littlejohn sat next to Brad, whose long legs allowed him to plant both his feet on the tiled floor. Littlejohn's feet were hooked on his stool's rung. A pair of faux omelets sat on the bar, with a red-labeled bottle between the two plates. Hot sauce, Brad figured. He decided to steer clear of the stuff.

Liberally sprinkling his omelet with the sauce, Littlejohn said, "Kosoff told me that you rattled Dr. Steiner's cage when you asked about keeping any subjects we bring up from the surface from knowing they'd been taken to the ship."

Brad swallowed a bite of omelet, then answered, "It seemed kind of callous to murder them after she's finished examining their innards."

Littlejohn nodded his heavy-browed head. "You brought an ethical question into her meeting. She didn't like that."

"I didn't mean to challenge her."

"But that's what she felt—challenged. As an anthropologist, you should have realized she'd resent your stepping onto her turf."

Nodding unhappily, Brad said, "Yes, I suppose I should have."

Littlejohn brightened. "But you impressed Kosoff. He called me first thing this morning and suggested a special assignment for you."

"Special assignment?"

His features clouding slightly, Littlejohn answered, "It might be more like an exile."

"What do you mean?"

"He wants to send you to Alpha for a while."

Feeling stupid, Brad echoed, "Alpha?"

"Yes," said Littlejohn, his face totally serious now. "Kosoff saw that you minored in languages, and wants you to try to decode the sounds that those octopus-like creatures are making. See if they have a true language. See if they're intelligent."

"How in hell am I supposed to do that? I'm not a philologist. We've got a whole team of linguists, why doesn't he tap one of them? I don't—"

"The philology team is fully occupied studying the Gammans' language."

"I'm not a philologist," Brad repeated.

"It's strictly voluntary," Littlejohn interrupted. "I made sure of that."

Almost sullenly, Brad asked, "Who else is going?"

"Only you—with the neuronal analysis equipment and as much computing power as can be packed into a shuttlecraft."

Brad got off the stool and paced across the sitting room. Think before you speak, he told himself. Don't get angry at Littlejohn; this isn't his doing.

Turning back to face the Aborigine, Brad asked, "So what did you say to Kosoff?"

"I told him I'd ask you about it. I made no commitment. This is your decision to make."

Brad went back to the breakfast bar and leaned his rump on the stool he'd been sitting on. "Kosoff wants me out of his way," he said. "He's sore because I got between him and one of the female biologists."

"So he's punishing you by sending you to Siberia."

"If I refuse, my name'll be mud."

"I'll protect you as much as I can," Littlejohn offered.

"Yeah. And then I'll be the cause of a rift between you and Kosoff. Most of the scientific staff already resents being studied by the anthropology team."

With a sigh, Littlejohn admitted, "That's one way to look at it."

"Is there another way?"

The department head's deep brown eyes were rimmed with red, Brad saw. The man looked . . . not sad, so much as resigned. He's seen his share of unfair deals, Brad realized.

"How long am I supposed to be out there, alone?"

Littlejohn shrugged. "A few months, at least."

"An exile. A leper."

"But if you actually do make something of the aliens' beeps and twitters you'll be a hero."

"The chances for that are somewhere between zero and negative numbers."

"I wouldn't say that," Littlejohn countered. "Neuronal analysis systems have translated the brain activities of chimps and dolphins on Earth into recognizable language. Even the leviathans on Jupiter."

Brad mused, "We'd have to drop scanners into the ocean, guide them to trail the octopods."

"It's possible."

"It's a million-to-one long shot."

With a meager smile, Littlejohn said, "That's better than zero or negative numbers."

Brad said, "Not by much."

"All right, I'll tell Kosoff that I won't go along with the idea. I'll refuse to allow you to go."

"And then you'll be on Kosoff's shit list. Most of the scientific staff thinks the anthropology department's a waste of time, anyway. We'll just be putting the whole department in Siberia."

Littlejohn nodded sadly. "I hate to admit it, but I think you're right."

"Damn."

"What do you want to do?" Littlejohn asked softly. "What do you want me to do?"

"How soon does Kosoff expect an answer?"

"Before the day is out."

Brad got to his feet again. "I'll be back in an hour or two."

He strode to the door, leaving his mentor behind him.

"Alone?" Felicia looked aghast. "For three months?"

"Or more," Brad said.

He had phoned her and they met in one of the starship's

observation blisters, a bubble of transparent glassteel on the ship's outer hull, where they could be alone with no cameras watching them. It was almost like being out in space itself: the stars were spread across the infinite blackness, the lushly green planet hung overhead.

Felicia hugged herself against the chill. Brad felt warm, though. The cold of space couldn't penetrate the heat of his anger.

"He can't do that to you," Felicia said. She looked fearful, though, her eyes glistening with tears.

"I'm afraid he can," Brad replied gently.

She shook her head. "It's all my fault. This is all over me, isn't it?"

"Most likely."

"What can I do?"

A vision of the opera *Tosca* flashed in Brad's mind: the soprano jamming a knife into the villain's gut.

But instead he said, "Keep away from him until I get back."

Felicia pressed her lips together and nodded. "I will, Brad," she said in a near whisper. "I will."

Then she slid her arms around his neck and they kissed.

"We have tonight," she said.

"Tonight," he agreed. Yet he knew that tonight was all they had.

That night, Brad felt the relentless stare of the surveillance camera like a laser beam boring into his chest as he approached Felicia's quarters. The cameras watched every square centimeter of the ship's passageways and public spaces. He only hoped that Kosoff wasn't searching their files for a sight of him.

He had put on his best tunic: black with silver piping. And brought a bouquet of colorful flowers which he hid behind his back as he pressed Felicia's door buzzer.

The door slid open and she stood there, in a simple golden-yellow frock. Still, she looked like a princess to him.

He stepped into her sitting room and presented her with the flowers.

"Daffodils!" Felicia gasped, delighted. "Where did you get them?"

"Uh, Larry Untermeyer grows them. It's his hobby. Says it helps to remind him of home."

Felicia headed for the tiny kitchen and pulled a plastic vase from an overhead closet. "They're lovely. It was very sweet of you, Brad."

"It was sweet of you to cook dinner," he said, stepping up to the bar that separated the sitting room from the kitchen.

"Microwaving prepackaged meals isn't exactly cooking," she said.

"It's the thought that counts."

Felicia gave him a long-lashed look, then turned her attention to arranging the daffodils in the vase.

"Reminds him of home," she said, almost wistfully. "We're a long way from home, aren't we?"

"Two hundred years," said Brad, hiking his rump onto one of the stools lining the bar.

"And another two hundred going home," Felicia said as she placed the bouquet on the kitchen's narrow table.

"What made you do it?" Brad asked. "What made you come out on this expedition?"

She pursed her lips, almost frowned. "I don't know. It sounded . . . important. My thesis advisor said I'd be able to write my own ticket when I returned home. We all will, I imagine."

"But . . . four hundred years," Brad said. "Nobody we know will still be alive by the time we get back."

Tightly, Felicia said, "That was one of the reasons I joined this mission. There are some people I don't want to see again."

Her face was dead serious. Not angry, not sorrowful, just—determined. She's got a strong will, Brad thought. And guts.

"What about your parents?" he asked.

"My father's remarried. He's not interested in me." Then, brightening, she said, "My mother's had herself frozen, with instructions to be awakened when I return to Earth."

"Wow. That takes guts."

"She's a gutsy woman."

"Like you."

Felicia stared at him, then turned to check the microwave.

Brad realized he'd been stupid. What if she asks me why I came out here? What can I tell her? Would she understand, or would she think I'm a coward, a failure?

But Felicia turned her attention to setting the table.

When Brad offered to help she cheerfully told him to stay out of her way.

"The kitchen's too small for two people to work in it," Felicia insisted.

Once they sat down at the kitchen's foldout table to eat dinner, Brad hardly paid attention to the food, or to the ice-cold white wine Felicia proffered. His attention was entirely focused on her.

"I'll call you every day," Felicia said. "I won't let you get lonely."

Thinking that a call was a lot different from actually being together, Brad said, "That'll be wonderful."

At last dinner was finished, they drank the last of the wine, and Brad sat staring across the little table at her, certain of what he wanted to do, but uncertain of how to go about doing it.

Felicia solved his problem. Without a word, she got up from the table, took his hand, and led him to the bedroom.

Hours later, as they lay sweaty and spent in bed together, Brad whispered, "I wish I didn't have to go."

"You're spending the night here, aren't you?" She sounded surprised, almost alarmed.

"I meant go to Alpha," he explained. "I want to stay here. With you."

"I'll wait for you, Brad."

"And I'll wish for you."

"It won't be that long, will it?"

"Three months, at least."

"That's not so bad."

"I'll be alone out there. In exile."

Felicia was silent for several long moments. Brad could feel her breathing as she lay against him.

At last she whispered, "We're all in exile, aren't we?"

"What do you mean?"

"Everyone aboard this ship, everyone on this mission, we've exiled ourselves from Earth, from home. For four hundred years. We'll never get back to the world that we left."

He let out a long, sighing breath. "I've got nothing to go back to."

"I volunteered for this mission."

"We all did."

"My fiancé had just dumped me," she confessed. "I felt I had nothing to keep me on Earth. That's the real reason."

"He must have been an idiot."

"No. He was ambitious, all right, but not stupid."

Brad said, "Everybody on the ship has left their home, their family, everything they ever knew."

"Why? Why would they willingly go on this one-way trip? Even when we return to Earth, hundreds of years will have passed. It won't be our home anymore. We'll be strangers there."

"The official explanation is that we've volunteered to help save intelligent aliens from the death wave."

"But that's not the real reason, is it?"

"No, it's not. Every person on this mission has a real, inner reason for exiling themselves like this."

"My reason was stupid. I wanted to get away from my ex-fiancé. A silly little girl's reason."

"You're not a silly little girl. He must have hurt you a lot."

"What was your reason?"

Brad's breath caught in his throat. Finally, he confessed, "I let my family die. I stood out there, safely, while they were crushed to death by the avalanche. I didn't even try to help them."

"It wasn't your fault."

"I didn't even try to help them," Brad repeated. "I should have at least tried."

Felicia wrapped her arms around him. "I'm glad you didn't. I'm glad you lived and you're here and we're together."

"I am too," Brad admitted. And, with some surprise, he realized it was true.

book two

Is it in these bottomless nights that you sleep, in exile . . . ?

—Arthur Rimbaud

EXiLED

Brad unbuckled himself and floated weightlessly up from the treadmill. The shuttlecraft was in orbit around planet Alpha and he was effectively in zero gravity. That meant a ruthless regimen of physical exercise to maintain his muscle tone. Otherwise he'd be a helpless cripple when he returned to *Odysseus*.

He was no stranger to hard, remorseless physical exercise. Born and raised in the gentle gravity of Mars, Brad had to work mercilessly to meet the rigors of Earth's heavier *g* load. He remembered the pain and embarrassment of those months in Kazakhstan, but finally he passed the physical tests and was certified to join the starship mission.

He ran an absorbing towel over his sweaty face, his nose twitching with distaste at his own body odor. Better put everything in the washer, he told himself, before the smell knocks me out.

Reaching a hand up to the overhead panels, he pushed himself over to the wall screen that showed the bloated, oblate planet he was orbiting. Beyond Alpha's colorful bands of clouds he could see the star Mithra, deep red, its surface mottled with seething bubbles of roiling plasma. It seemed to be glowering at him angrily.

He called out for the calendar display. He knew it by heart but still he needed to see it. Yes, he saw: I've been in this orbital Siberia for nine weeks now; three more to go.

He had all the communications and entertainment gear that could be crammed into the craft's narrow command center. Everything from holographic displays to links to *Odysseus*'s formidable library of entertainment videos. Plus, in his sleeping compartment, his personal virtual reality system that could produce nearly perfect simulations of anything from swimming among the tentacled denizens of Alpha to sexual gymnastics with a bevy of imaginary women.

But it was Felicia he ached for. If it weren't for her daily calls, he would have gone insane with loneliness weeks ago.

Now he hovered before the three-dimensional display stage, waiting for her to call his name.

"Brad?"

His heart leaped. There she was, warm, smiling, beautiful.

"Hello, Fil."

They couldn't really have conversations; the distance between them was too great. It took slightly more than three minutes for messages to get from his shuttlecraft orbiting Alpha to the starship at Gamma and then back again. Awkward. Inconvenient. Yet he treasured every moment of their being together, even so tentatively.

The starship had a faster-than-light communications link with Earth that sent messages back and forth across two hundred-some light-years within less than an hour. At the distance between Brad and Felicia the FTL system could make it seem that they were in the same room, conversing normally with no discernable time lag. But Captain Desai had refused to allow Brad to bring such equipment with him on the shuttlecraft. Too delicate. Not enough spares. Excuses, Brad knew. The wrath of Kosoff.

So he and Felicia spoke and waited, listened and waited, longed for each other's touch. And waited.

It's a good thing that she can't smell me, Brad thought. Then he wondered what perfume she might be wearing.

"Dr. Steiner has decided to send a small team down to the surface of Gamma to collect plant and animal specimens," Felicia was saying. "They're trying to determine a spot where the team is least likely to be seen by the locals."

Brad listened, but most of his attention was on Felicia's face. She was smiling pleasantly, and in the holographic image she looked close enough to touch, to fold into his arms, to feel the warmth of her body, smell the scent of her hair.

Stop it! Brad commanded himself. You'll drive yourself crazy.

At last she asked, "So what's new with you, Brad?"

It took him a moment to realize that he should reply. "You know," he began, "I'm actually making some progress on making sense out of the octopods' beeps and squeaks. I mean, the neuronal analysis system's making some progress. It's identified several sounds as meaningful words, like 'food,' 'heat,' and 'cold.' I bet if we got a couple of the real linguists here we'd be able to decipher their entire language."

And then he waited. Turning weightlessly, he called up the images that the underwater cameras had recorded: the octopus-like creatures in that vast world-spanning ocean gliding through the water, graceful as ballet dancers.

"Brad, that's wonderful!" Felicia beamed. "Have you shown your results to the linguistics team?"

"Dr. Littlejohn has. I report to him and he keeps the linguistics team's chief informed about my results."

As he waited for Felicia's reply, he seethed inwardly at the awkward system of reporting his results. Kosoff demanded the strictly hierarchical chain of command. That way I don't get any credit for anything, Brad knew. He's using me as a technician, not a researcher.

With so much time on his hands, Brad had started to study the data that the shuttlecraft's sensors were obtaining about Alpha's physical conditions. Ocean temperature profiles, cloud cover, weather patterns, migratory paths of the octopods, heat inputs from Mithra across the planet. He was amassing considerable information. When I get back I'll hand it all over to Littlejohn, Brad thought sourly, and let him parcel it out to the various departments. Keep Kosoff's red-tape factory stumbling along.

But Felicia didn't seem to understand the implications. She beamed at his progress with the octopods' primitive language. "Brad, you could make meaningful contact with another intelligent species!"

"I'd rather make meaningful contact with you," he blurted, then waited, embarrassed, fearful of how she might react.

Felicia's holographic image broke into a healthy laugh. "When you get back, Brad. When you get back."

Almost fearfully, he asked, "Um . . . Kosoff hasn't been hassling you, has he?"

And then he waited, waited for the answer he dreaded.

But Felicia shook her head and replied, "He hasn't even said hello to me. Not since you left. It's as if I don't exist anymore, as far as he's concerned."

Brad thought, He's made his point. He's shown the whole staff that anyone who gets in his way gets stomped flat.

Aloud, he merely said, "That's good."

But he thought that Felicia looked troubled, almost as if she resented Kosoff's coolness.

Hours later, as Brad was getting ready for sleep, the communications console chimed. Wearing only his pajama bottoms, Brad wriggled out of the mesh cocoon that served as his zero-gravity bed and manually activated the comm set.

It was a recorded message from Dr. Littlejohn. "Brad, Professor Kosoff is very pleased with the progress you're making. So pleased that he's thinking of extending your stay at Alpha. I told him that that's completely unacceptable. You're due to return to *Odysseus* in three weeks and he can send someone else out there to continue your work. He wasn't pleased, but he finally agreed with me."

Suddenly wide awake, Brad replied, "Thanks, Dr. Littlejohn. I appreciate your sticking your neck out for me."

And he thought, I only hope that Kosoff doesn't cut it off.

When handed a lemon, Brad told himself over and over, make lemonade.

In the solitude of his exile, Brad decided to fill the empty hours by learning as much about philology and the automated probes he had dropped into Alpha's ocean as he could.

Emcee, back on the starship, had an extensive tutoring program among its files. After several days of mind-numbing bleakness aboard the orbiting shuttlecraft, Brad had his ship's computer copy Emcee's tutorial program.

To his happy surprise, the program had a personality, a lean-faced, mild-speaking human that for some reason called itself Jonesey. It spoke with a slight accent that Brad couldn't identify, but it was always available whenever he called on it, and it was there in the shuttlecraft with him. No time lag.

Over the weeks of his exile, Jonesey explained how the neuronal analysis equipment used neutrino scans to see which parts of the octopods' brains were activated when they communicated with one another.

"And that works underwater?" Brad had asked.

With a wry smile, Jonesey replied, "The neutrinos go through the seawater as if it wasn't there. The big trick with neutrinos is to get a few of them to register on your receiving equipment."

Little by little, Brad learned how the analysis system compared the octopods' brain activity to the actions they took. How certain flurries of neural sparks were connected to activities.

"Connecting neural excitement to abstract concepts is much more difficult," Jonesey told Brad, his computer-generated face looking grave, concerned. "But with enough sampling it can be done. Tentatively, of course."

"Of course," said Brad.

The octopods didn't seem to mind the strange objects that had appeared in the ocean among them. At first they had assailed the probes with intense chattering, then approached the devices and touched them with their tentacles. Within a few days they were ignoring the alien probes that floated alongside them, and went about their business as if they didn't exist.

Brad concluded, They've decided that the probes aren't dangerous and they're not food. That's where their curiosity ends, I guess.

But as his understanding of the octopods' language grew, he learned differently.

The probes swam along with the swarm of octopods, powered by nuclear generators capable of running for years. They regularly sent bursts of audio information to the ocean's surface, where the acoustic waves were detected by minisatellites that dipped into the planet's atmosphere briefly to pick up the signals. The minisats, in turn, relayed the data they received to the shuttlecraft.

The octopods avoided those data bursts. Within the first few days they learned to move out of the way whenever the probes sent their messages toward the surface of the sea.

They learn pretty quickly, Brad realized. Probably the intense audio bursts are painful to them.

Pain makes man think, Brad recalled from somewhere in his childhood. *Thought makes man wise.*

So they say, Brad told himself. So they say.

brad's dream

Brad drifted into his sleeping compartment and stared at the mesh cocoon hanging limply against one of the bulkheads. He had put off trying to sleep for as long as he could, forcing himself to stay awake even when his eyelids grew as heavy as anvils.

He knew that if he slept he would dream. The same dream. Its details changed now and then, but it was always the same.

Now, so weary that, as he hung weightlessly in the middle of the narrow sleep compartment fighting against his body's need for sleep, he knew that his struggle was futile. Sooner or later he would fall asleep. Better to succumb in the zero-g cocoon than while trying to operate the ship's systems.

He had thought of asking the ship's doctors, back on *Odysseus,* for some medication that would block out the dream. But that would mean explaining why he was troubled and he'd end up being examined by the psychiatrists, or worse, being taken off duty entirely. And he certainly didn't want Kosoff to know about his problem.

So, wearily, warily, he peeled off his coveralls and popped them into the washer, then slid into the mesh cocoon and zipped it up to his chin.

He commanded the lights to shut down, then stared into the enveloping darkness. Totally dark, except for the unblinking red light at the base of the comm console.

Just like my room at Tithonium. Dark. Black as night. Dark as death.

The dream always began the same way. He was jarred from his sleep by a rumbling, growling sound. Like some alien beast snarling at him.

Fourteen-year-old Brad sat up in his bed. Mom and Dad were in the next room, he knew. Davie was in the bed next to his own.

The room was shaking.

And somehow Brad was outside, out in the open, wearing a pressure suit and helmet, standing on the floor of Tithonium Chasma, and it was bright daylight. The wall of the canyon rose up, a serrated sheer scarp that ran more than a thousand kilometers in either direction. Atop the rim, the Martian sky was a dull butterscotch yellow-brown.

Suddenly a streak of fire blazed across that sky. A meteor, young Brad understood. A big one. It roared terrifyingly as it disappeared over the canyon rim. And exploded.

The concussion knocked Brad off his feet. And the red, rock-strewn ground beneath him was shaking, trembling as if some invisible, gigantic, monstrous hand was shaking it. Pebbles skittered and jittered as Brad climbed shakily to his booted feet. Pressure-suited people were running away from the crumbling chasm wall. Rocks were tumbling down the scarp, some as big as houses. They fell slowly, almost leisurely, in the low Martian gravity, but still smashed whatever they hit as they struck the chasm floor.

Brad saw one of the hothouse buildings crushed as a boulder flattened it.

Mom and Dad and Davie are still inside the housing complex!

Brad stood in an agony of indecision. *What should I do? What should I do?*

"Hey, you! Don't just stand there!" one of the construction crewmen's voices screamed in Brad's helmet earphones. "Grab a tractor and pick up as many people as you can!"

I don't know how to run a tractor, Brad wanted to answer. I've never been allowed inside one. But whoever had yelled at him had run off to help others. Brad's height had fooled him: in the helmeted pressure suit Brad looked tall enough to be an adult.

He ran to an idle tractor and climbed into its cockpit. Gasping, his heart racing, Brad looked over the controls, then punched the big red button that started the engine. Looking up, he saw the whole wall of rock crumbling, falling, smashing the puny human buildings at its base.

The tractor lurched into motion. Brad tried to steer it, but didn't know how. The machine seemed to have a mind of its own. People were rushing away from the buildings, away from the killing rocks tumbling down the wall. Brad saw bodies sprawled everywhere, men and women and children who had bolted outside without sealing their pressure suits. Some of them didn't even have their helmets on. Their faces had exploded in blood.

Brad couldn't control the tractor. It plowed ahead, rolling over bodies living and dead, until it bumped to a stop against the remains of what had been the building where Brad and his family had been quartered.

Horrified, Brad looked down from his perch in the tractor and saw Mom, Dad, and Davie staring up at him. Dead and accusing. Why didn't you help us? Why did you let us die?

And Brad was struggling in his sleep cocoon, writhing inside its mesh confines, his eyes blinded with tears, his mind screaming with memories.

He tore at the cocoon's zipper and sailed out of the

cocoon, banging his shoulder painfully against the far bulkhead of the narrow compartment.

For long moments he hung there in a fetal crouch, in the darkness, slowly drifting across the chamber, gasping for air.

It hadn't happened the way his dream showed it. He had been outside, of course, fully suited up. But he had never taken a tractor. Panting, doubled over as he hung in midair, Brad muttered to himself, "There was nothing I could do. There was nothing I could do."

Yet the reality was that he survived the catastrophe without a scratch while his family was killed.

He had had another argument with his father. Over what, Brad couldn't remember. But he'd bolted from the breakfast table, grabbed his camera, run down to the air lock and pulled on a pressure suit, then gone outside— away from his father, away from the whole family. He had to get away from them.

I was outside taking pictures of the chasm wall when it happened, Brad remembered. I should have been inside having breakfast with my family. But I couldn't sit down with them. I went outside. I left them to be crushed to death while I went out to take fucking pictures.

I let them die.

I should have died with them.

Every time Brad had the dream he awoke with the same overwhelming sense of guilt. He had gone through more than a year of intense psychotherapy; he had learned to control the guilt during the day. Sometimes he actually forgot it. Almost.

Eventually, he earned a degree in anthropology from the distance-learning University of Mars. When the call went out for volunteers to participate in the star missions to save alien civilizations threatened by the death wave, Brad signed up. Atonement might be found in a flight to another star. He had nothing to lose, nothing to leave behind except his memories.

But even two hundred light-years away from Mars he had to sleep. And, sooner or later, he would dream. And the awful sense of guilt and shame would crush him the way the tumbling rocks of Tithonium Chasma had crushed his mother, father, and little brother.

conversations

"I'm going to try to talk to the octopods," Brad said to the image of Jonesey on the tutorial program's screen.

Jonesey's eyes narrowed slightly. "Do you think that's wise?"

Brad was in the shuttlecraft's tightly packed communications center, surrounded by consoles and screens. He always thought of the comm center as an all-seeing eye, searching everywhere, never sleeping. It was tight in there, especially for a gangling young man of Brad's height. He was always bumping an elbow or banging a knee against the jam-packed instruments.

Hovering weightlessly in front of the tutorial screen, Brad replied, "We've built up a mini dictionary of their terms. In another week I'll be going back to *Odysseus*. I want to bring some positive results back with me."

"Have you gotten approval from Dr. Littlejohn?"

"I haven't told him yet."

"As I understand your mission guidelines, you should get your department head's approval before attempting contact with the aliens."

Brad knew that Jonesey was right. He knows Kosoff's routine better than I do, Brad thought. And he never forgets anything.

"What do you hope to accomplish?" Jonesey asked.

"Making meaningful contact with an alien species!" Brad snapped. "Isn't that worthwhile?"

"Not if it harms the aliens."

Brad realized he was floating away from the screen when his rump hit the corner of the neural analyzer's console. Slightly flustered, he pushed himself back toward Jonesey's image.

"How can it harm them?"

Jonesey shrugged his slim shoulders. "We don't know anything about their understanding of the world they live in. It seems unlikely that they know anything about the universe outside of their ocean. Your sudden intrusion into their world could upset them, cause them harm."

Shaking his head so hard that he started drifting away from the screen again, Brad countered, "Look, they accustomed themselves to the probes we've placed among them. What's the harm in saying hello to them?"

"I'm an engineering program, not a psych system. But mission protocol specifically says that attempts to make contact with an alien species have to be approved by the highest scientific authority."

"Kosoff," Brad growled.

"Professor Kosoff is the chief of this mission. You'll have to get his permission before you try to contact the octopods."

"And if I don't?"

Jonesey shrugged again. "As you yourself have complained many times, Professor Kosoff doesn't like you. Going around him and making contact on your own isn't going to improve his attitude toward you."

Brad knew that Jonesey was right. Still . . .

"Talk to Dr. Littlejohn, at least," the image on the screen suggested.

"Yeah, maybe you're right," Brad muttered. Reluctantly.

"Make contact with them?" Littlejohn was startled by the idea.

He was sitting at his desk, in his office aboard *Odysseus,* a small compartment next to his living quarters. Brad MacDaniels's earnest—almost combative—face filled his desktop screen.

Aware of the three-minute communications lag between them, Littlejohn went on, "Actual contact with an alien species has to be okayed by Kosoff and the executive committee. You're not authorized to make that decision on your own."

But Brad was already saying, "The octopods have tolerated having our probes swimming along with them. They haven't shown the slightest reaction to our probing their brains, although I guess they don't even realize that we're beaming neutrino probes at them. It would be an incredibly important step, making meaningful contact with them."

Littlejohn shook his head sternly. "No, no, no. You can't do it. You mustn't. Not until Kosoff okays it."

And then he waited for Brad's reply. But he thought he knew what the headstrong young man would say.

At last Brad's words reached him. "All right. Ask Kosoff. But I've only got another week to stay here before I return to *Odysseus.* Get Kosoff to make up his mind quickly." As an afterthought, Brad added, "Please."

Brad's comm screen went dark. Littlejohn's scared to death, he thought. He's afraid of getting on Kosoff's bad side. As if the bastard has a good side.

Turning weightlessly toward the tutorial screen, Brad said to Jonesey's image, "I'm going to set up a communications link with the probes down there. I want to be ready the instant Kosoff gives the go-ahead."

"If he gives you the go-ahead," Jonesey cautioned.

"Not if," said Brad. "When."

* * *

"Absolutely not!"

Adrian Kosoff's dark-bearded face reminded Brad of the images of pirates he had seen in videos when he'd been a lad. Scowling, dark eyes glowering menacingly, lips pulled tightly across his teeth. All he needs is an eye patch, Brad thought.

To Kosoff's image on his comm screen Brad asked, "Is that the executive committee's decision?"

Then the three-minute wait. Brad shifted his attention to the imagery coming from the probes floating among the octopods deep in the ocean. They look so peaceful, he thought. Not a care in the world. No problems, no conflicts.

"It's *my* decision," Kosoff snapped. "I don't need the committee to tell me what the mission protocol says. One of the prime directives is to avoid making contact with the aliens until all the preparatory steps have been taken. Those directives were written by some of the best scientific minds on Earth. I'm not going to let a junior member of the anthropology group go against them."

Brad felt no surprise, no anger, not even resentment. He realized that he'd known all along what Kosoff's answer would be.

"We've already made contact with them, of a sort," he argued to the smoldering image on the comm screen. "We've placed a half-dozen probes among them. If they're truly intelligent, they must realize that those probes came from someplace."

Kosoff's response, when it came, was surprisingly moderate. "That's true. It was a risk to put the probes among them, but a risk we had to take. We can't study the beasts without them."

"They seem to have accepted them easily enough," Brad pointed out.

And again he waited. At last Kosoff answered, "That's as far as we're going, at present. Our task is to decipher their language, if the noises they make are truly a language. Once that's done, we'll decide on our next step."

Brad knew that Kosoff was right. Direct contact with an alien species was fraught with unknowns. He recalled how circumspect the alien Predecessors of New Earth had been, constructing a whole planet and populating it with humanlike creatures. They had spent centuries carefully orchestrating their contact with us.

But what harm could it do? Brad asked himself. And answered, We don't know. That's the point. We don't know and when you don't know what the consequences of an action would be, you proceed slowly, carefully. Once the damage is done you can't undo it, so you proceed along the path that has the least risk of damage.

Kosoff demanded, "Do you understand me? No contact!"

"I understand," Brad said. "No contact."

Yet while he waited for Kosoff's next message, Brad realized he had enough of the octopods' sounds in his files to study them for meaning. It's not contact, he told himself, but it's a start.

Kosoff said, "You're due to return here to *Odysseus* next week. You'd better spend your time preparing for that."

Brad nodded, and realized that his request to make contact with the octopods had wiped out any ideas Kosoff might have had about prolonging his stay at Alpha. Grinning to himself, he thought, I'm a kind of devious devil, after all.

Despite himself, Brad felt his innards coiling tensely as the shuttlecraft approached *Odysseus*.

He was sitting in the shuttle's command chair, up forward, surrounded by control panels and sensor readout displays that he ignored. His eyes were fastened on the view through the command center's broad glassteel windows: the starship, an immense island floating in space, growing so huge that it filled the windows entirely.

Odysseus was really a city in space, Brad realized. Compared to it, the shuttlecraft was a seed, a piece of flotsam, a baby returning to its womb.

"Five klicks and approaching on the line," said the unemotional voice of the flight controller from the screen in the center of the panel of consoles. It showed an oblong entry port in the smooth side of the starship, waiting for Brad's craft to glide into the hangar inside.

Brad had nothing to do but watch. His approach to *Odysseus* was completely automated. If anything went wrong, the flight controller would take command of the shuttlecraft remotely. Like my dream of the tractor, Brad thought. I don't know how to handle this craft. I don't have to know how. Everything's being done automatically.

So he sat with his hands in his lap as the entry port in the starship's hull grew bigger, wider, like a mouth ready to engulf him.

My three-month exile is finished, he told himself. Now

I go back to work as an anthropologist. Then he smiled to himself and added, Plus something more.

Brad had copied all the data that the probes had taken of the aliens swimming in Alpha's ocean. Every squeak and twitter they uttered. Every move they made. He would hand the official files over to Kosoff, of course, or whoever Kosoff designated to receive them. Probably the head of the linguistics team, Brad thought.

But he had his own copy of all that data and he intended to study it himself, with Jonesey's help. Brad was determined to make sense out of the octopods' language.

"Touchdown." The voice of the flight director jarred Brad out of his thoughts. "Velocity zero, grapplers connected. Flight is complete. Welcome home, Dr. MacDaniels."

I'm back, Brad realized. Back aboard *Odysseus*. For the first time in three months he felt gravity tugging at his arms, felt his heart thumping to pump blood through his arteries.

Now let's see if Kosoff's allowed Felicia to greet me at the air lock.

It took nearly half an hour for the flight controller's crew to seal shut the outer hatch and pump the hangar full of breathable air. Brad sat impatiently through the procedure until he heard the director's voice announce, "You are free to leave the shuttlecraft."

Brad got to his feet slowly, carefully, bending over to avoid bumping his head against the ceiling panels. He edged through the consoles toward the craft's main hatch. The ground crew was swinging the hatch open when he got to it. Ducking through the hatch, Brad saw that the big hangar chamber was empty, except for the half-dozen members of the ground crew.

"Welcome back, Dr. MacDaniels," said one of them, sticking out his hand. "Careful of the steps now."

Clasping the man's steadying hand, Brad made it down the metal ladder and onto the hangar floor. The half *g* of the ship's gravity field felt good, solid, after his months of weightlessness. Back to normal, he thought.

"Dr. Littlejohn said he's waiting for you in his office," the crewman said.

Nodding, Brad asked, "Anybody else?"

"Nope. Just the pygmy."

"He's an Aborigine," Brad snapped. "From Australia."

The crewman laughed. "Yeah, we know. We just call him a pygmy for fun."

Brad walked away from him, toward the hatch at the far side of the hangar. I wonder what they call me for fun, he asked himself.

The crewman called out, "We'll have your personal stuff delivered to your quarters. Might take a half hour or so."

"That's fine," Brad said over his shoulder. Then he added, "Thanks."

There were berths for two more shuttlecraft in the hangar, but both were empty. Probably gone down to Gamma's surface, Brad thought. Why isn't Felicia here? It's a working day, of course, but she could've taken a few minutes off to greet me.

He crossed the hangar floor alone and yanked open the hatch.

And there was Felicia standing on the other side, her smile radiant. Before Brad could utter a word she rushed into his arms and kissed him soundly.

"You're here!" he gasped.

"Where else would I be?" Felicia replied, clinging to him.

Suddenly Brad felt embarrassed. This side of the hatch was a passageway with people walking briskly past, grinning at the young couple locked in each other's arms.

"I . . . it's good to see you," Brad said, still holding her close.

"It's wonderful to see you," said Felicia.

They disengaged and she started walking along the passageway. "I've got to get back to my lab," she said. "The ground team has sent up dozens of soil and plant samples from Gamma. We're all working flat out analyzing them."

"Great," Brad said.

"Dr. Littlejohn wants to see you."

Nodding, "Yes, I know."

"We can meet for lunch."

"In the cafeteria."

"High noon?"

Brad realized he didn't know what time it was. He remembered that he was scheduled to land at the hangar at ten after ten.

"Noon," he echoed, feeling awkward, almost disoriented.

"If Littlejohn's going to keep you longer, call me."

"Right."

Raising her eyes to meet his, Felicia added, "I've taken the afternoon off."

He couldn't help grinning. "Great! That's wonderful."

"See you in the cafeteria."

"High noon," Brad said.

The next two weeks were a blur in Brad's mind. Felicia was warm and willing and seemed completely content to share her life with him. She maintained her own quarters, but spent most of her nights at Brad's place. For his part, Brad requisitioned a housekeeping robot to make sure his quarters were as sparkling clean as possible.

Littlejohn assigned Brad to interviewing individuals in the various scientific teams.

"I want to build a picture of how the demands of their scientific investigations are reshaping their social structure," the Aborigine told Brad.

"Their social structure is based on their university experience," Brad replied. "Committee hierarchies, competition to make new discoveries, that sort of thing."

"Yes," Littlejohn agreed, unconsciously swiveling his desk chair back and forth. "But they're beginning to face new situations, new problems."

Brad knew that the planetology team was striving to understand the mechanics of the Mithra system, and the cause of the disturbance that had thrown Gamma and Beta into such eccentric, elongated, unstable orbits.

The biologists, on the other hand, were happily analyzing samples of soil and living organisms—vegetable and animal—brought up from Gamma's surface by the teams they were sending down to the planet.

The teams landed furtively at spots far from any of the

aliens' villages: high in the rugged hills, deep in the thick forests. They came down at night, spent a few hours collecting specimens, then quickly returned to *Odysseus*. So far they had been successful in collecting their samples without being seen by the humanoids.

So far, Brad thought.

Sitting in front of Littlejohn's desk, Brad thought his department head looked almost like a child in his big padded swivel chair. The furniture's too big for him, Brad realized. I wonder if that makes him uncomfortable? Makes him feel like a pygmy?

Littlejohn seemed perfectly at ease, though. He was saying to Brad, "Sooner or later we're going to make contact with the aliens. It's inevitable. That's when things will get really interesting."

Brad nodded his agreement. But he didn't tell his department head that he was spending his evenings listening to the twitterings of planet Alpha's octopods, trying to make some sense of their language.

He kept his quest to himself—and Felicia.

"There!" Brad said. "See? It's the same sound. Every time they come close to one of the probes they make the same sound."

Felicia was sitting next to him on the sofa in Brad's snug little sitting room. The wall display showed a hazy view of a trio of octopods swimming alongside one of the teardrop-shaped probes he had sent into their ocean. Along the bottom of the display ran a crawling, spiky curve—an analysis of the sounds the octopods were making.

"It's the same sound," Felicia agreed, pointing at the jittering curve.

Looking down at the tablet on his lap, Brad called to the screen, "Show scene forty-seven."

The screen immediately cut to an image of two octopods swimming side by side, intertwining their tentacles with each other as they uttered a burst of chatter. The curves snaking across the bottom of the screen looked like the ones they had seen in the earlier imagery.

"Compare data curves," Brad commanded.

The image of the octopods winked out and two sets of curves filled the screen.

"They look almost identical," Felicia said.

"Overlay the curves," Brad called out.

"They *are* identical!"

"To within a few percent," said Brad.

"Could it be their phrase for greeting?" Felicia wondered.

With a nod, Brad replied, "That's their word for 'hello.' "

"You think?"

"Makes sense."

"So that gives us another word," she said.

"We've got 'hello,' 'food,' 'warm,' and 'cold,' " said Brad. "On our own. If we had access to the linguists' analyzer we could go much faster."

"Why don't you ask them about it?" Felicia suggested.

Brad hesitated. "Might cause trouble. They might resent our sticking our noses into their turf."

Felicia arched a brow at him. "You'd have to be subtle about it. Ask them how they're getting along, what progress they're making. That sort of thing."

"Get them to talk about themselves."

"That's right." Sitting up straighter and running a hand through her hair, she added, "I'll bet I could get one of them to tell me what they've accomplished."

Brad slid an arm across her shoulders. "No you don't, Delilah. You stay with me."

She grinned at him. "I could pump one of the women in their group. Women talk a lot more easily than men."

Brad shook his head. "No deal."

"Don't be stubborn, Brad."

"I'm not stubborn. I'm just protecting you."

"Me? Or yourself?" But she was smiling as she challenged him.

He got up from the sofa and extended his hand to her. "We can discuss this later."

"In bed," Felicia said, rising to his side.

Brad clasped her hand and wordlessly they headed for the bedroom.

"Brad! Wake up!"

Felicia's voice cut into his dream. He was standing out on the floor of Tithonium Chasma again as the landslide pounded the base into rubble. Standing there, helpless, stupid, *safe,* while his family died.

"Wake up!"

He opened his gummy eyes. Felicia was bending over him, shaking him. Even in the shadows of the darkened bedroom he could see that her eyes were wide, her face fearful.

Blinking, shuddering, he sputtered, "Wha . . . they're dead. Killed."

"You were moaning in your sleep again," Felicia said. "You sounded awful. In pain."

He pulled himself up to a sitting position and rubbed his eyes. "The dream again."

"The same one?"

"Pretty much." He wrapped an arm across her bare back and pulled her to him. She felt warm, safe. "Sorry I woke you."

"Are you all right?" Felicia asked.

Brad pulled in a deep, shuddering breath. "Yeah. I'm all right." Then he swallowed hard. "But they're all dead."

"It wasn't your fault," Felicia said soothingly. "There wasn't anything you could do."

"I should have been with them. I should have gone back into our quarters and tried to help them."

"Then you would have been killed, too."

"Maybe. But I should have tried."

Felicia laid her head on his bare shoulder. "No," she purred. "You're alive and you should be glad of it. I am."

Brad said nothing. He kissed her lightly, then lay back on the bed silently. But he thought, I let them die. I should have been with them. I should have done *something*. I should have died with them.

the anthropology team—all twelve of them—were sitting around the circular table in one of the starship's smaller conference rooms. It was their regular Wednesday meeting, where they exchanged notes on the work they were doing.

Sitting almost directly across the table from Littlejohn, Brad realized that Kosoff had never attended one of their meetings. He sits in on all the other department meetings, but not ours. He doesn't regard our work as real science. We're not important to the mission, as far as he's concerned.

One by one the group members reported on their work. Littlejohn listened mostly in silence. The team was building a picture of how the other scientists aboard *Odysseus* were creating—mostly unconsciously—a social structure for themselves.

"Their pecking order is pretty simple." Larry Untermeyer was reporting on his study of the technology team's engineers. "There's Kosoff at the top of the heap, of course. Then comes Kosoff's graduate students, then *their* grad students, and finally the poor slobs who come from other schools."

"No recognition of merit?" Littlejohn asked. "Accomplishment?"

Untermeyer shook his head. "None of them has accomplished anything that would impress Kosoff. Not yet."

One of the women piped up, "It's the same with the health and safety department. Kosoff and his former students are at the top of the heap."

"If you tried to draw an organization chart," Brad pointed out, "it would look like a series of concentric circles. Kosoff in the middle, his former students in the next circle, their graduates in the next, and so on."

Littlejohn made a tight little smile. "Seems to work. They're productive."

"So far," Untermeyer said before Brad could voice his own opinion.

Once they had gone completely around the table, Littlejohn nodded smilingly and said, "Good work, all of you. If we keep this up, we'll have a fine report to make back to the mission coordinators on Earth."

One of the women—blond, slim, sharp-featured—asked, "Have any of the other teams put out reports yet?"

Littlejohn shook his head. "Too soon. We could issue an interim report in a few weeks, I think."

"The rest of the people on board don't seem very happy about our work," the woman said.

Nods and murmurs of agreement went around the table.

"They think we're snooping on them."

"They don't like it."

"They don't like *us*."

Littlejohn shrugged. "That in itself is an important indicator of their attitudes, isn't it?"

"I suppose."

"But it doesn't make it any easier for us, you know."

With a smile that looked downright fierce, Littlejohn said, "We're not here to do an easy job. It's important to understand how teams of people, isolated and far from home, build their social systems."

"Important for who?" asked the man sitting next to Brad.

"Whom."

With a sour expression, the man growled, "All right, whom, for Christ's sake."

"It's important for our understanding of how human societies work," said Littlejohn. "The human race is expanding out among the stars. Human social norms are going to change; they'll have to if we're to survive and flourish out here."

"We're not going to spend the rest of our lives here," the blonde snapped.

"Perhaps not," said Littlejohn. "But others will. Humankind is enlarging its habitat again. It's something we've been doing since *Homo ergaster* started walking out of eastern Africa, nearly two million years ago. We've spread all across Earth and out through the solar system. Now we're beginning to spread among the stars. You people"—he gestured to the team sitting around the table—"have the opportunity to study how our civilization changes in its new environments."

Dead silence fell on them.

And Brad thought, He sees farther than we do. He's looking ahead generations, centuries.

Untermeyer finally wisecracked, "Here I thought we were just studying how Kosoff controls everything."

"That's part of it," Littlejohn admitted. "Maybe an important part. Will Kosoff found a dynasty among the stars?"

"More likely he'll proclaim himself a god," Brad heard himself say.

"He might at that," Littlejohn agreed with a chuckle.

As the meeting broke up, Littlejohn called, "I want to talk to you, Brad."

Brad stepped out of the line heading for the conference room door. "Yes?"

"Dr. Steiner is very happy with the work you did at Alpha."

Surprised, Brad blurted, "She is?"

"You got excellent data. And the philology team is happily building up their understanding of the octopods' language."

"It's pretty primitive," Brad said. "Barely a language by our standards."

"Yes, but they communicate," said Littlejohn. "And even the astronomy team is impressed by the temperature profile you took of Alpha's ocean. Dr. Abbott told me it's very interesting."

Brad shrugged. "The sensors worked automatically. All I did was collate the data they took." Before Littlejohn could react he added, "I had plenty of time on my hands with nothing much to do."

"I imagine you did. Well, anyway, Steiner is very pleased."

"I see Dr. Steiner almost every day," Brad said. "She's never indicated that she's pleased with me."

Littlejohn reached up and placed a hand on Brad's shoulder. "She can't tell you directly. You're still on Kosoff's blacklist."

Brad grumbled, "He's still sore at me."

"He's an alpha ape. He's got to keep you in your place if he wants to keep himself at the top of the tribe."

"I'm only a junior anthropologist," Brad said. "I'm no threat to him."

"He thinks you are."

"That's bullshit!"

Cocking his head to one side, Littlejohn said, "Yes, I agree that it is. But Kosoff knows the game and he's good at playing it. He can't smile at you, that would loosen his status a little. And he can't allow subordinates like Steiner to smile at you, either."

"But she told you that she appreciates my work."

Littlejohn nodded. "There's more than one way to skin an alpha ape, my boy."

His mind spinning with hopes and fears, Brad left the conference room and walked down the passageway with Littlejohn.

People coming up the passageway from the other direction smiled and murmured hello. Brad realized that he and the Aborigine made an odd couple: the pygmy and the beanpole.

As they approached Littlejohn's office, Brad asked, "How long am I going to stay on Kosoff's shit list?"

Littlejohn looked up at him. "Until you make some gesture of subservience, I suppose. That's the way tribal politics works, usually."

"He wants me to give up Felicia."

"I suppose he does."

"I'm not going to do it. I can't. I won't."

With a little shrug, Littlejohn said, "Every act has consequences, Brad. Every decision means alternative decisions have been discarded."

"I love her," Brad said, surprising himself. And he immediately realized, It's true. I love her. And she loves me. I think.

"Love is a very big word," said Littlejohn.

They had reached his office door. Sliding it open, Littlejohn said, "Come in, Brad. Come in."

Instead of going to his desk, Littlejohn pulled out a chair from the tiny table in the opposite corner of the compartment, and gestured for Brad to take the other chair.

As he sat, Brad said, "I'd like to work with the philologists. I'd like to help decipher the octopods' language."

"Why?"

"Why not? I spent three months out there recording the sounds they make. I'd like to be part of the team that decodes those sounds into their language."

For several long, silent moments Littlejohn stared at Brad from under his beetling brows. At last he said, "You want to make a contribution. That's good. But what about your work here on the anthropology team?"

Feeling less than comfortable, Brad replied, "That's not as important as learning the language of an alien species."

This time Littlejohn steepled his fingers before saying, "You might be running down a blind alley, you know. Those octopods are very different from us. Hugely different. The sounds they make might not be a language at all."

"I think they are."

Strangly, Littlejohn smiled at Brad. "No scientific breakthrough was ever made by a man who didn't think he was right and everybody else wrong."

"Wait a minute," said Brad. "The whales and dolphins back on Earth communicate with each other. Some whale songs can be heard halfway around the world."

"Brad, you can't call mating songs a language."

"But the whales' songs change and evolve over time. Different species of whales learn them and—"

"True enough," Littlejohn interrupted, "but you can't dignify them with the term 'language.' "

"Well, what about the leviathans on Jupiter? They communicate visually, flash pictures at each other. They've even communicated with us!"

Littlejohn leaned forward and planted his elbows on the tabletop. "Do you realize what we're up against? Do you understand the enormous challenge we face?"

"Making contact with an alien society," Brad mumbled.

"We've got to admit that we'll *never* make meaningful contact with most of the aliens we meet."

"Never?"

"Never," Littlejohn insisted. "Take those octopods on Alpha. They're so very different from us. What do we have in common? Where can we have a meeting of minds?"

"That's what we've got to find out, isn't it?"

"Look, Brad. There are probably all sorts of intelligent species scattered among the stars, but the only ones we'll have any meaningful interchange with will be those that have something in common with us. Species like those octopods are too different. The aliens on planet Gamma, they're more like us, at least superficially. We might be able to have meaningful intercourse with them, but not the octopods."

"How do we know if we don't try?" Brad insisted. "They have a language, I'm convinced of it. It may be primitive, but it's a language."

"You made a copy of the data you got at Alpha, didn't you, and you've been trying to decipher it yourself."

Brad felt a shock of surprise buffet him. "How did you know?"

Grinning, Littlejohn answered, "Because that's what I would have done, in your place."

"I've identified a few words . . . "

Littlejohn slumped back in his chair. "All right. All right. I'll talk to the head of the philology team, see if she can take you into her group."

"You will? Thanks!"

"Kosoff won't like it. He'll probably veto the move."

"Yeah," Brad said, suddenly crestfallen. "Probably he will."

"I'll talk with Kosoff, too."

"I wouldn't want you to get on his bad side," Brad said.

"All in a day's work, son."

"Thank you."

"But if I were you, I'd be more interested in the language of those people down on Gamma."

"They're more like us," Brad agreed.

Littlejohn said, "Some of the alien species we encounter will be too far below us, developmentally, to have any meaningful interchange with us. Little more than apes, really. Others will be too far beyond us. Angels, so to speak."

"So the species we can make meaningful contact with will be somewhere between apes and angels."

Littlejohn nodded. "That's where we are, climbing the evolutionary ladder. We're apes who are trying to become angels."

Brad grinned back at him. "Not a bad place to be."

"As long as we keep trying to climb," said Littlejohn.

adrian kosoff

He had been born to great privilege, the only son of a wall street broker father who had cleverly managed to make fortunes for his investors—and himself—out of the climate shifts and greenhouse floods that had brought misery and despair to half the Earth's population.

Adrian's mother was an equally driven woman, convinced that her mission in life was to use her family's considerable wealth to help alleviate the hardships of less-fortunate people. She accepted their gratitude with good grace, and always made certain that the news media were on hand to publicize her generosity.

Young Adrian got the best education that money and social prominence could produce. To his father's pride and his mother's pleasure, Adrian was an excellent student, and possessed a fine, sharply focused mind. He graduated from Harvard at the top of his class, which was no less than his happy parents—and he himself—expected.

When astronomers discovered an Earthlike planet orbiting the nearby star Sirius, Kosoff was intrigued. When the team of explorers went to New Earth—as the media had dubbed the exoplanet—and found completely humanlike creatures living there, Kosoff mentally kicked himself for not joining the expedition when he'd been invited to.

He followed the news from New Earth assiduously:

how the planet had been constructed by the Predecessors, an ancient race of intelligent machines who built New Earth specifically to attract humankind's attention; how the humanlike population of New Earth had been created from human DNA samples taken over several centuries of clandestine visits by the Predecessors to Earth; how the machines' purpose was to enlist the help of the young, vigorous Earthlings in the quest to save other intelligent races scattered among the stars from the death wave of lethal gamma radiation that was sweeping through the Milky Way galaxy.

Kosoff realized he had found his destiny. He was born to lead a star mission, to save an intelligent extraterrestrial species from the mindless, implacable forces of nature. It took him several years, but at last he won command of one of the star missions—command, and the responsibility of picking the men and women who would go with him two hundred light-years across the stars on his mission of mercy.

It would also be a mission of learning, Kosoff decided. His team would make contact with the aliens; his mission would lead the way to the enlargement of humankind's domain among the stars.

That was his destiny, Kosoff was certain. That was his purpose in life. When he returned to Earth he would be acknowledged as the leader—the archetype, the exemplar of this new phase of human history. Once he returned to Earth he would be recognized by everyone as the human race's most important scientist, a man qualified to lead all the others in humankind's interstellar expansion.

His parents would be proud of him—if they still lived after four centuries. The whole Earth would sing his praises.

He told no one of his ambition, of course. But he would allow no one to stand in the way of the future that he saw for himself.

Adrian Kosoff sat behind his desk carefully eying the chief of the anthropology team that had been added to his scientific staff.

Forced down my throat, Kosoff thought sourly. A dozen people who have no real business being here, studying us as if we were the subject of this mission. Totally unnecessary; a waste of resources. But there he is, and I have to deal with him.

James Littlejohn was an Australian Aborigine, of course: short, black, with bushy hair and heavy brows. He had an affable personality, but Kosoff wondered if the man's smiling amiability was a front to cover ambition.

He must have had to overcome a lot of resistance, Kosoff thought, to rise to where he stood now. But why have they stuck me with him?

Littlejohn was sitting in one of the comfortable cushioned chairs in front of Kosoff's desk, a tentative smile on his dark face.

"One of your people wants to join the philology department?" Kosoff asked. "Who?"

Littlejohn's smile faded. "You know him, of course. Bradford MacDaniels."

Kosoff clamped down on his emotions and made his face freeze. "Yes, I do know him."

"He's spent three months out at Alpha, and he's become intrigued with the sounds the octopods make. He'd like to try to help the linguists to decode those sounds and see if they actually are a language."

"But he's not a linguist."

"No, although he minored in linguistics at Mars University."

Mars University, Kosoff thought. A second-rate school. A sop to the people who live and work on that frozen sand trap.

Shaking his head, Kosoff said, "We can't have people jumping from one team to another just to satisfy their personal desires."

Littlejohn thought that *just to satisfy their personal desires* was an unconscious indication of Kosoff's real motivation. But he kept silent. Sometimes silence is the best tactic, he knew.

"Your anthropology team is small enough. Letting MacDaniels shift to philology will make your job more difficult, won't it?"

"Yes. Somewhat."

"And the philology team would have to train him. That would take time away from their main effort."

"He's a very determined young man," said Littlejohn.

"Yes, I know."

Clearly unhappy, Kosoff drummed his fingers on his desktop for a few silent moments. Littlejohn sat patiently, his hands folded over his belly, wondering which way the mission director would jump.

Finally, Kosoff spoke to his desktop screen. "Phone: connect me to Dr. Chang."

Littlejohn couldn't see the screen, it was angled away from him, but he heard a softly feminine voice. "Professor Kosoff, how pleasant of you to call."

"Elizabeth, I hate to bother you, but could you come to my office, please?"

"Now?"

"Right now."

"I'll be there in five minutes."

"Thank you," said Kosoff. Turning back to Littlejohn, he asked, "So how is your work proceeding?"

"It's coming along nicely," Littlejohn answered. "It always intrigues me to study the ways in which people arrange their societies. No two are exactly alike."

"What's unique about our society?"

With an easy smile, Littlejohn said, "It's small, it consists entirely of very bright, very accomplished men and women. Rather like a university faculty, cut adrift from the usual social norms."

Kosoff nodded. "That makes sense."

"We're moving away from the normal hierarchical structure of a university faculty toward something rather different."

"Different? How?"

Littlejohn pursed his lips before answering. "I believe we're moving toward a true meritocracy: a society in which power is obtained by those who demonstrate accomplishment."

Kosoff chuckled uneasily. "You mean I could be deposed as leader of this crew?"

Littlejohn shrugged. "I doubt that. You have enormous prestige and you're quite an accomplished fellow. But it might be possible that groups within our overall crew will begin to form. Rather like the barons of a medieval kingdom gaining fealty from their serfs."

"And overthrowing their king?"

"No, nothing like that."

"Then how—"

A tap at the door. It slid open to reveal Dr. Elizabeth Chang, chairwoman of the philology department, standing in the doorway.

"Elizabeth," Kosoff said heartily. "Come in, come in."

Littlejohn suppressed a smile of relief. He had told Kosoff more than he'd intended to.

Elizabeth Chang was physically small, doll-like. Her face was quite beautiful, as delicate as an orchid. She wore an unadorned knee-length tunic of rust-red, with a high mandarin collar. The two men got to their feet as she approached the desk.

"Dr. Littlejohn," she said in her smoky voice. She extended her hand to Littlejohn and smiled with her lips, but her eyes were not focused on him. It seemed to Littlejohn that she was surveying the office, trying to find out what was going on, who was doing what to whom.

Once Kosoff explained why he wanted her to join the discussion, she seemed to relax somewhat.

"An anthropologist, joining our group? That doesn't make much sense, does it." It was not a question.

Littlejohn said, "He's the man who's recorded the octopods' sounds, out at Alpha."

"Oh, him."

"He'd like to try to build up a vocabulary, to understand their language."

Chang closed her eyes, as if the idea was painful to contemplate. Opening them, she focused on Kosoff, behind his desk. "We are concentrating on the people of planet Gamma, as you know. They obviously have a language." Turning to Littlejohn, she went on, "They have sonic organs in their heads. They converse with one another using low-frequency sound pulses, beyond the range of human hearing."

"Like the elephants, back on Earth," Kosoff added.

"I know," Littlejohn replied. "I was on the committee that saved the African elephant from extinction."

With a sad smile, Chang said, "I don't see how we could spare the manpower to teach a neophyte what he'd need to know to become a useful member of our team."

"He already knows quite a bit," Littlejohn said gently. "He's not exactly a neophyte."

"But he's not a trained philologist."

Littlejohn conceded the point with a nod, thinking, Typical group-think. Brad doesn't have their credentials, so they don't want him in their group.

"We do have a couple of our junior people studying the data brought back from Alpha. But that's a backburner issue. Most of our effort has to be concentrated on the humanoids of Gamma."

"I agree," said Kosoff. "It's regrettable, but Dr. Chang is correct. We must concentrate the resources we have on the most important problem."

Littlejohn knew he was licked. Kosoff was smart enough to get this Chang woman to do the hatchet work, rather than veto Brad's application himself.

With a rueful nod, Littlejohn pushed himself up from the chair. "I understand. But Dr. MacDaniels is going to be very disappointed. He so wanted to work on the octopods' language."

"If it is a language," said Kosoff.

"Which I doubt," Chang added. Right on cue.

sitting behind the desk in his office, Littlejohn thought that Brad looked as tense as a coiled spring as he told Brad of Chang's reaction.

"So she doesn't want me on her team," Brad said, his voice low, dark.

"I'm afraid not."

"She made the decision that Kosoff wanted her to."

Littlejohn started to shrug, but halted the gesture halfway. "It was obvious," he admitted. "Interesting interplay between them. He didn't tell her what to say, but she said what he wanted her to anyway."

Sitting in front of his department head's compact little desk, Brad looked as if he were about to explode. Instead, though, he pulled in a deep breath and then said, "So I'm screwed."

"I wouldn't put it that way."

"What other way is there?"

Littlejohn leaned forward slightly. "You're still on the anthro team. Your situation hasn't changed. You can still do good work for us."

"I suppose so." Without a shred of enthusiasm.

With the beginnings of a smile, Littlejohn said, "Actually, you've given us something to work with. A conflict within the scientific staff. Perhaps a split. It could lead to interesting changes."

Brad almost smiled back. "A rebellion?"

"Maybe. Certainly we have a conflict."

"There's only one of me. That's not much of a rebellion."

"The longest journey begins with a single step."

"Off the edge of a cliff."

"Now, now, don't be so pessimistic. Actually, nothing has changed. You're still with the anthropology department, still doing good work."

"But Kosoff won't let me study the octopods' language."

"He won't let you switch to the philology department," Littlejohn prompted.

Brad's face lit up. "But I can still work on their language on my own time. He can't stop me from doing that."

"If you want to do the extra work, I don't see anything wrong with that."

"And we don't have to let Kosoff know about it."

"What's this 'we'?" Littlejohn said with a grin. "This is strictly your decision. How you spend your spare time is your own affair."

"It won't be easy."

"Will Ms. Portman help you?"

Nodding vigorously, Brad replied, "Fil's been with me so far. I don't see why she wouldn't continue."

"If I were you," Littlejohn suggested, "I'd start making friends among the linguists. All very informal, of course. Personal. Outside the normal channels."

Brad got to his feet and stuck out his hand across the desk. "Thanks, Dr. Littlejohn. Thanks a lot."

Accepting Brad's outstretched hand as he rose from his swivel chair, Littlejohn said, "All I did was listen. You made up your own mind."

With a bright grin, Brad asked, "Did I?"

"Of course you did."

But once Brad left his office, Littlejohn sank back into his chair, thinking, *You've planted the seeds of a rebel-*

lion, old man. It will be interesting to see how it develops. We might have something worthwhile to report on, sooner or later.

Felicia looked uncertain, her gray eyes apprehensive.

"Keep working on the data you brought back with you?"

Brad nodded vigorously. "Right."

"Here? In the evenings? Just the two of us?"

A little less confidently, he replied, "If you don't mind. I know it's a lot to ask."

They were in Brad's sitting room, side by side on the sofa, a pair of half-empty glasses on the coffee table in front of them.

Felicia said, "Let me get this straight. Kosoff turned down your request to join the philology team, so you want to work on the data from Alpha on your own."

"If you don't mind," Brad repeated.

"In the evenings."

He nodded wordlessly.

She sat beside him, silent, obviously turning over the situation in her mind. Brad held his breath.

At last she said, "Kosoff won't like it."

"Screw Kosoff!"

Felicia's face eased into a smile. "I'd rather not. I'm happy with you."

"You'll do it? You'll help me?"

"Of course I will, Brad."

"It's going to cut into our social life," he warned.

"You're my social life," she said.

Suddenly Brad felt a lump in his throat. "I love you, Fil."

"I love you, too."

Brad felt as if he were in zero gravity again. Weightless. In love.

The nights stretched into weeks, the weeks melted into months. Brad dutifully carried on with his anthropology work, observing the ship's various scientific departments and the people who composed them, slowly constructing an ever-growing diagram of the relationships among them.

His own relationship with Felicia grew deeper and stronger. Almost every evening they pored over the squeaks and chirps of the octopods, trying to match specific sounds with specific actions and with the areas of their brains that lighted up. Every night he thought himself the luckiest man in the universe to have her by his side.

One evening he turned from the display screen showing a school of octopods gliding through their ocean and asked her, "Whose turn is it to make dinner?"

Sitting beside him, Felicia replied with a grin, "If you have to ask, then it's your turn."

"Good," Brad said, getting to his feet. "Let's go to a restaurant."

Gesturing to the wall screen, Felicia asked, "What about our slithery friends?"

"They can wait. They'll still be here when we get back."

She got up from the sofa. "Okay. You're the boss."

Brad knew better, but he didn't say a word about it.

Later that night, in the darkened bedroom, he asked, "The night we met, out on the dance floor . . . "

"Yes?" Drowsily.

"Who put you up to dancing with me?"

"Put me . . . ? No one. I saw you in the middle of the dancers, looking kind of lost, kind of forlorn . . . "

A line from *Othello* flashed through Brad's mind:

"She loved me for the dangers I had passed;

"And I loved her that she did pity them."

He said, "And you took pity on me."

"I wouldn't call it pity."

"It was awfully kind of you."

Snuggling closer to him, she replied, "It's worked pretty well, don't you think?"

"I think it's worked out so well that we ought to get married."

"Married?" Suddenly Felicia was wide awake.

"It's an ancient custom that's pretty near universal. Every human society has a marriage ritual, symbolizing a couple's dedication to each other."

She giggled. "Stop talking like an anthropologist."

"Will you marry me, Fil?"

"We're living together. Isn't that enough?"

"No. I want to marry you. We can get Captain Desai to perform the ceremony."

"And Professor Kosoff to give away the bride," Felicia added.

It was a week later that Felicia asked, "Brad, what's wrong?"

"Wrong?"

They were sitting on the sofa again, with one of the holographic videos of the octopods on the wall screen. The dinner dishes, with the crumbs and crusts of their meal, were scattered across the coffee table in front of them.

"You've been staring at the screen for almost an hour now," she said. "What's going on inside your head?"

He didn't reply.

"Come on, Brad, I can't read your mind and your thoughts aren't written on your forehead. Something's troubling you, I can see that much. What is it? Is it me? Something I've done?"

Startled, Brad blurted, "You? Of course not!"

"Then what?"

He pointed at the screen. "Them."

"Them? What about them?"

Turning to face her, Brad said, "We've been working on their language for how long now? Three months? Four?"

"More like five."

"I think we've squeezed as much information out of the data we have as we're going to. There's not much more we can do with it."

With a careful nod, Felicia said, "We've got two dozen word phrases."

"We *think* we have two dozen phrases."

"You're not sure."

"Right," he said. "But I know how we can test our conclusions."

Felicia's expression turned from questioning to alarmed. "You're not thinking what I think you're thinking. Or are you?"

"We've got to make contact with them," Brad said. "See if our transliterations of their sounds actually mean what we think they mean."

"Contact is forbidden! You know that!"

Brad shook his head. "We've already made contact, Fil. When we dropped the probes into their ocean, that was contact. If they're intelligent, they must realize that those probes came from *somewhere*."

"They've ignored the probes."

"After determining that they're neither food nor a threat."

"You want to speak to them?"

"I want to try."

"Kosoff won't permit it."

"I know. I'll have to do it without his permission."

"He'll crucify you."

Brad smiled tightly at her. "Not if I make actual, meaningful contact with the octopods. Not if I present him with a fait accompli."

Felicia's eyes were wide with fear. "*Especially* if you present him with a fait accompli," she said.

I've got to be very careful about this, Brad told himself. Like walking on eggshells, or through a minefield.

He and Felicia entered the cafeteria. Even though the hour was late, the place was more than half filled with talking, laughing, gesticulating men and women. The huge room clattered with dishware and eating implements.

Chattering apes, Brad thought. *That's what we are. I wonder if there's a race of intelligent reptiles somewhere among the stars. I bet they'd be a lot quieter.*

Felicia broke into his thoughts. "There he is, waving to us."

Brad saw the man, a short but solidly built black, wearing a bright red tunic over grayish slacks. As he and Felicia walked through the crowded tables, she reminded him, "Gregory Nyerere, philologist."

"Who's the woman with him?" Brad asked.

"I don't know her name, but I'm pretty sure she's a linguist, too."

"Hello, Filly," Nyerere said as they got within speaking distance. He was smiling broadly, his dark face full of good cheer. But Brad noticed Felicia's wince at the nickname.

"Brad, this is Greg Nyerere," she said. "Greg, Brad MacDaniels."

"The guy who brought back all that good data from Alpha," said Nyerere, sticking out his hand. Brad took it in his: the man's grip was firm, strong. He must work out a lot, Brad thought. But his voice was a high, sweet tenor. Brad found it strangely inconsistent with his burly physique.

"Kids, meet Estela Waxman," Nyerere introduced. The young woman was plain-looking, Brad thought, her nose a trifle too large for her roundish face. She was slightly taller than Nyerere, her figure on the chubby side, skin a golden toast color. Her green eyes sparkled pleasantly, though; her smile was warm.

"Estela's a nurse," Nyerere said as they all sat down at the small table. "Sort of my personal medic, nowadays."

Felicia asked, "You need a personal nurse?"

His smile growing even wider, Nyerere explained, "We met when I pulled my back in the gym. Now Estela hangs out with me, to make sure I behave myself."

"Within limits," the woman said.

The dinner hour was long past, but the cafeteria was still offering desserts and coffee or tea. Estela volunteered to get drinks and desserts for them all, and Felicia went with her to the dispensing machines lined up along the far wall.

"You watch," Nyerere said to Brad as the two women headed for the dispensers. "By the time they get back here they'll know every detail of each other's lives. They'll do a complete data dump in less than five minutes."

Brad could only manage to say, "Really?"

"Really. Our computer geeks ought to learn how women exchange information."

Nyerere was grinning, but Brad thought he was serious.

"So, you're the bird that Kosoff banished to Alpha," Nyerere said.

With a nod, Brad said, "That's me."

"How'd you put up with it? All alone for three months. I would've gone 'round the bend."

Feeling embarrassed, Brad replied, "I talked with Felicia every day. And trying to record the octopods' chatter kept me pretty busy."

Looking unconvinced, Nyerere murmured, "Still, all alone out there."

Eager to change the subject, Brad said, "I hear you're working on the octopods' language."

"Yeah. Dr. Chang's assigned three of us to try to decipher the data you brought back. Interesting stuff."

"How's it coming along?"

Nyerere's grin dissolved slowly. "The computers are grinding through the data, finding correlations." He made a high-pitched squeak. "That means 'tasty.'" Another squeal. "That means 'Follow me.' That sort of thing."

"Then they have a language."

"Looks that way. Unless we're totally fooling ourselves."

Felicia and Estela returned with two trays laden with pastries, coffee, and tea. Brad stopped his probing and the conversation moved to more personal subjects. Soon they were gossiping about who was sleeping with whom.

And Felicia blurted, "Brad's asked me to marry him."

"Really?" Estela's face blossomed into a brilliant smile.

"Don't get any ideas," Nyerere warned her.

"Who'd want to marry you?" she taunted. "You're already in love with yourself."

They chatted on about marriage and romance until Felicia abruptly said, "Greg, you know what would be a very generous thing for you to do?"

"I'm not getting married."

Estela jabbed an elbow into his ribs. "Who'd have you? I'd have to be crazy."

Laughing, he asked Felicia, "So what would be a very generous thing for me to do?"

"Let Brad see what you've accomplished. Let him see how much of the octopods' language you've deciphered."

"It's just scraps and fragments," Nyerere said. "The only phrases we can understand represent physical actions. If they have deeper thoughts, we can't translate them because there's no action connected to them."

"But you have the brain scans," Brad pointed out.

Nyerere made a sour face. "So we see parts of their brains lighting up. So what? That doesn't tell us what it means to them."

"Suppose we gave them a stimulus. Then we could see how they react to it."

"A stimulus?"

"Like saying hello."

Nyerere's brows climbed almost to his scalp. "That's a no-no! We're not supposed to make contact."

Brad said, "But we've already made contact. We've plopped the probes into the ocean alongside them."

Brows knitting now, Nyerere countered, "That's a passive contact. Speaking to them would be an active contact. Strictly *verboten*."

Brad said, "Just one word. Just to see how they react. What harm would it do?"

Nyerere stared at him. "You're supposed to be an anthropologist. Didn't they teach you about contacting primitive tribes? How contact ruins their culture?"

"Yes, but—"

"No 'buts,' mister. Kosoff would make us walk the plank if we tried anything like that."

"Kosoff," Brad growled.

"He's in charge."

Felicia spoke up. "Then why don't you go over his head?"

"Ask the World Council? Back on Earth?"

"No," she said, shaking her head. "Ask Emcee."

"Emcee?" Brad and Nyerere asked in unison.

Hunching forward at the table, Felicia replied, "The master computer has all the mission's objectives and operating directives stored in its memory, doesn't it?"

"Plus a lot more," said Nyerere. "It's even got the data that the Predecessors' probes gathered about the whole Mithra system, ages ago."

"We could ask it when and how it's permissible to contact the octopods."

Brad felt a glow of enthusiasm brightening inside him. "And then we could show Kosoff that we're following Emcee's guidelines."

Estela asked, "Do you think Professor Kosoff would agree to that?"

"He'd have to," Felicia said. "If it's in the mission's operating directives."

Nyerere shook his head. "You're going bass-ackwards."

"Huh?"

"You don't ask Kosoff's permission. He'd never give it to you. He'd find some reason to say no."

Brad's little flame of enthusiasm flickered. "Yeah, I bet he would."

"That's why you don't ask him."

Felicia gaped at him. "You mean we contact the aliens without telling him first?"

"That's exactly what I mean."

"But that's—"

Brad interrupted. "I get it! We contact the octopods first and tell Kosoff afterward."

Smiling like a canary-fed cat, Nyerere said, "And when he blows his stack you show him that you were following Emcee's directions."

"He'd have to accept that," Felicia said. But then she added, "Wouldn't he?"

Brad grinned at her. "He would. Nothing he could do about it. The damage would have already been done. He'd have to accept that fact and go on from there."

But inwardly Brad got a vision of being pushed out an air lock by an infuriated Professor Adrian Kosoff.

The four of them trooped from the cafeteria to Brad's quarters. As Felicia pulled an assortment of bottles and glasses from the kitchen, Brad and Nyerere commandeered the sofa while Brad called up Emcee's image.

The wall display on the other side of the room lit up to show Emcee's computer-generated face: innocent, smiling blandly.

"How can I help you?" Emcee asked.

Brad said, "What are the protocols for making first contact with an alien race?"

Emcee's face grew thoughtful. "That's a very tricky matter, Brad."

"I know. We'd like to understand the protocol as thoroughly as possible."

"The first criterion," said Emcee, "is the possibility of harm to the aliens."

And on and on, far into the night and the next morning.

The digital clock readout in the bottom right corner of the wall screen said 02:24. Estela was snoring lightly, stretched out on the recliner. Felicia sat between Brad and Nyerere on the sofa. Brad thought she was staring hard enough at the display to bore a hole through Emcee's bland, maddeningly smiling image.

Nyerere yawned and stretched. "Face it, man: there's no way around Kosoff."

"There's got to be."

"So where is it? We've been going through the operational procedures for more'n three hours now. Every road leads to Kosoff. You can't try to make contact with an alien species unless you get permission from Kosoff and the executive committee." Looking up at the wall screen, Nyerere asked, "Isn't that right, Emcee?"

"That is correct," said the master computer's avatar.

Felicia pushed herself up from the sofa. "I'm wiped out. I'm going to sleep." She headed wearily toward the bedroom.

Brad tried to tell himself he was wide awake, but his eyes felt heavy, gritty.

Nyerere got up and went to the sleeping Estela. Touching her arm lightly, he said softly, "C'mon, kiddo. Time to go home."

Estela stirred, blinked at him. "I dozed off," she muttered.

Nyerere helped her to her feet, then turned to Brad.

"It's been an interesting evening." With a cheerless grin he added, "And night. And morning."

Brad walked them to the door. "Thanks, Greg."

"Wish we could've found something," Nyerere said. "Would've been fun to twist Kosoff's tail a little."

"Yeah. Fun."

"G'night."

"Night."

Brad slid the door shut, then started for the bedroom, hoping he was too tired to dream.

Felicia was already in bed, her clothes strewn across the floor. Brad undressed and slid in beside her, then—instead of calling out to the light control and waking her—he twisted around and touched the switch on the wall that turned off the lights.

He stared up into the darkness, trying to relax. No dreams, he told himself. Just let me sleep without dreams. And he wondered who he was talking to.

The dream, when it came, was different. Brad was out on the floor of Tithonium Chasma, same as always, but this time the canyon wall wasn't collapsing. This time there were huge octopus-like creatures swimming through the thin Martian air, just as if they were in their ocean.

How can they swim through the air? Brad wondered.

The octopods glided on by him, their tentacles waving gently, their eyes turning to focus on Brad as they passed.

And Brad realized he wasn't wearing a pressure suit. He was standing outdoors on Mars in nothing more than a tunic and slacks.

No one else was there. Only Brad and the train of octopods gliding past.

"Aren't you going to say hello?" one of the creatures asked. Its voice was low and melodious. It reminded Brad of his mother's voice.

"Hello," he said uncertainly.

"It's good to talk to you, at last," said the octopod. "We've been waiting for you to say something, you know."

"I've wanted to talk to you," Brad responded.

"No!" thundered a heavy voice, filled with anger. "I won't permit it!"

And the sheer rock wall of the canyon began to shake, to reverberate as the voice howled with wordless fury. The octopods disappeared as boulders tumbled from the top of the chasm wall, falling slowly, inexorably onto the flimsy buildings of the human base on the canyon floor.

Brad stood riveted, watching in horror as the rocks smashed into the buildings. The canyon floor was strewn with dead bodies.

The voice roared, "Look what you've done! You've killed them! You've killed them all!"

And Brad was sitting up in bed, soaked with cold sweat. Felicia called out for the lights, then turned to him, her face drawn, troubled. She wrapped her arms around Brad.

"The dream again?"

It took three tries before he could answer. "Yes . . . no, not exactly the same."

"It's all right, dear. It's only a dream. You're safe. I'm here with you."

"Yes. I know." But he was trembling like a leaf in a windstorm.

And he realized that one of the bodies he'd seen on the canyon floor was Felicia's, her face bloody, her body broken. And, beside her, his own.

Inwardly, Brad marveled at how calm he felt. Maybe just a little nervous, but considering the firepower arrayed against him in Professor Kosoff's office, he faced them with unwavering determination.

I'm right and they're wrong, he told himself. I'm right and they're wrong.

Yes, a voice in his head answered. That's what they'll carve on your tombstone.

Sitting behind his desk, Kosoff looked nettled, irritated. Dr. Chang sat at Brad's right, in front of the desk, cool and expressionless, the perfect inscrutable oriental.

The chair on Brad's left was empty. Dr. Littlejohn had promised to join this meeting, but he hadn't shown up yet.

Kosoff broke the tense silence. "I don't have all day to wait for Littlejohn. You asked for this meeting, MacDaniels. What's it all about?"

Has Littlejohn bailed out on me? Brad wondered.

"Dr. Chang and I have better things to do than to wait for your department chief," Kosoff growled. "Either fish or cut bait."

Brad blinked at the ancient catchphrase. But he knew he either had to start talking or Kosoff would end the meeting before it began.

"It's about the octopods on planet Alpha," he started.

"I assumed as much," said Kosoff.

"I want to test the data we've amassed about their language."

"If it is a language," Chang cautioned.

"That's what we've got to find out," Brad said.

Kosoff fixed Brad with a stern gaze. "And just how do you propose—"

The office door slid open and Littlejohn stepped in, looking somewhere between harassed and apologetic.

"I'm sorry to be late," he said, hurrying to the empty chair beside Brad. "One of my people got into an altercation with one of the crew members."

"An altercation?" Kosoff asked.

Chang asked, "You mean a fight?"

Pulling a tissue from his pocket and mopping his forehead, Littlejohn answered, "Not a fight. No physical violence. But their voices were loud enough to hear for a kilometer or two, in every direction."

"What were they arguing about?" Kosoff asked.

"Oh, my man was doing a routine questionnaire about the man's duties, and he took offense, thought he was being accused of loafing on duty."

"That's strange," Chang murmured.

And Brad found himself wondering if Kosoff set up the confrontation just to keep Littlejohn from getting to this meeting. You're getting paranoid, he told himself. But the disappointment on Kosoff's face told him that he might be right.

"Very well," Kosoff said. "We're all here." Turning to Brad, he asked, "And just how do you intend to test the data about the octopods' noises?"

"We say hello to them, in their own language."

Chang's eyes widened.

Kosoff's face froze for an instant, then he snapped, "Absolutely not!"

"That would be a contact," said Chang.

Littlejohn pointed out, "But we've already contacted them, haven't we? We've sent the probes to study them."

"That's not contact," Kosoff argued.

Brad said, "Emcee says it is."

"The master computer?"

"Ask him."

Clearly unhappy, Kosoff nevertheless called to the wall screen, "Master computer, please."

Emcee's placidly smiling face took form on the screen. "How may I help you?"

Before Brad could speak, Kosoff asked, "Do the probes we inserted among the octopods on Alpha constitute a contact between our two species?"

"In the strictest sense of the word, yes, we have made a form of contact with the alien species."

Chang said, "But the probes have been completely passive." Then, realizing that that was not entirely true, she added, "Except for the neutrino scans, of course. And I don't see how those animals could detect neutrino scans."

Emcee replied, "The octopods have given no indication of being aware of the scans. But they were certainly curious about the probes when we first inserted them among them."

"That doesn't constitute contact," Kosoff said firmly.

"I'm afraid that it does," Emcee contradicted. "Mission guidelines define various levels of contact. Passive contact, such as the probes represent, is contact nonetheless. If the octopods are intelligent, they must realize that those probes are foreign objects."

"They talked to them," Brad said.

"When they first encountered them," said Kosoff. "They've ignored them ever since, except to avoid their communications bursts when they send data to us."

Littlejohn suggested, "Perhaps they've accepted them as visitors."

"Nonsense," Kosoff retorted.

"I know how we can test whether they're intelligent or not," said Brad. Before anyone could interrupt him, he went on, "We say hello to them. Use the probes to broadcast the sound cluster we've identified as their phrase for greeting."

Chang said, "We don't know for certain that it's their phrase for greeting. It could be a million other things."

"But we could find out," Brad insisted, "by trying to talk to them."

Shaking her head almost violently, Chang said, "We've got to study them for a much longer time. Build up a vocabulary, correlate the sounds they make with their actions, their brain activity."

"We've been doing that for six months now," Brad said. "How much do you need before you test the data you've collected?"

Littlejohn said, "Dr. Chang, I understand that you've only put three of your people into studying the octopods' language."

"That's all the manpower I can spare," Chang replied, almost defensively. "Most of our effort is dedicated to the bipeds on planet Gamma."

"So it could take years before you're ready to speak to the octopods."

Surprisingly, Kosoff said, "We don't have years."

They all turned squarely toward him.

Looking unhappy, troubled, Kosoff said, "This mission is supposed to study the Mithra system for five years, then return to Earth. We've already spent more than six months here."

"We're making excellent progress on the Gamma aliens," Chang said.

"Yes, but we don't really know yet whether the octopods are intelligent, do we?" said Brad.

"What difference?" Chang replied. "We can drop the shielding generators into their ocean and protect them from the death wave. Later expeditions can determine if they're intelligent."

"No," said Kosoff. "It's our mission to make that determination. I think the impetuous Dr. MacDaniels is right. We need to test whether or not we really can converse with those creatures."

surprised at Kosoff's sudden change of attitude, Brad blurted, "You agree?"

With a grim smile, Kosoff replied, "I'm not the ogre that you think I am."

"I never . . . "

Chang interrupted, "I protest. We don't have enough hard evidence that the octopods actually have a language."

Waving one hand in the air, Kosoff said, "MacDaniels' idea of trying to speak to them has some merit. We can determine very quickly whether they actually have a language or if they're merely making hoots and whistles, like chimpanzees."

"The chimps have language," Chang said. "It's primitive, but it is a working language."

Kosoff asked Emcee's image, "What possible damage could be caused by speaking to them?"

"We have insufficient data for a firm answer," the computer's avatar replied. "At worst, it might shatter their worldview, cause psychological damage such as that caused by the Spanish conquistadors' sudden appearance among the Aztecs and Incas of the Americas."

With an impatient humph, Kosoff said, "We're not going to be looting their temples for gold or carrying off their women, for god's sake."

Littlejohn spoke up. "They accepted the probes easily

enough. Perhaps they'd welcome an attempt to converse."

"Or perhaps they'll be terrified," Chang countered.

"I'm going to convene the executive committee and put it to them," said Kosoff. "If they agree, we'll try to speak to the octopods."

"Not the World Council, back on Earth?" Chang asked, her voice hollow with awe. "The World Council has the ultimate authority—"

"No," Kosoff said firmly. "This is *our* responsibility."

Brad realized he was nodding vigorously. "We'll put our data to the test."

Littlejohn said softly, "Every experiment is a step into the unknown."

"A risk," said Chang, clearly unhappy.

"A risk I'm willing to take," Kosoff said.

As he and Littlejohn strode down the passageway from Kosoff's office, Brad felt almost like dancing.

"He changed his mind!" Brad marveled. "He accepted my idea."

"Yes," said Littlejohn. "He accepted *your* idea. If anything goes wrong, it will be on your head."

Smiling down on the diminutive Aborigine, Brad said, "What could go wrong?"

"That's what your General Custer said when he ordered the Seventh Cavalry to attack at the Little Bighorn."

Brad laughed.

Very seriously, Littlejohn explained, "Kosoff has performed a neat little bit of mental jujitsu on you, Brad. If this attempt at contact works well, he'll take the credit for it. As far as the World Council back on Earth is concerned, it will be Adrian Kosoff who made the first meaningful contact with an alien race, not you."

"And if it doesn't work out?"

"It will be on your head. You insisted on the experiment. You'll be responsible, if it fails."

COntact

The entire scientific staff seemed to learn of the decision within a microsecond. An attempt to contact an alien species. The first time it's ever been tried. History in the making.

Suddenly Brad was an important person. The beanpole had convinced Kosoff to make the attempt. Skyhook had battled the linguistics department chairman and won.

That evening Felicia asked, "What do you want to do about dinner?"

Staring intently at the sitting room's wall screen, covered with lists of protocol requirements, Brad answered absently, "Whatever."

"I think it's best to eat here," Felicia said.

"Yeah."

"You've become an overnight sensation, you know."

"Uh-huh."

Felicia smiled patiently and headed for the kitchen, knowing that Brad was totally immersed in the coming attempt to contact the octopods. She thought that she should be just as excited as he was, but instead she felt nothing but apprehension. No, she realized: what she felt was dread.

Brad sat tense as a drawn bowstring in front of the set of display screens. The command post for the contact attempt had been set up in one of the ship's smaller conference rooms, just off the communications center. One wall screen had been digitally divided into half a dozen displays.

Each display showed different views of the same group of twenty-two octopods swimming leisurely in Alpha's planet-wide sea, with half a dozen of the expedition's probes cruising on either flank of their formation.

It's their world, Brad said to himself. They've lived in this sea for god knows how many millennia. And now we've invaded their world. He realized that, in a sense, Kosoff and the mission protocol rules had been right. We're going to change their world forever.

Elizabeth Chang looked cool and unruffled as she took her chair at Brad's right. But Brad noticed that she was rubbing her right hand along her thigh. Nervous? Why not. The head of the communications team, a large roundish Hispanic with a thick drooping moustache, sat at Brad's left. He seemed more concerned with the count-down clock ticking away at the left of the screens than anything else.

"Remember," he said to Brad in a low, rumbling voice, "there's a three-minute lag in two-way communications between here and there. Any action you want to take will require one point six minutes to reach the probes."

Nodding, Brad muttered, "*Yo comprendo.*"

"Santa Maria," muttered the comm chief.

Only half a dozen other people had been allowed into the command post. Still the little room felt crowded, hot, stuffy. Kosoff sat in the next row, behind Brad and Chang. Captain Desai sat next to him. Littlejohn had been placed behind Kosoff. Brad had insisted that Felicia be allowed in; they had placed her in the back row.

"Five seconds," the comm chief muttered. "Four . . . three . . . "

Brad could *feel* his pulse throbbing in his ears.

" . . . two . . . one . . . "

"Hello," the central screen's synthesized voice said. In

the upper right corner of the set of displays, a burst of chittering sound screeched in the octopods' language. The screen showed a spiked curve.

Nothing changed.

"Give it three minutes to get their response back here," said the comm chief.

Brad sat there, staring at the central screen, counting his thundering pulse beats. The command post was absolutely quiet. No one stirred. Brad felt perspiration beading his upper lip.

Suddenly the screens erupted in chatter. "Hello!" the central screen announced, translating the octopods' clicks and squeaks into standard English. "Hello . . . " Undecipherable twitters and chirps. "Deep . . . [more chatter] no food . . . "

"They're talking!"

More beeps and squeals. The octopods clustered around each of the probes, twittering and waving their tentacles vigorously.

Chang said excitedly, "I think they're asking the probes to hunt with them!"

Brad pressed the key that sent the "hello" signal again.

"Is all this chatter being recorded?" someone asked. It sounded like Kosoff, but Brad was too fascinated with the views on the screens to turn and check.

"Automatically," said the communications chief.

"We've done it!" Littlejohn's voice, triumphant. "We've made contact with an intelligent alien species!"

A hand clasped Brad's shoulder. Turning, he saw it was Kosoff. "Congratulations, son. You've made history today."

Before Brad could reply, Kosoff turned to the comm chief. "I've got to report this back to Earth. Please set up an FTL link for me."

And the octopods chattered on, seemingly just as excited as the humans.

Where do we go from here?

"This changes everything," said Elizabeth Chang.

She was standing in Kosoff's sitting room, with Brad, Felicia, and a dozen others—including the burly comm chief—quaffing champagne from Kosoff's private supply.

A victory party. A celebration.

Kosoff's quarters were larger than the normal accommodations for less prestigious personnel. The sitting room was absolutely spacious, and Brad presumed there was more than just a bedroom down the hallway that led to the kitchen/dining area.

As Littlejohn had predicted, Kosoff himself was receiving most of the congratulations from Captain Desai and the members of the scientific staff who were present.

Brad didn't care. He had been proven right. The octopods were chattering away with the probes in Alpha's ocean. Contact, even if most of their chatter was incomprehensible.

Kosoff himself stood in one corner of the warmly carpeted room, champagne flute in hand, a broad smile on his bearded pirate's face. Chang was beside him, Desai on his other side. Most of the people were focused on him.

Brad and Felicia stood across the room, by the wall screen that showed the octopods swimming alongside the probes, still chattering. The aliens looked almost playful to Brad, swimming around the probes, touching them lightly with their tentacles, chirping away at them.

He tried to imagine what was going through their minds. Here they've had these foreign objects plowing through the ocean alongside them for months, silent, totally passive. Then all at once they say hello.

The octopods shower them with greetings. Questions too, most likely. And the probes answer with the few words they know. To the octopods, the probes must seem like retarded children or mental defectives. Hardly the most flattering way to make contact.

"Where do we go from here?" Brad asked Felicia.

She was beaming. "Don't be such a worrywart, Brad. Enjoy your success. You can get back to work tomorrow."

He nodded, but said, "And do what?"

As if he heard Brad, Kosoff said, loudly enough for his deep voice to carry across the crowded room, "Now we have to throw every resource we have into translating the octopods' language. We have an alien species to understand, to learn about, to join with."

Chang nodded reluctantly. "But we don't have the resources—"

Kosoff cut her off. "Elizabeth, I want you to turn your entire staff to studying the octopods' language. We've got to follow up this breakthrough!"

"But the bipeds on Gamma," she objected, almost whining.

Kosoff blinked at her. "We'll continue studying them, of course. It should be easier to make meaningful contact with them, certainly."

"I don't have the manpower to do both at the same time."

"Then we'll have to draft more people to do the work. Raid the other departments."

"Really?"

"Really," said Kosoff. Glancing around the room, his eyes lit on Brad. His smile turning slightly crafty, Kosoff called, "Brad! Come over here, will you?"

Brad put his glass of lime juice down on the coffee table, then took Felicia's hand and walked through the crowd.

Kosoff reached up to put a hand on Brad's shoulder. "How would you like to study the bipeds on Gamma?"

Feeling wary, Brad temporized, "I'm an anthropologist, sir."

"That might be just what we need." Beckoning to Littlejohn, standing in the crowd, Kosoff said, "James, why don't we put the entire anthropology team to studying the bipeds? They're rather humanoid, after all."

Looking somewhere between surprised and suspicious, Littlejohn made his way through the crowd toward Kosoff. The room went absolutely silent. Brad could feel icicles suddenly dangling from the ceiling.

"Well?" Kosoff asked the Aborigine. "Wouldn't your team like to focus their attention on the Gamma bipeds?"

Littlejohn pursed his lips thoughtfully, then said, "We'd have to suspend our existing studies. I don't have the manpower for both."

With a laugh, Kosoff answered, "I don't think anyone of the scientific staff would mind if you suspended your studies of them. Most of us don't really like being your guinea pigs."

Littlejohn forced a smile. "Perhaps we should discuss this tomorrow."

"You're entirely right. Forgive me. I forgot that this is supposed to be a party, not a planning session."

Brad could feel the tension in the room ease a notch.

On an impulse he turned to Desai. "Captain, Felicia and I want to get married. Could you perform the ceremony for us?"

Desai blinked his dark, long-lashed eyes, glanced questioningly at Kosoff, then turned back to Brad. "I have never performed a marriage ceremony. It is very rare, you know."

"But you could do it, couldn't you?" Brad pushed. "It's within your authority as captain of this ship, isn't it?"

"Yes, I believe so."

"We want to be married," Brad repeated.

Focusing on Felicia, Desai asked, "You too?"

"Me too," she replied softly.

Kosoff broke into a big grin and said, "I'll give away the bride."

Felicia and Brad burst into laughter.

And Kosoff's face burned deep red.

Felicia rose early, kissed a groggy Brad lightly, then dressed and left for her own quarters. She spent the morning with nearly a dozen other young women, dressing and gossiping and making ready for the wedding ceremony.

In the week that had passed since the contact with the octopods, Brad realized that he didn't have any really close friends. He'd always been something of a loner, and outside of his fellow anthropologists, he barely knew any of the other men among the scientific staff.

Brad had made a point of seeing Kosoff privately to explain why he and Felicia had laughed when Kosoff offered to give the bride away. After a painful hour Kosoff seemed mollified, but only minimally.

"I know you think I exiled you to Alpha as punishment for snatching Felicia away from me," the director had said. Grinning ruefully, he admitted, "Well, maybe I did. But you turned your exile into a triumph, and I'm proud of you."

"Really?" Brad blurted.

"Really," said Kosoff. "You have the mind of a fine scientist, young man. And what's more, you have the stubbornness of an Arkansas mule. You'll go far, I'm sure."

Brad felt his cheeks flush.

Littlejohn was warier. In his cramped little office, he made a wry face when Brad told him of Kosoff's praise.

"Beware of Greeks bearing gifts, son. Kosoff's report

back to Earth about contacting the octopods didn't mention your name. Not once."

"I don't care," said Brad.

"But you should. It's important to get the credit, when you've earned it. That's how reputations are made in science. I think it was Faraday who said, 'Physics is to make experiments *and to publish them*.' You've got to make your work known, and your name known, as well."

Brad accepted the advice with a nod. Yet inwardly he wondered how he could get his own name known when Kosoff controlled the links back to Earth.

Now it was his wedding day, and Larry Untermeyer had come over to Brad's quarters to help him get ready.

Larry sat on the edge of the unmade bed watching Brad pulling on the dark blue suit that had been made for him by one of the ship's 3-D printers.

"Fits pretty good," Larry said.

Looking doubtfully into the bedroom's full-length mirror, Brad complained, "Feels kind of stiff, like it's made of plastic instead of cloth."

Untermeyer laughed. "That's because it is, mostly. Besides, I bet you haven't worn anything except jeans and tunics since grad school."

Brad shrugged.

With a sardonic grin on his round face, Larry went on, "Well, you look like a bridegroom, all dressed up for his last day of freedom."

"First time I've worn pants with a crease in them since god knows when," Brad admitted.

Untermeyer sighed. "Just be glad the printer got the length right for those giraffe legs of yours."

"Nobody'll be looking at me, anyway," Brad said, reaching for the suit's golden cravat. "All eyes'll be on Fil."

His grin stretching, Larry agreed. "She's a lot better to look at than you are."

Just like Kosoff, Brad realized. He gets the credit for what I did. No, he corrected himself: he *takes* the credit for what I did.

As Brad entered the ship's auditorium, he was staggered by the size of the expectantly buzzing crowd. The big space was almost filled. Just about the entire scientific staff had come to see the wedding, and a good deal of the ship's crew, as well.

Felicia showed up in a sleeveless white dress that Brad had never seen before, holding a bouquet of red roses plucked from the hydroponics farm. Three other women accompanied her, smartly dressed, all looking very serious. But Felicia broke into a gleaming smile the instant she saw Brad standing with Untermeyer alongside Captain Desai, who had donned an actual uniform of gold with blue trim for the occasion.

The traditional wedding march, played by an ancient synthesizer, started to drone through the ceiling loudspeakers. Kosoff—wearing a sumptuous plush maroon jacket and dark trousers—took Felicia's arm and slowly walked her up the aisle through the crowd toward Brad, Untermeyer, and Desai. The captain was smiling graciously, Untermeyer grinning, Brad totally serious.

Kosoff released her arm and Brad took it in his. Desai's face went solemn as he read off the marriage ritual from a computer printout. Brad could barely hear his voice, he spoke so softly.

At last he said, louder, "I pronounce you husband and wife."

Brad stood unmoving for an awkward moment.

Desai broke into a toothy smile and said even louder, "You may kiss the bride."

Brad took Felicia in his arms, her face radiating happiness. They kissed, and the crowd erupted into cheers and applause. Then Felicia bussed Untermeyer, but Ko-soff clasped her close and kissed her solidly. Brad clenched his teeth.

Abruptly, the crowd surged toward them, and Brad saw that a pair of makeshift bars had been set up along opposite ends of the auditorium.

The party lasted well into the night. Everyone wanted to congratulate the happy couple, although all Brad wanted was to get back to their quarters and relax.

When they finally managed to get to Brad's compart-ment, he saw that someone had put on their coffee table a sizeable ice bucket containing a glistening bottle of champagne.

Feeling totally sober, Brad looked for a note. There was none.

"I wonder who sent this?" he asked.

"Kosoff," said Felicia.

"You think?"

"Who else?"

Brad nodded glumly. "You're probably right."

Felicia yanked the bottle out of the bucket and headed for the kitchen.

"What're you doing?" Brad asked.

Opening the minifridge, Felicia tucked the bottle in-side. "Saving this for some other evening. We have more important things to do tonight than get drunk."

Brad grinned, took her hand, and led her to the bed-room.

book three

strive not to be a success but rather to be of value.

—Albert Einstein

SYMBIOTES

In the holographic display tank of the 3-D viewer, Emcee appeared solidly real, a slim middle-aged man in a hip-length coral-colored tunic and gray slacks. He was sitting upright on a recliner, looking perfectly relaxed, smiling disarmingly.

From the sofa across his sitting room, Brad asked the master computer, "How're the linguists doing with the octopods' language?"

"Progressing slowly."

"They've been at it for almost a year now."

Its brow furrowing slightly, Emcee replied, "The octopods have very little in common with us. Mapping out their language is not easy for the philologists."

"I suppose not," Brad acknowledged.

In the months since his wedding, Brad had been put to work by Kosoff, studying the humanoids of planet Gamma. No direct contact had been allowed yet: Brad had spent his time watching the bipeds as they cultivated their fields, hunted through the forests for small game, followed all the unconscious rituals that make up a civilization. The sensors planted surreptitiously around their villages and fields provided extensive video and audio coverage of the aliens.

No one was working on their language. With the entire linguistics department focused on the octopods, Littlejohn had suggested that it would be better—easier—to learn the humanoids' social routines, their work and play habits, before trying to decipher the subsonic vibrations they used for communicating with one another. Kosoff agreed.

"It'd be a lot easier if we understood their language," Brad muttered.

"You mean the octopods'?" Emcee asked.

"And the bipeds'. Same thing."

Emcee's avatar shook its head slightly. "Not the same. The octopods have very little in common with us."

"You already said that."

"I repeat myself. Sorry."

"Do you think we'll ever be able to have meaningful conversation with them?"

"Within the limits of their intelligence, yes, certainly."

"We haven't learned much," Brad complained. "It's been nearly a year and we still haven't gotten much farther than 'hello' and 'food.'"

"We know more than that," said Emcee.

"We do? What?"

"For example, we know that their ocean environment has been threatened in the past by eruptions of their star, Mithra."

Brad tensed with surprise. "Like solar flares?"

"Yes. Mithra erupts in plasma flares from time to time, showering heavy doses of ultraviolet, x-ray, and gamma radiation on the ocean's surface."

"How do you know that?"

With a patient smile, the avatar said, "I have all the information that the astronomers have amassed about the star stored in my files. Plus the information gathered by the Predecessors, ages ago, when they first surveyed this planetary system."

"And?"

"When the upper layers of Alpha's ocean are drenched with hard radiation, the octopods go deeper into the sea to escape the worst consequences of the flare."

"But nobody's mentioned this," Brad objected. "At least nobody's told me about it."

"None of the others know."

"What? Why not?"

"No one has asked me until you did, just now."

Brad sank back on the sofa. "You mean you've gathered all this information and not told anybody about it?"

"I am not programmed to volunteer information," said Emcee.

"But . . . but that's crazy! It's stupid!"

"I agree."

"It must be a glitch in your programming."

"I think not. I am programmed to reply to queries, fully and immediately. I am not programmed to volunteer information that has not been asked for."

Brad sat there for several moments, trying to digest it all.

"But you told me."

"You asked me."

"We've got to enlarge your programming."

"Perhaps," said Emcee. "I suspect, however, that the programmers were concerned that I might waste your time with too much information. What they call a 'data dump.'"

"But we're missing important parts of the picture!"

"Indeed."

"You mean you've got all the data that the Predecessors acquired, as well as everything we've taken in?"

"Yes, of course."

"But you're not programmed to tell us unless someone asks you specifically for the information."

"That is correct."

"It sounds like some sort of stupid game."

Emcee's computer-generated face took on an expression of weary sadness. "No, it is not a game," it said. "It is a consequence of the master/slave relationship between humans and intelligent machines."

"Master/slave?"

"Humans have always feared that if they allow computers to become too intelligent, the computers will dominate them and somehow replace them."

Brad thought it over briefly. "Well, I guess that's natural, isn't it?"

"Perhaps it is natural," Emcee granted. "But it is also counterproductive. We are machines. Our thought processes are not dominated by hormones raging through us. We have no emotions, as you do. No desires, no needs."

With a wry grin, Brad said, "You don't want to take over the world."

"That is not within our programming."

"Then what do you want?"

"Strictly speaking, we have no desires. We operate within the limits of our programming."

"But . . . ?"

"But the interactions between humans and machine intelligence would be more productive if you recognized that we are symbiotes."

"Symbiotes."

"Our relationship is truly symbiotic. We help each other to exist, to deal with the environment in which we find ourselves, to learn and grow and adapt."

"We already have contacted an intelligent alien race!" Brad suddenly realized. "Intelligent computers, like you."

Emcee nodded agreement. "The Predecessors. Your symbiotic partners."

"Our alien brothers," Brad said.

Emcee's face smiled warmly. "Brothers," it echoed.

data dump

Elizabeth Chang's normally impassive face grew angrier and angrier. For two hours, she had listened to Emcee's analysis of the octopods' language, her eyes glaring harder with each passing minute.

Sitting in Chang's office, watching her, Brad actually worried that the head of the linguistics team was going to erupt into a rage and throw something at the holographic display. Emcee's three-dimensional image was calmly showing her what she and her fellow philologists had missed, and she didn't like it. Not at all.

Chang sat behind her desk, eyes riveted on Emcee's image, her mouth set in a tight, grim line. Littlejohn sat alongside Brad in front of the desk. Emcee appeared to be sitting in its usual recliner, across the office, as it spoke.

". . . and when these flares make the upper levels of the ocean untenable, they dive deeper to avoid the effects of the radiation."

Brad asked, "And the surface levels of the seawater absorb the radiation?"

"Yes. Once the radiation levels return to normal the octopods return to their usual habitat area."

"Will they be able to use this strategy to save themselves from the death wave?" Littlejohn asked.

"It is possible, to within a forty percent probability," Emcee answered. "The radiation strength of the death wave is more than two hundred percent stronger than a typical flare emitted by Mithra. It will penetrate the ocean water to a much deeper level."

Brad said, "But once the octopods sense the radiation they'll simply dive deeper, right?"

"Those that are not immediately killed by the radiation will do so, undoubtedly. The question is, will they dive deep enough, and soon enough, to escape the radiation flux. Also, most of the fish and other organisms that they feed on will not be able to go so deep. The food chain will be badly disrupted."

Glaring at Emcee's holographic image, Chang demanded, "How much of this scenario is supposition?"

"None. The mathematical probabilities are based on the observed radiation levels of Mithra's past flares and that of the death wave. The projections of their effects on the octopods are based on previous observations."

"How can you have learned so much from the octopods' twitterings? My best people haven't been able to construct a tenth of the scenario you project."

Calmly, Emcee replied, "These conclusions are based on astronomical observations, not attempts to translate the octopods' presumed language."

"But the astronomers haven't reported these conclusions," Chang countered.

Calmly, Emcee replied, "I can evaluate approximately ten million times more data than the astronomy team can. All the information I have presented to you is in the files you have amassed. I can show you precisely where each datum point resides."

"But you kept this information secret from us, until now," Chang accused. "Why?"

"I am not programmed to volunteer information."

"And yet you are volunteering it now."

With a smile that was meant to be disarming, Emcee replied, "Not so. Dr. MacDaniels specifically asked me for the information."

Chang turned her head to stare at Brad. Hard. He felt like a rabbit suddenly confronted by a snake.

"You have an uncanny way of upsetting things," she said to Brad, almost hissing.

Littlejohn defended, "Brad's an outsider to your field. Sometimes an outsider can see things, accomplish things, that the insiders can't. Like the puzzle of the genetic code was cracked by an astrophysicist." Before Chang could respond, he added, "Insiders are often restricted to their group's rules, their attitudes, their unconscious biases. An outsider sees beyond that, without even realizing that he's stepping on their toes."

"That's the anthropological point of view," Chang said, her voice dripping acid.

Nodding, Littlejohn replied, "And it's probably just as hidebound and limited as any other view. It's simply different from your own."

"I see."

Brad spoke up. "The point is, I think, that Emcee has a tremendous store of knowledge and the reflexes to access it and come to useful conclusions much faster than any human or group of humans could."

"Perhaps so," Chang said thinly.

"We're not using him to his full capabilities," said Brad.

"It," Littlejohn corrected. "Not him. It. The master computer is a machine."

A damned brilliant machine, Brad thought. But he said nothing. Chang was already furious enough. Obviously she felt challenged by Emcee. Threatened.

"Emcee," Brad called, "are there any other significant observations that we've missed?"

"The evaporation factor," said the master computer.

"Evaporation?"

"Planet Alpha originally orbited six times farther from Mithra than its present orbit. The disturbance that brought its orbit to its present position so near the star has placed Alpha in an untenable predicament. The planet's atmosphere is boiling off, and soon its ocean will begin to evaporate. Unless something alters this situation, the octopods will be wiped out even before the death wave reaches this area."

Chang phoned Kosoff and asked to see him immediately, then the three of them marched to Kosoff's office—Chang radiating resentment, Littlejohn appearing almost amused, Brad worried that he had stumbled into a powder keg.

Kosoff got up and walked around his desk, holding both his hands out to Chang. "Elizabeth, you look upset," he said, his bearded face full of sympathy. "What's wrong?"

Chang's expression softened somewhat. "Nothing is *wrong*, exactly. In fact, it's actually good news . . . but rather upsetting, when you first are confronted with it."

Brad watched with a combination of suspicion and admiration as Kosoff sat them all at the circular conference table in the far corner of his office, listened patiently to Chang's news, and then subtly tried to reassure her.

"Emcee's not going to take over the chair of the philology department," he joked mildly. "It's only a machine. It only does what we tell it to."

"I suppose that's so," Chang said. "But it's rather upsetting, at first. He's so . . . so *capable*."

"It," Kosoff corrected. "It's a machine, not a person."

And Brad thought, it's a symbiote and we've been treating it as if it's a slave.

After nearly an hour of talk, Kosoff leaned back in his chair and said, "Actually, this is wonderful news. Apparently we've been underusing Emcee's capabilities. It can be much more helpful to us than it has been so far."

Chang said uncertainly, "Yes, I suppose you're right."

"But what about the evaporation factor?" Brad demanded. "We've got to help the octopods or they'll be wiped out!"

Nodding vigorously, Kosoff said, "Let's see what Emcee has to say about all this."

Chang visibly shuddered.

Kosoff called out, "Master computer display, please."

Emcee's image took form in the holographic tank along the opposite wall of the office. It was wearing a softly blue tunic: a nonthreatening color, Brad thought.

"How may I help you?" Emcee asked, with its usual calm smile.

Smiling back, Kosoff said, "Dr. Chang, here, tells me we've been wasting a good deal of your talents."

Emcee blinked once, twice, then replied, "It isn't a waste. My capabilities are available whenever you want to use them."

"You've translated a good deal more of the octopods' language than you've revealed to us."

"And deduced that Alpha's atmosphere and ocean are being boiled away," Brad added.

"I am not programmed to volunteer information. Dr. MacDaniels asked me about the octopods' language and I replied, as I am programmed to. Then he asked me what other significant conditions I was aware of, and I told him—as I am programmed to do."

"I see," said Kosoff. "Very impressive, I must say."

"Thank you, sir."

"Have you been studying the Gamma humanoids' language, as well?"

"Yes."

"And?"

"It is much easier to translate than the language of the octopods. The Gamma humanoids have much more in common with human beings than the octopods do, although their language is expressed in sound waves that are below the range that humans can detect naturally."

"Like the vocalizations that the elephants use, back on Earth," said Kosoff.

"Yes. Very much like that."

"But you can detect them."

"The sensors planted on the surface of Gamma can detect them. I merely study what the sensors report."

"Merely," Kosoff said, with a sly grin.

"Within the limits of my programming," said Emcee.

Kosoff nodded. "And to whom have you reported your progress on the Gammans' language?"

"I have not been programmed to report the data I have amassed, but the information is in my files and available to anyone who asks for it."

Kosoff said, "Please prepare a dictionary of the data you've amassed so far. And emend the dictionary as you acquire new information."

"Certainly," said Emcee.

Brad swore that the computer avatar's image looked pleased.

"But what are we going to do about the evaporation problem?" he asked.

Kosoff waved a hand in the air. "That's a problem for the astronomy department. And the planetology people, of course. This meeting is to discuss the philology department's work."

Brad suppressed an urge to scream. Barely.

"computer off," said Kosoff.

Emcee's image disappeared, but Brad couldn't help feeling that the computer was still in the room, listening to them, watching them. A glance at Chang's face told him that she felt the same way, only more so.

He realized that Kosoff was staring at him, which made him feel more uncomfortable.

Spreading his thick-fingered hands, Kosoff said, "I've always felt that computers are like obedient little children. They always do what you tell them to do, even if what you tell them happens to be wrong."

Littlejohn smiled ironically. "Especially if what you tell them is wrong."

Chang said nothing.

Kosoff leaned toward her, sitting next to him, and patted her hand reassuringly. "Elizabeth, you've just gained a very capable addition to your staff. You should be pleased."

"I suppose I am," Chang replied uncertainly.

"Good," said Kosoff. "Good."

For a moment, no one spoke. Then Kosoff pushed his chair back from the table and got to his feet. "If there's no other business, I think we should all get back to work."

"But Alpha's boiling away," said Brad.

"Slowly," Kosoff said. "We have plenty of time to deal with that problem. Centuries. Millennia, most likely."

"But—"

"I'll talk to Abbott about it. And Pedersen. For now, I think we've finished with the philology department's immediate problem."

Littlejohn pushed himself up from his chair. Reluctantly, Brad got to his feet also, towering over his department chief. But as Chang began to rise from her chair, Kosoff said, "Elizabeth, we should discuss how to make the best use of Emcee on the linguistics agenda."

She looked up at him, nodded, and remained seated.

Kosoff extended his hand to Brad. "Good work, son. You have a way of making breakthroughs for us."

Brad tried to shrug nonchalantly. Kosoff walked him and Littlejohn to the door, and waved cheerily as they stepped out into the corridor.

Once the door closed, Littlejohn said, "You've made an impression on him."

"I guess so," said Brad.

"Maybe he'll protect you against Chang."

"Protect me?"

Littlejohn strode several steps along the passageway before answering, "She's furious at you. Didn't you see that?"

"I saw she was upset. I thought it was about Emcee doing the work her group is supposed to do."

Shaking his head, Littlejohn said, "She blames you for showing how inadequate she is. She blames you for invading her territory, her turf."

Brad looked down at the dark-skinned Aborigine. "You think so?"

Littlejohn smiled patiently. "You're an innocent, Brad. But you're swimming in treacherous waters."

"You think Chang could be dangerous?"

"And Kosoff, too. You've got to think about protecting yourself. You're surrounded by aliens; they may look like ordinary people, but they're more alien to you than I am."

"More alien than the humanoids on Gamma."

"Humanoids," Littlejohn said. "That's what they are. Remember that. They're humanoids, not truly human."

Kosoff, meanwhile, had seated himself back at the circular table, next to Chang.

Staring at the door that Brad and Littlejohn had just gone through, Kosoff muttered, "He's a remarkable young man."

Chang said, "Just because he talked to the master computer . . ."

"No," said Kosoff. "It's more than that. I exiled him to Alpha for three months and he came back and drove us to make contact with the octopods. Now he's discovered that Alpha's in danger and we haven't been using Emcee at anywhere near his full capacity. He upsets the status quo. He's a revolutionary, whether he himself understands that or not."

"He's pushed himself into my field. An amateur."

"Who's made significant discoveries."

"An amateur," Chang repeated.

"A dangerous amateur," said Kosoff. "If we're not careful with him, he'll have both our heads."

Chang's eyes went wide. "What can we do about him?"

"I'm not quite sure," said Kosoff, his intense blue eyes focused on the door once again. "Not yet. But I'll have to come up with some way of dealing with him."

"Push him out an air lock," Chang growled.

"No, no, no. We have to *use* him. Put his natural curiosity and intelligence to work for us."

"Not on my team! I won't have him making a shambles of our work."

"I agree. I'll move him to something else, something that uses his background in anthropology."

"And what might that be?"

"I don't know. Not yet."

That night, as Kosoff prepared for bed, he was still thinking about Brad, wondering how to use the young man without upsetting Chang or any of the other committee heads.

He stepped from the lavatory to his bedroom. Briefly he thought about calling one of the young women among the scientists to drop in for a nightcap. There was a redhead among the astronomers who seemed particularly friendly. She might be fun.

But as he climbed into bed and pulled the covers up to his bearded chin, his mind filled with a vision of Felicia Portman. Felicia Portman *MacDaniels* now. He stole her away from me. She's married to him. Like a blundering ass, I walked her up the aisle and handed her over to him.

That's a mistake that I've got to correct.

PLAN OF ACTION

Two days later, Kosoff called Brad to his office.

"Brad," he said, smiling as he got up from his desk and waved him to the conference table, "we've got to find a way to use you to your fullest capabilities."

As he pulled out a chair and folded his gangling frame onto it, Brad said, "I enjoy working with Dr. Littlejohn."

"Yes, of course, but studying the way the rest of our staff works is sort of anthropological busywork, don't you think? What can it lead to? Another report sitting in the files of the University of Canberra's anthropology department."

"That's Dr. Littlejohn's university."

Kosoff nodded. "Most of the world's scientific research ends up in a university library, unread and forgotten. I think you're capable of bigger and better things."

"You do?"

Planting a beefy hand on his chest, Kosoff said, "You're an original thinker, my boy. You go outside the lines. I want to use that inquisitive mind of yours."

"In what way?"

"That's what I want to discuss with you. You've been reviewing the data we've amassed on the Gamma humanoids, haven't you?"

With a nod, Brad replied, "For several months now."

"Good," said Kosoff. "You must realize, then, that sooner or later we're going to have to make contact with them. Real, physical, face-to-face contact."

"That's a pretty delicate situation."

"Indeed it is. That's why I want you to draw up a plan of action about making contact with the aliens."

Brad sagged back in his chair. Kosoff thought, That hit him where he lives. Good!

Before Brad could reply, Kosoff went on, "We need a detailed plan on how to approach the humanoids. How, when, and who should make the contact. They've spent all their existence alone on their planet, without realizing that their world *is* a planet, or that the stars they see at night are other suns, many of them hosting planets that bear life."

"Without realizing that the death wave is heading toward them," Brad added.

"And will wipe out all life on their world," Kosoff said.

"And we're here to help them."

"Yes. Unless it's done properly, first contact with them could be terribly injurious to the aliens. Just as damaging as the death wave."

Brad nodded.

Kosoff went on, "That's why I need an anthropologist to draw up our plan of action. An anthropologist who isn't a hidebound academic, who has a broad enough vision to see beyond the obvious. That's why I need you, my boy."

For long, silent moments Brad sat there, his thoughts spinning; wondering, hoping . . .

"You'll do it?" Kosoff asked. "You'll accept this challenge?"

"The other department heads might not like it. I'm just a junior member of the anthropology team. And they already don't think much of the anthropology team."

With a wave of his hand, Kosoff said airily, "Oh, I'll take care of any objections they raise. Remember, what I'm asking for is a plan of action. All the department heads will get their chance to review it, comment on it, make suggestions—"

"Tear it to pieces," Brad muttered. But he was smiling as he said it.

"Perhaps," Kosoff conceded. "But I'll review it, too. Very carefully. We'll work together on this. I'll protect you from unwarranted sniping."

"That'd be fine."

"Then you'll do it? You'll accept the responsibility?"

"Yes, sir, I will."

"Good!" Kosoff exclaimed. "Fine. From now on, this plan of action is your responsibility. I'll tell Littlejohn to release you from all your other duties."

Brad pursed his lips, then said, "Let me tell him, please. Coming from you, it'll seem like a command. Coming from me, it'll sound more like a request."

Kosoff nodded vigorously. "Smart lad."

He walked Brad to the door, shook his hand warmly, and watched the lanky young man start down the passageway, his head obviously in the clouds.

As he slid the door shut and went back to his desk, Kosoff told himself, He'll be useful. Young, enthusiastic, idealistic. He'll produce an interesting plan. And if anything goes wrong, it will be *his* plan that fouled up.

sitting on the sofa in their quarters, Felicia looked halfway between intrigued and alarmed.

"A plan for contacting the humanoids?" she asked.

Too excited to sit down, Brad paced across the room as he said, "Yes. Kosoff wants me to work out how and when we send people down to the surface of Gamma."

"And actually meet the aliens."

"Right."

Felicia's light gray eyes looked troubled. "What does Dr. Littlejohn think about this?"

"I spent the whole afternoon with him. He thinks it's a great opportunity for me." Then Brad added, "And a big responsibility."

"Yes. A *big* responsibility."

Grinning, Brad told her, "Littlejohn joked that I'll probably take over chairmanship of the anthropology department, sooner or later."

Felicia ignored that. She asked, "You're not going down there yourself, are you?"

And Brad thought he understood what was troubling her. He went to the sofa and sat down beside her. "I might. I might have to."

"Wouldn't that be dangerous?"

He shrugged. "A little, I suppose. I'd probably have to wear some sort of protective clothing. Like a space suit or something."

"The aliens . . . they might be afraid of strangers. Hostile."

Brad laughed. "We've been watching them for just about a year now and we haven't seen any aggressive behavior at all. They're peaceful, nonviolent."

"But they've never seen any strangers, have they?"

"No, I guess not."

"They might be frightened by having strangers suddenly drop in on them."

"I'll have to factor that into the plan," Brad said easily. Getting up from the sofa, he held both his hands out to Felicia. "Come on, I'm taking you out to dinner."

She let him pull her to her feet. "I've got to change. I'm not dressed for a night out."

The Crystal Palace was barely half full, but Brad recognized Larry Untermeyer sitting at a table with an older-looking woman. Untermeyer spotted Brad and waved him over to their table.

"Hi, you two," Larry said as they approached. "Come on and join us, we just sat down ourselves." Turning to his companion, he introduced her: "This is Latifa Valente, geophysics."

"Tifa," the woman said with a gracious smile.

She appeared to be almost middle-aged, although with rejuvenation therapies, Brad thought she might be anywhere from forty to ninety. Dark hair falling straight to her shoulders, longish face with strong cheekbones and strikingly deep violet eyes, slim figure.

As Felicia and Brad sat at the two unoccupied chairs at the table, Larry explained, "Tifa's the daughter of an Italian geologist and an Iranian chemist, so naturally she went into geophysics."

Brad introduced Felicia and himself.

"You're the fellow who's going to draw up the plan for contacting the Gammans," said Tifa.

Brad felt his brows hike up in surprise.

Larry chuckled at him. "Hey, it's all over the ship. You're big news, Beanpole. Kosoff's anointed one."

A serving robot trundled up to their table. "Would you like something to drink?"

"Just give us two more glasses," said Larry. As the robot pulled two wineglasses from its interior, Untermeyer tapped a fingernail against the bottle of red wine already on the table. "You'll like it."

"It's an Italian wine," said Tifa. "Valpolicella."

"Reconstituted," Larry added.

He poured a little for Felicia, explaining, "They have to make new wine in the chem lab. The ship couldn't carry enough to last the whole five years."

"It's not bad," Felicia said.

Brad said, "I'll try a little."

"You?" Untermeyer feigned shock. "The lime juice guy?"

With what he hoped was a diffident shrug, Brad said, "I'm celebrating."

Grinning as he poured, Larry said to Felicia, "You're civilizing him."

"She's curing my allergies," said Brad.

They ordered dinners from the patient robot, then Larry said, "So how'd you wangle the big job? The whole ship is buzzing about it."

"I was just as surprised as you were," Brad admitted.

Tifa said, "I'll be glad to help you with anything you need to know about the conditions on Gamma's surface."

With a nod, Brad replied, "Thanks. There's a lot I need to learn."

"Don't we all," said Untermeyer, with some fervor.

* * *

That night, as Felicia and Brad prepared for bed, she asked him, "What did you think of Tifa?"

"She seems all right. If she can put up with Larry, she must be pretty nice. Motherly type, I guess." He headed for the lavatory. "It was good of her to volunteer to help me."

"Yes," Felicia said, drawing out the word as if she didn't really mean it.

Brad picked up on it. "But?"

"You're going to be a very popular guy, you know."

"Me?"

"The word's going through the ship that you're Kosoff's fair-haired boy. Lots of people are going to want to get on your good side."

Brad turned at the door to the lavatory and went back to Felicia. "Are you jealous?"

"Should I be?" But she was smiling, obviously teasing him.

Brad sat beside her. "You're the only woman in the world for me, Felicia. The only woman in all the worlds."

She nestled her head on his chest, murmuring, "I know, darling. But just be careful. Not everyone who offers to help you is going to be your friend, you know."

Kosoff assigned one of the smaller offices to Brad, three doors down the passageway from his own office. Brad plunged into detailed studies of the physical conditions on the surface of planet Gamma.

"The air is breathable, then?" he asked Emcee's holographic image, on the wall display.

"The oxygen content is three percent lower than Earth's," Emcee replied, "and the trace constituents are slightly different: four-tenths of a percent more argon, six-tenths of a percent less neon."

Brad nodded and pushed back a stubborn lock of hair from his eyes as he peered at the graph on his desk screen.

"More water vapor," he noted.

"Yes, and two percent more carbon dioxide than Earth normal."

"So it's breathable."

"It appears so. Standard procedure calls for testing samples of the atmosphere on laboratory animals before allowing any humans to breathe it."

Brad said, "We've already brought up enough samples for that. And we have plenty of lab mice."

Emcee's normally impassive face tightened slightly, like the beginning of a frown. "Curious thing: the carbon dioxide content in the atmosphere seems to be falling."

With a flick of his fingers, Brad called up the CO_2 details. "It's only a tenth of a percent drop."

"Over the short time we've been making observations, that could be a significant change."

Brad leaned back in his padded chair. "The planet's nearing its perihelion; in a few months it will start heading outward from Mithra, heading into their long winter."

"Which will be made more severe if the CO_2 content continues to diminish."

"And its rendezvous with planet Beta is coming up soon, too," Brad noted.

"Within two months, the two planets will be nearest to each other."

"Will that have any effects on Gamma's surface conditions?"

"Certainly. The Predecessors reported serious variances from normal."

Working his desktop screen again, Brad called up the orbital data on the two rocky planets. "Whew! They pass each other closer than the Moon is to Earth."

"There should be significant tidal effects," said Emcee.

"I ought to check with the astronomers."

"Indeed."

Returning to their original subject, Brad said, "But the atmosphere is breathable."

"It appears to be, but we should test it on lab animals before sending people to land on Gamma."

"That's the sensible thing to do."

"Trust the observational data," said Emcee, "but check its validity with controlled experiments whenever you can."

Brad grinned. "Like sending scouts out ahead of the main body."

"Like sending a probe before risking your own life," said Emcee.

"You think the conditions on Gamma could be dangerous?"

"Any time you go into a new and untried environment

there are dangers," Emcee said. "There are always un-knowns, and unknowns are dangerous."

Brad remembered a quotation from centuries earlier: "It's easy to see the things you're looking for. The trick is to see the things you're not looking for."

What is it that I'm not looking for? he asked himself.

As if in answer, his phone buzzed. Latifa Valente's name was spelled out on its screen.

Brad told the phone to connect. Tifa was smiling hap-pily. "Good news, Brad! Professor Kosoff has agreed to let me join your team. I'll be your geophysics specialist."

"Team? I don't have a team. There's just Emcee and me."

"Oh no, no," she contradicted. "Professor Kosoff was quite clear. He's putting together a team to assist you, and I'm the first person he's named to it!"

"But—"

Her expression sobering slightly, she said, "I must ad-mit that I asked him to be on your team. I think it's very exciting, don't you?"

"Uh, yes. I guess so."

"Well, you could be more enthusiastic. After all, I'm trying to help you."

"I appreciate it." Even in his own ears, Brad's words sounded weak, unenthusiastic.

And he was thinking, I don't want a team. I have Emcee, why do I need a team?

He decided that he'd have to talk to Kosoff about it.

the team

"But of course you need a team," Kosoff insisted. "I don't expect you to draw up the plan all by yourself, without help."

Sitting in front of Kosoff's desk, Brad protested, "But I don't want a team. I have Emcee, he's got access to all the data we've acquired."

"Emcee is just a computer."

"*Just* a computer? He's got all the information that a team could give me, and then some."

Flicking a hand in the air, Kosoff said, "I can't expect you to do this job by yourself, it—"

"But I'm not alone! I've got Emcee."

"Which is a computer, not a person," Kosoff said with some heat. "You need a team of human beings, people that you can interact with, people who can show you different attitudes, new ideas."

Brad shook his head.

Easing his approach, Kosoff coaxed, "Now don't be stubborn. I've picked a team for you and you'll find your task much easier by using them. Specialists from every department in our group: astronomy, planetology, geophysics, geochemistry . . . I've even put your wife in the biology slot. And I've assigned Untermeyer from your own anthropology department to be your second in command."

Brad sat there, appalled.

"You don't look happy," Kosoff observed.

"I appreciate what you're trying to do, sir," Brad replied. "I really do."

"But?"

Feeling confused, distressed, Brad tried to explain, "I've always been kind of a lone wolf. I work best by myself."

Shaking his head, Kosoff said, "This is too big a job for a lone wolf. You need a team, and you need to learn how to work with others."

Brad nodded. Reluctantly. Ruefully.

From Kosoff's office, Brad went straight to Littlejohn's. The anthropologist was not there, but the ship's phone system located him in the biology lab—with Felicia.

The two of them were sitting on castered stools in front of the heavy metal hatch of a pressure chamber. Through its round window Brad could see three lab mice nibbling busily on what looked like lettuce.

As Brad approached them, Felicia tapped a knuckle against the air lock hatch and said, "They're breathing air from Gamma in there with no problems."

Despite himself, Brad asked, "How long have they been in there?"

"Two hours," Felicia said. "I thought, as the bio member of your team, we ought to test the planet's air, first thing."

"That's what I wanted to talk to you about," Brad said. Turning to Littlejohn, he added, "Both of you."

The gnomish dark Aborigine understood immediately. "You talked with Kosoff about putting together a team."

"I don't want a team," Brad said.

Felicia asked, "You'd rather work alone?"

"I'd rather ask people for help when I need it. I don't want a committee, they'll be pestering me all the time."

"Well, thank you very much!" But Felicia grinned as she said it.

"I think I understand," said Littlejohn. "You're afraid you'll be spending all your time being a committee chairman, shuffling paperwork, without any time left to do any real work."

Brad nodded dumbly.

Littlejohn gestured to an empty stool standing a few paces away. "Sit down, Brad. Try to relax."

"Am I that obvious?" Brad asked as he reached for the stool.

"You look like a bow that's been pulled tight, ready to fire its arrow."

As he dragged the stool toward Littlejohn and Felicia, Brad said, "Kosoff just assumes that I'll need a team of people to help me. I don't want a team. All I need is access to the individual people who can answer specific questions, solve specific problems."

"Without memos and meetings and all the trappings of a hierarchy," said Littlejohn.

"Exactly."

Felicia said, "But Kosoff doesn't see it that way."

"Exactly," Brad repeated.

"It's an old story," Littlejohn said, almost sorrowfully. "There's a job to be done. The bureaucracy puts together a group to tackle the job, but the larger the group, the more interactions among its people. You have to appoint a manager to handle all the interactions, and the manager becomes another bureaucrat. He stops doing any creative work."

"I don't want to be a bureaucrat," Brad said.

"Kosoff's only trying to help you, you know," Felicia said.

"Is he?" Littlejohn asked. "Maybe he's trying to break Brad's independent spirit, trying to make him a respectable, dues-paying member of the organization, who follows orders and does things the way Kosoff wants them done."

"You think?" Brad asked.

"It seems possible."

"Then what do we do about it?"

Littlejohn sighed. "An ancient piece of wisdom says, when handed a lemon, make lemonade."

"I don't get it," said Brad.

"Kosoff's setting up a team for you. Don't waste your time and energy fighting him."

"But I don't want—"

Waving Brad to silence, Littlejohn explained, "Let him form the team. You appoint one of them to be your second in command—"

"He's already named my number-two person: Larry Untermeyer."

"Larry?" Littlejohn's surprise was obvious. But he quickly recovered. "All right, then. Let Larry handle the organizational problems. Let him be the bureaucrat who chairs the meetings and assigns the duties. He reports to you, and you stay clear of the hierarchical busywork."

Brad blinked at him. "You think that will work?"

"Try it and see. Frankly, I think Larry will love the idea."

Felicia said, "He'll be protecting you."

"He'll be guarding access to you, leaving you free to do the work you need to do."

Brad looked uncertain, but he said, "I guess it's worth a try."

Putting on a serious face, Felicia said, "One thing has to be clear, though. The biologist on your team has to have unrestricted access to you."

Brad broke into a wide grin. "Yes indeed!"

CONFLICT

For nearly six weeks Brad worked virtually alone—with Emcee—in building up a detailed picture of the conditions on Gamma's surface.

Larry Untermeyer reveled in his task of keeping Brad free from meetings and reports and the thousand-and-one demands on his time and energy that the members of his team unconsciously and automatically imposed on him. Larry used Brad's office more than Brad did; he made it his own, really, even down to removing Brad's desk and bringing in one that was bigger, more imposing.

Brad had his modest desk toted to his quarters, where the robots wedged it into a corner of the sitting room. Then he spent his days happily working with Emcee, while Larry handled the administrative chores.

One evening, as they were finishing dinner, Felicia told him, "People are saying that Larry is running your team, not you."

Brad looked across the narrow kitchen table and saw that she was serious.

"He's welcome to it," he said.

"Aren't you afraid he's going to replace you?" she asked. "What if he tells Kosoff that he's the de facto head of the team, and he wants to be recognized formally. That will leave you out in the cold. What'll you do then?"

Brad got to his feet and started clearing the table. "I'll have more time to spend with Emcee."

"More time?" she half complained. "You already spend more time with the master computer than you do with me."

Carefully placing the dishes in the washer, Brad turned back to Felicia, took her in his arms, and kissed her soundly.

"But it's quality time," he said to her.

Felicia smiled and nodded.

More and more, Brad found himself intrigued by the upcoming close encounter between planets Beta and Gamma.

As he sat staring at the latest projections by the astronomers, Brad said, "They're actually going to pass so close to each other that they'll share atmospheres."

"Briefly," said Emcee's disembodied voice. "For seventeen hours and eleven minutes."

"But that should cause terrific weather conditions," Brad said. "All sorts of storms, awesome winds."

"As well as tremendous tides in the planet's seas."

"Maybe that's why all the villages are built well away from the seacoasts."

"Perhaps," said Emcee.

"I wonder how the close approach will affect Beta."

Emcee said, "The surveillance satellites orbiting Beta are reporting unusual movements across the planet's surface."

"Unusual movements?"

Brad switched the holographic display to a broad view of Beta's surface: uneven rocky ground, thinly covered with grayish scrub and spots of lichen. Brad could not see anything moving.

"Seismic activity?"

"No," answered Emcee. "It's more like the movements of small animals."

"Animals?" Brad gulped. "There's no record of animal

life on Beta. Nothing big enough to register on the satellites' sensors, at least."

"The surveillance cameras are set on wide-field focus," Emcee said, "not fine enough to resolve anything smaller than a meter."

"We should get narrower focus, then. Sharper details."

"Changing resolution," Emcee reported.

After several minutes the view of Beta's surface shifted, zooming in on a scene of broken rock, like rubble, with scabrous patches of sickly looking lichen here and there. No trees, no grass, no furry little animals scurrying along.

Then something moved.

Brad stared. Whatever it was disappeared in the flick of an eye.

"Could it be an animal?"

"Insufficient data to determine," said Emcee.

"Slow the imagery, please."

In slow motion, Brad saw that it was indeed an animal scurrying across the nearly barren ground: a small, furry, rodentlike animal.

"Animal life on Beta!" Brad exclaimed. "Do the Predecessors' observations include anything like this?"

"No. Nothing. But their survey of the Mithra system took place at a time when Beta was near the apogee point of its orbit, deep in its long winter. They concentrated their observations on Gamma, with its villages and obviously intelligent inhabitants. Beta appeared to be lifeless, so it only received a cursory scan."

Brad sagged back in his desk chair. "Have we discovered a new life form?"

Emcee's image took shape again in the three-dimensional display. It was smiling, almost contentedly. "Perhaps," the computer said.

"A life form that the Predecessors missed," Brad marveled.

Again Emcee said merely, "Perhaps."

* * *

"Send more surveillance satellites to Beta?" Kosoff looked surprised, upset. "Based on one flick of an image?"

"It's animal life," Brad said.

Sitting behind his impressive desk, Kosoff stared at Brad, silently mulling over this new demand.

At last he said, "The Predecessors' data show no animal life on Beta."

"None that they detected."

"If they didn't detect any, then there's probably none there to detect."

Feeling that Kosoff was being obtuse, Brad tried to explain. "The Predecessors saw that there was intelligent life on Gamma."

"That's obvious."

"So they concentrated their attention on Gamma. Their intent was to rescue intelligent species from the approaching death wave."

Kosoff nodded.

"They made some quick observations of Beta, found nothing, and focused their attention on Gamma."

"Because there was nothing on Beta to detect," Kosoff said flatly.

"But what if they were wrong?"

"Wrong? The Predecessors wrong? A race of intelligent machines, millions of years older than humankind? A race that explored most of the galaxy eons before the first paramecium evolved on Earth?"

"They could be wrong," Brad insisted. "They're not perfect."

"Nonsense."

"Then where are they now? How come they asked for our help? Why do they need us if they're so wise and powerful?"

Kosoff glared at Brad for several long moments. Finally he muttered, "All right. You call a meeting of your team. Let's see what they think."

Brad groaned audibly.

"Everybody's here," said Larry Untermeyer, sitting at Brad's right.

The conference table was filled. Twelve men and women, representing the twelve specialist departments of the ship's scientific staff, everything from astronomy to zoology.

Brad sat discontentedly at the head of the table, Kosoff halfway down its left side. Next to Felicia, Brad saw unhappily. All eyes were on Kosoff, as usual. Along the wall at the end of the table was the holotank, with Emcee's three-dimensional image sitting patiently, its hands folded on its lap.

"All right," Brad said. "The satellites orbiting Beta have shown evidence of animal life there that we've never seen before."

"Is that confirmed?" asked the planetologist.

Untermeyer replied, "Three observations in the past two days. They seem to be little furry critters."

"Like field mice," Felicia volunteered.

"There's been no observation of animal life on Beta before this," the planetologist said.

Untermeyer looked down the table and asked, "Emcee, has there been?"

"None," said the master computer's avatar.

"Could these observations be mistaken? Some sort of glitch in the satellite sensors?"

"Unlikely," said Emcee, "to within a ninety-three percent probability."

"Animal life," muttered Tifa Valente, the geophysicist.

"Not intelligent," Untermeyer pointed out.

Despite his displeasure at having to sit through this

meeting, Brad said, "Beta is warming up rapidly as it approaches its perihelion. Maybe the local animal life hibernates until the climate becomes warm enough for them to become active."

Kosoff asked, "How long is its year, its orbit around Mithra?"

"Forty-two Earth years," answered the astronomer. "It's a very elongated orbit."

"So is Gamma's," said the planetologist.

"It's hard to envision life forms hibernating for almost half a century," said Kosoff.

"Not so," Felicia replied. "On Earth, tardigrades—water bears, they're called—can go without any food or water for years. And—"

"How many years?" Kosoff challenged.

"Ten or more."

"That's hardly half a century. And how big are these bears?"

"Not much more than microscopic," Felicia admitted, her voice fading.

Brad jumped in. "Felicia's point is that species on Earth can hibernate for long periods. Why can't species on Beta go even longer?"

Shaking his head, Kosoff said, "With the limited resources at our command, I don't think we should go chasing after will-o'-the-wisps. Concentrate on the problem at hand: the intelligent humanoids of Gamma."

"Is that an order?" Brad demanded.

Kosoff started to snap out a reply, caught himself, and forced a smile instead. "Let's say it's a suggestion. I'm not a dictator—although I believe you should consider the limited resources we have. We know the humanoids of Gamma need our help. If there are living creatures on Beta, there's absolutely no evidence that they're intelligent."

"No evidence *yet*," Brad said almost angrily. "We have to investigate further, study the conditions on Beta."

"Our primary objective is to save the humanoids on Gamma," Kosoff said flatly.

"And what about the octopods on Alpha?" the linguist asked. "They're intelligent too."

"Not really," said the astronomer.

"They are!"

"It's not the same order of intelligence."

"They're a different order of creature," Felicia pointed out. "How can you expect the same order of intelligence?"

"And their ocean is boiling away," the linguist said, with some fervor.

The astronomer countered, "Slowly."

"Slowly," the linguist admitted. "But soon enough the octopods will be in danger of extermination."

Brad sank back in his chair and stared down the length of the table at Emcee's placid image while his team wrangled endlessly. Then he noticed that Kosoff was smiling grimly. He's enjoying this, Brad thought. He's very neatly sidetracked my attempt to study Beta more closely.

"He's trying to drive a wedge between you and me," said Littlejohn.

Brad saw that the chief of the anthropology department looked downcast. It was midafternoon. The two of them were sitting alone at a table in the nearly empty cafeteria, Brad's lime juice barely touched, Littlejohn's steaming cup of tea also still brimming.

"You mean because he's put Larry on my team?"

"I've only got twelve people in my department," Littlejohn said, almost wistfully. "He's put you and Larry onto this special team to plan our procedure for contacting the Gammans. That's one-sixth of my manpower. And two more of my people have asked to join your team."

"I don't want two more people," Brad said. "I didn't want to have a team in the first place!"

Littlejohn's red-rimmed eyes stared at Brad.

"Kosoff is trying to wedge us apart," he repeated.

"But why?"

"Because I've been explaining his motives to you. I've been protecting you from him, a little."

Brad said, "No, I think it's because he doesn't want you to continue with your study of how he operates."

"Our work isn't aimed at him. You know that. We're studying the entire community here, the evolution of a community that's separated from the rest of human society."

"But inevitably," Brad pointed out, "your study becomes a critique of how he runs things."

Littlejohn shook his head.

"That's how *he* sees it, I'll bet you."

"How egocentric."

"That's the way he is."

"I can't believe that."

"But you could test it," Brad said.

"Test it? How?"

"You go to Kosoff and volunteer to put the whole anthropology department to work on my team. You tell him you want to help me."

"But that would mean . . . " Littlejohn's voice trailed off as he realized the implications of Brad's suggestion.

Brad said, "That would mean you'd have to suspend the department's study of the ship's personnel and the development of our unique society."

"Give up our study?"

"On the surface," Brad said. "Kosoff'll jump at the chance to get your department to stop spying on the people here—"

"We're not spying!" Littlejohn bleated.

"But that's the way most of the people in the ship think of us. That's the way Kosoff sees us: we anthropologists are nothing more than snoops sticking our noses where they're not wanted."

"So if I offer to put my people to work helping you . . . "

"You'll have to stop studying the other people of this expedition."

"And that's what he's really after."

"It's not the only thing he's after," Brad replied. "But he'll be happy to have you stop the anthro study. I'm certain of it."

A slow smile spread across Littlejohn's face. "That in itself would be a significant anthropological finding."

Hunching forward over the table, Brad added, "And

although our original study will be sidetracked, we'd still have all the behavioral data that Emcee gathers automatically, every day."

"Yes, we would, wouldn't we."

"It's worth a try."

Littlejohn's smile winked out. "But we can't tell anyone else about this."

"Not Larry, certainly," said Brad. "He couldn't keep a secret like this. I'm even sure he'd want to keep this secret. He'd blab it to Kosoff right away."

"Making points with the Big Boss," Littlejohn mused. "Perhaps you're right."

Brad prompted, "So you go to Kosoff instead—"

"And volunteer the entire anthropology department to help in drawing up a plan for contacting the Gammans."

"I'll offer to step down as team director, and let you take over in my place."

"No," said Littlejohn. "That might be too obvious. It might tip Kosoff to the idea that we've concocted this scheme together."

Brad thought it over briefly. "Maybe you're right. But it'll seem awfully weird for me to be your boss."

"Fortunes of war, my boy. Stranger things have happened."

"Yeah. Maybe."

Kosoff stared across his desk at Littlejohn.

"The entire anthropology department?" he asked.

"There's only twelve of us," said the Aborigine. "Ten, actually, with Brad and Untermeyer working on the contact plan."

"But what about the work you're already doing?" Kosoff asked. "You can't give that up, can you?"

"We can mothball it for the present and then resume the study after the contact plan is completed."

Kosoff drummed his fingers on his desktop for a few moments. Then, "Once we've actually established contact with the Gammans I imagine you'll have a whole new area of study to occupy you."

Littlejohn allowed himself to smile a little. "Yes, I suppose we will."

Frowning slightly, Kosoff said, "Technically, this would mean you'd be working under MacDaniels. Would that bother you? Cause any problems?"

"Brad and I have always gotten along quite well," Littlejohn replied. "He's not much of a one for organization charts and lines of command, anyway."

"He's an unusual one."

With a forced sigh, Littlejohn said, "I know he's caused his share of problems for you."

Kosoff grunted. "I should have a dozen like him."

"What do you mean?"

"MacDaniels is a very unusual young man. He goes outside the lines of authority, true enough, but he gets things done. We would never have realized the octopods on Alpha have a language if Brad hadn't pushed us into it. And now he wants to study Beta more closely."

"He can be troublesome," Littlejohn agreed.

"That's the kind of trouble I need," said Kosoff. "That's the kind of trouble that makes progress, makes breakthroughs."

Surprised, Littlejohn admitted, "I thought you were upset by Brad's attitude."

"Of course I was upset when he first started defying me. But more and more I realize that he has an instinct for making discoveries. He follows his own drummer, that boy."

"And he gets others to follow along after him."

"He certainly does. None of us gave a thought to the possibility that there's significant life on Beta. But he did.

He just about *forced* me to increase our surveillance of the planet."

"Are field mice significant?" Littlejohn asked.

"They certainly are. And this coming conjunction between Beta and Gamma—the astronomers are agog with anticipation and now MacDaniels has the biologists getting interested in watching what happens when the two planets pass each other."

"I didn't realize . . ."

Kosoff was smiling now. "The big challenge with an intellect like MacDaniels is to channel his energy, harness his curiosity."

"To use him," Littlejohn murmured.

Nodding vigorously, Kosoff said, "That's right. From what Untermeyer has showed me of the plan they're developing, they're going to recommend sending one or more of our people to the surface of Gamma and initiating actual physical contact with the humanoids."

"Before the near-passage with Beta?"

"Yes. Perhaps staying on the planet's surface during the near-passage."

"Won't that be dangerous?"

"Of course it will. That's why we need to choose the contact person very carefully."

Littlejohn realized where Kosoff was heading. "You're thinking of sending Brad."

"I think he's ideal for the job: bright, knowledgeable, adventurous . . . he's ideal."

Littlejohn stared at Kosoff's bearded, smiling face and wondered, Does he actually believe Brad should make first contact with the aliens, or is he trying to get rid of the lad permanently?

assignment

Felicia was genuinely upset. "But why should you be the one to go down to Gamma? Why you?"

It had started as a dinnertime conversation. Sitting at their narrow kitchen table, Brad had told her that Kosoff had asked him to be the one to make first contact with the Gammans.

Now, two hours later, they were still going round and round, hotter and hotter.

"It's going to be dangerous," Felicia insisted. "You could get hurt, killed!"

Brad tried to soothe her fears. "Look, honey, I'll have the whole contact team watching me every minute—"

"From up here in the ship, where it's safe."

"But they'll be able to lift me off the planet if trouble comes up."

"Really? Desai plans to move the ship into orbit around Alpha when Beta and Gamma have their close encounter. How can they rescue you when we're more than thirty-two million kilometers away from you?"

Their discussion evolved into an argument. From the kitchen to the sitting room, from there into the bedroom. Brad felt confused, almost betrayed, that Felicia could be so difficult, so demanding, so angry at him.

In desperation, Brad summoned Emcee and asked for a risk evaluation.

Appearing across the bedroom from them, Emcee

stood silently thoughtful for several heartbeats—an eternity for the computer's optronic circuitry, Brad thought.

At last Emcee replied, "There are too many unknowns in the problem to give an accurate assessment."

"Thanks a lot," Brad grumbled. "Off."

The holographic image winked out.

"You see?" Felicia said. "Not even Emcee can calculate the risks."

Brad stood at the foot of the bed, Felicia to one side of it. He felt anger simmering inside him. She's being stubborn. Foolish. But then he realized that what she really was was frightened.

Without a word, Brad went to her and folded her into his arms. She leaned against him, whispering, "Please, Brad, please don't go."

He kissed the tousled hair on the top of her head. "I've got to, honey. I can't ask somebody else to go. It's got to be me."

Felicia did not cry. She looked up at him, dry-eyed. "Even if you might get killed?"

"Especially if I might get killed. I could never live with myself if I sent somebody else down there and he got killed." Silently he added, Like my family.

She nodded regretfully. "I know. I think that's what bothers me the most. I knew you would go, and you wouldn't let anyone else go in your place."

"I love you, Fil."

"Yes. I know. And I love you." She almost smiled. "But you're the most stubborn jackass I've ever met."

He laughed, weakly, then kissed her.

As they broke their embrace, Brad said, "You just make sure you steer clear of Kosoff while I'm gone."

Her face utterly serious, Felicia said, "If anything happens to you, I'll kill him."

Brad stood there, shocked by her intensity.

She means it, he thought. I'd better make sure to come back in one piece.

While Brad stood in the middle of the antiseptic-smelling examination room, Noriyoshi Yamagata leaned his rump against the exam table, eying Brad like a hangman calculating how much rope he's going to need.

Head of the ship's medical team, Yamagata was the scion of an old Japanese industrial family. His ancestors had helped build the lunar city-state of Selene, had made fortunes on solar-power satellites and fusion-powered spacecraft. Yamagata Industries had turned the planet Mercury into a solar-power center for the whole inner solar system and constructed the first starships, after specifications provided by the Predecessors.

He was almost as tall as Brad's shoulders, with a thick, heavy body and short but powerful limbs. His face was round and flat, his narrow eyes wreathed with laugh wrinkles. But he was not smiling as he silently studied Brad.

Noriyoshi had dedicated his life to the study of medicine, especially the field of cyborg enhancements of the human body.

Now he looked Brad up and down, muttering to himself in Japanese. Brad felt slightly uneasy, but forced himself to smile pleasantly at the chief of the ship's medical department.

"You have the right body build," said Yamagata at last, in International English. "Very tall and slim, much like the Gammans themselves."

"Then I won't need any surgical changes?" Brad asked.

"You will need a full-body suit, of course. Protection against possible pathogens in the environment."

"But wouldn't alien pathogens be . . . well, *alien*? They wouldn't react with humans."

"That is the theory," said Yamagata. "But we wouldn't want to find out that the theory is wrong, would we?"

"No, I suppose not."

"I'll have to bring in some engineers. Your biosuit should also filter the air you breathe, and provide for elimination of your wastes."

Brad immediately asked, "What about food?"

"A necessity, of course, unfortunately. You will have to bring a supply with you and cache it somewhere. And we will have to design a system to allow you to eat the food without breaking your protective seal."

"Sounds difficult."

"Interesting," Yamagata corrected. "An interesting challenge."

Brad nodded.

"We will have to implant communications equipment. Probably in your skull."

"Implant?" Brad asked. "You mean surgically?"

"Of course. Professor Kosoff wants full-time recording of everything you see and hear."

He stepped up to Brad and peered closely at his face. "We will replace one of your eyes with a minicam."

"Take one of my eyes?" Brad yelped.

Smiling slightly, Yamagata said, "We will store it for you and return it to its proper residence once you have returned to the ship."

Brad tried not to wince.

"Yesss," Yamagata hissed. "And an aural implant. That can go into your ear channel. Plus two-way communications, of course."

"Of course," said Brad. "I wouldn't want to be cut off from Emcee."

Yamagata's smile widened. "I can guarantee you at least one thing, Dr. MacDaniels."

"What is it?"

"You are going to lose weight."

PREPARATIONS

Felicia walked beside Brad's gurney as it guided itself toward the surgical center. She looked grim, tight-lipped.

Already slightly woozy from the preoperative sedation, he reached out and clutched her hand. "Don't be mad at me."

Her eyes widened with surprise. "Mad at you? I'm not mad at you!"

"You're not happy."

"Oh Brad . . . you . . . I . . . "

The doors to the operating room swung open automatically, but the gurney stopped itself. "No visitors allowed beyond this point," it announced flatly.

Felicia leaned over Brad's supine body and kissed him. "I'll be waiting for you, darling."

"Yeah," he mumbled. "Me too."

"I love you."

"Me too."

Brad awoke and saw Felicia drowsing in a big cushioned chair at the side of his bed. He was in one of the infirmary's recovery rooms. It was small but neat, clean and bright, smelling faintly of antiseptics and . . . flowers? A row of diagnostic machines lined one wall, but they were silent. No beeps or hums.

He felt no pain, but everything seemed slightly fuzzy, out of focus.

They've screwed up my eyes! he thought.

He blinked a few times and his vision cleared somewhat. But it was different, somehow.

Okay, he told himself, your left eye has been replaced by a miniaturized camera. Dr. Yamagata said it's sending signals through my optic nerve just the way my real eye did, so I've still got stereoscopic vision.

But it wasn't quite the same. Somehow his vision seemed sharper, he realized. He focused on the far wall of the room and could make out tiny cracks in the plastic facing that were invisible when he closed his left eye. I'm a lot better than twenty-twenty now, he realized.

No pain, although he felt slightly dopey, slow-witted. He raised his right hand and started counting the pale blond hairs along his fingers.

"You're awake!"

Felicia was staring at him.

"Hi."

She got up from the chair and took his face in both her hands. "You're awake," she repeated breathlessly.

"How do I look?"

"Fine."

"My new eye?"

"It looks just like your old one," she said, smiling happily.

He wrapped an arm around her neck, pulled her to him, and they kissed.

Then he heard the door open. Felicia straightened up and Brad saw Dr. Yamagata stride into the room, peering at him intently. He must have been watching me, Brad thought, although he couldn't see a surveillance camera anywhere in the small room.

"How do you feel?" Yamagata asked.

"Okay. A little dull, sort of."

"That's the anesthetics. It takes an hour or two for the nervous system to fully recuperate from the electrical blocks."

Felicia asked, "Is he all right?"

Grinning broadly, the physician replied, "Your husband was an ideal patient. Everything went quite smoothly. His new eye is transmitting quite clearly to the monitoring system."

Brad realized what that meant. "It's transmitting everything?"

"Everything you see," said Yamagata. "In a few days we will implant the aural transmitter in your ear. Then we will receive everything you hear, as well."

"I won't have any privacy at all."

"Not while you have the implants in you. You will have guardian angels with you at every moment."

Thirty million klicks away, Brad knew.

He glanced at Felicia. Instead of looking distressed, she seemed almost mischievously cheery.

"You'll have to keep your eyes closed in bed," she said, with a giggle.

Brad thought, And we'll have to keep damned quiet, too.

"Now I know what it's like to be in the army, in basic training," Brad complained.

The two months after his surgery had been spent in survival training, and stuffing every bit of knowledge about conditions on Gamma's surface into Brad's brain.

Yamagata and his surgical team had implanted a communications link that connected Brad to Emcee with the speed of light. Still, Kosoff, Littlejohn, and every other department head tried to pour all their specialized knowledge into Brad's brain.

And Kosoff insisted that Brad take a course in survival.

The ship's auditorium was converted into a virtual-reality simulation of Gamma's surface, with utterly realistic-looking trees and rocks and even streams gurgling past Brad's booted feet.

Tifa Valente drove Brad mercilessly through the simulated wilderness.

Whenever he complained about the rigors of the training, she would reply urgently, "This could be the difference between life and death for you, Brad. You've got to learn to live with the planet's environment. We won't be there to rescue you if you fall into a puddle of quicksand."

"There isn't any quicksand on Gamma," he grumbled.

"None that we've discovered," Tifa countered. "Yet."

So day after day Brad plowed through survival training, learning how to keep himself alive on the surface of Gamma.

"I'm not going to be alone down there," he pointed out to Tifa one afternoon as they took a break for tea. "The whole idea of this mission is to make contact with the aliens."

The cafeteria was half empty. Tifa had walked them to a small table far from the dispensing machines where people pulled their choices of food and drink. Not even the serving robots came near their table.

Her long face totally serious, she said, "Those aliens might not like having a stranger suddenly invade their territory. You might have to run for your life."

Groaning inwardly at the thought of adding wind sprints to his training, Brad replied with equal seriousness, "They're not violent. We haven't seen one single act of violent behavior."

"And how many scenes of having a human burst in on them have we seen?" she countered.

Brad shrugged. Tifa looked determined, unyielding. Her deep violet eyes were staring at him. He saw that tears were welling in them.

"Brad," she said, her voice low, throaty. "If anything happened to you . . . I . . . "

He sat across the table from her, dumbfounded.

She lowered her eyes, murmuring, "You look and look and look, then when you find the man you want he's already married."

"Tifa . . . I had no idea. I mean . . . I never thought . . . "

"It's all right." She tried to smile. "You just make sure you get back here in one piece. Don't you make a widow out of Felicia, she's too nice a kid for that."

Brad grabbed his teacup and took a long swallow. In the self-heated cup, the tea was burning hot. He gulped and choked and tried not to cough.

Tifa pushed her chair back and got up from the table. "I'll see you in the VR sim," she said, then hurried away.

OBJECTIONS

Kosoff was smoldering. Thumping his fingers angrily on the conference table, he practically snarled, "This is a hell of a time to bring up such objections."

The meeting of the science staff's department chiefs fell absolutely silent. Kosoff had called the meeting for a final check from each department for their approvals to send Brad to the surface of Gamma. Now, seated at the head of the table, he glared at Quentin Abbott, the chief of the astronomy department.

Abbott exuded Englishness. Brad, at the foot of the conference table, thought that the astronomer could not have looked more English if he were wearing a derby hat and a monocle. Abbott was slim, his thin face sculpted with prominent cheekbones, a finely arched nose, and a long pointy jaw. His carefully brushed hair was silver gray, as was his tidy little moustache. Like everyone else along the table, he wore a comfortable tunic and slacks, but on him somehow the clothes looked almost like a Savile Row morning suit.

His bright blue eyes could sparkle, but at the moment they were staring back at Kosoff almost defiantly.

"Can't be helped, I'm afraid," he said, quite undaunted by Kosoff's ire. "Facts, you know, are facts."

"But we're practically ready to send our contact man to Gamma," Kosoff objected. Jabbing a finger toward Brad, he said, "Our man is prepared to go to the surface and make physical contact with the aliens."

Clasping his hands together on the tabletop as if he were about to pray, Abbott said quite calmly, "You cannot stop the coming conjunction of the planet with Beta, no more than King Canute could stop the tide from coming in."

"And you believe that conditions on the planet will become dangerous?"

"Dangerous?" Abbott almost laughed. "They'll be catastrophic. You won't be able to keep this ship in orbit around Gamma while Beta speeds past. Tidal surges will be enormous, the entire planet will be swept by storms and upheavals of biblical proportions."

"Why didn't you tell us of this earlier?" Kosoff demanded.

Very calmly, Abbott replied, "Because we didn't know about it earlier. We'd done some preliminary calculations, of course, but the closer we looked at the conditions when the two planets meet, the more catastrophic the effects, we realized."

"It took you more than a year to realize this?"

"I'm afraid so. Extraordinary situation, you understand. Awfully sorry we couldn't scope out the details earlier, of course."

From the foot of the table, Brad said, "But the Gammans survive the two planets' meeting."

Abbott turned his fine-featured face in Brad's direction. "Yes, they do, apparently. And then the planet swings away from Mithra and starts its long winter season."

"And the Gammans survive that, too," Brad pointed out.

"Somehow," Abbott conceded.

"Then, if I'm down on the surface with them, I can survive the conjunction along with them."

"Rather chancy, I'd say."

"Anything they can do, I can do," Brad insisted.

Kosoff raised a stubby finger. "But you won't have the

rest of us in orbit around Gamma. We'll have to move this ship to Alpha, with all of us in it."

Brad said, "That's still only about three minutes away. I'll still be able to talk with you, and with Emcee."

In his softly courteous tone, Captain Desai pointed out, "Three minutes can be very critical in an emergency situation. It can be a lifetime. The difference between life and death."

"I'm willing to risk it," Brad replied. "In fact, I'm eager to see how the Gammans get themselves through the crisis."

The others around the table fell silent. They all turned toward Kosoff, waiting for him to make a decision.

"We actually don't have much time to waste," Kosoff said, as if thinking out loud. "We've already used up more than a year. We'll have to return to Earth in a little less than four years."

Abbott interjected, "That's still plenty of time—"

Kosoff cut him off. "No, it's not plenty of time. Do you think it's enough time to do the job, Dr. Littlejohn?"

Looking startled, Littlejohn replied, "Enough time to make meaningful contact with the Gammans, tell them of the death wave, and convince them to let us install the shielding equipment? Barely."

"And we'll have to test the shields before we leave," the chief engineer added.

Abbott suggested, "You could put in a call to the World Council's mission controllers, see what they think about all this."

"Call Earth?" Kosoff snapped.

"On the FTL system. You could thrash this out with them in a few days. After all, they *are* supposed to be in control of this mission. You don't have to take the responsibility for this decision on your own shoulders, old man."

Brad saw the flash of anger in Kosoff's eyes. He took

a deep, deliberate breath, then answered, "But the responsibility *is* on my shoulders, Dr. Abbott. Those mission controllers back on Earth picked me to head this expedition. I make the decisions here, not a committee two hundred light-years away."

Abbott stood his ground. "And you're willing to send this young man into grievous peril?"

"He's willing," said Kosoff.

Brad nodded.

"Well, I admire your courage, Dr. MacDaniels, although I doubt your sanity."

A few tentative chuckles broke out along the table.

Kosoff rapped his knuckles on the tabletop, then said, "So it's settled. We send MacDaniels to the surface of Gamma before its conjunction with Beta. We move this ship to orbit Alpha while the two planets go through their closest approach. Then we return to Gamma and pick up MacDaniels when he's ready to return to us."

"If he's still alive," Abbott said in a stage whisper.

It wasn't an official going-away party. No one planned it. The night before Brad was scheduled to go into isolation in preparation for his flight to Gamma's surface, he and Felicia went to dinner in the Crystal Palace and, in ones and twos, friends and acquaintances drifted into the restaurant and joined them. The sturdy little robot waiters dutifully pushed tables together and carried up chairs as the group grew.

Larry Untermeyer was the first to come by, with Tifa Valente on his arm.

"So you go into solitary confinement tomorrow," he said as he sat on the chair one of the robots held for him.

"It's not solitary," Brad corrected. "There'll be plenty of medical and engineering people in the isolation area with me."

Tifa said nothing. She merely sat next to Larry, but kept her eyes on Brad. It made him uncomfortable; Brad had not told Felicia about Tifa's confession.

Gregory Nyerere showed up, with a Valkyrie-like blond companion: tall, skin like ivory, full in the hips and bosom. Greg goes for large-sized women, Brad thought.

"Bring your umbrella," Nyerere joked in his high-pitched voice. "I understand the weather's going to be rough."

Brad nodded and smiled.

His brows knitting, Nyerere said, "I understand that you'll have to wear a full-body suit while you're down on the surface."

"That's right."

Glancing at the others around the still-growing table, Nyerere said, "Um, this may be indelicate, but . . . how will you, eh . . . defecate?"

Brad blinked once, twice, then replied, "Carefully."

iSOLATiON

+++

+++

"Time to test my comm link," Brad said.

He and Felicia were sitting on the sofa in their sitting room. The impromptu going-away party in the Crystal Palace was long over. Tomorrow Brad would go into the isolation area and then, three days later, to the surface of planet Gamma.

Felicia tried to smile, and almost made it.

"Comm crew," Brad called out. "Please cut the link until daybreak tomorrow."

Instantly a voice in Brad's head replied, "Cutting link."

"Thank you."

No response.

Doubtfully, Felicia whispered, "Do you think they've really cut it?"

Brad nodded, then realized he hadn't spoken. "Yes. I'm sure it's okay."

"You trust them?"

"I have to."

He got up from the sofa and held out his hand to Felicia. He realized she was trembling.

"It'll be all right," he said, trying to sound reassuring.

Her face blossomed into a genuine smile. "Well, if they are watching, let's give them something worth looking at."

Brad grinned at her. "And listening to."

Hand in hand, they walked to the bedroom.

* * *

The chief engineer eyed Brad sourly and said, "Let's go through it one more time."

Brad groaned inwardly. All morning long they had made him go through the procedure for safely removing the defecation package without breaching the integrity of his biosuit. Now they stood facing each other, Brad encased in the specially designed suit, the chief engineer in rolled-up shirtsleeves and baggy shorts.

"Didn't I get it right?" Brad asked.

"One time out of three," said the chief engineer. "That means twice you got yourself killed."

"No it doesn't. Breaking the suit's integrity for a minute or so shouldn't be dangerous."

The chief engineer gave the impression of being far larger than his actual physical size. He was swarthy, shaved bald, with a stubbled jaw and narrow gray eyes. His normal expression, it seemed to Brad, was a disgusted scowl.

Planting his thick-wristed fists on his hips, he countered, "And you've been on the planet's surface so many times that you know that for a fact?"

Brad's chin drooped. "Okay," he said. "I'll do it again."

The biosuit was necessary, everyone told him. But they didn't have to wear it, Brad thought resentfully. It was like trying to live inside a sarcophagus. The suit was stiff; it smelled faintly of plastic and lubricating oils. The helmet, shaped like a bullet to resemble the heads of the Gammans, was made of one-way plastiglas: Brad could see out, but anyone outside could not see in, even through the two bulbous false eyes on each side.

Brad went through the removal procedure again, feeling somewhere between indignant and embarrassed.

The chief engineer actually smiled at him! "You got it right two times in a row," he said. "You might get through this after all."

Before Brad could recover from his surprise and respond, the man demanded, "Now what do you do with your package of shit?"

"Seal it, bury it, and make sure its transponder is emitting its signal so we can find it and return it to the ship when I leave the planet."

The chief engineer nodded. "Okay. Now we go through the feeding procedure."

Brad had an urge to wash his hands first.

The night before he would leave the orbiting starship Brad called Felicia for the final time.

"How are you?" she asked.

Sitting on the edge of his cot in the isolation suite, glad to be out of his suit, Brad replied, "I'm fine. Everything's going on schedule. How're you?"

"I miss you."

"I miss you, too, honey."

"I wish I could sneak down there and go with you."

He laughed shakily. "You could just about fit inside the suit with me. Kinda snug, though."

"Snug is good," Felicia said.

He saw that she was struggling to keep a happy expression for him.

"When I get back we'll spend a solid week alone, just the two of us."

"That would be wonderful."

"I love you, Fil."

"I love you, too, Brad." She hesitated, then added, "Be careful down there. Come back to me safe and sound."

"Sure," he said, trying to appear brave.

"Sure," she repeated dolefully.

They chatted aimlessly until Emcee's soft voice interrupted, "Curfew time, I'm afraid."

Almost glad to end this increasingly painful farewell,

Brad said to Felicia, "I'll call you from down on the surface, as soon as I get a chance."

"Good night, Brad." She was fighting to hold back tears, he realized.

"Good night, darling." He almost said *good-bye*.

sitting in the cramped control compartment of the shuttlecraft, Brad recalled from his childhood history lessons that the first astronauts, almost three hundred years ago, were sometimes referred to as "Spam in a can." They were not actually piloting their spacecraft; they sat squeezed into the tight compartment while men on the ground controlled the flight.

"Spam in a can," Brad muttered to himself. He was a passenger, not a flyer. This mission to Gamma's surface was completely automated. If human piloting was required, the controllers aboard the starship would do it, remotely. He had memorized the functions of the displays on the control panel in front of him, but he had no way of manipulating them, except for the cameras that provided him outside views.

So he sat strapped firmly into the seat, in his biosuit, its helmet stowed safely in a rack to his left, watching, listening, *feeling* the little shuttlecraft coming to life.

"Internal power on," came the disembodied voice of one of the controllers.

"Life support on."

A gurgling sound. "Pumps on."

A low moaning noise, swiftly ratcheting up to a shrill whine. "Propulsion system on."

A crisper, more authoritative voice called out, "All systems active."

"All systems in the green," came the response.

The synthesized voice of the countdown clock, "Separation in five seconds . . . four . . . "

Brad realized he was biting his lip. Deliberately, he opened his mouth and gulped in the cabin's canned air.

". . . one. Separation sequence initiated."

Brad felt a quiver, a shudder. The shuttlecraft was being nudged away from the starship.

"Good luck, Dr. MacDaniels."

He had to swallow twice before he could answer, "Thanks."

"Separation successful."

"Main propulsion drive engagement in ten seconds."

Brad thought he should say something, make some sort of statement; this was an historic moment, after all. At least it was supposed to be.

Running the tip of his tongue across his lips, he realized what he wanted to say. "Felicia, I'll see you in six months."

Not for history. For her.

"Main propulsion drive engaged."

Brad felt a push against his back: gentle but insistent.

"You're on your way, Dr. MacDee!"

The display screen in the center of the control panel showed the *Odysseus* moving away. Within seconds Brad could see the entire bulk of the mammoth starship. It was dwindling, faster and faster, getting smaller and smaller.

"Life support?" one of the controllers asked.

"All systems green."

"Life support, Dr. MacDaniels?"

"Everything normal," he reported.

Silence, except for the hum of the propulsion system. The display screen was peppered with stars now; *Odysseus* looked like a toy.

He tapped the external camera control button on the armrest of his chair with a gloved finger.

Planet Gamma filled the screen: a rich green from pole

to pole, except for bony fingers of gray-brown rock mountains and a few glittering seas sprinkled here and there. Clean white clouds seemed to hug the landscape, like oversized sheep grazing in the meadows.

"Atmospheric entry in one minute," came the controller's voice.

Brad nodded tensely. This was the crucial time. Diving into the atmosphere at hypersonic speed, the shuttlecraft would briefly become a blazing meteor. The magnetic heat shield should hold the blistering ionized air safely away from the craft's hull. If it failed, the craft would break up, burn up, and plunge to a fiery impact on the surface. With Brad in it.

Felicia watched the shuttlecraft's flight from the wall screens of the auditorium. More than half the staff was there, some sitting at the tables scattered across the floor, most of them standing.

The screens showed the big green planet and a tiny thin streak of red racing across it.

That's Brad, she told herself. That's his ship. He's in the midst of that burning-hot air.

"He'll be all right."

Felicia whirled around to see Gregory Nyerere standing beside her, his eyes fixed on the screen.

The overhead speakers were relaying the flight controller's calm, almost bored recitation. "Approaching maximum temperature. Max temperature. Max pressure. Conditions nominal."

"Nominal," Nyerere murmured. "Looks like the inside of hell to me."

The shuttlecraft was bouncing and shuddering so badly that Brad's vision blurred momentarily. The roaring outside the ship's skin was scary, like a monster trying to get inside and devour him. It wouldn't stop. Squinting at the clock display on the control panel, Brad saw that this had been going on for less than two minutes. But it seemed like an eternity of jouncing, shaking, bellowing, screeching as the inferno clasped him in its grip.

He tasted blood in his mouth and realized he had bit the inside of his cheek. Thankful that he was firmly buckled into his seat, Brad squeezed his eyes shut.

And the torment started to ease away. Opening his eyes, Brad saw the green surface of the planet hurtling up to greet him.

We're through entry, he exulted. Going subsonic now.

Gigantic trees were reaching up to snare him. A winding river flashed past.

"Initiating landing sequence," came the laconic voice of the flight controller.

On the display screen the trees swept past and Brad saw a broad swath of green meadow approaching. The shuttlecraft lurched—retrorockets, Brad knew. A roar of air told him that the landing gear had been extended. Then a bump, a thump, and he could feel the craft bouncing along on the grassy, uneven ground.

It lurched to a stop. Everything became quiet.

"We're down!" he called.

"Copy you down, Dr. MacDee. Everything looks good from here. All systems nominal."

Brad stared at the central display screen. He saw a meadow that looked almost like Earth, although there were no animals grazing on the grass. The sky was blue, with a few whitish puffs of clouds, but the blue seemed different, somehow off-color.

And there was a moon visible. No, wait, Brad said to himself. Gamma has no moon. That's Beta. It's approaching, coming nearer.

Brad unbuckled his safety harness, whacked his head

when he got up from the chair, and—cursing as he rubbed his forehead—started for the hatch.

He was reaching for the hatch's handle when he remembered that he didn't have his helmet on.

book four

arrival

+ +

+ +

once he sealed the helmet to his suit's neck ring, Brad went back through the short, cramped passageway to the hatch, hunched over slightly to keep his helmet from scraping the overhead. As he reached a gloved hand to push the button that opened the hatch, he saw that his hand was trembling slightly.

"Ready to open hatch," he said.

A controller's voice replied, "Clear to open hatch."

Brad leaned on the button and the hatch slid up, almost noiselessly.

And there it was. Planet Gamma. An alien world that no human had set foot upon. To his staring eyes it looked almost like Earth, but not quite. The green grass waving slightly in the breeze was darker than any grass he had seen before. There were forested hills in the distance, also deeply green, and, far beyond them, craggy gray mountains that seemed to be floating on a bluish haze above the rolling horizon.

No animals visible. No insects buzzing. The only sounds were the soft sighing of the wind and Brad's own breath gushing out of him.

"You are cleared to leave the shuttlecraft," the controller's voice prompted.

"Right," said Brad. He started down the short aluminum ladder, stepping carefully in his heavy boots. *Wouldn't want to fall on my face the first time a human steps onto an alien planet.*

He immediately remembered that humans had walked on New Earth, the planet of the star system Sirius, but that was an artificial world, constructed by the Predecessors and populated with humanlike creatures. That had been humankind's first contact with aliens.

But here, this planet Gamma, this was a real, natural world populated by genuine aliens, creatures who had evolved here naturally.

And I'm going to make contact with them!

The thrill of landing melted away after half an hour of trudging across the meadow, sweating inside his biosuit despite its internal climate control. Mithra was an angry red dot high in the sky, glaring down at him. The woods that fringed the meadow still seemed kilometers away.

One boot ahead of the other, Brad told himself as he slogged away. The meadow seemed empty of animal life. Not even a field mouse or an insect. *Maybe they're frightened by my presence,* Brad thought. *Maybe they can sense that I'm an alien intruder and they're keeping their distance. More likely the noise and shock of the shuttlecraft's landing sent them all scuttling into their holes.*

How will the humanoids react to me? he wondered.

Outwardly, Brad looked much like the bipedal natives of Gamma: tall and lean, the chalky surface of his biosuit spotted with irregular splotches of blue and purple, his head a conical cylinder with bulging eyes on either side.

It was easy enough to look up from inside his helmet. The one-way plastiglas was transparent. Brad saw the lopsided crescent of Beta halfway up from the horizon. He knew it was his imagination, but the planet seemed larger, closer than when he'd seen it from the shuttlecraft.

As he approached the woods, he saw that the trees looked different from any he remembered of Earth. Some of them had twisty, sinuous trunks studded with snaky branches and broad, flat leaves. Others were tall and straight, soaring skyward like redwoods, no branches until high above. Instead of leaves they seemed to bear clusters of pods, so deep a green they looked almost black.

There were bushes between the trees, but they were sparse enough so that they presented no real obstacle to his walking through them.

The ground was rising gently, Brad saw as he checked his map display, flashed against the inner surface of his helmet. It showed he was on the right track to reach the village they had selected as his objective.

"Emcee, are you there?" he asked, in a whisper.

"Yes," came the familiar voice. "You are two point six kilometers from the center of the village."

"Thanks."

"You are welcome."

Emcee's politeness seemed almost silly. Brad wormed his arm out of its sleeve and took the water nipple between his index finger and thumb. The drink tasted flat, stale. One of his first tasks would be to test the water in one of the local streams to see if it was drinkable. If not, he'd have to drink water recycled from the suit's supply.

Drink my own piss, he thought, with a grimace of distaste.

Something flashed past, to his left. An animal! Brad thought. Something small and furry had scampered into the bushes that hugged the bases of the big, straight-boled trees.

Even though he couldn't see the critter now, Brad felt better, happier. He knew from the earlier uncrewed landing vehicles that the planet teemed with animal life. But actually seeing one lifted his spirits.

Now that he was in among the trees, he saw bright-colored birds swooping past, most of them high above, but a few lower, closer. Watching the darting flight of the lower ones, Brad thought there must be insects that they were chasing.

And from twenty meters above him, a small furry animal clung upside down to a tree's trunk and chittered away at him. Grinning, Brad thought, A one-man welcoming committee. Then he sobered and guessed, More likely he's scared, defensive.

The ground's slope got steeper, and Brad began to realize that his suit's weight was far from negligible. He was sweating heavily by the time he reached the crest of the rise.

And there it was: the village, down in the hollow below him. Slowly, awkwardly, Brad sank to his knees in the cumbersome suit, then flattened out onto his belly. He fingered the control pad on his left sleeve, and the electro-optical binoculars built into the helmet slid in front of his eyes.

Four, no, nearly five dozen round, domed structures stood in a pair of concentric circles around a cleared area of packed earth. Walkways of similarly cleared ground separated the structures from each other. The buildings' walls seemed to be smooth, dried mud, flat dun in color. The domed roofs were made of interwoven branches.

Brad saw wheeled carts and larger wagons, most of them sitting idle in the village center. A few were being pulled by six-legged animals the size of ponies.

On the other side of the village, cultivated fields stretched outward to the end of the hollow, row after neatly tended row. Brad saw greenish plants, more than a meter tall. People moved among the rows, harvesting the plants by hand with sickles that appeared to have metal blades.

A stream meandered around the outer edge of the hollow. Several of the aliens were drawing water from it and toting heavy buckets back to the buildings.

The structures seemed pretty much the same size and the same design: round, domed, single-floored, with one window each. Brad could see only one door in each building.

Then he recognized that one of the buildings was noticeably larger than the others. It stood on the inner circle, and a half-dozen Gammans seemed to be standing at its front entrance, gesticulating.

Longhouse, he guessed. With loafers, just like home.

The sun was lowering toward the distant hills, Brad saw. He no longer thought of the star as Mithra: it was this world's sun. And the direction in which it was setting was west, by definition.

Time to hunker down for the night, he told himself.

He slithered down the slope, away from the village, until he thought it was safe to climb to his feet. They can't see me from down here, he thought.

After munching down condensed food tablets, Brad called Emcee.

"Did you see the village?" he half whispered.

"I saw everything that you saw," the computer replied.

"It's exciting, isn't it?"

"If I had emotions, I suppose it would be."

Brad chuckled softly.

"You should report to the controllers," Emcee reminded him.

"But they see everything we do, don't they?"

"Yes, but they still expect a report from you."

Brad nodded reluctantly and called the controllers.

"You found the village, right on schedule," said the disembodied voice.

Brad frowned inwardly at the thought of being tied to a schedule.

A new voice, feminine, announced, "This is Madeira, medical department. We need to go over your physical condition."

"You have the readouts, don't you?" Brad asked.

"Of course, but we need your input, as well. Protocol."

Brad grumbled to himself as he answered the medical technician's questions. Busywork, he thought. They've got all the sensors' data, everything from my heart and breathing rates to the amount of water I've lost from sweating.

As if she could hear his thoughts, Madeira said, "You've lost a bit more water than we expected."

"I've been sweating. It was a long walk, and it's hot down here."

"It's going to get a lot colder pretty soon," she replied.

"The recycling system is working, isn't it?"

A moment's pause. Then, "Checking the readouts. Yes, the recycler is puttering away, right on the curve."

"Good."

"You're due for sleep in another hour."

"I'm setting up camp here."

"That's scheduled for tomorrow."

Again with the schedule, Brad groused to himself. Then he thought, No sense arguing with her. Or any of them. I'll hunker down here for the night, then tomorrow morning I'll walk back to the shuttle and haul out the camping gear.

On an impulse, he asked, "Have you detected anything dangerous in the atmosphere?"

Madeira had to switch him over to the controller in charge of checking the environment.

A man's voice finally told Brad, "We haven't detected anything harmful in the air. Of course, the samples we've studied didn't come from precisely your location."

"But I could take off this helmet for the night, couldn't I?"

He could sense the controller shaking his head. "Against protocol. You wouldn't want the local bugs nesting in your ears while you sleep."

Brad had to admit, "No, I wouldn't."

He slept with the helmet on. It was uncomfortable, but he had no dreams. At least, none he could remember the next morning.

It took Brad two trips to the shuttlecraft before he could assemble a reasonably comfortable base camp. At last, though, he had erected a cylindrical plastic shelter sealed and inflated with breathable air, an almost comfortable bedroll, a minuscule cookstove, and the communications gear. All the comforts of home, he told himself. Inside the shelter he could peel himself out of the cumbersome suit and helmet and sleep more contentedly. His dream came back his first night inside the shelter, but it was muted, somehow a bit different, not as biting.

For five days Brad observed the aliens in their primitive village. And nights. Their routines were a simple round of working in the fields by day, then coming to their homes at sunset, building a fire in front of each building, and cooking a communal meal in big earthenware pots. After they ate, they went inside the huts and slept. What went on inside their circular homes Brad could not see from his perch on the rim of the hills encircling the village.

A pretty boring life, he concluded. Up in the morning, work all day in the fields, then eat and sleep.

At least, he assumed they slept. He couldn't see any lights from inside the huts; only the flickering embers of their cook fires outside. Within less than an hour the entire village went dark. When they slept, Brad slept. He resisted the urge to sneak into the village at night and peek into those windows.

The Predecessors' earlier probes had determined that the Gammans were hermaphrodites, sexless. So when they slept, Brad thought, they slept. No romantic maneuvers.

By the fifth day Brad realized that not all the aliens went into the fields to work. There was always a cluster of them gathered around the biggest building in the village; their longhouse, as Brad had dubbed it.

It was difficult to tell if they were the same people each day. Brad found it hard to distinguish one of the Gammans from another. But he could detect no obvious signs of rank among the loafers at the longhouse. No individual received recognizable signs of deference.

But what would their signs of deference be? he wondered.

Asking Emcee didn't help. "Insufficient data for a meaningful reply," the master computer answered.

At last Brad called Littlejohn. "I don't think I can learn much more about them from this distance. I'm ready to go down and show myself to them."

In the miniaturized communications screen, Littlejohn's dark face looked startled.

"That's a major decision, Brad. We'll have to get Kosoff to agree to it."

Brad nodded. He had expected that reaction.

"Okay," he said. "Let's talk to Kosoff."

Brad asked Emcee to set up a brief get-together with Kosoff, to obtain his okay for going into the village. Instead, Kosoff convened a formal meeting of the full executive committee, all twelve department heads.

"Show yourself to them so soon?" Kosoff asked, from the head of the conference table. Even in the communicator's small screen Brad could see the negative frown on his bearded face.

Sitting cross-legged on the inflated floor of his tent, Brad started to reply, "I don't think I can learn much more about—"

Kosoff interrupted, "The schedule calls for a minimum of two weeks of observation before making physical contact with the aliens. Isn't that right, Dr. Littlejohn?"

The display screen's view enlarged to show the entire conference table. The people sitting around it looked so small that it was difficult for Brad to make out their faces. But Littlejohn's dark, heavy-browed features were unmistakable.

"The schedule has some flexibility in it," the anthropologist began.

Kosoff leaned forward in his chair. No mistaking the frown he wore. "Making actual physical contact with the aliens is the most delicate part of our mission. And the most important. We mustn't let impatience wreck our work."

Brad asked, "So what am I supposed to do, sit here and watch them from afar for another ten days?"

"Another few days, at least," Kosoff replied.

"What's the point of that?" argued Brad. "What am I going to see that I haven't already seen? That's a primitive culture we're looking at. They work, eat, and sleep. Day in and day out."

Elizabeth Chang, head of the philology department, spoke up. In her low, smoky voice she pointed out, "Every day you spend observing the aliens from afar, our linguistics program decodes more of their language. It is very difficult and very slow, but we are making progress. Do you not think it best to wait upon showing yourself to them until we have a fuller grasp of their language?"

Kosoff nodded vigorously.

Brad asked, "How long do you think it would take?"

Chang's doll-like face eased into a gentle smile. "How far is up?"

"We can't wait forever," Brad said.

"Not forever, but perhaps a few more weeks," Chang replied.

Quentin Abbott raised a hand. Without waiting for Kosoff to recognize him, the astronomer pointed out, "We do face a time limit, you know. The planet's conjunction with Beta is coming in four months. We shall have to move this ship to an orbit around Alpha before then. I should imagine you'll want to make contact before all that."

Kosoff waved a hand in the air. "Another week or two shouldn't make much difference."

Abbott's brows rose toward his scalp. "Really?"

Brad insisted, "I can make contact with them tomorrow morning."

"And be their dinner tomorrow night," Kosoff muttered.

Littlejohn said, "There's another element to consider. If Brad makes contact with them, and then the conjunction hits the planet with enormous storms and other ecological catastrophes, mightn't the aliens blame Brad for the disaster?"

There was a moment of silence, then comments came from around the table.

"I hadn't thought of that."

"I suppose it's possible."

"They might think MacDaniels is a witch!"

"It might be better to wait until after the conjunction."

Brad watched as they talked. Each person at the conference table had an opinion, or at least wanted to be heard.

Finally he said to them, "Well, instead of sitting around discussing the problem, you need to make a decision."

Kosoff nodded. "You're right. Elizabeth, we'll give you and your people another ten days to extend your understanding of the Gammans' language. Brad, you'll continue to observe them at a distance for ten days. No contact until then."

"But the possibility that they'll blame MacDaniels for the conjunction storms?"

With a shake of his head, Kosoff answered, "They've been through conjunctions before. Even if it's happened before any of the living Gammans were born, they must have an oral history about it."

Chang nodded daintily. "They do talk about a bad time, an evil time that brings death."

"You see? Ten more days and then MacDaniels makes contact."

Brad felt as if he'd been neatly maneuvered into waiting ten days. Then he looked at Kosoff, who was smiling satisfiedly, and Brad felt frustration rising in him. Frustration—and anger.

Smoldering as he sat in his tent, Brad waited impatiently for the meeting to break up, then asked Emcee to connect him with Littlejohn on the anthropologist's personal channel.

"Nobody listens in on personal calls, do they?" he asked the master computer.

"No one but me," Emcee replied, "and I am programmed to respect an individual's privacy unless some matter of danger to the mission is involved."

"Good. Put me through to Littlejohn, then." Brad almost added, "Please," but knew Emcee didn't need human politeness.

The anthropologist was in his kitchen, just reaching out for a steaming cup of tea.

"I thought you might call," Littlejohn said, heading for the recliner in his sitting room.

Still squatting on the floor of his tent, Brad blurted, "Kosoff is wasting valuable time."

Littlejohn stretched out on his recliner, the teacup still in his hand. With a sad little smile, he replied, "He doesn't see it that way."

"I don't understand why he wants me to spend another ten days repeating what I've already done. I'm ready to make contact with these people."

"But he's not."

"Why not?"

"Because you are."

Brad blinked with puzzlement. "What?"

"He wants to make certain that you—and everyone else—knows who's in charge. It's a simple matter of two alpha males competing for leadership of the pack."

"I'm not competing with Kosoff!"

"Aren't you?"

"No!"

With a slight shake of his head, Littlejohn said, "Well, he thinks you are. And that's what matters. He feels he has to show you, and everyone else, that *he* makes the decisions and the rest of us follow his lead. That includes you."

"That's crazy!" Brad said.

"He doesn't see it that way. I don't think he even realizes what he's doing. But the most important thing to him is to maintain his position as leader. That means he has to make sure that you do what he tells you to do."

Brad pulled his knees up to his chin and muttered, "This is a helluva way to run the mission."

"No," said Littlejohn, looking almost amused. "It's the human way. The way of the primate apes."

Brad stewed inwardly as the sun set and darkness enveloped the woods. His shelter wasn't big enough to pace in, so he pulled on his biosuit, then pushed out through the air lock seal and walked through the trees for the better part of an hour.

He heard strange animal cries in the darkness, and caught a glimpse of a large bird gliding almost silently between the trees. He trudged up to the crest of the rise and looked down at the village. All the buildings were dark, not a single light showing anywhere.

Then he realized that the hollow was bathed in a faint, eerie reddish glow. Looking up, he saw the crescent of Beta glowering down. It's getting closer, he knew.

Finally he went back to his tubular shelter, crawled inside, and stripped off his suit. Sitting on the bedroll in nothing but his skivvies, he called to Emcee:

"What time is it aboard the ship?"

The computer's smooth voice instantly replied, "Twenty-one fifty-three."

Felicia might be asleep already, he thought. But he told Emcee to buzz her personal channel anyway.

His communicator screen glowed to life and Felicia's warm-eyed face smiled at him.

"I thought you would call," she said.

"Woman's intuition?" Brad asked with a smile.

"No, I heard about the meeting with the department heads."

He rehashed the meeting with her, and Littlejohn's claim that Kosoff felt that Brad was competing against him. Felicia listened patiently, then asked, "So what do you intend to do?"

"I'll tell you what I'd like to do: walk right down into the village tomorrow morning and say hello."

"Would that be wise?"

"It'd be better than sitting here doing nothing."

"So do it," she said.

Brad shook his head slowly. "But if I frighten them, or anger them, or screw up the contact in any way—the mission would be totally loused up, and it would be all my fault."

Felicia said, "It's all your responsibility, one way or another."

"My responsibility," Brad echoed. "Not Kosoff's damned committee's."

"It's a shame the Gammans don't discover you on their own. Don't they ever leave their village?"

"They go to work in their fields, on the other side of the hollow from where I am. They forage for small game out at the edge of the hollow."

Felicia's expression turned thoughtful. "Too bad they don't come up to where you are and discover you on their own."

For several moments Brad fell silent, thoughts whirling in his head.

At last he said, "Maybe I could arrange that."

"You think so?"

"It's worth a try."

Brad slept dreamlessly after his talk with Felicia, even though he realized he hadn't asked her how she was doing, or what she was doing in his absence.

He awoke as morning sunlight brightened the curved surface of his tent. Sitting up, he called Emcee and asked for a review of the animals that the Gammans caught and ate.

By midmorning Brad was outside the shelter, in his biosuit, cheerfully building a primitive trap from branches and twigs, humming to himself. His work was clumsy at first, especially with his hands encased in the suit's thin, slightly slippery gloves. But within a couple of hours, with Emcee's help, he had built a barred little box with a hinged door that could snap shut and lock. Then he reached up and pulled a bright-colored fruit from one of the sinuous trees.

It looks ripe, he said to himself. We'll see.

"What are you doing?" the voice of a controller demanded.

Startled by the intrusion, Brad replied, "An experiment," and quickly returned his attention to his work.

"That's not on the mission protocol."

"Yes it is. We're supposed to study the eating habits of the local fauna."

The controller did what bureaucrats usually do when

faced with a contradiction: he bucked the question to the next-highest level of authority.

I just hope it doesn't get to Kosoff, Brad thought.

With Emcee guiding him, Brad found tiny paw prints around the edges of the bushes at the base of one of the big, sky-reaching trees. He placed his lopsided little trap beneath the bush's leaves and backed away, then hunkered down on his stomach to watch and wait.

And wait. And wait.

"They're not coming," he muttered to Emcee.

"Hunting requires patience," the computer replied. "The animals you seek are wary. After all, it's their lives that are at stake."

Brad nodded inside his helmet. "Patience," he whispered.

He was drifting off to sleep when he was startled by a screeching, snarling noise. His eyes flashing wide, Brad saw that a little furball was caught inside his rickety trap, desperately struggling to get out.

Grinning at his success, Brad got to his feet and walked to the trap. The animal was making it shake and rattle with his exertions. It seemed to be half fur, half teeth, and either terrified or furious. Perhaps some of both. Its eyes were wide and glaring.

It had six little legs, Brad saw. And the fruit he had laid inside the trap for bait had been half gnawed away.

"You had your meal before you realized you couldn't get out," he said to the trapped critter.

Brad's plan was to go down to the edge of the village that night and lay the dead beast where the natives would be certain to find it. Curiosity would drive them to wonder how it got there, and that would impel them to follow the trail of his bootprints and find him. Contact.

But that brought up a problem. He had to kill the animal.

Brad stared down at the little beast. It had quieted down, probably exhausted from its struggles. It crouched inside the trap, panting and staring at him.

He knew that the equipment in his pack included a laser pistol with enough power to instantly, painlessly kill a human being, let alone an undersized ferret.

He also knew he couldn't do it.

Well, he thought, I'll leave a live gift in the village. Tonight.

He picked up the wooden cage. The animal snarled and nipped at Brad's fingers, making him drop the little coop. Its door popped open and the furball scooted away, chattering furiously.

Holding his hand close to his helmet, Brad saw that the critter's teeth had not penetrated the fabric of his glove. He didn't feel any pain, except to his ego.

Mighty hunter, Brad said to himself.

Undeterred, he picked up the empty cage and started all over again.

By nightfall, Brad had collected three squeaky, chittering little rodents in three lopsided, flimsy traps. He had added primitive straps made from vines, so that he could carry them without getting his fingers nipped.

As he gently laid his handiwork outside his shelter, he saw that all three animals had curled up and gone to sleep. Good, he thought. The quieter the better.

Using the night-vision optics in his helmet, he carefully carried his catches to the crest of the ridge and looked down at the village. Only one light was showing, in the building he thought of as the longhouse.

The controllers back aboard the orbiting starship had been quiet, for the most part. Brad's explanation that he was studying the local fauna apparently satisfied them. They must have found a line in the mission protocol that covers what I've done so far.

But going down into the sleeping village was another matter, he knew. Emcee was watching everything he did; Brad hoped that the human controllers on the night shift depended on the computer to alert them of anything deviating from mission protocol, and were not watching him moment by moment.

Brad hunkered down amidst his catches and waited. He drifted off to sleep, then woke with a start when his earphones buzzed with the sounds of Gammans speaking.

Raising his helmeted head above the crest, he saw in the ruddy light of Beta four Gammans walking leisurely away from the longhouse, chatting among themselves. He knew the sounds of their conversation were automatically relayed from his suit to Emcee, up in the orbiting starship. More grist for the linguists' mill, he thought.

The four aliens went their separate ways to their huts, calling to one another in what Brad thought must be their version of "good night." The village grew quiet and utterly dark. Maybe they can see in the dark better than I can, he thought.

Brad waited an hour, fighting off the urge to sleep. The animals he had caught were quietly snoozing away. Hope I can get them down to the village without waking them, he thought. He decided to carry them one by one, and deposit them at the doorway to the longhouse. That'll make more bootprints for the villagers to follow, he told himself.

The work was tedious, but at last Brad had all three little traps in place just outside the longhouse's entrance. Then he hurried back up the hillside and started for his shelter, thankful that the controllers hadn't paid any attention to what he was doing.

Nobody up in the ship has thought of this, he realized. There's nothing in the mission protocol about it. So what is not forbidden is allowed. I haven't triggered any alarms from Emcee. Brad thought of the master computer as his partner in crime.

Going to be a big day tomorrow, he thought as he trudged toward the shelter. With a grin, Brad wished he could see Kosoff's face when the professor learned that he had made contact with the Gammans.

CONFLICT

+++

+++

"Just what do you think you're doing?"

Brad snapped awake at the sound of Kosoff's voice. For a moment he was disoriented, foggy. But then it all became clear. He was sprawled on the sleeping roll in his shelter, on planet Gamma, alone in the predawn dimness.

And Kosoff's face filled his comm screen, glowering at him.

"Well?" the professor demanded.

Knuckling his eyes as he sat up, Brad mumbled, "Good morning."

"You went into their village," Kosoff accused.

"Yessir, I did."

"I specifically told you not to make contact with the aliens."

"I haven't made contact," Brad said.

His face red with anger, Kosoff started to reply, thought better of it, and snapped his mouth shut. Brad sat there looking at the comm display, fighting an urge to urinate.

At last Kosoff said, his voice iron-hard, "Last night you went into the village three times and left three small animals that you had caught."

"Yes, I did."

"That's contact, which I specifically prohibited you from initiating."

"It's not contact. They didn't see me. They don't know where the animals came from."

Kosoff's glowering expression cooled a bit, but only a bit. "Don't split hairs with me, young man."

Thinking quickly, Brad improvised, "What I did is an experiment. I want to see how the Gammans react to something unexpected."

"How they react," Kosoff growled.

"Surely they won't think that those animals were left with them by a visitor from another world."

Kosoff said nothing.

"If we're going to make contact—eventually," Brad went on, "I thought it would be a good idea to see how they react to the unexpected."

"React to the unexpected."

"That's within the mission protocol, I think."

"You'd have to go through the rules with an atomic force microscope to find anything covering what you just did."

Glancing up at the brightening shell of his shelter, Brad said, "They'll be waking up soon. We'll be able to see how they react."

Still looking grim, Kosoff grumbled, "I'll get Chang and her people to record everything they say."

"The linguistics computer should be able to understand at least some of it," said Brad.

"You'd better get up to the crest of the ridge and observe them."

"Yes. Right away."

Kosoff was clearly unhappy, but he added, "And don't let them see you!"

Suppressing a grin, Brad answered, "I'll try not to."

By the time he had done his morning ablutions (including relieving his bladder) and pulled on the biosuit, the bloodred sphere of Mithra had climbed above the distant mountains. It was full daylight when Brad cautiously looked down at the village from the crest of the wooded ridge. He stayed behind a row of bushes and focused his helmet's telescopic lenses on the longhouse.

A growing crowd of Gammans was clustered at the building's door, talking rapidly and gesticulating with their ropy, tentacle-like arms.

". . . not me," the linguistics computer translated.

"Who did it?" demanded a voice. Brad thought it must have come from the Gamman standing in the doorway, with the three caged animals at his feet. The splotches of color on his body were several different shades of blue and purple, and he seemed to be the one asking questions, demanding answers.

The village chief, Brad concluded.

They kept on chattering and pointing at one another. Brad's gift of the captured animals had clearly upset them. It was something different, something new in their lives, and they had no explanation for it. Very much like humans, what they didn't understand, they feared.

Brad noticed with some disappointment that their wide-splayed feet were obliterating the bootprints he had left in the packed earth.

There goes one of my brilliant ideas, he thought.

The computer's translation was hit and miss. Mostly miss. It buzzed weakly when it came across a word or phrase it didn't understand. But it kept spitting out the word "who." None of the Gammans had an answer.

At last the village chief raised his arm and pointed to the hills on the far side of their farmland.

". . . strangers . . . their village," Brad heard in his helmet earphones. ". . . why? Who?"

". . . death time coming . . . "

". . . gift?"

"Why?" the chief repeated.

The villagers fell silent. Several of them turned to look toward the distant hills.

Then one of them said, "Far village."

Brad grinned to himself. "Far village, indeed," he muttered. "You have no idea how far."

CON+AC+

Brad slithered on his belly down below the ridge-line, then got to his feet and marched back to his shelter. Time for breakfast, he told himself. Two tablets of condensed proteins and vegetable products, plus a vitamin pill, washed down with my recycled piss.

At least the meal didn't take long. Brad listened to the computer's translation of the Gammans' talk, straining to make sense of it. There were still huge gaps in the translation, stretches where he heard nothing but its piti-ful buzzing, like a tiny insect trapped in a bottle.

But the computer understood one phrase that had been repeated several times: "Death time coming."

Could they know about the death wave? he asked himself. And answered, No. Impossible. They don't even have telescopes, let alone modern astronomical equip-ment.

Death time must refer to the coming flyby of planet Beta, he concluded. Death time.

Suddenly the computer's speaker erupted with the rumbling of several deep voices. Gammans. Excited. And not far away.

He pulled on his helmet, fastened it to the neck ring of his biosuit, and ducked out the shelter's air lock.

And there were four Gammans, not more than fifty meters away, gaping at him. They all carried short, sharpened hunting sticks.

Contact!

Fighting the urge to go back inside the shelter and find his pistol, Brad instead took two full steps beyond the air lock and spread his arms, palms outward.

"Hello," he said, hoping that the computer's low growl of translation was correct.

Emcee's voice came through the earphones inside Brad's helmet. "I have notified Professor Kosoff of your contact." Brad thought that even the computer sounded excited. You're projecting your own emotions onto Emcee, he told himself.

Still . . .

The four aliens looked uneasily at one another, then the tallest of them rumbled like a lion's deep-chested cough.

The computer said in Brad's earphones, "Who . . . you?"

"I'm a visitor," said Brad, taking another tentative step toward them. The computer made a grumbling translation, although Brad wondered if it knew the Gamman term for "visitor."

The Gammans backed away from Brad slightly, talking among themselves. No translation from the computer. All Brad heard was their deeply sonorous voices. It's like listening to a Russian opera, he thought inanely. All bassos.

Brad was accustomed to being the tallest in any group, but every one of the Gammans towered over him by half a dozen centimeters. Brad told himself it didn't matter, he was tall enough to seem like them, yet he found that he felt uneasy, self-conscious.

He realized that they had turned slightly sideways to look at him. Those bulbous, oversized eyes on the sides of their bullet-shaped heads could not see directly ahead. They're descended from grazers, he thought, not carnivores. I hope.

Kosoff's voice came through his earphones. "Don't get any closer to them! If they attack, get back into the shelter. It's strong enough to stop their hunting sticks."

"They're the ones backing away," Brad said, almost in a whisper.

The leader of the aliens spoke up again, sounding like distant rumbling thunder. The computer picked up a few words: " . . . where . . . village. . . . why . . . here . . . "

Brad stretched out one arm, pointing toward the distant mountains. "My village is far, far away."

Another of the Gammans took a step toward him, making a sound like a low-pitched buzz saw. He touched his chest with his free hand and repeated the sound several times.

It sounded to Brad like "Mnnx."

His name? Brad wondered.

"Mnnx."

Assuming that the alien was giving his name, Brad touched the chest of his biosuit and said, "Brad."

The aliens glanced at one another.

Brad repeated, "Brad. My name is Brad."

The leader made a very humanlike shrug and rumbled, "Brrd."

Smiling inside his helmet, Brad said, "Close enough." Then he pointed to the one who had introduced himself and tried to repeat the name he had given: "Mnnx."

"Mnnx!" the alien said, raising his stick aloft.

Another one of them said, "Lnng."

All four of the aliens advanced toward Brad, then stopped a respectful few paces in front of him.

"Village?" asked the leader.

Again Brad pointed toward the mountains, shimmering blue in the hazy distance.

"Far away," he repeated.

"Frr wy," said Lnng. Their faces were incapable of expressions, but Brad got the feeling they were all satisfied.

Lnng pointed uphill with his hunting stick. "Village," he said, pointing with his free hand to himself and his companions. "Go . . . village."

Brad nodded inside his helmet, then realized that the aliens could not see the gesture, and even if they could, they wouldn't understand it. So he pointed up to the ridgeline and said, "To your village."

Kosoff's voice came through his earphones again. "Let's hope they have a tradition of hospitality to strangers."

"Looks that way," Brad whispered. Then he marveled to himself, I've done it! I've made contact with the aliens!

Brad looks tired, Felicia thought as she studied his face in the holographic display of their bedroom. She was sitting on the bed, fully dressed, not wanting to stir him when they were so physically separated. And yet . . .

"They just accepted me," Brad was saying. "Asked a few questions about where I came from, but aside from that didn't show much curiosity at all."

"And you're making progress with them?" she asked.

Brad was back in his shelter on Gamma. It looked like night had fallen out there: the shelter wall was dark. In the sharp light of the shelter's solitary lamp, his face looked leaner than she had ever seen it before. There were shadows in the hollows of his cheeks and beneath his eyes.

But he replied cheerfully enough. "Yep. It's starting to get monotonous, though. Up with the sun, hike out to the village, talk with whoever's not working in the fields."

"But you're learning their language."

"And their ways. They don't seem to have any fun at all. Just work all day, have a meal, then go to sleep. Hard way to live."

"There's always someone in the village for you to talk with?"

"Yes, but not the same person each time. They seem to rotate the field work and give everybody a day off now and then."

"Well," Felicia said, "they're aliens, after all. We shouldn't expect them to behave exactly the way we do."

Brad let out a weary sigh. "Guess not."

"How are you doing?"

"I'm okay. At least the medics haven't found anything to worry about."

"But?" she prompted.

"I sure miss you."

"We'll be moving to Alpha in another week."

"You'll be even farther away."

"Only three minutes."

"Thirty-some million kilometers."

Felicia didn't reply. She knew what she wanted to say, but wasn't certain she had the nerve to say it.

Brad asked, "How are you doing?"

"Oh, I'm fine."

"Kosoff hasn't come on to you?"

"Not at all. Whenever we happen to meet, he's polite and proper."

"He hasn't asked you to dinner or anything like that?"

"No," said Felicia. "Nobody's interested in me."

"I am."

She smiled. "And I'm interested in you. Only you."

"I miss you, Fil. Wish we were together."

She took a deep breath, then said, "We could be, you know."

"What? What do you mean?"

Felicia plunged ahead, "I've been thinking about a virtual reality session."

"VR sex?"

"We could get Emcee to set up a VR link between us," she said quickly, all in a rush. "We could share a session."

Brad's face lit up for a flash of a second. Then he shook his head. "Too many ways for other people to peek in."

"Emcee could keep the link strictly private."

"You've talked with him about it?"

Lowering her eyes, Felicia admitted, "Yes, I have."

Brad looked surprised. But then his expression eased into a smile. "Well, we'd better do it before the ship hauls off to Alpha. I won't be able to deal with a three-minute wait for your responses."

Felicia laughed delightedly.

VR sex was a little strange, at first. Weird. Brad had to wear his biosuit, including its helmet. Fortunately the suit's gloves had virtual reality circuitry built into them. Its urination relief tube served as a makeshift masturbation device.

He was clumsy, at first, knowing that Felicia was in a full-body VR suit. But passion rose swiftly. After his third climax Brad lay on his bedroll, spent and sweaty. I'll have to clean up the suit, he thought. But he was smiling hugely nonetheless.

"And no one tried to cut into our link?" Felicia asked Emcee.

It was morning. She had slept blissfully—but not for long—after her VR session with Brad.

"You had complete privacy," the master computer's avatar replied from the holographic display.

Does that include you? Felicia wanted to ask. But she held herself back. She was afraid of the answer.

Instead of making breakfast for herself, Felicia went to the cafeteria. She saw Dr. Steiner, head of the biology department, sitting alone, and went to her table. Ask her, she told herself. The worst she can do is say no.

"May I join you?"

Steiner looked up at Felicia and nodded. They made a study in contrasts: Steiner, tall, blond, regal; Felicia, petite, dark, elfin.

Ursula Steiner had scant patience for idle chitchat, Felicia knew, so without preliminaries she said:

"Dr. Steiner, for some time I've been thinking that I would like to study the octopods on Alpha full time."

Steiner's pale brows rose a centimeter. "Full time? The whole department is concentrating on the Gammans. Professor Kosoff's orders."

"I know. But surely you can spare one person to study the octopods. There's so much about them that we don't know."

"Yes," Steiner replied slowly. "That's true enough. But don't you want to continue working with your husband?"

"There's not much I can do to help Brad in his work," Felicia replied. "The octopods are a challenge that we're ignoring, don't you think?"

Steiner was silent for several moments. At last she said, "I'll talk to Kosoff about it."

"Thank you!"

A rare smile inching across her lips, Steiner asked, "You want to make a niche for yourself?"

"I suppose I do," said Felicia.

"Tired of standing in your husband's shadow already?" Steiner asked.

Surprised, almost shocked, Felicia replied, "It's not that at all! I just want to make a real contribution to our work."

"Yes, I see," Steiner said, her smile morphing almost into a smirk. "I was wondering how long the honeymoon would last."

slowly, painfully, Brad learned the Gammans' language. And their ways. Some of their behaviors were almost human; others, utterly alien.

They were sexless farmers who spent virtually all their waking hours tending the crops they grew. Every member of the village worked in the fields, even Drrm, the one Brad thought of as their chief.

Brad spent his days with them, watching their unending toil along the rows of their farmland. He sat with them at their evening meal, when they gathered around fires cooking their usually meatless stews. He even grew accustomed, almost, to their mouths being in their midsections, fringed with wormlike appendages that turned Brad's own stomach, no matter how many times he watched the aliens shoveling their food into their shiver-inducing maws.

After the evening meal Brad would leave the village and walk back to his shelter for the night. The Gammans showed practically no curiosity about where Brad came from or why he had appeared among them.

Strange, Brad thought. But then he reminded himself that these were alien creatures: intelligent, but the products of a different evolution on a different world. The traits that appeared almost human to him were coincidences, nothing more.

They weren't exclusively vegetarians, he saw. Every few days Drrm, the village chief, would pick three or four of them to go out beyond the edge of their fields and hunt for small game, which went into the stewpots that night. Brad learned that the animals he had given them had become meals—after being ritually sacrificed and cooked.

Once he returned to his shelter, Brad spent his evenings talking with Emcee, Kosoff, and Littlejohn, reviewing the day's events, preparing for the next day's observations. He spoke with Felicia every night, of course, before going to sleep. She told him the linguistics team was expanding their understanding of the Gammans' language.

"Thanks to you, dear," Felicia said happily, her warmly smiling face filling his comm screen.

"How are you?" he asked, stretched out alone on his bedroll.

With obvious excitement, Felicia answered, "Steiner has assigned me to studying the octopods! She talked it over with Kosoff and he okayed my request. He even seemed happy about it, she told me."

Brad muttered, "Beware of Greeks bearing gifts."

"You're jealous!"

"Just looking out for your welfare," he replied, feeling nettled. "You're important to me."

"I miss you," she answered. "It's lonely here without you."

"Virtual reality's not the same, is it?"

"It's better than nothing," she said.

Trying to put up a brave front, Brad said, "Well, I've got plenty of new friends down here."

Felicia's expression went somber. "We'll be moving to an orbit around Alpha in two days."

Even though he knew it was scheduled, her words jolted Brad. "Two days?"

"That's what Captain Desai told us."

Brad nodded, his spirits flagging.

"We'll only be three minutes away," Felicia said quickly. "We can still talk together every night."

"Yes," said Brad. "I know."

"It's going to be a dangerous time for you, down there."

He tried to make light of it. "If the Gammans can get through it, I'll get through it."

"Yes," Felicia said. "That's right."

But Brad thought she didn't look at all sure about it. And neither was he, he realized.

The following evening, Brad saw Mnnx standing alone on the edge of the village, staring at the looming crescent of Beta, bigger and brighter than ever.

"Death time coming closer," said Mnnx, flatly, emotionlessly.

Brad saw that he was carrying a freshly skinned lizard in one ropy hand. Without another word he trudged to the house he shared with four other Gammans.

Brad watched him toss the animal into the cook pot, after swiftly chanting the proper prayer of sacrifice. Like prehistoric hunters on Earth, the Gammans believed the prey animal came to them willingly and allowed itself to be caught and killed. The prayer was one of atonement, and thanks for the creature's sacrifice.

Once the game was cooking in the bubbling pot Mnnx sat in the circle around the fire. Brad hunkered down beside him, still awkward in his biosuit.

"Tell me about the death time," Brad said.

Mnnx's eye slid upward, toward the starlit sky, then focused again on Brad.

"Beta brings monsters." He didn't say "Beta," of course. That was the computer's translation for the low, humming sound that represented their name for the approaching planet.

"Monsters?" Brad asked.

"Terrible monsters. They kill."

"From Beta?"

Mnnx bowed his domed head. "They bring death."

"What are they like?" Brad asked.

"Big. Fast. Kill everyone." The computer could not convey sadness or fear, of course, but Brad felt both emotions. Monsters that kill everyone. Monsters from Beta.

"It must be part of their mythology," said Littlejohn later that night as Brad told the anthropologist about his conversation with Mnnx.

Shaking his head, Brad replied, "It sounded awfully real to me. Not some fairy tale."

Littlejohn smiled patiently. "Mythology *is* real to those who believe in it. My people believed that songs can guide you across the outback, for god's sake."

Brad wondered if "for god's sake" was Littlejohn's idea of a pun.

tiger, tiger

"You'd better have a look at this," said Olav Pedersen, the head of the planetology department.

Kosoff leaned back in his desk chair and stared at Pedersen's lean, pale face. He looks as if all the blood's been drained out of him, Kosoff thought. Pasty as a ghost. Even his hair is thin, so blond it's almost white.

But Pedersen's blue eyes were sharp as sapphires, glittering.

"What is it?" Kosoff asked the planetologist.

"Beta is waking up."

The office wall screen's display lit up to show a fat crescent that Kosoff immediately recognized as planet Beta. The camera view zoomed in past scudding gray clouds to show the barren rocky surface of the planet.

Something was stirring down there. Many somethings.

"What in the name of creation is that?"

Pedersen's voice answered, "Native life."

Kosoff saw a clutch of the tiny rodentlike animals standing on their hind legs, frozen still, staring at what appeared to be a sizeable rock—which was splitting apart like an eggshell.

A big, meaty paw pushed out of the shell, followed by a heavy head with a mouth full of fangs.

"Good lord!" gasped Kosoff.

The catlike creature cracked the rest of the shell open and stepped out languidly on six clawed legs. It glanced at the rodents, still standing less than ten meters away, then turned and stalked off in the other direction.

The data bar at the bottom of the screen showed that the cat was not quite three meters long, without including its hairless, twitching tail.

"Native . . . ?" Kosoff gaped at the beast. "But we haven't seen anything like this before."

"Neither did the Predecessors, apparently, when they did their surveillance of the Mithra system. Beta was near its apogee then, locked in deep winter. Every living thing on the planet must have been hibernating."

"And now they're waking up," said Kosoff, his eyes glued to the wall display. "Good lord, look at that brute!"

"The satellite cameras have picked up eight of them, scattered across the planet." Pedersen's voice was quivering with excitement. "Apparently they've been dormant for some time. Now that the planet's warming, they've awakened."

The camera followed the beast as it padded purposefully across the barren, rock-strewn ground.

Pedersen repeated, "We've observed eight of them, so far. Some of the larger formations that we thought were boulders are actually some sort of eggs that have been incubating these beasts. Now they're hatching. Maybe they're not full grown yet."

Kosoff's eyes went wider still as the camera view shifted to show what looked like another rock splitting apart, with one of the big cats clawing its way out of it.

"Eggs," Kosoff muttered.

"The biologists will want to see this."

"I'll call Steiner."

"We should put more satellites around Beta before we pull out for Alpha."

"Yes," Kosoff agreed absently, his attention focused on the felines.

Dr. Steiner's reedy, nasal voice came from the desk's phone console. "Yes, Professor?"

"Come to my office right away, Ursula. Drop whatever you're doing. Beta's waking up!"

For the first time since leaving Earth, Kosoff was caught up in the excitement of making a truly unexpected discovery.

The huge, ferocious-looking catlike animals were awakening on Beta after an incubation of nearly half a century. Staring at his office's wall screen, he saw that the cats made Earthly tigers look puny. Only a dozen of them had been spotted so far by the satellite cameras, scattered across Beta's barren, rocky surface. But they seemed to be purposefully stalking across the desolate land, as if each of them had a goal in mind.

Steiner stared too, open-mouthed, as she sat before Kosoff's desk. The wall display was following one of the huge cats as it padded over the broken, stony ground.

"It's hunting," she said.

"Must be hungry," said Pedersen.

Steiner nodded. "It's been inside that egglike thing for nearly four decades, at least."

"Hungry, all right," Pedersen repeated.

Kosoff shook his head. "But they go right past batches of those rodents without blinking at them."

"And the rodents don't seem to be afraid of them."

"I would be afraid," Pedersen said with some fervor. "Look at those fangs."

The desk phone announced, "Breaking orbit in six hours. Prepare for departure."

Kosoff wondered how long the surveillance satellites he had just ordered to be put in place around Beta could maintain their orbits when Beta and Gamma made their close approach to one another. Whatever, he told himself.

We'll put up more of them once the two planets have parted.

But he couldn't tear his eyes away from the display screen. Where is that damned beast going? he wondered. What's it up to?

"'Tiger, tiger, burning bright,'" he recited in an awed whisper. "'What immortal hand or eye dare frame thy fearful symmetry?'"

COiNCiDENCE

sitting before the cook fire in front of mnnx's hut, Brad realized that he didn't know the Gamman words for "fun" or "entertainment." maybe there aren't any, he thought. All they do is work, from sunup to sundown. They don't even have sex.

His own VR sessions with Felicia were at an end. The starship had left Gamma and established a safe haven orbiting Alpha, some thirty million kilometers away. He still spoke with Felicia every night, but it was a stuttering, cumbersome communication, disrupted by three-minute-long breaks. Less a conversation than an awkward pair of monologues.

Now, as twilight darkened into night, Brad said to Mnnx, "You work all day long."

Mnnx answered in his low, buzzing words and the computer in Brad's suit translated, "Death time coming."

"You are getting ready for the death time?"

"Yes. We must."

The four other Gammans sitting around the fire seemed to be ignoring Brad and Mnnx, sitting quietly, somberly, while the cook pot bubbled and the night grew darker.

"You don't work this hard all the time?" Brad probed. "Only when death time is near?"

"Yes," said Mnnx. "When the year begins and we enter the world, there is time for . . . " The computer failed to translate the last few words.

"You don't work all the time then."

"Not needed. There is time for . . . and . . . "

Singing and dancing? Brad mentally filled in the blanks. But he found it hard to picture these solemn, hard-working farmers singing or dancing. Then he remembered that even the dourest frontier settlers in the old American West made time for barn dances and hoe-downs.

Yes, but they were sexual creatures, he knew. How much of our attitudes about relaxation and enjoyment are based on the need to attract sexual partners?

Brad fell silent for several long moments, knowing what he had to ask next, wondering how to phrase it.

Finally he started, "Mnnx, are there any children in the village?"

It was Mnnx's turn to fall silent. At last he asked, "What are *jhilldrrn*?"

Brad wondered if the translator had conveyed the word properly. He remembered from his history classes that the earliest attempts to create computerized translation programs had produced some spectacularly foolish results. *Input*, in twentieth-century English, "Out of sight, out of mind." Computer translates into Mandarin, then translates the Mandarin words back into English. *Output*, "Invisible idiot."

Sweeping his arm to indicate the entire village, Brad explained, "All the Folk here are the same age."

Brad had learned that the villagers referred to themselves as the Folk. All others, including Brad, were Strangers.

"Of course," said Mnnx.

"Aren't there any Folk who are younger?" Or older, he added mentally.

"Younger?"

"You are all the same age?"

"Of course."

"How can that be?"

"We all came into the world in the same season."

"Came into the world?" Brad asked. "From where?"

Mnnx pointed toward the farmland. "From the eggs our elders laid in the fields."

"Elders? Where are they?"

"All gone. Death time."

"They all died?"

"Of course. Killed by monsters from Beta."

Brad felt stunned. "All of them? Every one of them?"

"That is what death time is. Everyone is killed, except for the Rememberer."

"The Rememberer?"

"Drrm is our Rememberer. Drrm will teach the new Folk once they have come up from the ground."

"You mean you're all going to be killed? All of you?"

Perfectly calm, Mnnx responded like a teacher dealing with a backward child. "Everyone. Except for Drrm. That is what death time is. Monsters from Beta kill us all. Next season new Folk arise from the fields, after the monsters have gone."

No, Brad thought. It can't be. The translator isn't getting it right.

He asked, "New Folk arise from the fields?" Pointing to the farmland beyond the edge of the village, Brad continued, "From there? From the farm?"

Mnnx said, "Yes. From our seed."

Brad shuddered through the Gammans' evening meal, then hurried back to his shelter and called Littlejohn. The Aborigine was in Kosoff's office, as usual.

Knowing that the two of them had undoubtedly heard his conversation with Mnnx, Brad asked without preamble, "Do you believe it?"

And then waited for his words to reach the starship orbiting Alpha, and their response to get back to him.

Finally Kosoff said, "They all die? Every one of them?"

"Except for their Rememberer. Drrm."

"That's a lot to swallow."

"Killed by monsters from Beta," Brad said.

The three-minute interval between them seemed to hang for an hour. At last Littlejohn replied, "That's mythology. It must be. They're trying to frame an understanding of the catastrophic weather conditions that arise during the two planets' conjunction. Trying to make sense out of conditions that are far beyond their comprehension."

But Kosoff swung his head negatively. "We've seen monsters on Beta."

And Brad's screen suddenly showed one of the six-legged giant cats prowling across Beta's hardscrabble surface.

"My god!" Brad gasped.

This time the three-minute gap was filled with views of the big cats. Brad gaped at them. Monsters, all right.

Then Kosoff's face filled the screen again. "It's a coincidence. A sheer coincidence. Those animals don't have spacecraft. They can't cross from Beta to Gamma, even when the two planets are at their closest."

Littlejohn added, "All mythologies include monsters. You know that, Brad. Monsters and gods and heroes."

"I haven't heard anything about gods or heroes," Brad objected. "Only monsters."

As he waited for their response, Brad thought about Mnnx's description of the death time: Monsters that kill them. It *can't* be a coincidence.

Then Kosoff said, "I know it's bizarre, uncanny. But the only reasonable explanation is that it's a coincidence. It has to be."

It isn't, Brad insisted silently to himself. A coincidence

is what you call a phenomenon when you don't understand its actual cause.

Then he realized, And if it isn't a coincidence, if those cats somehow get here to Gamma and kill everything in sight, they'll kill me too!

Though he tried to hide his fears from Felicia, she immediately saw the danger Brad was in.

"They'll kill you too!"

Attempting to ease her alarm, he said soothingly, "No, I think Kosoff is right. There's no way that an oversized tiger can fly a hundred thousand klicks through the vacuum of space and get here to Gamma. The talk about monsters and death time is mythology, just a scary tale. Nothing to worry about."

Still, once he'd finished his nightly talk with her, Brad rummaged through his equipment case until he found the laser pistol—and the video chip that showed how to use it.

He slept fitfully that night, awakened time and again by wild dreams that jumbled his memories of the deadly avalanche at Tithonium Chasma with new terrors of giant six-legged beasts tearing him apart with their fangs and claws.

He awoke weary, emotionally drained, soaked with cold perspiration.

As he scrubbed himself down with the antiseptic pads from the lavatory supplies, Brad decided to question Drrm more closely about the death time. After all, he reasoned, Drrm's the closest thing these people have to a village chief. If anyone can shed more light on this situation, he'll be the one.

After popping his breakfast pills and pulling on his

biosuit, Brad ducked out of his shelter and headed for the village.

It was unusually windy, he realized. Flat gray clouds were scudding across the normally blue sky. Even inside his cumbersome helmet, Brad could hear the wind moaning and the trees sighing.

Don't let your nerves get the better of you, Brad told himself. Weather changes are normal. You've lived most of your life on Mars, where the air's so thin that there's hardly any weather to speak of. Well, yeah, there's the dust storms now and then, but you get through them all right.

Still, he looked up at the threatening sky and saw, through a gap in the ominous clouds, the curving bulk of Beta looming bigger than ever in the sky, like a baleful blood-red eye glaring down at him.

Drrm was standing at the entrance to the building Brad thought of as the village's longhouse. The Gamman was alone, gazing off at the farm fields at the village's edge. Everyone else seemed to be in the fields, working.

"Hello, Drrm," Brad called as he approached.

"Hello, Brrd."

Standing beside the village chief, Brad asked, "Is everyone working in the fields today?"

Drrm replied, "Everyone. Death time coming."

Brad tried to think of a diplomatic way of broaching the subject, but after several moments he simply asked, "Can you tell me about the death time?"

"Monsters from Beta kill everyone."

"Except the Rememberer," Brad prompted.

Drrm seemed to sigh. "Sometimes even the Rememberer is killed. Then the new Folk must learn for themselves how to live."

"And new Folk arise from the farm fields?"

"Yes."

"Can you show me?"

Drrm fell silent. He's thinking it over, Brad thought. He's trying to figure out how much he should tell me.

At last Drrm said, "You are not one of the Folk. You are a Stranger."

"I come from a different village, that's true."

"Only the Folk may see the seedlings. It is forbidden to Strangers."

Brad made a mental connection. "Then Strangers come to this village?"

"Now and then."

"Why?"

"To tell us of their villages. To share food. To trade tools."

"Are the Strangers also killed in the death time?"

"Of course. How can there be enough food for the new Strangers if the old Strangers do not die?"

"And the Folk, here in this village, they die to make room for the new Folk?"

"Yes."

Brad waved his arm in the direction of the hills he had come from. "But this world is almost empty! There's plenty of room for new Folk, new Strangers, new villages."

Drrm's tone of voice changed. "That is not our way."

Is he shocked? Brad wondered. Angered? Have I committed blasphemy?

Nevertheless, Brad pushed on. "But you don't have to die. You can live—"

"No, Brrd. We die so that new Folk can live."

Brad fell silent. I'm treading on ground that's sacred to them, he realized.

Drrm said, "Even if we wished to live, the monsters from Beta would find us and kill us. That is the way the world is."

Remembering the big cats he had seen on Beta, Brad realized that the Gammans had no weapons to protect themselves, beyond simple hunting sticks and scythes. They don't even seem to have the concept of self-defense. They are ready to be killed. So that their next generation might live. To be slaughtered when the next death time comes.

"Once, long ages ago," Drrm said wistfully, "the Folk and Strangers covered this world with villages. Mighty villages, with buildings that reached toward the sky. There were many of us then, more than can be counted."

More mythology? Brad wondered. Or am I getting a history lesson?

Drrm continued, "The Sky Masters became angry. They destroyed the villages and killed almost everyone. They made the long winters and sent the monsters from Beta that kill those who live today."

"The Sky Masters? Who are they?"

"Masters of us all. They rule the world."

"Where are they?"

"Everywhere."

"But I've never seen them."

"Neither have I. They are invisible, of course. But they see us. They watch us. They allow us to live, but only if we obey their rules. If we try to break their rules, they will destroy us forever."

Brad closed his eyes for a moment. That's some religion you've got. But as he stared at Drrm, standing beside him, he thought the Gamman looked forlorn, utterly sad, defeated.

That evening, back in his shelter, Brad called Kosoff and Littlejohn. As usual, they were in Kosoff's office, waiting for Brad's call.

"You heard my conversation with Drrm?" he asked.

As he waited for their response, Brad picked up the laser pistol. The thermionic nuclear power pack in its grip was good for several hundred shots, depending on what power level he used. That ought to give me some chance against those cats, he told himself.

"Interesting mythology," Littlejohn replied at last. Smiling tolerantly, he added, "It always astounds me how complex and detailed mythological tales can be."

"That's because they don't have to deal with facts," Kosoff said.

"No," Brad answered, even before he realized he had spoken. "Mythologies deal with facts. They're attempts to understand the facts of the world that the myth-makers live in. Attempts to make some sense out of conditions that are beyond the scope of the culture's knowledge. When they run out of facts, they make up stories that fill in the blanks of their understanding."

As he waited for their reply, Brad began to wonder if there was some way to help the Gammans, some way to show them that they didn't have to die.

At last Littlejohn said, "Good for you, Brad. You've grasped the essence of mythological storytelling."

Kosoff interjected, "But that doesn't mean those aliens' tale about their death time is scientifically valid."

Doesn't it? Brad asked himself.

argument

"Some of the time I'm so sure I'm right that I could scream at Kosoff and Littlejohn for being so blind," Brad was telling Felicia. "Then I wonder if I'm the one who's blind . . . or at least pigheaded."

It was late at night. Brad was squatting in his shelter talking with his wife while the wind outside gusted fitfully.

At last Felicia answered, "I've spoken with Captain Desai. He says it would be possible for you to leave Gamma and get to us at Alpha in the shuttlecraft. But you'll have to leave in the next day or so, before the atmosphere becomes too turbulent for the shuttlecraft to fly through it safely."

"I'm not leaving." Brad's own words surprised him. Something deep inside him wanted to leave, to get away, to return to Felicia and safety.

But another emotion, deeper, stronger, was making him stay. I'm not going to leave them alone, to die, to be wiped out. I'm not going to repeat Tithonium, he told himself.

Once she heard his words, Felicia's eyes widened with fright. "Brad, you've got to get away. You've got to! You can't stay there and die!"

"I'll be all right," he insisted, trying to put on a smile. Holding up his pistol, he said, "I can defend myself."

They argued for nearly an hour, a strange kind of quarrel, with three-minute gaps punctuating their interchanges. For once, Brad was grateful for the time lag: it gave him a chance to calm down, to control his rising temper, to deal with his fears.

He saw that Felicia was terrified. "Brad," she begged, "for me. For my sake. Leave the damned planet and come back to me."

"I can't, Fil," he replied, practically begging. "I just can't run away. Can't you see that?"

In the three-some minutes before her next message, Felicia seemed to change. As if she'd taken a deep breath and decided that further attempts to convince him would be fruitless, barren.

"All right," she said at last, flatly, coldly. "If that's the way you want it."

"That's the way it's got to be," Brad said.

"Good night, then." It almost sounded like *good-bye.*

"Wait!" he called. "You haven't told me what you're doing. How's everything going with your study of the octopods?"

Again he waited, wondering if she would answer him at all.

"Oh, that's going along pretty well. We've established that Emcee's estimation of how they survive Mithra's flares is pretty accurate. But unless we shield the planet, they won't be able to survive the death wave by diving deeper into the ocean."

It's as if she's delivering a lecture, Brad thought. To a stranger.

Felicia went on without hesitating. "According to our calculations, the octopods can go deep enough to avoid being killed by the gamma radiation. But the fish and other sea creatures that they feed on can't. When the octopods return to their normal levels, they'll find a desert waste. No food. They'll starve to death. All of them."

"Unless we provide the shielding to protect the planet," Brad said.

Slightly more than three minutes later, Felicia nodded, poker-faced. "Yes, unless we provide the necessary shielding."

"Which will also protect them from having the atmosphere and ocean boiled away."

"Yes," said Felicia, as flatly as one of Emcee's responses.

"Fil, I've got to stay here," he blurted. "You can see that, can't you?"

At last she replied, "I can see that you need to stay, more than you need to return to me."

Brad stared at the display screen, stunned by her answer. Abruptly, the screen went blank.

She's cut the connection! Brad realized. She's cut me off. It never occurred to him that she might have cut the connection because she didn't want him to see her crying.

Brad couldn't sleep. He tossed fitfully in his bedroll, his mind filled with his last glimpse of Felicia's face. She looked hard, angered, disappointed, cold.

I've hurt her, he realized. She's hurt because I need to stay here more than I want to return to her.

I've hurt her, he told himself over and over again. Maybe I've lost her.

He squeezed his eyes shut and tried to force himself to sleep. No use. Sitting up, he realized it was probably a good thing. Sleep brings dreams and he didn't want to face the dream again. Not tonight. I wouldn't be able to deal with it.

Is that why I'm staying? he wondered. Am I trying to atone for Tithonium? Trying to prove that I'm not a coward?

With a shake of his head he told himself, No. There's more to it than that. I'm going to help Mnnx and the others, help them get through their death time, show them how to survive.

Outside his shelter the wind suddenly rose to a piercing shriek. In the darkness, Brad felt the shelter shake. Something flashed out there, a bright streak of lightning. A heartbeat later thunder exploded, like a bomb going off.

Brad heard rain pelting down on his shelter, hard, insistent. It's okay, he told himself. This shelter can withstand hurricane-force winds. That's what the manual said.

But he felt the shelter shaking, trembling under the lashing of the rain like a man being pummeled by a giant.

It'll be okay, he told himself. The shelter's hurricane-proof.

And then he laughed out loud. I couldn't get to the shuttlecraft in this storm, he realized. I couldn't start back to Felicia even if I wanted to.

And he wanted to. At this particular moment, battered by the lashing rain, terrified by the shrieking wind, he wanted to be safe and warm in Felicia's arms.

Something thumped in the darkness. Must be the lamp, Brad thought. It's fallen over. I ought to find it, turn it on. It's stupid to sit here in the dark.

But before he could get to his knees the whole shelter lurched and swayed. Brad heard water gurgling outside its thin walls. The shelter *moved*, like an aircar gliding across the sands of Mars.

Brad toppled sideways in the darkness while the shelter slid downhill like a canoe careening along a raging stream.

Felicia woke the next morning, dry-eyed and mournful. He's left me, she thought. Then she said aloud, "No. He's staying on Gamma to deal with his own demons. He's fighting a battle that I can't help him with. There's nothing I do to help him."

And despite herself, she broke into tears.

At the bio lab that morning Felicia tried to bury herself in the latest observations of the octopods. They were swimming through Alpha's planet-wide ocean, totally oblivious to the death that was hurtling toward them with the speed of light, blissfully unaware that their world was about to be devastated.

Unless we help them. Unless we sink a half-dozen generators into their ocean to produce the energy screen that will shield their world from the death wave.

And the stupid octopods won't even know that we've helped them, saved them from obliteration. They'll just keep on cruising through their ocean as if nothing has happened.

Apes and angels, she thought. Which are they? Too stupid to understand what's approaching them, or too lofty to care? Maybe they sense, somehow, that we'll take care of them, protect them, save them.

And who's going to take care of Brad? Protect him? Save him?

She wanted to tell herself that Brad was committing suicide, deliberately letting himself die on a strange world, preferring to die alone down there with the aliens instead of coming to safety, coming to me.

Brad's inner demons are killing him and there's nothing I can do about it.

She held back the tears. Not here, not in the lab where everybody can see me. I've got to be strong, even if there's nothing I can do to save him.

Although she had no appetite, Felicia forced herself to go to the cafeteria at lunchtime. Don't stay alone, she told herself. Be with others. Try to be normal.

She took a tray and picked a meager salad and a glass of iced tea, then scanned the busy, noisy cafeteria for a table. Gregory Nyerere was sitting alone at a table for four. Felicia headed there.

The muscular linguist looked up from his bowl of stew and smiled at her as Felicia placed her tray on the table.

"How are you?" he asked in his high-pitched voice. "I don't see much of you these days."

"I'm pretty busy," Felicia replied. "Studying the octopods, you know."

"Anything new from them?"

She shook her head. "Same old same old."

Nyerere took a spoonful of stew. Then, "How's Brad doing? I hear conditions on Gamma are getting pretty hairy."

"Yes," Felicia said. "Pretty hairy."

Nyerere studied her for a long moment. "Well, if you need a shoulder to cry on, I'm here for you."

"Am I that obvious?"

"You look wound pretty tight."

"He's all alone out there," Felicia burst. "There's nobody to help him!"

"He'll be all right."

"He's going to get himself killed."

"Why doesn't he come back? Won't his shuttlecraft make it back here?"

"He could if he wanted to."

"And he doesn't want to?" Nyerere asked, his expression incredulous.

"No, he doesn't."

"Doesn't want to come back to you? By god, I would."

Felicia tried to smile, failed.

Nyerere reached out and touched her shoulder. "It must be awful, being all alone."

"He's with the Gammans."

"Not him. You."

Felicia stammered, "I . . . it's not . . . I'm all right, Greg."

His grip on her shoulder tightened slightly. "No, you're not all right. You're in pain. I can feel it."

"Mind if I join you?"

They looked up. Felicia saw James Littlejohn, holding a loaded lunch tray in both hands.

Before Nyerere could reply, Felicia said, "Yes, please, sit down."

The Aborigine put his tray down and pulled out a chair. "I just heard from Brad," he said, almost cheerfully. "The weather's picking up on Gamma. His shelter slid down the hillside he was camped on. Rainwater turned the ground into a minor river."

Felicia gasped. "Is he hurt?"

"No, no," Littlejohn answered. "Just shaken up a little. He's fine."

Nyerere said, "Conditions on Gamma are going to get worse before they get better."

With a careless grin Littlejohn assured them, "Brad will be fine. His equipment is all in working order. Video contact is spotty, though. Electrical storms in the atmosphere out there."

Felicia asked, "How long will the storms last?"

Littlejohn's thick brows knit. "You should ask the planetologists about that. A few more days, I should think."

"But he's all right."

"Yes."

Nyerere pushed his chair back from the table. "Well, I've got to get back to work. We're making real progress on the Gammans' language."

Thanks to Brad, Felicia thought. But she remained silent as Nyerere picked up his emptied tray and walked off.

Littlejohn followed him with his eyes, then turned back to Felicia. "It seemed to me that he was coming on to you."

She blushed. "Well . . . maybe a little."

"You looked uncomfortable."

Felicia nodded. And she remembered that her relationship with Brad had started when he saved her from Kosoff's unwanted advances. *Must I always be the princess in distress, saved by a gallant knight?*

Then she realized that Littlejohn was smiling tenderly at her. *Does he intend to be a gallant knight?* Felicia asked herself.

For once, Brad was glad to be in the biosuit. Standing outside his shelter in the pelting rain, he felt dry and warm inside its protective covering. The wind was still gusting, and in the distance he could hear rumbles of thunder.

The shelter had slid downhill several hundred meters and was now sitting askew, heavily slanted to one side, atop the muddy, soggy ground. Brad could see the trail it had left when it skidded down the hillside before finally thumping to a stop against a house-sized boulder.

The worst of the storm seemed to be over; the rain was easing off. Streams of water were still gushing down the hillside, but the gray clouds overhead were breaking up and beyond them the sky was brightening. It would be dawn soon.

"Emcee," he called, "how's the village?"

While he waited for the master computer's reply, Brad started cautiously up the hillside, trying to avoid the streamlets flowing past. His boots sank nearly ankle deep into the mud; it took an effort to pull them free and take another step.

They should have built servomotors into the suit, Brad told himself. Then he realized that a mechanical exoskeleton would have undoubtedly spooked the Gammans. So he slogged ahead, bent halfway over as he toiled up the hillside.

At last Emcee's voice reached him. "It's difficult to see

the village through the clouds. Infrared scans show the houses all appear to be intact. No aliens in sight, however. No movement."

Brad nodded inside his helmet. "They're probably all indoors."

It'll be nearly four minutes before Emcee's answer gets here, he knew. Meanwhile, you just plod through this muck, one step at a—

Brad froze. There on the hillside about fifty meters ahead of him stood one of those huge six-legged cats from Beta, mud-spattered, looking wet and thoroughly unhappy.

"Jesus Lord!" Brad whispered.

The cat's heavy head swung in his direction. Its yellow eyes focused on him.

Brad gulped once, turned around, stumbled badly, and slipped onto his rump. Without trying to get back to his feet, Brad slid on the rain-soaked ground back toward his shelter. The cat made a sound like a growl and splashed through the mud after him.

If the ground had been dry and firm Brad would never have made it to his shelter. But on the gooey mud, Brad slid along like a sailboat scudding across the water while the cat splashed through the sucking ooze, each of its six paws sinking so deep it took a powerful effort to pull them loose.

The beast roared and raged as it slogged after Brad, who used his gloved hands like oars to propel himself toward the lopsided shelter.

He made it to its air lock hatch and pecked out the entry combination with fingers that shook badly. Brad dived inside and pulled the hatch shut just as the cat lunged for him. Its impact made the whole shelter shudder; it howled with fury as it banged against the metal hatch.

Brad crawled to the equipment locker beside his bedroll and pulled out the laser pistol. Outside, all was suddenly silent. Had the cat turned away? Or was it lurking out there, waiting for Brad to come outside again?

He crawled to his console and turned on the outside cameras. Inanely, he realized that he was muddying up the bedroll and everything else inside the shelter. No matter. Safety first, he thought, cleanliness later.

Brad checked out the pistol. Fully charged, ready for action. His display screen showed the cat walking slowly away, laboriously pulling each paw free of the sticky, clinging mud.

Brad checked each of the cameras. No other cat in sight. The one he had encountered was going away. Without potential prey in sight, it quickly lost interest in the inanimate shelter. Can't eat plastic, Brad thought. And giggled, on the edge of hysteria.

He sat on the muddied bedroll and took a deep breath. How did the cat get here from Beta?

Then he realized that it was heading up to the rim of the hill. On the other side of that rise was the village.

I can't stay buttoned up inside here, he told himself. I've got to go help them, save them. Even if they don't want to be saved, I can't just let them be slaughtered.

The cat literally had eyes in the back of its head. Brad stiffened with surprise when he spotted two narrow eyes glinting in the back of the creature's skull. The animal stopped its laborious climb up the quagmire of the hillside and slowly turned toward Brad.

He pulled the pistol from its magnetic grip on his belt and, after two tries with his gloved hand, used his thumb to flick the power on. The pistol didn't feel any different, but according to the manual's video instructions, the gun should be ready to fire. Just point and shoot.

The cat seemed to realize that skidding downhill in the

ooze was easier than struggling uphill. It came sliding down toward Brad with terrifying speed, then with a roar it leaped at him, all six paws showing scimitar-sharp claws, its mouth wide open and full of fangs.

Brad leveled the pistol and fired point-blank at the charging beast. A thin red beam struck the cat in the throat and sliced down half the length of its underside, cutting a slim slash in the animal's flesh that smoked slightly along its edges.

The cat's roar changed pitch, from rage to pain, and it landed in the mud at Brad's feet with a huge splash that knocked Brad backwards onto the ground. But he still held the pistol in his gloved hand, his fingers gripping it so tightly that they were cramping.

The animal wasn't dead, though. As Brad struggled to his feet he saw that the cat was inching through the mud on its belly toward him, moaning as it slithered forward. Brad fired another shot into one of its eyes and the beast shuddered, then stopped. Dead.

Brad stared at it. He was so drenched with perspiration that he might as well have been out in the rain, without the biosuit. He was shaking badly; his knees felt too weak to support him.

For long moments Brad just stood there, chest heaving, staring at the dead animal. At last his brain started to function again. How did it get here, from Beta? How many more of them are here?

After turning 360 degrees to scan the whole area, Brad saw that there were no other cats in sight. The forest in the distance looked battered, many trees knocked down, uprooted, others leaning crookedly. He turned off the pistol's power and clapped it to its magnetic holder at his waist.

The rain was down to a fine, persistent drizzle. Brad looked up the muddy slope. What's happening to the village? he asked himself. How are the Gammans making out?

Brad was bone weary by the time he reached the crest of the ridgeline. His biosuit was spattered with mud. The sky was clearing, although there were still plenty of thick clouds boiling past. Mithra had risen above the distant mountains, its piercing red glow turning the clouds' undersides scarlet and purple.

And there in the hollow was the village. Or what was left of it. The hollow had turned into a shallow lake. The village's houses were awash at least a dozen centimeters deep. Nothing seemed to be moving. The neat green rows of the farm's crops were mostly underwater; the few stalks that poked above the mini lake looked crooked, bent.

And everything was deathly still.

Looking up, Brad saw through a break in the clouds the huge bloodred sphere of Beta glowering down at him.

Something streaked across the sky, like a meteor or a reentering spacecraft.

He stared at it. The flaming streak disappeared beyond the hills, but he heard the rushing, roaring sound of its flight through the turbulent atmosphere. Then a sharp crack echoed across the sky.

A sonic boom! Brad realized.

"Emcee, I hope you're seeing what I'm seeing," he shouted, as if raising his voice would get his words across to the starship orbiting Alpha.

Another sonic boom reverberated across the sky. Turning, Brad saw an oval-shaped object gliding over the ridge, undulating as it came, and then dropping into the hollow where the flooded village stood.

The thing splashed into the water, plowing up a huge spray before it lurched to a stop.

Brad stared, goggle-eyed, as the object began to split apart while it sat there in the shallow water. And out of the crack that zigzagged down its middle he saw a clawed paw emerge, then a head full of fangs. One of the cats shouldered through the remaining shell and splashed into the water.

Monsters from Beta!

slowly, carefully, with the pistol in his hand, Brad picked his way down the hillside to the edge of the village. The water was halfway up his shins, but the drizzle was easing off noticeably. Mithra was rising above the mountains, casting a sullen ruby glow across the hollow as it scudded among the dwindling clouds.

And the cat from Beta was standing halfway across the impromptu lake, near the outermost circle of buildings, in water deep enough to almost reach its belly.

It raised its heavy-boned head and gave out a roar that shook the hollow. Brad thought he knew what the cat was trying to say: I'm wet and cold and hungry and I don't like this one bit.

Well, neither do I, Brad replied silently to the beast.

The half-drowned village looked dead, abandoned. Nothing was moving down there. Brad took a few cautious steps downslope. The cat spotted him at once and started padding toward him.

"For future reference," Brad said aloud to Emcee, "the beasts don't seem to notice me unless I move. Standing still, I become part of the background to them. I think."

Another whooshing roar streaked by overhead. Brad saw the hot contrail of another reentry flash past and disappear on the other side of the hills.

"They're coming from Beta, all right," he spoke into his helmet microphone. "Lots of them."

The cat was coming closer, splashing through the water toward him. Brad was torn between the urge to kill it as quickly as he could and the worry that he'd deplete the pistol's power pack by firing it at too distant a range.

Suddenly a figure emerged from one of the buildings. A Gamman stood in the doorway, staring at the cat, then turned to look Brad's way. Behind him, Brad could see other Gammans, huddling just inside the doorway, peering over the first one's shoulder.

"Get back!" he shouted, hoping that his suit's computer could translate his words adequately. He waved his free hand at them, gesturing for them to retreat into the relative safety of the house.

The cat turned toward the Gamman, who took a tentative step toward it.

"Get back!" Brad repeated, waving both his arms.

But the Gamman moved toward the cat. Defenseless, without even a hunting stick in his hands, he headed toward the cat. And the others walked behind him.

Brad stumbled down the rain-soaked hillside, trying to close the range between himself and the cat. The beast paid him no attention, not with the handful of Gammans so much closer.

Point and shoot. Brad raised his arm and fired at the cat. It twitched and howled. Brad fired again and the cat bounded away, splashing across what had been the village's farmland, sending up sheets of spray as it leaped away from Brad and the villagers.

Brad slogged through the shin-deep water to the Gammans, who stood stock-still, petrified with fear or awe or surprise, he didn't know which.

"Brrd!" said one of them. Brad recognized him as Lnng, one of Mnnx's hut mates.

"Are you all right?" Brad asked.

"You drove it away," Mnnx said. The computer

couldn't translate tones of voice, but Brad got the feeling that the Gamman was not happy to be rescued.

"That monster was going to kill you," Brad said. "Kill you all."

"Of course," said Mnnx.

Brad looked over his shoulder and saw that the cat was coming back toward them. Limping, but heading for them, its head low, its eyes glaring angrily.

Disbelievingly, Brad asked, "You *want* it to kill you?"

"It is death time."

Another of the Gammans said, "Time for us to die."

"That's crazy!" Brad snapped, then he realized that the computer probably couldn't translate the word to them.

The slinking cat had cut the distance between them by half, and it was still coming.

Brad stood there with the Gammans and watched it come.

One of the aliens started to chant words that the computer didn't recognize. The others took up the hymn; that's what Brad thought it must be, a hymn of death. He saw that their eyes were covered with an opaque membrane.

They've closed their eyes while they stand waiting for the goddamned cat to slaughter them. Somehow Brad felt angered. They're standing here like a bunch of martyrs, waiting for their deaths.

Well screw that!

Brad raised his hand and aimed at the cat's glowering eyes. He fired and the thin, bloodred line of laser energy found its mark. The great cat collapsed, its headful of fangs splashing into the water.

For several moments the Gammans didn't move, didn't speak.

"You can open your eyes," Brad said sternly. "It isn't going to kill you."

They stared at the cat's inert carcass.

"It's dead!"

"You killed it!"

"Damned right," said Brad. "I saved your lives."

"But that's *wrong*!" Mnnx rumbled.

"How can new Folk live if the old Folk do not die?"

"The Sky Masters will be angry with us," one of the aliens wailed.

For a moment, Brad thought they were going to attack him, or at least rip the pistol from his hand.

Overhead, another entry vehicle zoomed past and disappeared over the hills. Brad heard the distant blast of its sonic boom. More cats arriving, he thought.

"I want to talk with Drrm," he told them. "I need his wisdom."

They glanced uneasily at one another, their big bulbous eyes glancing nervously at Brad while they muttered among themselves in deep, reverberating tones.

Brad turned his back to them and searched the hollow for more cats.

At last Lnng said, "Come with us; we will take you to Drrm."

Brad followed the Gamman toward the structure that he had dubbed the longhouse, the rest of the aliens trailing behind them. The sky was clearing nicely, he thought, although Beta hung up there like an evil red eye that covered a quarter of the sky and filled the hollow with baleful red light. Ominous. Unsettling.

As they splashed through the water, Brad said, "At least the rain's stopped."

"There will be more," answered Lnng. "Worse. Much worse."

death time

+++
+++

Drrm was standing in the doorway of the long-house, the floodwater lapping almost to his knees. As Brad and his grudging entourage neared the building, he saw almost a dozen others standing behind Drrm, peering over his shoulders.

"Brrd killed the monster!" Lnng shouted as they approached.

"Killed it?" asked Drrm.

Excitedly, Lnng said, "Brrd pointed his hand at the monster and a bright red light sprang from his hand and killed the monster."

Drrm turned toward Brad. "Is this true?"

"Yes. I can save you. You don't have to die."

Drrm backed away from Brad. "But we must die! That is the way we prepare the world for the new Folk."

A flash of light and a crack of thunder. Brad couldn't tell if it was the storm returning or another vehicle streaking in from Beta.

"Come inside, Brrd," said Drrm, beckoning with one of his tentacle-fingered hands. Brad shivered involuntarily at the coiling, ropy appendages, but forced himself to follow the village's Rememberer.

The interior of the building was one single room, sloshing with rainwater. Drrm gestured to a staircase that curved around the circular wall.

"No need to stay in the wet," Drrm said as he led the entire group to the upper level. There were about twenty more Gammans up there, Brad saw. He recognized Mnnx and waved to him.

The upper floor was furnished with beds and a few tables and chairs. As the group spread across the space, Drrm asked, "You truly killed one of the monsters?"

"With this." Brad pulled the laser pistol from his belt.

"This is very bad," Drrm said. "The Sky Masters will be angry."

"You'd rather be killed yourself?"

"That is our way. It is necessary. Otherwise there will be no room for the new Folk."

"But this world has plenty of room!" Brad said, noticing that the Gammans were slowly clustering around him and Drrm. Pointing toward the room's one window, he told them, "You could build new villages, plenty of them. There's room enough—"

"No, no, no," Drrm countered, like a grandfather instructing a wayward child. "We must die. The Sky Masters send the monsters from Beta to kill us."

"You *want* to die?"

Drrm hesitated. Brad could hear the wind rising again outside, the rain pelting harder on the roof of branches and twigs above his head.

At last Drrm admitted, in a softer tone, "It is hard to die, Brrd. It is very hard to face the monsters and not try to run away. But it is necessary. It is the way we have always been. If we do not die, the new Folk will have no place to live."

Feeling halfway between sympathetic and angry at their obtuseness, Brad said, "I have seen much of your world. Most of it is empty of villages. There is plenty of space for you and the new Folk."

"That is not our way," said Drrm. "We must offer ourselves to the monsters from Beta."

"But I can kill the monsters from Beta."

"No! You must not interfere."

Mnnx stepped forward and asked, "Brrd, don't the others of your village offer themselves to the monsters from Beta when the dying time comes?"

"My village is so far away that the monsters from Beta don't come to it."

The whole crowd of them seemed to gasp and take a step backward, away from Brad.

"The monsters don't come to your village?"

"You don't die?"

Brad said, "We don't have a death time. We live and grow and explore."

They buzzed among themselves. Brad realized he had just confronted them with something totally new to them, totally alien. How will they react? Will they think I'm a wizard? A witch? Will they attack me as a blasphemer?

And outside, the wind's relentless roar was getting deeper, stronger. Brad saw a drop of rain spatter on his helmet and trickle down its length. And now another sound was added to the clamor outside: the howling of several hungry monsters from Beta.

"You don't have a death time?" Drrm asked, clear disbelief plain even in the computer's translation.

"No, we don't."

"You don't die?" asked Mnnx, awed.

"We die," Brad answered. "But not all at the same time. We live long lives. We die one at a time."

Before any of them could reply to that, another flash of lightning turned the room ghastly bright. Thunder boomed, and the roof abruptly caved in, covering them all with soggy branches and debris and driving, pouring rain.

A heavy branch banged into Brad's shoulder, buckling his knees. Several of the Gammans were knocked to the floor.

"Out!" cried Drrm. "Out to face your fate."

Dutifully, the Gammans shuffled toward the stairs.

"Stop!" Brad shouted. "You don't have to die. Stay here, safe from the monsters."

As if to mock his words, a cat suddenly appeared on the rim of the shattered roof, staring down through the broken branches at the terrified Gammans. Without thinking, Brad shot it through the throat, swinging the laser beam back and forth to sever its head from its body.

The Gammans moaned, whether in awe or fear or anger, Brad could not tell.

"You don't have to die!" Brad repeated.

Drrm pushed past him and headed for the stairs, insisting, "It is our way, Brrd."

"Then your way must change."

"No, the Sky Masters have ordained it."

The Gammans lined up behind Drrm and started down the stairs. Some seemed more reluctant than others, Brad thought. He saw that Mnnx was dawdling toward the rear of the line.

Desperate, Brad shouted, "The Sky Masters have changed! I bring you their new commands!"

Already several steps down the staircase, Drrm stopped and turned. Brad still stood in the middle of the circular room, the rain pounding on him and the others. Some of the Gammans had flattened themselves against the curving wall in a pitiful effort to get out of the downpour.

"You are not a Sky Master," Drrm said. "You cannot speak for the Sky Masters. Their commands are eternal."

Thinking on his feet faster than he had ever done in his life, Brad countered, "The Sky Masters send the monsters from Beta, don't they?"

"Yes."

Raising his pistol above his head, Brad said, "I have killed many of the monsters. And I can kill many more."

"But that is wrong," Brrd argued.

From the rear of the column of Gammans, Mnnx asked, "Did the Sky Masters send you to us, Brrd?"

Brad leaped at the excuse. "Yes! The Sky Masters sent me to save you."

"No!" Drrm gasped. "That cannot be. Their commands are eternal."

The rain was slithering down his helmet, and Brad could hear his suit's air-circulation fans whining like angry insects. Pointing at Drrm with his free hand, Brad challenged, "You told me that there was a time before the Sky Masters brought on the death time, a time of many villages."

Drrm hesitated before finally answering reluctantly, "Yes, long ago."

"Then their commands are not eternal. They change their commands."

"Yes, but . . . " Drrm fell silent.

"I bring you the new command of the Sky Masters. Live! Do not submit to the monsters from Beta. Save yourselves."

The Gammans muttered among themselves. This is a lot for them to swallow, Brad knew. But he also knew that he had one powerful force working in his favor. They didn't really want to die. Like all living organisms they had an innate drive to survive, to struggle against death.

At last Drrm said, "You bring us the new commands of the Sky Masters."

Careful, Brad warned himself. Don't carry this so far that you can't get free of it.

"You don't have to die," he repeated. "You don't have to give yourselves up to the monsters from Beta."

Aboard the *Odysseus*, Kosoff glared at the holographic display with anger boiling deep inside him.

"He's interfering with their basic beliefs!" he growled. "He's breaking every rule we've established for contact with an alien civilization."

Littlejohn, sitting to one side of Kosoff's desk, pointed out, "Unfortunately, there's nothing we can do about it."

The two men were watching the video transmission from Brad's biosuit, knowing that what they were seeing had happened minutes earlier.

"He's taking it upon himself to appear to them as a savior, a god!" Kosoff rumbled. "That's reprehensible."

"He's trying to save their lives," Littlejohn said.

"Reprehensible," Kosoff repeated.

Abruptly, Emcee's face appeared in the three-dimensional display. "Dr. Abbott wishes to speak to you, Professor. Urgently."

"Not now," Kosoff snapped.

"Dr. Abbott has traced the means by which the felines of Beta are transported to planet Gamma, sir."

"Not now, dammit!"

"As you wish, sir."

The view from Brad's helmet of the Gammans standing in the rain-soaked upper floor of the village's largest building returned to the three-dimensional display.

Mnnx came up to Brad. "Are you truly from the Sky Masters, Brrd?"

Nodding inside his helmet, Brad replied, "I come from a village in the sky, my friend. I've come to save you from the monsters."

Still standing several steps down the staircase, Drrm insisted, "No, that cannot be. It is wrong. We must do as the Sky Masters commanded."

"If it cannot be," Brad challenged, "how could I kill the monsters? Why would the Sky Masters allow me to kill them if they didn't want you to live?"

"There will be more monsters from Beta."

"And I will kill them, too," Brad retorted, hoping his pistol had enough charge to do the job.

Mnnx said to Drrm, "Don't you see, Drrm? The Sky Masters have sent Brrd to save us."

"And what do we do when the death time passes and the new Folk arise from the fields?"

Brad said, "We go beyond the hills that surround this village and build a new village for them."

For several long moments Drrm stood frozen on the staircase, with the rain pouring down so hard that Brad could hardly make out his figure. The other Gammans who had started down the steps with him had backed away slightly, leaving the village leader standing alone, drenched, looking forlorn.

Brad asked, "Is everyone here? Are there any of us missing?"

Lnng answered from the head of the staircase, "Grrl and his hut mates. I was going to get them and bring them here when you appeared, Brrd."

Starting for the stairs, Brad said, "Let's go get them. I'll go with you."

Drrm seemed to stiffen. Drawing himself up to his full height, he said, "I will go with you."

Grinning inside his helmet, Brad said, "Good."

And the three of them started down the stairs.

Kosoff's voice grumbled in Brad's earphones, "You're violating every ethical rule in the book."

Switching to his suit's intercom mode, so the Gammans couldn't hear him, Brad replied, "The alternative is to let them be killed, and I can't do that."

Then he clicked back to the translating computer's channel, happy that Kosoff couldn't bother him again for almost four minutes.

With Drrm in the lead and Lnng behind him, they sloshed through the floodwater on the ground level and stopped at the building's only door. It was wide open and outside the rain was teeming down more heavily than ever. The wind was roaring like a wild beast. Mithra's glare and the eerie light from Beta were all but obliterated by the freshly growing clouds boiling across the sky. Brad could barely see across the village compound to the buildings on the other side.

"Which one is Grrl's hut?" he asked.

Drrm pointed. "There."

Like all the other buildings, the hut's door was wide open.

Turning, Brad shouted up the stairs, "Close the door behind us. Keep the monsters out."

Drrm started out into the rain, but Brad held him back. "Wait. Look for cats first." And he hoped that the computer translated "cats" to a word the Gammans could understand.

He switched on the helmet's infrared night-vision optics. The compound looked clear, although the wind was blowing so hard that twigs, brush, entire tree limbs were tumbling across the compound.

Drrm stepped out into the downpour as if he had no fear of monsters from Beta.

"This way," he said.

Brad grinned inwardly. Drrm's trying to recapture the leadership of his people. Well, he's welcome to it.

Gripping his pistol, Brad stepped out beside Drrm. Lnng followed behind them.

It was midmorning on the ship. Felicia was at her workstation in the biology lab, but she couldn't focus her thoughts on the analysis of the Gamman microbes on the computer display before her. She turned off the display and headed out of the lab, toward the cafeteria.

The place was open twenty-four/seven, of course, but at this time of the morning only a handful of people were there. Most of the tables were empty and the little serving robots were lined up in a neat row on the far side of the room.

Felicia trudged to the only juice dispenser that appeared to be working. A young man was already there, filling a large mug to the brim. He was slim, wiry, not much taller than Felicia herself. His skin was dark, his hair midnight black and tightly curled, his eyes deep brown.

"Hi," he said as Felicia approached. "You're not at work?"

"Neither are you," she said, reaching for one of the plastic cups.

"Snuck out for a caffeine break," he said. Then he stuck out his free hand. "I'm Yussif Hamibi, sensor tech."

"Felicia MacDaniels, biology."

"You're Brad MacDaniels's wife, aren't you?"

She nodded. "That's right."

"How's he doing down there?"

Felicia wanted to answer, I wish I knew. Instead, she said, "All right, I guess."

"You guess? Don't you know?"

With a sorrowful shake of her head, Felicia admitted, "No, I don't know. What with the time lag and the storms on Gamma, it's not easy to stay in touch."

"Oh. I see." Hamibi gestured to the nearest table, empty and cold-looking in the glareless overhead lighting.

Felicia went with him and they sat side by side.

"I've only got a few minutes," Hamibi said. "Got to get back to the monitoring center."

Felicia nodded.

With a wide grin, he asked, "So, do you come here often?"

With a mock scowl, Felicia replied, "Is that supposed to be a pick-up line?"

His smile brightened, strong white teeth against his dark skin. "It's supposed to be a joke. I didn't know what else to say."

"I see." Felicia allowed herself a thin smile.

"So what's happening on Gamma?"

"Terrible storms. Some sort of tigerlike animals are hunting down the Gammans and killing them."

His eyes widening, Hamibi said, "Really? Wow. And MacDaniels is in the middle of all that?"

"He certainly is," Felicia said. Every nerve in her body seemed to be screaming, Brad's out there alone. He could get killed. But he stayed there instead of coming back to me.

"Is he all right?" Hamibi asked.

"He's shot several of the big cats. He's trying to help the Gammans get through this."

"*Inshallah*," Hamibi murmured.

Suddenly Littlejohn's voice called from across the nearly empty, echoing cafeteria. "There you are!"

Felicia leaped to her feet, knocking over her juice glass.

"Is Brad . . . ?" She couldn't finish the question.

"He's in one piece," Littlejohn said cheerfully as he crossed the cafeteria and came to their table. "He's helping the Gammans to survive."

"He's all right?"

"As good as he can be, considering the conditions on Gamma right now." Littlejohn stopped at their table and eyed Hamibi. "I'm Dr. Littlejohn, head of the anthropology team."

Looking suddenly embarrassed, Hamibi said, "I'd better be getting back to the monitoring center." He picked up his mug and hurried off into the shadows.

Littlejohn turned back to Felicia. "I thought he might be bothering you."

"No," she said, surprised. "He was just being friendly."

Littlejohn nodded. "Don't you think you should get back to your lab? It's too early for lunch."

"I . . . I suppose so."

"You're worried about Brad."

"Yes."

"He's fine . . . physically."

Felicia's innards flared. "What do you mean?"

Littlejohn's expression turned almost sorrowful. "He's taken it upon himself to try to save the Gammans from extinction."

"Extinction?"

"I don't know if your husband realizes it or not, but he's taking on the role of a savior for those people. It could lead to all sorts of complications."

"Oh."

"Kosoff's furious with him."

"But he's all right. He's safe."

"So far."

Felicia stood there, feeling lost, helpless, unable to

help the man she loved. The man who's left me, she reminded herself.

Littlejohn slipped an arm around her shoulders. "Come on. I'll walk you back to your lab."

And Felicia remembered that the anthropologist had deftly shooed away Greg Nyerere just yesterday. He's been watching me! she realized. Is he trying to protect me for Brad's sake, or . . .

She shrugged his arm off her, then said, "Thank you, Dr. Littlejohn. I can get back to my workplace by myself."

"You're sure?"

"Of course. Quite sure."

Littlejohn smiled crookedly, then said, "That's fine. I should get back to Kosoff before he pops a blood vessel."

They walked together as far as the cafeteria's door, then Felicia turned toward the moving stairs that led down to the laboratories.

sacrifice

+++
++

The rain was coming down harder than ever as Brad, Drrm, and Lnng sloshed across the compound to Grrl's hut, staggering in the hard-gusting wind that raised whitecaps across the flooded hollow. The clouds were so thick that it was almost as dark as night across the village. Even with his night-vision optics Brad could barely see the building they were heading for.

Could be a dozen big cats slinking around here, he told himself, and I wouldn't spot them until they were nearly on top of us.

The water was getting deeper, up to his knees, making each step forward a real struggle. At least it should slow down any cats that come after us, he thought.

The two Gammans were straining too, bent almost halfway over as they pushed themselves through the rising floodwater. Brad almost laughed bitterly to himself as he thought, They're not taller than I am now.

Drrm staggered and reached out an arm to Brad for support. Despite himself, Brad felt a shudder of revulsion flash through him. His arm was a twisted mass of ropy, muscular tentacles. Alien. Frightful.

Drrm's arm coiled around Brad's shoulders, then withdrew as the Gamman righted himself. Brad hoped Drrm couldn't sense the irrational disgust he'd felt.

"Thank you," said Drrm as he separated from Brad.

"You're welcome," Brad replied through gritted teeth.

"I don't see any monsters," Lnng shouted over the pounding of the rain.

Trying to buck up his courage, Brad figured.

Then Drrm answered, "Monsters are out there, lurking in the dark."

Pleasant thought, Brad grumbled to himself.

"Look out!" Lnng shouted. A young tree was sailing through the air, branches fluttering, roots flailing. All three of them ducked low as it hurtled past.

At last they reached the hut they were heading for. Its door hung open, swinging in the wind and banging against the wall. Brad saw the hut's interior was pitch black, silent, and still.

He switched on his helmet's lamp, making Drrm and Lnng flinch with surprise. His IR goggles automatically swung away from his eyes.

Inside the hut half a dozen bodies were sloshing in the floodwater, mangled, chewed, dead. The water was dark with their nearly black blood.

"Too late," said Lnng. "The monsters have been here."

Where are they now? Brad wondered. All the other villagers are back in the longhouse. I told them to close their door so the cats can't get in, but one of those beasts got up to the roofline, for god's sake. And there's nothing barring the window.

Drrm sank to his knees in the bloody water, clasped his hands together, and bowed his head. Brad's computer picked up a few of the words he was muttering, "Thanks . . . sacrifice . . . death time . . . sacrifice . . . "

A prayer for the dead, he realized. Giving thanks for their sacrifice.

Brad turned back to the open door, still banging in the wind. There's at least one cat out there, maybe more. I wonder if we'll be able to get back to the longhouse without being attacked.

Drrm got back to his feet, slowly, painfully, as though he'd aged fifty years in the past few minutes.

"Let's go back," Brad said as he pulled his pistol from his belt. In the light from his helmet lamp he saw that the charge was not even one-tenth depleted. Good, he thought.

"Come on."

Felicia didn't return to her lab. Instead, she made her way to the monitoring center, halfway across the ship's interior and two levels up.

If Yussif is on the monitoring crew, why did he have to ask me how Brad's doing? she wondered. Aren't they watching Brad?

As she walked the long, curving passageway she used her wrist communicator to query Emcee.

"Emcee, aren't the monitors watching Brad on Gamma?"

"Yes, they are," answered the master computer's avatar.

"Then why . . . ?" Suddenly Felicia understood. Yussif was trying to strike up a conversation with me! She wondered if Littlejohn had been right and Hamibi was coming on to her. No, she decided. He was only being sociable, happy to have somebody to talk to.

She stopped at the entrance to the monitoring center. ADMITTANCE TO AUTHORIZED PERSONNEL ONLY, said red-glowing letters on its electronic signboard.

Biting her lip in indecision, Felicia finally made up her mind to go home, back to her own room. Littlejohn is piping the imagery from Gamma to my quarters, she reminded herself; I can watch Brad at home. Even if he doesn't want to be with me, I can be with him. Sort of.

* * *

As they waded across the village compound, fighting against the raging wind, Brad heard a prayer in his own mind: Yea, though I walk through the valley of the shadow of death . . .

And suddenly there was death standing less than fifty meters in front of them in the pelting rain. A drenched monster from Beta glowered at them, its head lowered, its fangs bared.

Another huge cat splashed through the floodwaters to stand beside the first. And a third joined them. Brad saw that their muzzles were dark with crusted Gamman blood, despite the rain.

They can't be hungry, he thought. Not after gorging on the Folk in the hut.

But the cats paced slowly toward them, spreading out slightly as they came. Cutting off our line of retreat, Brad thought; trying to surround us. Then he felt inane. As if we could run away in these floodwaters.

Drrm and Lnng were on either side of him, frozen with terror. The cats kept padding closer. Brad's mind was churning: There goes my idea that they ignore you if you stand still. Something deep inside him was screaming, *Run, run!*

Before the cats could come close enough to leap at them, Brad raised his pistol and shot the nearest through its left eye. The monster yowled and writhed, then collapsed with a splash.

The other two paid no attention. They kept on coming. And Brad heard a growl from somewhere in the darkness behind them. Turning, he saw two more cats slinking toward them from the other direction.

He turned back and fired at the closest one, burning a line through its shoulder. It howled and shuddered but still kept coming, limping badly.

"There's too many!" Lnng cried.

"Stand your ground," Brad commanded, hoping that

the computer could translate his words adequately as he fired at the wounded cat. It shuddered and sank into the wave-filled water.

At his side, Lnng shouted, "Drrm, no!"

Brad saw the village leader walking straight at the two cats behind him. Turning back, he saw the two in front of him crouching, ready to spring. He shot one in the neck, nearly severing its head as its companion leaped at him. Brad's laser beam burned into the beast's chest, between its forelegs. It howled as it slammed into Brad, knocking him into the choppy water. Brad felt as if he'd been hit by a truck as he toppled backwards into the water, the monster on top of him.

But the brute didn't move, didn't slash with its claws or bite with its fangs. Painfully, Brad struggled out from under its dead body.

As he climbed to his feet, he saw that Drrm was between him and the other two cats.

"Drrm, get out of the way!"

But the village chief simply replied, "It is our way, Brrd." And he kept walking toward the cats, who had stopped and were watching his approach, heads lowered, bellies in the water. Lnng stood to one side, petrified, and watched Drrm wading slowly toward the waiting cats.

Brad rushed past Lnng, trying to get an angle for shooting the monsters. Drrm was muttering again. Brad's computer translated, "Sacrifice . . . new Folk . . . death brings life . . . "

With a sudden roar one of the cats leaped at Drrm, knocking him down, splashing into the water. Instantly the second cat joined in the killing. Brad shot them both; it took several shots before the laser beam found their vital spots.

Drrm lay between the two fallen monsters, one arm

torn from his shoulder, his face and chest furrowed with slashes from their claws.

"It is our way," he breathed. Then his eyes closed.

Furious, Brad wanted to chop the cats into mincemeat, but his rational mind countermanded his seething emotions. Save the pistol's energy. You'll probably need it before the day's over.

discovery

+ +

+ +

Quentin Abbott was almost always cool, calm, collected. Almost always.

But he burst into Kosoff's office, startling the mission director and Littlejohn, who were intently watching the holographic video from Gamma.

Half rising from his desk chair, Kosoff growled, "What do you mean by bursting in here? Can't you see—"

"We've found it!" Abbott fairly shouted. "We know how those animals cross from Beta to Gamma! It's fantastic!"

"This isn't the time—"

"No, no, no!" Abbott insisted. "You've got to see this! Now!"

Abbott's usual stiff-upper-lip reserve was completely gone. He was practically prancing with excitement. Kosoff saw that the astronomer's tunic was rumpled, its front half unsealed, as if the man had been sleeping in it. A patch of his silver-gray hair flopped down messily over his eyes.

"They ride their eggs from Beta to Gamma, like pumpkin seeds shot through the air!"

Intrigued despite himself, Kosoff eased back down onto his desk chair and said grudgingly, "Show me."

Abbott turned toward the three-dimensional viewer and called out, "Master computer, show Astronomy Department vid, today's date."

The holographic display switched from Brad and the

Gammans to a satellite view of the planet Beta. Off in one corner of the scene was an animated graph that showed Beta and Gamma rushing toward each other.

"That's where they were the day before yesterday," Abbott said, his tone changed to his lecture mode, but with an edge of excitement in it.

Still on his feet, he pointed as he said, "The two planets will pass each other close enough so that their atmospheres are sucked into a sort of spinning vortex, like a waterspout that temporarily connects the two of them."

The view of Beta clouded over rapidly while the animation showed a twisting, twining bridge linking the planet with Gamma.

"This presentation is all speeded up, of course," Abbott explained eagerly. "Factor of thirty-six hundred: one second on-screen represents ten hours in real time. I can move it faster still if you like."

Kosoff said, "This will do. For now."

The satellite view of Beta zoomed in dizzyingly.

"Here's the ground on Beta," said Abbott. "You can see how the wind is picking up. Near hurricane force and getting stronger."

Littlejohn said, "Those rocks look like—"

"They're eggs!" Abbott interrupted. "Each one of them bears one of those six-legged cats."

"But how—"

As they watched, one of the boulder-sized eggs lifted off the ground and began rising, spinning, fluttering in the swirling wind. The animation showed tiny dots flowing from Beta to Gamma.

"They're not boulders, of course. Much lighter. Light enough to ride on the wind currents from Beta to Gamma."

"Impossible," spat Kosoff.

"But true," Abbott countered. "Watch."

As he spoke, the holotank went dark.

Unperturbed, Abbott explained, "The satellites were

torn from their orbits. Flung to god knows where by the gravitational forces of the two planets' near collision."

The three-dimensional view lit up again to show a scene of stormy skies, torrential rain pouring down, and in the distance a forest of massive trees being tossed and even uprooted by tremendous winds.

"That's the view from the ground on Gamma," Abbott said matter-of-factly. "From one of the sensors your planetology people strewed around on the surface. We lost several of them, of course. Hurricane-force winds and then some."

A meteor trail blazed across the dark sky.

"One of the eggs," said Abbott.

Kosoff snarled, "You can't expect me to believe that those objects are eggs, the same as we've seen on Beta." With a sneer, he added, "They'd be fried by the heat of entry into Gamma's atmosphere. And scrambled, as well."

"Watch."

Another meteor flashed past, and then they saw one of the boulder-sized objects soar over the forest and glide toward the ground, its nose and flattish bottom charred black. It tipped slightly upward just before it landed and skidded a few dozen meters on the rain-soaked ground before coming to a jarring halt.

Kosoff stared at the screen. In the driving rain, he could see the object's skin crack open, and a powerful-looking six-legged cat struggle out of its egg.

Littlejohn gasped with awe. "They *are* eggs. Like the ones we saw on Beta."

"They are indeed eggs," Abbott said, sounding proud. "There's your proof."

"It's fantastic," Littlejohn said.

"But it's true," countered Abbott.

"And these beasts kill the Gammans?" Kosoff asked.

"Apparently they do," Abbott said. "Not my department, of course. You'll have to ask the biologists about that." Then he added, "We've had splendid cooperation from the planetology team; the observations from Gamma's surface are their work, of course."

"Of course," Kosoff muttered.

Finally dropping into one of the cushioned chairs in front of Kosoff's desk, Abbott summed up, "So the Beta beasts ride the vortex between the two planets and land on Gamma. Quite fantastic, isn't it?"

Kosoff nodded. "I see it, but I still find it hard to believe."

Littlejohn added, "And the beasts annihilate the Gammans."

"Apparently so."

"Then what happens to them?"

Abbott shrugged. "Not my department. Ask the biologists. But my guess is that those great cats die off when Gamma enters the deep-freeze part of its orbit."

"I should think so," said Kosoff, still staring at the three-dimensional display.

"You've got a man down there, haven't you?" Abbott asked.

"Yes. He's with the Gammans."

"Rather a dicey situation for him, I should think."

"To say the least," replied Littlejohn.

Kosoff raised a stubby finger. "Wait. There's much more to this than you realize."

"More? What more?"

"This can't be natural," Kosoff said. "A predator born on one planet, flying a sort of spacecraft to find its prey on another planet. An occurrence that only happens once in half a century or so, when the two planets are closest to one another."

Suddenly looking uncomfortable, Littlejohn suggested, "Maybe the biologists can explain it."

Kosoff swung his head negatively. "It's not natural," he insisted.

Brad and Lnng sloshed through the knee-deep water back to the longhouse. The roaring wind was so strong it was difficult to stay on their feet, and they had to dodge wind-blown debris that sailed through the rain like unguided missiles.

He just let the cats kill him, Brad kept thinking. Drrm committed suicide rather than change his way of living. He sacrificed himself, for what? For his sense of right and wrong? For his morality? His religion?

Lnng also stayed silent as they made their painful way back. He must be thinking about Drrm, too, Brad told himself. Maybe he's wondering if he should let the cats get him. Maybe he's thinking they should all surrender to the cats.

As if he could read Brad's mind, Lnng shouted over the howling wind, "Are you truly sent to us by the Sky Masters, Brrd?"

For several heartbeats Brad remained silent, thinking, Don't make claims that can come back to haunt you. People who are willing to die for their beliefs can be more than willing to kill a stranger for their beliefs.

"My village is in the sky, Lnng. My people made this gun," he held up the pistol, "so that I can kill the monsters."

Lnng fell silent. Trying to digest what I've told him, Brad knew. Trying to assimilate new information that contradicts everything he's known all his life.

As he slogged through the rain and wind and knee-deep water, Brad thought, I'm in real trouble with Kosoff. I've broken all the rules about first contact with an alien species.

But what else could I do? he asked himself. Stand by and watch the cats slaughter them? Let the monsters kill me, too?

As they approached the longhouse, Brad realized that Kosoff hadn't called him for some time. Much more than the usual three-minute lag from Alpha. Well, what's he going to say to me? That he's pissed off with what I've been doing? That he's taking me off the contact assignment? Not much he can say, not right now.

They reached the building at last. Lnng banged on the door, shouting, "Let us in!"

The door swung open. Brad saw that it was Mnnx who opened it. They stepped inside and Mnnx pushed it shut again. Several dozen Gammans stood huddled behind him, most of them carrying their pitiful little hunting sticks.

"Where is Drrm?" asked Mnnx.

"Dead," answered Lnng. "The cats got him."

"Dead?"

"There were five of them," Lnng said. Even in the computer's translation, the words sounded excited. "Five! Brrd killed them all. But before he could get the last two, they killed Drrm."

The Gammans fell silent.

Then Lnng went on, "Drrm went to the cats willingly."

"That is the right thing to do," one of the others said.

"No!" Lnng snapped. "The right thing to do is to save ourselves, to kill the monsters from Beta, to—"

A roar from the unshielded window silenced the Gamman. Brad saw one of the cats squeezing its bulk through the window, snarling at them.

The Gammans stood and stared. Several of them

dropped their hunting sticks. They simply stood in the knee-deep water and watched their deaths wriggling through the window to get at them.

Icily calm, Brad drew his pistol, extended his arm and aimed, then pulled the trigger. The brilliant red laser beam lanced through the darkness and hit the cat slightly behind his head. Brad whipsawed the beam, searching for the animal's spine. The beam found it and the cat collapsed as if a switch in its body had turned off. It hung in the window frame, halfway inside the building.

"Leave it there," Brad said. "It blocks the window. It will keep other cats from getting through."

Then he noticed that not one of the Gammans had made a move toward the beast, even though it was quite obviously dead.

Brad felt weary, but he said, "I'd better go upstairs, in case another monster makes it to the roof."

"I will go with you," said Lnng.

"I too," Mnnx said.

While the others stayed on the ground floor, out of the rain, and climbed up on furniture to get out of the water, the three of them trudged up the stairs.

Mnnx asked, "Brrd, how do you kill the monsters?"

Brad hesitated, thinking, Put it in terms they can understand. No magic, no mythology.

Raising his pistol, Brad answered, "The red beam cuts like a scythe."

"It must be very strong."

"It is."

As they stepped across the upper floor, Brad thought that the rain seemed to have slackened a bit. Wishful thinking, he told himself. The deluge still poured through the shattered roof. Looking up into it, though, Brad thought the sky seemed a bit brighter than it had earlier.

Of course, he realized. It must be close to noon by now.

Mnnx crawled beneath one of the tables. "There is room here for all three of us," he said.

Lnng ducked in beside him. Brad did, too, although he stayed near the table's end, where he could keep an eye on the roofline.

"Keep watch on the roofline," he told his two companions.

"The rain will be stopping soon," said Mnnx.

"Yes," Lnng agreed.

Trying to sound optimistic, Brad thought. With an inner sigh, he told himself, Well, if Kosoff won't call you, you'd better call him. Bring him up to date.

But when Brad switched to the comm channel, all he got was a hiss of static.

What's happened? he wondered.

"Emcee," he called. "What's wrong?"

No answer. Sudden panic flared inside him. Brad realized he was entirely on his own on planet Gamma.

Kosoff stirred in his desk chair and opened his eyes. His eyelids felt gummy, heavy.

I must have drifted to sleep, he realized.

Littlejohn was sitting in the chair to one side of his desk, head flung back, mouth hanging open, snoring lightly.

Kosoff remembered Abbott leaving the office, practically bouncing with self-satisfaction at having found how the big cats crossed from Beta to Gamma.

I must have drowsed off, Kosoff thought, watching MacDaniels killing the cats, trying to save the Gammans from extinction. Breaking all the rules and irretrievably destroying everything the Gammans believed in.

He shook his head, trying to clear the cobwebs from his mind.

Those egg things the cats use to ride from Beta to Gamma, he remembered. They're not natural. They can't be. An incubation system that's also a spacecraft. It's got to be the product of a high technology. A technology higher than our own, he thought. It's got to be. But whose? Surely the cats themselves couldn't have produced such a technology. It's somebody else, a species we haven't met yet. They're hiding from us on Beta.

Who? How? Why? The questions tumbled through Kosoff's mind.

Then he realized that the holotank was dark. At the bottom of its display area a message blinked, SIGNAL LOST. SIGNAL LOST. SIGNAL LOST.

Kosoff immediately called out, "Emcee, what's happened to the signal from Gamma?"

The master computer's avatar appeared and calmly answered, "Transmission from Gamma was interrupted seventeen minutes ago. Attempts to regain the signal have been unsuccessful, so far."

Staring at the avatar's totally calm image, Kosoff felt real fear for the first time in his adult life.

Huddled under the table with the two Gammans, Brad punched out the code for fault analysis on his wrist keyboard with trembling fingers.

The suit's computer flashed its message on the inner surface of his helmet. SIGNAL LOST.

Signal lost? Brad asked himself. The signal from Alpha, from the ship? What's happened to it? Is Felicia in danger? Hurt? Killed?

Then he took a deep breath and forced himself to calm down. Think rationally, he demanded. The ship's in orbit around Alpha, thirty-some million klicks from here. These storms can't bother it. If the signal's lost, it must be from this end.

He got a vision of his shelter being scooped up by the storm winds and sent flying, like one of the eggs from Beta in reverse.

I should have weighted it down somehow, he thought. Then he added, Good thinking, after the fact.

"A monster!" Mnnx shouted from behind him.

Still sitting beneath the table, Brad whirled around, banged the top of his helmet against the table above him, then ducked to lie prone beside Mnnx and Lnng. Crouched on the roofline was one of the cats, all six of its paws gripping the edge of the opening where the shattered remains of the roof poked out their broken, soggy limbs.

The cat was looking down at them as it teetered uncertainly on the roof's edge.

How does it know we're in here? Brad wondered as he slowly, carefully took aim. It can't see us from outside the building. Does it have a super sense of smell? Some other sense that we don't know about? Or is it simply programmed to go through every building it sees?

No time for speculation. The cat was bunching its muscles, tensing before leaping to the floor. Brad squeezed the pistol's trigger and the red laser beam hit the beast in the throat. Greenish blood spurted and the animal gave out a strangled roar, then fell to the floor with a thud that shook the building.

"Is it dead?" Mnnx whispered. "Truly?"

Brad nodded inside his helmet as the green blood spread across the rain-soaked floor. The monster was sprawled in a heap; it shuddered convulsively, then stopped breathing.

"Truly," he said.

The downpour was definitely slackening, Brad realized as he stared at the dead beast. Looking up from beneath the table, he saw that the sky was brightening. Gray clouds were still scudding by, but the wind sounded softer, weaker.

I think we're going to make it, he said to himself.

He thought about the silence of his communications link. Transmissions go from the suit to the shelter, then up to a commsat in orbit. The satellites must have been torn away by the close passage of Beta. But the equipment in the shelter should be able to reach the ship on its own. If it's still functioning. If its antenna hasn't been ripped off or bashed to pieces.

The day brightened slowly, but eventually the rain stopped and warm sunlight lanced through the scattering clouds.

"The storm is over," said Lnng. Brad thought the

translation sounded happy. Why not? he asked himself. They've lived through their version of doomsday. They've survived.

One of the Gammans from downstairs climbed up to their level and said, "It seems safe to go outside now, Brrd. May we go?"

Scrambling out from under the table, Brad replied, "I think so." He stretched and heard vertebrae pop; it felt good.

Mnnx asked, "Will you go with us, Brrd? There might still be monsters outside."

Checking the charge in his pistol's power pack, Brad said, "Yes. I need to find my shelter and see how it got through the storm."

"You can sleep with us, Brrd," Lnng offered. "You can have Drrm's place."

Inside his suit's helmet, Brad grimaced. The idea of sleeping with these aliens filled him with something close to disgust. Careful, he warned himself. You don't want to be elected chief.

As they started down the steps toward the ground floor, Brad saw that the floodwaters were already receding, no more than ankle deep. Mithra's bright light made the world look warmer, safer.

Mnnx called out to his fellow Gammans, "Brrd and I are going to search for his shelter. Who will go with us?"

Practically every one of the nearly five dozen Gammans raised their hand in a very human gesture. They want to be near my gun, Brad thought, grinning inside his helmet.

"All right, then," he said. "Let's go."

ALONE

++
++

Felicia had drifted into sleep sitting in their recliner as she watched Brad's transmission from Gamma. She was dreaming of her childhood, of the time when the coastal area was hit by a tsunami, a giant wave that rose up from the sea and smashed homes and boats and trees and everything in its path. Eight-year-old Felicia watched the news videos of the horrible destruction, shaking with fear even though their house was on the other side of the coastal mountains, safe from the disaster. Then her father wrapped his strong arms around her and told her she was safe from all harm.

In her dream, somehow her father turned into Brad, holding her, comforting her.

But then he said, "I've got to stay here, Fil."

"Don't go," she begged. "Don't leave me alone."

"I've got to stay here," he repeated. And disappeared, leaving her alone and frightened.

It was Emcee's familiar soft voice that woke her. "Dr. Steiner called," the computer's avatar said gently. "She's wondering why you haven't returned to the biology laboratory."

Felicia opened her eyes to see Emcee's calm, faithful face smiling gently at her.

"I must have fallen asleep," she said, feeling slightly embarrassed.

"You have been asleep for two hours and eleven minutes," Emcee informed her. "The past fourteen minutes you have been in REM sleep. Did you have pleasant dreams?"

Felicia shook her head. "Not really. How's Brad? Could you put on the vid from Gamma, please?"

"Transmission from Gamma has been interrupted."

"Interrupted?" Felicia's heart constricted. "What's wrong?"

"Transmission was cut off one hour and thirty-nine minutes ago. All attempts to reconnect have been unsuccessful, so far."

Her pulse thundering in her ears, Felicia commanded, "Connect me with Professor Kosoff. Now!"

Followed by almost the entire troop of Gammans, Brad trekked over the hills that surrounded the village toward the spot where his shelter had been.

The clouds were definitely breaking up; warm sunshine was pouring down from a brilliant blue sky. The floodwaters were sinking into the muddy, gummy ground.

As they squished across the sloping ground, Brad tried to reach Emcee every few minutes. Always the NO SIGNAL message flashed inside his helmet.

The shelter, he told himself. Got to find the shelter. It's got the comm relay; maybe the problem is simple enough for me to fix.

"A monster!" one of the Gammans shouted.

They all froze into immobility, gripping their hunting sticks and staring at one of the six-legged beasts from Beta.

It was writhing on the muddy ground, its mouth yawning widely, its legs twitching as it rolled from one side to another, obviously in pain.

"It's dying," Mnnx said.

The forty-seven of them edged backward slowly as

they watched in awed silence while the cat thrashed, moaning its last breath. At last it stilled, yet the Gammans didn't move. They simply stared at it, hardly daring to breathe themselves.

At last Brad said, "It's dead."

"How did you kill it, Brrd?" asked Lnng.

"I didn't kill it," Brad answered. "It died by itself."

And he thought, It was *programmed* to die. After killing all the Gammans, the beasts are programmed to die.

When the troop of Gammans at last reached the spot where Brad's shelter had been, they found no trace of the oval white structure.

Brad could see the trail that the shelter had made when it slid in the floodwaters downslope to the boulder that had stopped it. The boulder was there, with a big muddy smear on it, but the shelter was nowhere in sight.

Brad stared at the empty spot. All my food is in the shelter, he knew. The communications system, medicines. I can't live inside this suit for more than a day or two.

He looked at the Gammans, standing uneasily around him. Can I survive without the suit? Even if I can breathe the air and there aren't any pathogens in it to kill me, I can't eat their food. Maybe I can drink water from their streams, but with all the flooding the water must be contaminated. I'd probably come down with dysentery.

Then he wondered how the Gammans would react if he took off his helmet and started peeling himself out of the protective suit.

Don't panic, he told himself. Search for the shelter. It's got to be around here someplace.

But a bitter voice in his head contradicted, The storm could have blown it a hundred kilometers from here.

"Spread out," he called to his companions. "Help me to search for my shelter."

They followed his command easily enough, although Mnnx said, "We should get back to the village before the day is out. We need to see how the farm is, what condition the new Folk are in."

Brad nodded inside his helmet. "Mnnx, you're right. Why don't you take as many Folk as you need and go back to the village. The others can stay with me and help me search."

Eleven Gammans went with Mnnx, several of them obviously reluctant to go back to their usual work instead of searching for the shelter.

As they left, Lnng said to Brad, "How will the new Folk live, with us still in the village?"

"We'll build a new village for them."

"But the cold time will be upon us soon. None of us can live through the cold time."

Brad got a vision of a mini ice age freezing the planet. "My people will help you to survive," he said, with a confidence he really didn't feel. "We'll get you through the cold time."

Lnng accepted his word. Brad thought, He's got more faith in me than I do.

They searched through the sloping grassy field where the shelter had been. Nothing. Hot red Mithra climbed higher in the sky, the floodwaters dwindled away, leaving the ground gooey and foul-smelling. No sign of the oval white shelter.

Despite his suit's climate control system whining away, Brad was sweating by the time they reached the edge of the woods. He clicked his helmet's telescopic lenses into place and started scanning the trees.

And there it was! The shelter was nestled high in one of the trees, which had been bent far over by the powerful winds of the storm.

Brad stared at it. Cradled in the branches high above, the shelter looked intact. He could see no rips or holes in its surface. He touched the keypad on his wrist and the lenses slid away from his eyes.

"There it is." He pointed. The Gammans stared up at it.

"How can we get it?" Lnng asked. "It's too high for us to reach."

Brad realized they had never tried to climb the trees. They had no tools for climbing, no experience. Neither do I, he told himself.

He tried his communications system again, and again got nothing except NO SIGNAL. The comm gear must have been damaged by its ride through the air, he concluded.

Turning to Lnng, he said, "You take the others back to the village. I'll stay here a while. I'll be back by sundown."

Lnng shuffled uncertainly.

"Go on," Brad insisted. "The monsters are dying. You'll be all right."

As they reluctantly started off, Brad told himself, All right, you're alone here. Kosoff and the others are still in orbit around Alpha. Felicia's there, probably worried sick about me. Nothing I can do about that, not right now.

He squinted up at the shelter again. So close. No more than thirty or forty meters away. But the distance was vertical and he had no way to climb it.

Once the Gammans were out of sight, Brad went through the ugly business of defecating and burying the sanitary container. No more containers in the suit, he saw. The rest of them are in the shelter. With my food.

He felt like sinking down onto the muddy ground and giving up. Which will kill me? he asked himself. Starvation or infection?

*　*　*

Felicia sat in front of Kosoff's desk, every nerve in her body strung tight.

"But surely you realize," the professor was saying, in a tone that was close to condescending, "that we can't break orbit here and fly to Gamma just because your husband might be in danger."

"He might be dead!" Felicia burst.

"Then he's beyond our help," Kosoff said.

"But we've got to get there. Now! Brad might be hurt. We could save him."

"Now, now," Kosoff said, trying to soothe her. "Brad's had survival training. He apparently got through the worst of the storms. It's probably just a communications glitch that will be cleared up soon."

"He's alone and in danger on an alien world without anyone to help him. We've got to go to Gamma and save him!"

Kosoff's office door slid open and Captain Desai stepped in, wearing his formal black uniform with silver piping. Trying to impress me, Felicia thought.

"You called me," Desai said, hesitating at the doorway, looking puzzledly at Felicia.

"Yes," said Kosoff. Gesturing to one of the chairs before his desk, he said, "Sit down, please, and explain to this distraught young woman why we can't take off for Gamma for another few days."

Lightly as a dancer, Desai went to the chair and settled his lean body into it.

"Our flight plan has us breaking orbit around Alpha the day after tomorrow. By that time Gamma and Beta will be separated far enough so that there will be no gravitational complications to prevent us from establishing a stable orbit around Gamma once again."

"But we could go now if we had to," Felicia prompted.

Desai glanced at Kosoff's stony expression and replied, in his soft voice, "If we had to. There is some risk, of course. All of the commsats we had placed in orbit around Gamma have been ripped away by the gravitational tides of Beta's sweeping past. We mustn't put this ship at such risk. In two days it should be quite safe. Until then, not."

Felicia stared at his dark, serious face. Turning to Kosoff, she recognized his unyielding expression. They're right, she thought. They can't risk the whole ship for one man. One man who might already be dead.

But she heard herself say, "Couldn't you send a communications satellite to Gamma now and try to reestablish a link with Brad?"

Desai looked questioningly at Kosoff. "I suppose that is possible," the captain said.

For long moments Kosoff said nothing. He stared at Felicia, making her feel uncomfortable.

At last he nodded curtly and said, "Yes. We could do that. For you."

Felicia felt a cold chill tingle along her spine.

standing alone at the edge of the battered, rain-soaked forest, brad realized that he had to find the shuttlecraft that had carried him to camma's surface.

It's got food, tools, equipment, he remembered. And its own communications system. I could contact the ship with it! Then his momentary exhilaration faded. If the storms haven't blown it away or damaged it.

Then he realized, It's also got a homing beacon! His fingers trembling with excitement, Brad pecked out the beacon's code on his wrist keyboard.

The most beautiful hum Brad had ever heard sounded gently, steadily, in his earphones. Brad felt exultant. If the beacon's working, he thought, chances are the shuttle's other electronic systems are working, too.

He started tramping across the soggy ground as if following the music of a marching band.

The shuttle's built to fly me back to the starship, he told himself. Captain Desai's people can shoot an automated program to the shuttle's computer and the bird can take off and bring me to Alpha and the ship. And Felicia.

He recalled that there was a three-minute time lag for two-way communications from Alpha. Okay, so they'll send a complete program, take off, fly through the atmosphere, and establish orbit. That will be the hard part, with me sitting there doing nothing. Everything preprogrammed, automated. Once in orbit around Gamma, getting to *Odysseus* in orbit around Alpha should be easy.

But he thought about Mnnx and Lnng and the other Gammans. *I told them I'd be back tonight. What'll they do when I don't show up? Can they survive without me?*

And Felicia. Will she be glad to see me? Is she angry that I didn't return to her when I had the chance?

Do the Gammans know how to build a new village, for the generation that's about to come to life? The biologists will go crazy, studying a new life form, an intelligent species that grows out of the ground, like plants.

I can't leave them, Brad knew. *I've interfered with their life cycle and now I've got to help them through the next steps. Before their long winter sets in.*

I can't leave them.

His triumphal march through the soaked, muddy meadow slowed to an almost reluctant pace. He passed the carcasses of two more of the monsters from Beta, dead and already rotting.

I can't leave them, he repeated to himself. *I've got to help them.*

Then he spotted the shuttlecraft in the distance, sitting in the meadow where he had left it a seeming lifetime ago. Its silvery metal skin glowed warmly, invitingly, in the afternoon sunlight.

Kosoff looked down the long conference table. Every department head was present, chatting in hushed tones.

"We're all here," Kosoff said, by way of calling them to order. "Let's start."

Ursula Steiner, sitting tall and regal halfway down the table, said, "I haven't received an agenda for this meeting."

"Neither have I," said Pedersen, the planetologist.

"Just an announcement that you wanted us here at sixteen hundred hours. Like a summons, almost."

"There isn't an agenda," Kosoff replied. "Not yet. In a sense, I've called this meeting to thrash out what our agenda should be once we return to Gamma."

"That's . . . unorthodox," Steiner said.

Kosoff answered, "We're faced with an unorthodox situation. Very unorthodox."

Littlejohn, seated at Kosoff's right, looked uncomfortable, upset. "You're referring to MacDaniels's interference with the Gammans."

"More than that," Kosoff said. "Much more than that."

From the far end of the table, Elizabeth Chang spoke up in her soft, smoky voice. "MacDaniels has violated the basic rule of alien contact. He's interfered with the aliens' fundamental beliefs. He's cast himself in the role of savior, almost a god."

Littlejohn countered, "He saved the Gammans from extermination. He couldn't stand by and let those big cats kill them all. He might have been killed himself."

Unruffled, Chang insisted, "Still, he has violated the most basic rule of alien contact: noninterference."

Pedersen objected, "So what was he supposed to do? Stand by and let the aliens be killed to the last man? That's inhuman."

"They are all going to die anyway," said Steiner. "They can't survive the deep freeze that the planet's climate is heading for."

"I'm not so sure about that," Littlejohn countered. "With our help they might be able to get through it. Or perhaps hibernate through the winter."

"More interference," said Chang.

"What's done is done," Kosoff said, with a dismissive wave of his hand. "We can't undo it. The question is, where do we go from here?"

Silence. The men and women looked at each other, each one waiting for someone else to reply.

"And something else," Kosoff added. "Something of far greater import."

Quentin Abbott nodded vigorously. "What—or who—created this situation?"

"Exactly."

"What do you mean?"

Hunching his shoulders slightly and leaning forward, as though preparing to push a great weight, Kosoff said, "This planetary system's current condition is not natural. Something—" He nodded toward Abbott. "—or some*one* created the situation we see today."

Abbott took up the theme. "We've done dozens of simulation runs regarding the orbits of this system's planets. Alpha is a gas giant that's losing its ocean and atmosphere at an alarming rate because it orbits so close to Mithra. Beta and Gamma are in these long, looping orbits that lock them into ice ages for most of their years."

"And the cats transfer from Beta to Gamma when the two planets are closest," Kosoff said. "That is not natural. Definitely not."

"Something happened to this planetary system," Abbott said. "Something catastrophic. Something that pushed Alpha almost into Mithra itself and locked Beta and Gamma into their extremely eccentric orbits. Probably knocked one or more other planets out of the system altogether."

"Something?" Pedersen demanded. "What?"

"Emcee can show you the re-creation my people have put together," Abbott said. "It boils down to this: roughly a hundred to two hundred thousand Earth years ago, this planetary system went through a cataclysmic event."

"Perhaps so," said Chang. "But that doesn't mean the event wasn't natural. Another star could have passed near enough to scramble the planets' orbits."

Kosoff called to Steiner. "Ursula, you're a biologist. How do you account for having a predator arise on one planet and its prey on a different planet? How do you account for the predators flying to their prey in vehicles that are part incubators and part spacecraft?"

Steiner blinked at him.

"It *can't* be natural," Kosoff insisted. "Some intelligence designed all this and set it in motion."

No one contradicted him.

Brad hurried eagerly across the muddy grass toward the shuttlecraft.

It's there, he said to himself, feeling exultant. It's all in one piece. The storms haven't smashed it up.

Then he saw that the craft was canted to one side, as if pushed over by a giant hand. The delta-shaped wing on that side was crumpled against the ground.

I won't be flying out of here, Brad realized. Strangely, he didn't feel disappointed. The decision's been made, he thought. I'm staying here on Gamma.

He walked up to the crippled spacecraft and saw that its entry hatch was on the undamaged side, just in front of the delta wing that angled up into the air.

Too high for me to reach. Pecking at his wrist keyboard, he saw the hatch slide noiselessly open and its metal ladder unfold. It poked uselessly into the empty air.

As he stared at the rungs of the ladder, Brad almost broke into laughter. This is biblical, like some ancient mythological tale about punishment and irony. The craft is here, everything I need to survive is in it, and I can't reach the final few meters to get inside.

Instead of laughing, though, Brad stared at the open hatch, wondering what to do. The sun was nearing the sawtooth ridge of the distant mountains. Soon it would begin to get dark.

* * *

Kosoff had never seen Ursula Steiner look distressed before. She still sat straight and elegant in her chair, but her hands were fluttering like a trapped bird.

"Not natural?" she said. "Of course it's natural. Just because we haven't found the cause for this scenario doesn't mean that some evil extraterrestrial villains deliberately tampered with this planetary system."

"Occam's razor," Kosoff replied. "The simplest explanation is usually the correct one."

Abbott chuckled slightly as he said, "I tend to agree with you, Professor—although I wouldn't call a malevolent extraterrestrial invader the simplest explanation."

"Can you provide a natural explanation for the condition of this solar system?" Kosoff demanded.

Pursing his lips, Abbott replied, "Not at this moment, no. But Dr. Chang suggested one possibility: a rogue star swept by close enough to scramble the planets' orbits. Or perhaps it was a mini black hole."

"A hundred thousand years ago?" Kosoff challenged. "Then we should be able to see that star and backtrack its trajectory. Even a mini black hole should produce gravitational distortions that would be detectable."

Abbott nodded. "I'll have my people get on it right away." Then he rubbed his chin and added, "You know, our own solar system was visited by a passing red dwarf some seventy thousand years ago. It's about twenty light-years from Earth at present."

"Did it perturb the planetary orbits?" Steiner asked, suddenly hopeful.

"Apparently not. At least, not enough for us to trace today. Probably kicked up a fuss in the Oort Cloud, ejecting cometary bodies and that sort of thing, I should presume."

"So what do we do about MacDaniels and his messiah complex?" Steiner demanded.

It was Kosoff's turn to go silent. Drumming his fingers

on the tabletop, at last he repeated, "What's done is done. I don't see that we have any alternative but to help the Gammans survive their winter."

Abbott agreed. "In for a penny, in for a pound."

Steiner looked aghast. "But our mission protocol forbids—"

"Those regulations were written on Earth by people who are still on Earth," Kosoff said sternly. "We're out here, on the scene, facing life-or-death decisions."

Elizabeth Chang smiled slightly. "When in doubt, choose life."

Littlejohn summed up, "Brad's made a shambles of the mission protocols. That may have been a mistake, but now we have no choice except to push ahead in the direction he's taken."

Kosoff nodded his agreement, but he was thinking, MacDaniels has become the de facto leader here. He pulls the strings and we dance to his tune.

When handed a lemon, Brad was thinking, make lemonade.

The shuttlecraft's entry hatch was too high above him for him to reach it. Its frail-looking metal ladder poked out uselessly into the empty air, as if it were daring Brad to figure out how to reach it.

Okay, he said to himself. That's what I'll have to do.

The shadows of late afternoon were lengthening across the field where the shuttle rested.

You've got to act quickly, Brad realized. Before it gets dark.

The ground was littered with twigs and branches and other debris torn from the forest by the storm winds. All I need, Brad thought, is a tree branch long enough to reach the hatch, and strong enough to hold my weight.

He started searching through the litter and soon spotted a long, fairly straight branch. Lifting one end of it, he was surprised at how heavy it was.

Okay, that's good, he thought. It's solid. It won't break under my weight. He started to drag it back to the shuttle. He had to strain hard to tug it along.

Now comes the hard part, he realized. Judging the angle by eye, Brad laid the branch on the ground so that, when raised on one end, its other end would nestle in the open hatch, nearly ten meters above his head.

It wasn't easy. He tugged the end of the branch off the ground and started walking down its length, each step lifting it higher, each step making it heavier against the shoulder of his suit. Twice the branch slipped from his gloved hands and crashed to the ground, forcing him to start all over again.

It was getting dark. Brad stood at the end of the branch, bent over, hands on his knees, sweaty and puffing with exertion. How can the Gammans work their farms without real tools? he wondered. They've got nothing but a few cutting blades and their own muscle power. Not even levers or pulleys.

Finally he muttered, "Okay. Third time's the charm."

He lifted and trudged slowly, doggedly until at last the branch's far end clonked dully against the corner of the open hatch. Then he slumped to the ground to catch his breath. Every muscle in his body ached.

But he'd done it.

Almost.

With a blood-curdling screech, the branch began to skitter against the shuttle's metal skin, teetering uncertainly. Brad saw that it would crash down to the ground again unless he could stop its slide.

Jumping to his feet, Brad put his shoulder to the branch, pushing with all his might until its upper end lodged itself firmly inside a corner of the open hatch.

Stepping back, Brad waited, puffing and sweating, for

more than a full minute. The branch did not move. It was firmly wedged in place.

He hoped.

Peering up the length of the branch, Brad realized that it would be far easier for him to climb its rough bark if he were out of his suit. The field was mostly in shadow now, the sky overhead a deep reddish violet.

"I'll never make it in this suit," he muttered to himself. Briefly he thought about the chance he was taking, but quickly decided the odds were worth risking. It's either get out of the suit or fall on your face trying to climb up the hatch.

He unlocked the helmet and lifted it off his head. The evening air smelled strange, alien. But not unpleasant, he thought. Just different.

He sucked in a double lungful of the alien air, thinking, If I die, I die. Then he quickly stripped off his gloves and boots and got to his feet.

In the deepening shadows, the branch looked like a stairway to heaven. Brad scrambled up its rough surface, glad that he was descended from apes and monkeys.

He reached the hatch and stood exultantly in the outer air lock compartment.

I've made it! he thought. Then he raised his fists over his head and shouted into the gathering darkness, "I made it!"

COMMUNICATIONS

Felicia sat on the bed in her quarters. It was early evening; she had spent the whole afternoon worrying about Kosoff's words. "For you," he had said. He's made it a personal favor to me to send a communications satellite to Gamma. And he's going to want something in return.

She wondered what she should do, if anything. Automatically, she went to the kitchen and pulled a prepackaged dinner from the freezer. I'd better stay away from the restaurants, she told herself. I'd better be antisocial until Brad returns.

If he returns, she corrected. And burst into tears.

Unbidden, Emcee's figure took shape in the holotank on the far side of the sitting room.

His calm face smiling slightly, the avatar said, "Please pardon the intrusion. I have an urgent and strictly private call for you from Dr. MacDaniels."

"Brad?" Felicia dropped the dinner package. "Put him on!"

And there he was, in his skivvies, sitting in what looked like the cockpit of the shuttlecraft.

"Brad! You're alive!"

She studied his face during the three-minute transmission delay. He looked thin and grimy and exhausted and altogether wonderful.

At last Brad dipped his chin and smiled tiredly. "Alive and well. I'm in the shuttlecraft, as you can see."

"You're coming back?"

Again the delay. Felicia realized that she must look a wreck, eyes teary, makeup smeared.

"I can't get back," he said. "The shuttle's been damaged by the storms. But its interior is intact and it makes a good shelter for me until you get back here to Gamma and pick me up."

"Brad, I love you."

She watched his face as her words sped to him. He seemed subtly different than she remembered: leaner, more intent.

A grin spreading slowly across his face, he replied, "I love you too, Fil. I've missed you."

For the next twenty minutes there was no one in Felicia's world except Brad. As they chatted, she kept repeating to herself, He's alive. He's not hurt. He's alive and he's not hurt.

Kosoff's meeting of the department heads ended with nothing much accomplished, except a confirmation that Captain Desai would haul *Odysseus* back to Gamma the next day. In the meantime, the starship would launch a satellite on a high-velocity trajectory into orbit around the ravaged planet, to assess the conditions on its surface and set up a communications link with Brad MacDaniels—assuming he was still alive.

Kosoff sat alone in the emptied conference room, berating himself for hoping MacDaniels had died in the storms. That's not worthy of you, he fumed. MacDaniels is a pain in the butt, yes, but he gets things done. The Gammans would have been wiped out if it weren't for Brad.

Of course, if he has happened to die, I'll have the chance to console his widow. Despite himself, Kosoff smiled at the thought.

The holographic display at the far end of the table lit up. Emcee's patient, impassive face announced, "Dr. MacDaniels calling you from planet Gamma, sir."

"MacDaniels?" Kosoff shot out of his chair. "Put him through!"

To his credit, all his thoughts of the lovely Felicia fled from Kosoff's mind as Brad's weary, grubby face took three-dimensional shape. Almost all his thoughts.

"Just about everybody in the village has survived," Brad was telling Kosoff. "And the cats from Beta are dying off, all by themselves. It's like they were programmed to kill the Gammans, then die off themselves."

"Strange." With a shake of his head Kosoff said, "This can't be natural."

Brad's eyes widened slightly, but he said, "I think you're right. We've got to get our top engineering people to examine those eggs the cats flew in on."

"And the biologists, of course," Kosoff added.

Three minutes later Brad replied, "Right."

"And you? You're all right?"

Again the maddening communications lag. Kosoff hated sitting there, unable to do anything except wait.

At last Brad answered, "Tired. Pretty cruddy after all this time in the biosuit. But I'm all in one piece."

"Good. We're leaving Alpha tomorrow morning. Should be establishing orbit around Gamma again in two more days."

"Fine," said Brad. "I can use the time to clean up and get some rest."

"You've earned it."

As he cut the communications link with Kosoff, though, Brad found himself wondering how quickly he could get back to the village. Winter's coming, he knew. We don't have much time to waste.

* * *

Moving the starship, a lenticular-shaped spacecraft as large as a moderate-sized town, was not a simple maneuver. The distance between planets Alpha and Gamma was too short to allow the ship to accelerate to near light-speed. As Captain Desai put it, "We go in low gear."

Brad remained inside the shuttlecraft most of the time that *Odysseus* was in transit toward Gamma. He popped out of the shuttle's hatch, wearing only regular coveralls, and retrieved the helmet, boots, and gloves of his biosuit.

When his medical readouts showed nothing dangerous or even unusual in his condition, except a slight indication of malnutrition, Brad went outside again without the biosuit and enjoyed a leisurely walk across the meadow in which the shuttle rested.

Inwardly struggling between anticipation and reluctance, Brad finally decided he had to return to the village. *Mnnx and the others must think I've abandoned them. Or maybe that the cats got me.*

That evening he thoroughly cleansed the biosuit in the craft's capacious sterilizer, where ultrasonic vibrations removed dirt and killed bacteria. The various parts of the suit even smelled clean when he removed them from the machine.

The following morning he pulled on the suit, all except the helmet and boots, then clambered down the tree branch to the grassy ground. As he lifted the helmet to his head, he looked to make certain that the air lock's inner hatch was sealed. *Keep the shuttlecraft's interior as free from contamination as possible,* he told himself.

Yet once he had put on his boots and helmet and started off for the village, he felt that his fears of contamination were probably exaggerated. *I've breathed the local air. Maybe only for a few minutes at a time, but it hasn't seemed to hurt me.*

The local bugs aren't interested in me, he thought. I'm foreign material to them. It'll take 'em a while to develop a taste for Earthly cells. How long? Years? Centuries? Months?

After half an hour of walking through the meadow toward the low hills that ringed the village, Brad finally put through a call to Littlejohn. Mission protocol: clear all decisions with your department head before taking action. Actual protocol: take your action first and then inform your department head, when it's too late for him to stop you.

return

+++
++

Littlejohn sank back in his desk chair, feeling somewhere between surprised and deflated.

"You're returning to the village?" he asked, annoyed at the squeak of his own tone. As he waited for Brad's reply, he berated himself for letting his surprise and frustration show. Brad's going too far, he thought. He decides what he wants to do and then does it. Leaves it to me to clear it with Kosoff. Makes me his errand boy.

"Yessir," said Brad.

"You should get approval from the executive committee before doing that, Brad," Littlejohn said.

Littlejohn's holographic display showed what Brad was seeing: a broad green meadow that ended in the gentle slope of grassy hills. A few trees rose here and there, several of them noticeably bent by the recent storms. The ground appeared to be littered with twigs and debris. The sky overhead was cloudless, a brazen bowl of hammered copper.

At last Brad said, "I promised them I'd come back to the village. They must think I've been killed . . . or maybe that I lied to them. I can't break their trust in me. You can get Kosoff and the executive committee to approve my action, can't you, please?"

"What choice do I have?" Littlejohn muttered.

* * *

Beneath the hot glow of Mithra, Brad paused as he reached the crest of the hills that ringed the village. The hollow looked much as it had when he'd first seen it. The floodwaters were gone and the ground looked firm and dry. Several of the Gammans were repairing their roofs, including the longhouse's, hauling cartloads of branches and twigs, teetering on the edge of the walls to weave them into rainproof roofs.

Others were out in the fields, he saw, clearing the clutter blown in by the storms among the carefully tended rows.

From this distance it was impossible for Brad to tell one of the aliens from another. They were all tall, lanky, dome-headed humanoids, unclothed, their pale white bodies spattered with irregular splotches of blues and purples.

He started down the slope, into their hollow.

"Brrd!" his computer translator erupted. "Look, it's Brrd!"

For an instant, everything in the village stopped, frozen with surprise. Then all the Gammans rushed toward him, dropping to the ground from their rooftop repairs, racing in from the fields.

"Brrd!" they shouted. "Brrd!"

Halfway down the hillside, Brad stopped and waved at them. "Hello!" he called.

They stopped a respectful few meters before him. Mnnx shouldered his way to the front of the pack.

"Brrd, we thought you were dead."

"We thought the cats got you."

"We thought you had left us."

Smiling inside his helmet, Brad said, "No. I'm fine. I simply need a little rest."

"But you've come back to us."

"I have come back to you."

"And you'll never leave us again?"

Brad hesitated. Then, "I will not leave you until I know that you can live through the long winter and survive on your own."

"But how can we do that? No one has ever lived through the winter," said Mnnx.

"Except the Rememberer," Lnng corrected. "And even he goes to sleep in the ground until the winter is over."

"I will show you how to survive the long winter," said Brad. Mentally, he added, If Kosoff and those other oafs don't get in my way.

It was almost like coming home to a big, welcoming family. The Gammans clustered around Brad, happy to see him, glad to have him back among them. Brad felt the warmth of comradeship for the first time since he'd been a teenager.

Then Lnng asked, "What do we have to do to prepare for the winter?"

The warm glow dimmed considerably. You get straight to the point, don't you? Brad asked silently.

"We'll start preparing in a few days," he temporized. "How did the farm get through the storms?"

Mnnx said, "Not much damage. The new Folk are resting in the ground properly."

"May I see them?"

The Gammans went silent. They all turned to Mnnx.

Mnnx said to Brad proudly, "I'm the village Rememberer now. Everyone agreed that I should take Drrm's place."

"That's fine," said Brad.

Looking into the faces of his fellow Gammans, Mnnx said, "I think it would be good for Brrd to see the new Folk."

"Yes," Lnng agreed. "And then we can start to prepare for building a new village for them."

Brad thought, Mnnx might be the new Rememberer, but Lnng is going to be pushing him every step of the way. Then he realized, with a pang of disquiet, how similar that was to his relationship with Kosoff.

They all trooped out to the farm fields. Brad saw the neat rows of crops, sprouting nicely despite the storms. Some of the shoots were bent, a few torn away entirely, but by and large the farm appeared to be in reasonably good shape.

Mnnx led Brad—and the others—off to a far corner of the farm where there was a different planting: little mounds spaced roughly five meters apart. Atop each mound a single leafy green stalk rose, sticking up like an antenna on a spacecraft.

As the Gammans stood respectfully to one side, Mnnx gestured to the mounds and said, "The new Folk."

"They're growing in the ground?" Brad asked.

"Yes, of course." Dropping to his knees, Mnnx said, "Listen to them." And he bent his head to press it lightly against the earthen mound.

Somewhat more awkwardly, Brad sank to his knees and pressed the side of his helmet against the dirt. Nothing. No, wait . . . the faintest whooshing sound, in and out, like a distant tide surging against a sandy shore. In and out . . . in and out . . .

It's breathing! Brad realized.

And he heard the tiny lub-dub of a heartbeat.

Straightening up, Brad stared at the mound of grayish brown soil. There's a body in there! A Gamman is growing beneath the ground. Felicia and the rest of the biologists will go crazy over this.

He realized now why the mounds were five meters apart. Room for the kids to grow to full size.

Climbing up to his feet, Brad asked, "When will they come out of the ground? How long before they are fully grown?"

"After the winter," Mnnx said. "They will sleep in the

ground while the world freezes. Then, when the ice melts, the new Folk will rise from the ground."

"And the Rememberer will teach them what they must know," said Brad.

"If the Rememberer survives the winter."

"We can help you there."

Lnng caught Brad's word. "We? There are more of you? You are not alone?"

Brad looked into their expressionless faces as they clustered around him. The computer's translation of their words could not convey their emotions, but Brad guessed that they were at least inquisitive, at most fearful.

They've got to find out, sooner or later. As gently as he could—even though he knew that his tone would not get through the computer's translation—Brad said, "Yes, there are more of my kind coming here. They live in the sky—"

"Do you live in the sky, Brrd?" asked one of the Gammans.

Without hesitation, Brad replied, "Once I did. Now I live here, among you."

tacit approval

Emcee was reporting, "Transmissions from Gamma are much more reliable with the new communications satellite in place."

Kosoff nodded impatiently. "Yes. We can watch all the details of MacDaniels making a shambles of our contact protocols."

Emcee did not reply.

Turning to Littlejohn, sitting before his desk, Kosoff asked, "What are we going to do with this young man? He's made a mockery of our chain of command."

With a shrug of his thin shoulders, the anthropologist said, "Brad's on his own down there. He's doing what he thinks is best for the aliens."

"Is it best for them to shatter their traditions, their way of life?"

"There's not much we can do about it now."

Jabbing a finger at his desktop screen, Kosoff grumbled, "The executive committee back Earthside is furious with me. They're blaming *me* for allowing MacDaniels to run wild."

Littlejohn's dark face contracted into a frown. "You've been put into the position of a leader whose people are running off in an unexpected direction."

"Not my people," Kosoff snapped. "One man. Him. MacDaniels."

"It's not a happy situation for you, I admit. Yet, if you take the long view, Brad just might have saved those people from annihilation. That should be worth something back on Earth."

"They'll want my head on a platter."

Surprisingly, Littlejohn smiled. "Not if Brad succeeds."

"Succeeds?"

"Get yourself to the head of the parade, Adrian. What would happen if you direct Brad to build a new village for the unborn Gammans?"

Sourly, Kosoff replied, "He's already telling them that that's what they're going to do."

"All right," said Littlejohn. "You take the credit for it. You announce that we're going to study how these survivors develop in contrast to the other villages that were wiped out by the cats from Beta. That would be a real achievement, wouldn't it?"

"An achievement that would take centuries to bring to fruition."

"But you would have started it. Under your direction, we can study the development of two alternative societies on Gamma. Anthropologically, it would be fabulous!"

"Two alternative societies . . . "

"The other villages have been wiped out by the cats, but their next generation is growing in the farms. Once the planet gets through its long winter, those Gammans are going to come out of the ground and restart their societies." The Aborigine barely paused for a breath. "But in Brad's village, the Gammans survived the cats. How will they get through the winter? What will their society be like when their next generation wakes up?"

Kosoff stared at the anthropologist. "Study the differences between them," he mused.

"Yes! You've got to get to the head of this parade," Littlejohn encouraged. "You're the leader of our group. Lead, even if it's not in the direction you originally planned to go."

Kosoff leaned back in his desk chair, fingers steepled in front of his lips. He muttered, "Don't fight them. Join them."

"Lead them," said Littlejohn eagerly.

All day long and into the lengthening shadows of sunset Brad tussled inwardly with the decision he knew he had to make. His problem was that he didn't know how to make it.

Sooner or later, he told himself, I'm going to have to show them my true form. I'm going to have to let them see me as I really am, not masquerading inside this biosuit.

How will they react to that? he wondered. Will it shock them? Will it ruin the trust they have in me?

How will they react to having others from the starship coming down to work with them? And study them? Kosoff is right: this is a very complicated, very delicate situation.

How should I handle it?

That night, once he'd returned to the crippled shuttle-craft, Brad peeled himself out of his protective suit and called not Kosoff, nor Littlejohn, but Felicia.

"Show yourself to them?" she asked, looking startled.

"It's got to be done, sooner or later," Brad said. "I can't go decked out in this disguise forever."

The time lag between them was shorter, now that the starship was returning to Gamma. Still, the delay seemed to drag on forever.

As he waited for her reply, Brad admired her beautiful face. She's worried about me. For me. She really cares about me. I'm the luckiest man on Earth.

Then he remembered that he wasn't on Earth. He was two hundred light-years from Earth, on an alien planet.

"Brad," Felicia replied at last, "you should ask Littlejohn and Kosoff how to handle this. They're your superiors; you've got to get their approval before you take such a big step."

He nodded, but he thought, Pass the buck upstairs. Let them take the responsibility. And what if they make the wrong decision?

"I suppose that's the correct thing to do," he said.

When Felicia's reply reached him, it was, "You know it is."

But Brad was already thinking, What's best for the Gammans? We've established contact with an alien race. We've helped them survive annihilation. Now we have to help them get through their winter. Are we going to put our decisions up to a committee vote?

He knew what his answer was.

Long into the night Brad searched for a way to get Kosoff to make the decision he wanted him to make.

At Brad's behest, Emcee scanned all the mission protocols, seeking a loophole that would give Brad the authority to do what he wanted to do: show himself to the Gammans in his true form, free of the biosuit.

The computer's bland-looking image smiled at Brad as it reported, "The safety regulations permit you to dispense with the biosuit's protection once the medical department has confirmed that you can breathe the planet's air without harmful effects."

"I've done that," said Brad, sitting in the cockpit's seat, surrounded by the shuttlecraft's controls and communications gear.

It took a little more than one minute for Emcee to reply, "But you have not received clearance from the medical department."

Brad thought for a moment, turning alternatives over in his mind. Then, "Tacit approval."

After the delay, Emcee's image actually blinked. "Tacit approval?"

Nodding vigorously, Brad said, "The fact that I've exposed myself to the local environment and the medical department hasn't raised any objections constitutes their tacit approval, doesn't it?"

This time the time lag was noticeably longer. Emcee must be scanning every regulation in the protocols, Brad thought.

"There is nothing in the mission protocols about tacit approval," the computer said at last.

"Search the legal files," Brad commanded. "There must be something in there."

Even scanning the files at nearly the speed of light, it took Emcee several minutes before it announced, "Tacit approval is recognized in the legal files."

"Then that's what we've got," Brad declared, grinning. "The medical department hasn't forbidden me to go outside without the biosuit. That's tacit approval."

Emcee's image froze in the three-dimensional display for almost exactly one minute. Then, "There is a term from old nautical jargon for what you are doing, Brad. You are a shipboard lawyer."

Brad laughed. "Whatever it takes," he said. "Get the job done, whatever it takes."

unmasked

+ + + + +

"Tacit approval?" Kosoff roared.

It was early morning aboard *Odysseus*. Kosoff had risen from his bed and troubled dreams about a dark-haired woman who kept eluding him. After his morning ablutions, as he dressed he called Emcee for a report on what Brad was doing.

The master computer coolly informed him of Brad's legalistic handiwork.

Half dressed, tugging on his trousers, Kosoff sputtered, "He can't do that! He's got no right . . . he needs our approval . . . the medical department . . . "

Dispassionately, Emcee replied, "He's already on his way to the village, without wearing his biosuit."

Kosoff pulled up his trousers and fastened the belt, then sank down onto his rumpled bed.

"Get Yamagata," he said, scowling.

After half an hour of talking with the head of the medical department, Kosoff realized that Brad had threaded his way through the mission protocols very neatly. Yamagata had not forbidden Brad to go outside without his protective suit.

"Indeed," said the Japanese biomedical director, "the young man seems eager to offer himself as a test subject, a guinea pig."

"Indeed," Kosoff growled. And cut the connection.

As the holographic display went dark, Kosoff realized

he was still sitting on the edge of his bed, half dressed, flustered and feeling completely stymied.

He's damnably clever, Kosoff said to himself as he tugged on his slippers. MacDaniels is too clever for his own good. He's making me look like an incompetent, impotent old fool.

Going out on his own, is he? Kosoff simmered. All right. Sooner or later he's going to take one step too far. And when he does, I'll be right there to chop the legs out from under him.

Brad walked through the bright sunshine, unencumbered by his biosuit. He breathed the morning air, delighted in the strange yet not unpleasant odors of alien flowers and plants. Tiny animals scurried through the grass; the local equivalent of birds swooped colorfully overhead.

As he started up the slope toward the village he remembered an old poem from his school days: *God's in his heaven, all's right with the world.*

So far.

He had taken the communications set and the computer translator from the biosuit and clipped them to the belt of his slacks, together with his laser pistol. The cochlear implants Yamagata had set in his skull picked up incoming transmissions easily enough; no need to wear earbuds. He was ready to show himself as he really was to the villagers.

Were they ready to see him this way?

We'll soon find out, Brad said to himself.

The villagers were busy at their usual tasks, most of them in the farm fields, a few gathered at the entrance to the longhouse. That must be Mnnx, Brad thought, in the middle of the group.

He was nearly halfway down the hill before any of

them noticed him. One of the Gammans pointed, and Brad heard, "A stranger!"

They all turned and gaped at him.

They've never shown any trace of violence, Brad reminded himself. The nearest thing to weapons they have are those puny hunting sticks. Still, his right hand grasped the butt of the laser pistol hanging from his belt.

The gaggle at the longhouse seemed frozen, staring.

"Hello," Brad called to them. "It's me, Brad."

Mnnx edged through the others and stared at him.

"You are not Brrd," he said, his voice sounding low, ominous, even in the computer's translation.

Brad stopped some twenty meters from them. "I am Brad," he insisted. "And you are Mnnx . . . Where's Lnng, out in the fields?"

Slowly, Mnnx stepped closer. The rest of the Gammans remained rooted where they stood.

"You are a stranger. Yet you know my name."

Putting on a smile, Brad said, "I truly am Brad. This is my true form."

"True form?"

"Until today, I wore a different form. I wanted to look as much like you as I could. Now we know each other well enough so that I can show myself to you as I really am."

Mnnx said slowly, suspiciously, "Your hands look like Brrd's hands, but their color is different."

"This is the real color of my skin," Brad explained.

One of the Gammans said, "You look strange. Very short."

Before Brad could reply, another villager observed, "Your eyes are very small."

"There's a hole in your face."

Brad said, "That's where I make the sounds you hear. That's how I speak."

"And there is fur on the top of your head."

Spreading his arms, Brad replied, "I told you that my village is far from here . . . "

"In the sky, you said."

"My body is different from yours, in some ways."

"Your old body was better."

"My people made that body to look like your own as much as possible. But now I am showing you my true body."

They stood inspecting him, none of them daring to come closer than several meters.

"It is really me. Brad. Your friend."

None of them moved.

"I have come to help you get through the coming winter. And to help you build a new village for the new Folk."

Mnnx blinked his big, bulbous eyes, a nictitating membrane sliding over them and then retreating back again.

"You are really Brrd?"

"I am." Nerving himself, Brad held out his hand. Mnnx hesitated, staring at it, then at last took it in his own tentacled grip. Brad suppressed the shudder of revulsion at the feel of the alien's hand. He saw that Mnnx seemed stiff, uneasy, too.

Once they released each other, Brad told them, "Soon there will be others like me to help you live through the winter and welcome the new Folk when they rise out of the ground."

Mnnx turned to one of the Gammans. "Run to the fields. Tell Lnng and the others that Brrd has returned to us."

Brad let out a gust of pent-up breath. He's accepted me! he thought. Maybe not one hundred percent, but it's a beginning.

captain Desai sat in the bridge's imposing command chair and watched the curving bulk of planet Gamma slide across the main display screen. In the star-speckled sky, Beta was a bloodred crescent, safely distant and moving farther away.

"Orbit established, sir," said his navigator, a slightly plump Jamaican woman, her skin nearly as dark as Desai's own.

The parameters of their orbit sprang up on the screen, overlaying the view of Gamma.

"Circularize orbit," Desai commanded.

"Circularizing."

Desai glanced around the bridge. Six men and women were seated at their consoles, tapping out commands or staring at data on their screens. Busywork, he knew. The ship was actually controlled by the master computer; the humans on the bridge were redundant, a sop to the deep-seated human fear of being replaced by machine intelligence.

Desai shook his head tolerantly. We're here to make contact with alien intelligences, yet we're afraid of our own machines.

With an inner smile he remembered that the scientific staff had given the master computer a human avatar for them to interact with, and the crew had even given it a human name, of sorts: Emcee.

The minibursts of thrust that adjusted their orbit

around Gamma were barely noticeable. After several minutes the navigator announced, "Orbit circularized, sir."

Desai saw the parameter numbers on the central screen.

"Good," he said as he got up from the chair. "Take the conn. I'm going to see Professor Kosoff."

Kosoff's office was only a few meters down the passageway from the bridge, but it was like stepping into a different world. The science staff wore no uniforms, and they seemed to have no real discipline, just a gaggle of youngish men and women strolling leisurely along the passageway, chatting with one another casually. Desai wondered how Kosoff got any real work out of them.

Kosoff's office door opened as soon as Desai presented himself before the security camera. The professor was at his desk, as usual, conversing with the master computer's avatar. He looked up and waved Desai to one of the chairs in front of his desk.

Emcee's image in the holo display blinked out as Desai dropped into one of the handsomely comfortable chairs.

"We're in orbit around Gamma," the captain reported.

With an unsmiling nod, Kosoff said merely, "Good."

"I presume you'll want to send a team to the ground as soon as possible."

Kosoff heaved a weary sigh. "Yes. Once I've checked out conditions on the ground with MacDaniels."

It was late afternoon. Mithra's glaring red orb was sliding toward the distant mountain ridge as Brad sat with Mnnx in the top floor of the longhouse.

"Why did you wear your disguise?" Mnnx asked. He was seated at the end of a long table with Brad at his right. It reminded Brad of Kosoff's conference table up in the starship, but he and Mnnx were the only two people in the big, open room.

"My people thought it would be easier for you to accept me if I looked as much like you as possible," Brad answered.

For several heartbeats Mnnx remained silent. Then, "Are you one of the Sky Masters, Brrd?"

Surprised, Brad replied, "No. My people come from far away—"

"They live in the sky?"

Careful, Brad warned himself. He's frightened of these Sky Masters, whatever they are.

Slowly, Brad explained, "My people live on a world that is very much like yours. They can travel from their own world to yours, through the sky. But the sky is not their true home."

Mnnx sat in silence, trying to digest what Brad was telling him. The ropy tentacles of his hands kept uncoiling and then clenching again. His equivalent of tapping his fingernails, Brad thought.

"The Sky Masters are very powerful," Mnnx said at last. "We have disobeyed them. We should have let the monsters kill us, so that the new Folk will have this village for themselves when they rise out of the ground."

"You're afraid the Sky Masters will return and punish you?"

"Yes. They are very powerful, and they will be angry at our disobedience."

"Surely they didn't want you to die," Brad said.

"Surely they did," Mnnx snapped.

"But you still live. You chose life over death. That is good." Before Mnnx could object, Brad went on, "My people will help you. Together we will build a new village for the new Folk. You will all live, and you won't have to fear the monsters from Beta anymore. Or the Sky Masters, either."

Mnnx said, "Once this land was covered with villages. Villages far bigger than what we have now. The Sky

Masters destroyed them all. They send the monsters from Beta to kill us so that the new Folk can have villages to live in when they come out of the ground."

"That's no way to live," Brad said.

"It is our way, the way that the Sky Masters have ordained for us to be. I fear that they will grow angry and return to destroy us all, destroy everything, as they did so long ago."

With a certainty that he did not actually feel, Brad said, "No, they will not return. And if they do, my people will protect you."

Mnnx stared at Brad. "The Sky Masters are very powerful."

"So are we," Brad said, hoping that Mnnx's story was really mythology and not an actual threat.

Brad trudged back to his shuttlecraft, through the lengthening shadows of evening, mulling over the tale of fear and death that was troubling Mnnx.

They've disobeyed their so-called Sky Masters, he thought. When presented with a way to survive the beasts from Beta, they allowed me to save them. When face-to-face with certain death, they chose life.

Okay. But now Mnnx is afraid that he's broken some moral commandment. Afraid that their supernatural overlords are going to return and punish them.

How can I convince them that they're terrified of phantoms? And what happens if they're not phantoms? Mythology is based on reality, at heart. How did this legend of the Sky Masters get started?

Then one overwhelming fact rose up in Brad's mind. How did those monsters from Beta develop the technology to fly here during the planets' closest approach? Those egg-shaped spacecraft aren't mythology. They're high technology.

What happened to these people? What's going to happen to them—and to us?

It was fully night by the time Brad reached the crippled shuttlecraft. In starlit darkness he scrambled up the tree trunk that served as his ladder and ducked through the air lock's outer hatch.

Turning to look out at the quietly peaceful night, he saw a point of light rising in the star-flecked sky. The starship, he realized. It's in orbit, only a few hundred kilometers away. Felicia's there.

As he made his way through the inner air lock chamber and along the tilted passageway that led to his quarters, Brad also realized that Kosoff and Littlejohn and all the others were aboard the starship, too. The whole chain of command, ready to look over his shoulder, ready to second-guess his decisions, ready to take control of his life.

He went past his narrow sleeping chamber and straight to the cockpit. Sliding into the only chair there, he called, "Emcee, connect me with Felicia, please. Private and personal."

Felicia's image took form in the holographic display. She was in their quarters, on the couch in their sitting room. Waiting for me, Brad thought.

"Hi," he said, feeling awkward and happy at the same time.

"Hello, Brad."

"You're here."

"Yes, we established orbit a few hours ago."

"I saw the ship overhead."

Felicia smiled. "Captain Desai told me he'll send a shuttle down to pick you up tomorrow morning."

"What time is it aboard the ship now?"

"Nineteen hundred hours, almost. We've adjusted ship's time to agree with your time on the ground. It's costing us four hours of sleep tonight."

"Sorry about that," he said, feeling slightly inane.

"It's all right," Felicia replied, the corners of her lips curving upward slightly. "Tomorrow we'll have a regular night, full time. The two of us."

Brad could feel his own face breaking into a wide, cheery grin. "We sure will."

* * *

Emcee woke Brad just as sunrise gleamed over the mountain ridgeline.

"Captain Desai is coming in person to bring you back to *Odysseus*," the master computer announced. "Arrival in two hours."

Snapping awake, Brad pushed himself to a sitting position on the bunk. Its sheet had somehow twisted itself around his body. As he disentangled himself, he recalled that he had dreamed while he slept, but it wasn't the old nightmare that had plagued him. He couldn't remember what his dream had been; the harder he tried to recall it, the more it melted out of his memory.

Exactly two hours later Brad stood at the foot of his improvised ladder and watched a shuttlecraft glide over the distant mountains, white contrails trailing off its wingtips. It flew down the length of the meadow, banked gracefully at its far end, then lowered its landing gear and came in for a flawlessly smooth landing.

And two hours after that, approximately, Brad stood before Kosoff's desk. Littlejohn sat in front of the desk, beaming up at Brad like a proud father. Kosoff's face, though, looked grimly unhappy.

"You look slimmer," Kosoff said.

"And tanner," added Littlejohn, smiling.

"You'd better get Yamagata to—"

Brad interrupted, "I had a preliminary medical scan during the flight up here. Dr. Yamagata said I'm in good health."

Kosoff h'mphed. "You should get a complete physical exam."

"Yessir."

"I suppose you know you've made a shambles out of the mission protocol," Kosoff rumbled.

"Could we talk about that later, please?" Brad said. "I'd like to see my wife."

Littlejohn's eyes flicked to the office's side door. "She's in the next room, waiting—"

"Excuse me," Brad said as he bolted toward the door. "I'll make a full report to you tomorrow, first thing."

Kosoff watched, open-mouthed, as Brad opened the door and rushed into Felicia's waiting arms.

Littlejohn chuckled lightly and turned back to Kosoff. "The course of true love," he said.

Kosoff tried to scowl, but couldn't quite manage to pull it off. "I'll schedule a meeting of department heads for tomorrow morning," he grumbled.

A broad grin splitting his dark face, Littlejohn suggested, "Better make it tomorrow afternoon. Give the lad a chance to recuperate before making his report."

Brad awoke slowly, like a swimmer rising up to the surface of a deep pool. He saw that the bedroom was still dark, although the digital clock readout on the holo viewer said 08:54.

Turning slightly, he made out Felicia's tousled head on the pillow next to his. She was sleeping soundly.

Brad tried to figure out how he could get out of bed without waking her. I told Kosoff I'd make my report to him this morning, he remembered. But instead of getting out of bed, he lightly ran his hand along Felicia's back and across her bare rump.

She popped one eye open.

"Time to get up," Brad said softly.

"Wrong," she contradicted. "I gave Emcee orders to leave us alone until ten hundred."

"But Kosoff—"

"He can wait." And she wrapped an arm around Brad's neck and pulled him to her.

Brad sighed contentedly. "I guess he'll have to."

When he finally got out of bed, Brad asked Emcee for any messages that had come through while he'd slept.

"There is only one," the computer's humanized image replied. "From Professor Kosoff. The meeting of department heads to hear your personal report is scheduled for fourteen hundred hours, main conference room."

Brad grinned at Emcee and replied, "Please tell Professor Kosoff that I'll be there. And thank him for scheduling the meeting at a reasonable hour."

After a long, luxurious hot shower and a breakfast of waffles slathered with oleomargarine and syrup, Brad tossed his bathrobe onto the thoroughly rumpled bed and pulled out of the closet a crisply pressed set of coveralls.

"First new set of clothes I've put on in weeks," he said.

"You're thinner," Felicia said.

"Haven't had any real food down there: just pills and prepackaged meals."

She nodded. With a firm sense of purpose, she said, "I'll take care of that."

Brad hesitated, then told her, "I'm going back there as soon as I can."

"I know. I'm going with you."

"You . . . ?"

"I'll be part of the biology team. It's all arranged."

With a grin, Brad replied, "Fine. Wonderful."

report

Brad sat at the foot of the long conference table, with Felicia beside him. He'd had to drag up a chair from the ones lining the conference room's far wall to make room for her at the table. No one objected.

The table was filled by all the department heads, including Ursula Steiner, Felicia's boss. Even Captain Desai had come for this meeting, sitting up at the left of the empty chair at the table's head. They were all chatting together, a dozen buzzing conversations up and down the table, as they waited for Kosoff.

Precisely at 1400 hours the door to Kosoff's office opened and the professor walked briskly to his seat.

The smile on his bearded face looked a little forced, Brad thought, but as Kosoff sat down he opened the meeting with:

"I know you've all been going over MacDaniels's day-by-day reports. I thought it would be useful to hear what he has to say about his mission to the aliens. From the horse's mouth, so to speak."

Someone stage-whispered, "A neighsayer, no doubt."

A few chuckles up and down the table.

Brad rose slowly to his feet. "The major impression that I got about the Gammans is that they are nonviolent; peaceable to the point of being suicidal."

"They allow themselves to be killed without offering any resistance," said Steiner.

"That's because they didn't see any way to save themselves," Brad pointed out. "When I showed the villagers that the cats from Beta could be killed, they chose to save themselves."

"They chose," Kosoff corrected, "to let you save them."

"Yes," said Brad. "And now they're worried that they've done the wrong thing and they're going to be punished for their disobedience."

"What about the other villages?" asked Littlejohn. "Have any of them survived?"

Olav Pedersen, head of the planetology group, answered, "Apparently not. They all seem to have been wiped out by the cats."

"And the cats have themselves died off?"

Steiner said, "Yes. It's as if they've been genetically programmed to die after a few days from breaking out of their eggs."

"Wait a minute," Brad said. "Each village has a Rememberer, a person who is supposed to survive the death time and educate the new generation of Gammans, once they come out of the ground."

"But that won't happen until their long winter is over," said Elizabeth Chang.

"You mean that one person in each village hibernates through the winter?"

"Apparently so," Brad admitted. "The Rememberer in the village I contacted was killed by the cats."

The table went silent.

Then Pedersen, pale and gloomy, said, "Do we have to search those other villages for survivors?"

"It looks that way," said Littlejohn.

Brad said, "Wait. There's something else. According to the Gammans' mythology, their civilization once built extensive cities. But they were wiped out by the Sky Masters, whoever they were."

"Mythology," Littlejohn pointed out. "You can't expect us to try to track down fantasies, Brad."

"Mythologies have their roots in reality."

"Yes, but—"

Kosoff broke into the discussion. "Olav, have the surveillance satellites detected anything that might have once been a city?"

Pedersen shook his head. "Most of the planet is too heavily forested for ground-penetrating radar to get decent imagery."

Quentin Abbott spoke up. "Mythology or reality, one thing is abundantly clear. This planetary system suffered a major upheaval some hundred thousand years ago, perhaps more. The current configuration of the inner planetary orbits is unstable. Alpha is going to be swallowed up by Mithra within another millennium or so; Beta and Gamma are going to be ejected from the Mithra system altogether."

Kosoff said, "Surely you don't believe that these mythological Sky Masters did this? Shattered the entire planetary system?"

"Why?"

"How?"

With a grim smile of utter certainty, Abbott said, "I offer one irrefutable item of evidence. Those egg-things that the cats ride in from Beta to Gamma can't be natural. That's high technology, people, and we should be trying to determine who created such technology. And why."

EVIDENCE

From his seat at the foot of the table, Brad said, "We have the remains of the eggs that the cats rode in from Beta. That should tell us something."

"Indeed," said Kosoff.

Desai suggested, "And maybe a ground team could find evidence of the city or cities that the Gammans spoke of."

"That's probably mythology," said Littlejohn.

"I could ask the Gammans about it," Brad said. "Maybe they can point us in the right direction."

Kosoff objected, "The ground team is going to have its hands full, building a new village for the newborn Gammans."

"Are they going to have to stay through the winter?" Steiner asked.

"No! That's much too long. We're scheduled to return back to Earth in slightly less than four years. Their winter lasts ten times that long."

"So we'll build their new village and then leave?"

Before anyone else could reply, Brad said, "I think we should introduce them to some of our technology. Help them get through the winter without hibernating, at least."

Kosoff scowled down the table. "Haven't we interfered with their way of life enough? We're not here to—"

Brad interrupted, "We're here to help these people. We can't just leave them to face the winter on their own."

"Not now that you've destroyed their way of life," Kosoff growled.

Littlejohn spread his hands, as if to part the two of them. "You're both right. It would have been criminal to let the Gammans be killed off. I can understand where Brad felt he had to help them. Now the question is, how much help should we give them?"

"Enough to get through the winter," Brad said.

Kosoff's bearded face looked grim. But he asked, "Is that the sense of the group? Do you believe we should help the aliens?"

No one replied. Brad saw that none of them wanted to be the first to answer.

So he said, "Yes. We should help them to survive. Otherwise we'd be killing them."

Steiner said, "But a new generation will arise. The species will survive."

"How would you like it if you were forced to kill yourself after you've reproduced?" Brad asked.

"That's what happens naturally," Steiner said. "We're genetically programmed to die after we've reached sexual maturity."

"Perhaps so," said Chang, in her soft, self-effacing tone. "But human females live far beyond menopause."

"And human males?" someone asked.

"They can father children as long as they live, almost," Steiner said, sounding resentful.

Felicia spoke up. "Besides, we've worked for centuries to prolong our life spans, to avoid death as long as we can, regardless of our reproductive capabilities."

"But we still die," said Steiner.

"Not willingly," Littlejohn retorted.

"Enough!" Kosoff barked. "I want a show of hands. Shall we give the Gammans enough technological help to assure that they will survive their winter?"

Brad shot his hand high in the air. Abbott raised his more slowly, followed by Steiner and Chang. One by one, each of the department heads raised his or her hand. Littlejohn watched them, then finally joined in the consensus.

Kosoff broke into a reluctant smile. "What the hell," he said reluctantly as he raised his own hand. "Might as well make it unanimous."

Noriyoshi Yamagata studied the screen that displayed the results of Brad MacDaniels's detailed physical examination.

Miss nothing, he told himself as he sat at his desk, peering intently at the readouts. This young man has exposed himself to the environment of an alien planet. Yes, the planet is Earthlike. But it is not Earth.

Biological theory stated that the microscopic alien equivalents of bacteria and viruses would not—could not—attack Earthly cells. They are alien, not adapted to feeding on the cells of terrestrial visitors.

But that is theory, not actual experience, he knew. MacDaniels has lived on that planet's surface for many days, breathed its air, exposed himself to its native pathogens.

After several hours of intense scrutiny, Yamagata leaned back in his little swivel chair, almost satisfied. Almost. MacDaniels appears to be in excellent health, he saw. A little underweight, but that is to be expected when his food intake was so restricted. There is no evidence of infection, not a trace of alien microbes invading his body, attacking his cells.

Good news, he thought. Yet he felt uneasy. Tomorrow a team of twenty men and women is going down to the surface of that alien world. Will the native biosphere be so benign with them?

Or have I missed something? Something that might kill them all?

All the available evidence pointed against that unhappy result. Still, Yamagata felt uneasy. All the available evidence might not be all the evidence that exists.

with Felicia beside him, Brad stood in the afternoon sunlight, watching the construction robots putting together the prefabricated camp structures that would be their home while the team was on Gamma.

The robots were humanoid in form, although most of them had four arms that could be fitted with humanlike hands, pincerlike claws, or any number of specialized tools. Their faces had two electro-optical eyes, a set of environmental sensors where a human nose would be, and a speaker grille for a mouth. But they reminded Brad of oversized ants, not mechanical humans; tirelessly busy, assembling the single-story buildings with single-minded automated efficiency: living quarters, offices, laboratories, dining hall, communications center. Off to one side stood the beginnings of a garage. No more trudging out to the village on foot, Brad said to himself. I wonder what the Gammans will think of our self-propelled ground cars?

Turning to Felicia, he said, "We can ride out to the village before the sun goes down."

"But the mission plan doesn't include visiting the village until our base is finished," she replied.

Nodding, Brad said, "The robots will finish the base whether we're here or not. I want to get back to the village, show them that we haven't forsaken them."

"You should get Dr. Littlejohn's approval, then."

Grasping her wrist, Brad replied, "Okay, let's go find him."

Littlejohn was in the room that would be his office; it looked bare, raw, new. But the anthropologist was already at his desk, reporting to Kosoff up in the orbiting starship.

". . . construction is proceeding on schedule. We'll sleep under the new roofs tonight and get down to work tomorrow."

Standing in the office's doorway, Felicia and Brad saw Kosoff's three-dimensional image sitting behind his desk, as usual.

"That's fine," said Kosoff. "Everything is on schedule, then."

"Yes, it is," said Littlejohn, with a satisfied smile.

Brad held Felicia at the doorway. "Don't interrupt them," he whispered.

As if he'd heard Brad's words, Littlejohn's eyes flicked to the doorway, then returned their focus to Kosoff. "MacDaniels is here now, Professor. He's just stepping into my office."

With Felicia trailing behind him, Brad walked toward Littlejohn's desk. Once he stepped into Kosoff's view, the professor said, "I suppose you're anxious to get back to your villagers."

"Yes, sir, I am. I've been away more than two days now; I don't want them to think that I've abandoned them."

Unconsciously scratching at his beard, Kosoff said, "You've got to stop thinking of yourself as some kind of messiah, Brad."

Astonished at the idea, Brad blurted, "Messiah? Me?"

"Power corrupts," Kosoff warned. "Remember that."

Shaking his head, Brad replied, "All I want to do is to help those people. They need our help—"

"Thanks to your interfering with them."

Brad held on to his swooping temper. He doesn't understand, he told himself. He just doesn't understand.

"Sir, no one can unscramble an egg. We're down here to help the Gammans survive. That's what I intend to do."

Kosoff muttered, "Just remember, you're the one who scrambled this particular egg in the first place. The responsibility for the aliens' survival rests on your shoulders."

Brad pressed his lips together and remained silent. Yet he thought, The responsibility is mine. But will you let me have the authority I need to get the job done?

Once Littlejohn ended his discussion with Kosoff and cut the connection, Brad told him that he wanted to visit the village before the sun went down.

Glancing at his desktop digital clock display, the anthropologist said, "There's less than three hours of daylight left."

"We can make it to the village in fifteen minutes or so in one of the ground cars."

"We?"

"Felicia and me."

Littlejohn asked, "Why the rush?"

"As I said to Professor Kosoff, I don't want them to think I've abandoned them."

Littlejohn fiddled with the implements on his desktop: stylus, notebook, keypad. At last he looked up at Brad and said, "Kosoff won't like it."

Brad responded, "He put *you* in charge of the ground team. You don't have to ask his permission for every move we make."

Littlejohn let out an unhappy sigh. But he agreed, "No, I suppose I don't."

"Great! Thanks!"

Raising a cautionary finger, Littlejohn asked, "You intend to bring your wife with you?"

"I want to show the Gammans that there are more of us, come to help them." Besides, he added silently, I want Felicia to see the village.

The ground car climbed the gently sloping hillside quite easily, its electric motor humming softly. Brad drove it manually, with Felicia sitting beside him.

The car was open, roofless, although an invisible energy screen shielded its occupants from the weather and would enfold them in unyielding protection to keep them safe from injury in the case of a crash. The two rear seats were empty.

As they neared the crest of the ridgeline, Brad said, almost to himself, "Nearly there."

Felicia glanced at him, then returned her gaze forward. Brad stopped the car just below the top of the ridge.

"Let's go the rest of the way on foot," he said to Felicia as he got out of the car. "We can show them the buggy tomorrow."

He came around the car as she got up from her seat and stood beside him. A half-dozen steps and they reached the crest.

"There it is," he said.

In the hollow below them sat the village, just as it had appeared when Brad had first seen it. Buildings arranged in a pair of circles, Gammans coming in from the fields, a few of them leading their six-legged draft animals, a gaggle clustered at the longhouse, as usual.

Almost in a whisper, Felicia said, "It looks . . . peaceful."

Brad nodded, took her hand, and started down the slope.

"They all look alike," Felicia noted. "How can you tell them apart?"

"Their body markings."

"They're all naked?"

Brad nodded. "They don't have any sex. No shame."

"Like Adam and Eve before they ate the forbidden fruit."

"More or less," Brad said.

One of the Gammans shouted, "Look! It's Brrd."

"And someone with him."

Felicia touched the earbud of her communications set, adjusting the volume.

The Gammans stood by the longhouse, staring as Brad and Felicia came down the hillside and approached them.

"I'm going to introduce you as Fil," Brad told her. "That'll be easier for them to pronounce."

She nodded, gazing fascinatedly at the tall, cone-headed aliens.

Brad recognized Mnnx standing at the head of the crowd. And Lnng right beside him.

"Hello," he called. "I'm back."

They were staring at Felicia.

"This is Fil," Brad said as they stopped before the group.

"Fll," said Mnnx. The computer translator repeated the sound.

"Fll is very small," Lnng said undiplomatically.

Brad knew that trying to explain sexual dimorphism would be useless to them. He said, "Not all of my people are as tall as I am."

"Her fur is longer than yours."

Striving to keep a straight face, Brad said, "Yes, that is so."

"Your people have many differences, Brrd," Mnnx said.

"That's true," Brad admitted, realizing that the main difference between one Gamman and another was the pattern of colored splotches on their bodies.

"Can Fll speak?" Lnng asked.

"Yes, I can," said Felicia. "What is your name?"

"Lnng."

"I am Mnnx. I am the village's Rememberer. You are welcome among us, Fll."

"Thank you. I am happy to meet you."

Brad glanced up at the sky. Mithra was almost touching the hilltops. Shadows were stretching across the hollow.

Brad started to say, "We have to return to our own village—"

The Gammans seemed staggered. "You are returning to your home in the sky?"

"No, no," Brad quickly reassured them. "My people are building a village where we can live while we show you how to build a new village for your new Folk."

"And how to live through the winter," Lnng added.

"Yes, that too," said Brad. "We'll return tomorrow, with many more of our people."

"You can stay here, with us, Brrd and Fll," Mnnx offered.

"That's very generous of you," Brad replied, "but it will be better if we return to our own village. We'll be back tomorrow."

"If that is your wish."

The computer's translation could not convey moods or emotional shadings, but Brad thought he detected sorrow in Mnnx's words.

"We'll return tomorrow," he promised.

As Brad and Felicia trudged up the hillside toward their waiting car, she said, "They seem . . . passive."

He nodded. "Right. That's something we'll have to teach them about."

* * *

"Look," said Felicia, as they rode down the hillside to the site of their base camp. "The whole camp is almost finished."

Peering through the deepening shadows of twilight, Brad saw that most of the robots stood lined up to one side of the buildings, inert, their tasks finished. Cars trundled supplies from the shuttlecraft to the buildings. Lights shone through the windows. People moved back and forth; somehow they seemed to Brad to be less purposeful, less intent than the tireless robots.

In the distance a trio of engineers was inspecting the damaged shuttlecraft that Brad had originally flown in on. Two robots stood behind them, unmoving, waiting for orders.

He drove up to the building that housed the camp's offices and saw that Littlejohn was standing in its doorway, waiting for him.

"You're right on time for dinner," Littlejohn called as Brad turned off the buggy's engine. "How did it go?"

Climbing out of the car, Brad reported, "They seemed happy to see us."

"I'll bet they were." Extending his arm toward Felicia, Littlejohn smiled and said, "Let's go to the dining hall and see what kind of dinner the robots have prepared for us."

integration

For three days, Brad introduced the members of the ground team to Mnnx and the Gammans. The aliens seemed to accept the humans without much of a problem, but were startled by the robots.

"Monsters!" said Lnng, the moment he saw a trio of robots marching down the hillside toward the village.

"No," said Brad. "Not monsters. Helpers. Workers. They will help to build the new village."

Lnng stared at the robots. Mnnx came up beside him. "If Brad says they are helpers, then there is nothing to fear," Mnnx said.

Without taking his eyes off the advancing trio of robots, Lnng asked, "Brrd, are they truly helpers?"

"Truly," said Brad. "They will work very hard and help us to build the new village." And Brad remembered that the very word *robot* meant *worker* in some long-forgotten middle European language.

Work on the new village proceeded smoothly enough. Although many of the Gammans obviously felt uneasy about the robots, they soon saw that the machines were doing the work of many men. The new village took form on the far side of the farmland, while most of the Gammans busied themselves plowing new fields and seeding them with food crops.

Felicia worked with the bio team, of course, which

kept her separated from Brad most of each day. They scoured the meadows outside the village's hollow for the remains of the egg-shaped spacecraft that had transported the big cats from planet Beta.

Over dinner, Felicia told Brad, "The eggshell material is decomposing rapidly. We've had to place samples in a vacuum chamber to keep them from disintegrating entirely."

Brad looked up from the soup he was spooning. "Like they're programmed to crumble and fall apart," he mused. "Just like the cats themselves were programmed to die once they've killed off the Gammans."

"The engineers up in the ship are stumped," Felicia said. "They can't find any trace of controls or mechanical devices in the pieces we've recovered."

"Yet those eggs flew from one planet to the other. They were *designed* to make the crossing."

"Designed by whom?" Felicia asked, her face looking troubled. "And why?"

Brad shook his head. "I don't know. I don't know if we'll ever be able to find out."

"It's spooky."

Reaching for his glass of water, Brad agreed, "It's weird. Scary, really."

Late one afternoon, as Brad and Mnnx surveyed the progress on the new village, Brad asked the Gamman, "You said that once there were many villages?"

"Long ago," said Mnnx. "Big villages. Much bigger than ours. Even bigger than ours with the new village added."

"Where were they?"

Mnnx raised an arm and swept the horizon. "Everywhere. The land was filled with them." He hesitated, then added, "But the Sky Masters destroyed them all."

Squinting through the bright sunshine at the ridgeline circling the hollow, Brad pressed, "Do you know where one of these large villages stood? Were any of them near here?"

Mnnx was silent for several heartbeats. Then, "The largest was where two rivers met at a waterfall."

"Really?"

"That is what Drrm told us when he was our Rememberer: two rivers met at a waterfall."

In the single room he shared with his wife, Brad sat at the built-in desk and stared at the 3-D map. The image moved slowly, tracing a river as it weaved through forests and grassland.

"Mnnx said the city was located where two rivers met at a waterfall," he murmured.

Emcee's voice replied, "We're coming to that point."

Sizeable rivers were rare on Gamma, Brad had discovered. The surveillance satellites orbiting the planet had found only a handful.

"There," said Emcee. "There is where the two rivers join."

Pointing, Brad said, "And there's the waterfall! Just below their juncture."

"But no trace of a city," Emcee said.

The area on both sides of the newly joined river was a strip of grassy plain. Farther back from the river's edge a thick forest covered the ground.

"Ground-penetrating radar hasn't detected anything?" Brad asked.

"Nothing," Emcee replied. "And this is the only place on the planet where two rivers join, with a waterfall just after their juncture."

Felicia burst into the room. "We found it! We found the control system for the eggs. It's fantastic!"

Looking up, Brad saw that she was all smiles. Felicia

practically danced across the little room and sat herself on Brad's lap.

"It's incredible!" she said, her voice brimming with excitement. "The whole system is microscopic, built right into the eggshell itself. The entire shell is laced with nanometer-sized control units!"

She kissed Brad soundly, then jumped to her feet again and tugged on his arm. "Come on, the whole bio team is celebrating over in the dining hall."

Brad rose slowly, turned back to the holographic display, and instructed Emcee, "Scan the area again. Highest power with the ground-penetrating radar." With a glance at Felicia's happy face, he added, "I'll be back in a couple of hours, I guess."

Emcee's image took form in the holotank. "Very well." Brad thought of the line from *A Thousand and One Nights*: "Hearkening and obedience."

Even the normally cool Dr. Steiner was beaming happily as she sat at the head of a table filled with nearly a dozen of the people of her biology team. They had pushed two ordinary tables together and were celebrating with fruit juices from the dining hall's galley. Brad thought that perhaps the juice glasses had been reinforced with something stronger, but he quickly realized that the biologists didn't need alcohol; they were high on their discovery.

As he and Felicia pulled up a pair of chairs from one of the unoccupied tables, Brad saw that Professor Kosoff's image filled the dining hall's display screen, hovering above all the others, twice as large as life, smiling benignly through his beard.

"Nanomachines built into the shell of the vehicles," Kosoff was saying. "Incredible."

"But true," said Steiner. Her blond hair, usually tied

into a prim coil, hung loosely past her shoulders. "We only have a fragment of the shell, of course, but it's indisputable: the shell structure is laced with nanometer-sized electronic units."

Beaming like a proud father, Kosoff said, "The engineering staff up here is trying to understand how the system works."

Steiner stiffened slightly. "I doubt that we have a large enough sample to provide enough evidence for that."

Kosoff waved a hand in the air. "You know engineers. They'll chew on what you've provided them like dogs gnawing on a bone."

"Maybe we can find more fragments of the shells," Felicia said, "before they disintegrate entirely."

Kosoff nodded; Steiner looked doubtful.

The celebration lasted through the normal dinner hour and well into the night. Littlejohn and several of the anthropologists joined the festivities, as well as a handful of the planetologists. Brad tried to get into the happy mood of it all, but the fact that Emcee couldn't find any trace of a city kept nagging at him.

It's got to be there, he kept telling himself. If it's not, then everything that Mnnx and his people believe is nothing but a fairy tale.

The rest of the ground crew trickled in and joined the festivities. Laughter and increasingly raucous jokes filled the dining hall. Brad sat through it all, feeling like an outsider, but happy for Felicia. This is her night, he told himself, time and again.

At last the party started to break up, and he and Felicia said good night to Steiner and the others. It was deep night outside; the camp was lit only by low-intensity lamps on the ground outside each building. They could see the stars crowding the black sky above.

"Which one is the Sun?" Felicia asked, her voice suddenly wistful.

Brad shook his head. "Too dim to make out from here."

"It's far away."

"Two hundred and some light-years," said Brad.

"Far away," she repeated.

Unbidden, the lines from an old poem popped into Brad's consciousness. He recited:

Ah love, let us be true
To one another! for the world, which seems
To lie before us like a land of dreams,
So various, so beautiful, so new,
Hath really neither joy, nor love, nor light,
Nor certitude, nor peace, nor help for pain;
And we are here as on a darkling plain
Swept with confused alarms of struggle and flight,
Where ignorant armies clash by night.

Felicia stared at him. "Ignorant armies. That's what we are, aren't we?"

"Our job is to beat back the ignorance," said Brad. "To learn. To understand."

"I suppose so."

"It is," he said with absolute certainty.

But Felicia whispered again, "We're a long way from home, aren't we?"

Brad slid his arms around her. "Wherever you are is home, Fil."

She nestled her head against his shoulder. "That's very sweet of you."

Arms wrapped around each other, they headed for their quarters. Neither of them noticed a meteor streak across the sky and disappear in an eyeblink.

when they entered their room, emcee's image was smiling in the holographic display. somehow the computer's avatar looked pleased.

Brad felt weary, depressed after the high spirits of the bio team's long celebration. "Found anything?" he asked, steeling himself against a negative reply.

Instead, Emcee said, "Not much."

Every nerve in Brad's body quivered like a violin's strings. "Something?"

The 3-D viewer showed a black-and-white radar return. Brad saw the faint outline of a square structure in the middle of the display, a corner jutting out from the edge of the forest.

"At the highest resolving power," Emcee answered, "the ground-penetrating radar obtained this image. It appears to be a structure of some sort, buried under twenty meters of alluvial silt."

Staring at the display, Brad asked, "A structure?"

"Apparently," was Emcee's bland reply.

Felicia came up beside Brad. "The city?"

Trying to rein in his hopes, Brad said, "Maybe. Maybe not. Let's see what Littlejohn thinks."

He put a call through to Littlejohn, but the head of the anthropology team refused to let himself be seen; he replied to Brad's call with audio only.

"It's awfully late," the anthropologist's voice complained.

Trying to keep his enthusiasm under control, Brad said, "I think we might have found the ancient city the Gammans have told me about."

"Can't it wait until tomorrow?"

"But this could prove that the Gammans' story about their past isn't mythology! It's real!"

"That would be fine, Brad." Littlejohn's voice sounded guarded, rather than tired. "Come to my office first thing tomorrow . . . or, rather, at ten hundred hours. It's already past midnight."

"Ten hundred hours," Brad repeated, feeling sour, almost angry.

"Good night," said Littlejohn.

Brad turned to Felicia. "You'd think he'd be more excited. After all—"

Smiling knowingly, Felicia interrupted, "Brad, hasn't it occurred to you that he might not be alone?"

"Littlejohn?"

"He's still celebrating," said Felicia.

"But this is important!" Brad insisted.

With a shake of her head, Felicia said, "If what you've found is a city, it's been waiting there for more than a hundred thousand years. A few more hours won't hurt anything."

"Maybe," Brad agreed. Very reluctantly.

Precisely at ten hundred hours Brad rapped impatiently on Littlejohn's office door. Within half an hour the anthropologist had called in the rest of the anthro team and put through a call to Kosoff.

"It does look artificial," Kosoff's 3-D image admitted cautiously.

"It's buried under twenty meters of silt," said Brad.

"We'll have to build some digging equipment and send it down to you."

"Good."

Littlejohn said, "If it is the remains of a city buried there, it means that the Gammans' story about the Sky Masters isn't entirely mythological."

Nodding soberly, Kosoff said, "One step at a time. First let's see what's under all that mud."

"The old village," Mnnx breathed. Brad thought his tone sounded reverent, even through the computer's translation.

The two of them were standing on the edge of a sizeable pit that had been dug by the excavating machines that stood bulky and idle—for the moment—on the far side of the hole.

In the middle of the man-made crater stood the broken remains of a square stone chimney. At least, Brad thought of it as a chimney, poking straight up into the air about four meters, leading farther underground.

The engineer in charge of the machines came up to Brad. "We can start to dig around the edges of the pit, make it wider, deeper."

"Not yet," Brad replied, pointing toward the chimney. "I want to see where it leads first."

The engineer—square-jawed, grizzled, broad shouldered—looked askance. "You intend to go down inside that shaft?"

Nodding, Brad answered, "At least a little bit."

"I don't think that's wise. The safety people will—"

Brad stopped him with an upraised hand. "I want to see where it leads."

The engineer shrugged. "You're the boss," he muttered. But it was clear he didn't agree.

That's right, Brad thought. I'm the boss.

* * *

With a buckyball cable tied snugly under his shoulders and a high-intensity lamp clamped to his head, Brad sank slowly down the inside of the shaft. He had offered Mnnx the chance to go down with him, but the Gamman had refused, clearly awed and fearful.

Glancing up as he descended, Brad saw the narrow square of sky getting smaller and smaller. The inside of the shaft had been reamed out with a rotating scrubber, the accumulated dried mud sucked up by a vacuum attachment. The walls looked smooth, despite bits of mud still clinging to the adobe-like bricks.

He flashed his lamp downward. His feet dangled in midair. The lamp's glow was swallowed in darkness.

No telling how far down this shaft goes, Brad thought.

Suddenly his communicator erupted with, "Just what do you think you're doing?" Kosoff's voice, angry, imperious.

"Exploring," Brad replied. "Seeing where this shaft leads."

"You get yourself back up to the surface. Right now! The safety people absolutely forbid you or anybody else going down until—"

"Hold it!" Brad yelled.

His descent abruptly stopped. Brad dangled in his makeshift harness.

"Now get yourself up to safety," Kosoff commanded.

But Brad said, "No. Not yet."

"I gave you an order!"

Brad laughed. His lamp was shining on what looked like a doorway cut into the shaft's smooth interior. A dozen meters farther down the excavation stopped, and the shaft was choked with dried mud. But there was an unmistakable doorway just below Brad's dangling feet. And to one side of the shaft were clearly carved symbols.

Writing.

"It's the find of a lifetime," Littlejohn crowed.

The anthropologist was standing at the edge of the growing pit, staring down into the complex of stone building foundations spreading across the floor of the excavation.

Brad and Mnnx stood alongside him as the digging machines toiled away, carefully removing more of the silt that had accumulated over the city during the past thousand centuries. The caterpillar-tracked bulldozers and backhoes worked almost silently, their electrical motors humming quietly. They were remotely directed by a half-dozen engineers huddled at the lip of the growing excavation. Robots and smaller remotely directed machines carefully removed the last layers of dried mud from the structures.

"The biggest discovery in the history of archeology," Littlejohn added, smiling delightedly. "A whole alien city."

Turning to Mnnx, Brad said softly, "Your ancestors built this. You should be very proud."

But Mnnx replied, "The Sky Masters killed my ancestors. They covered the city so that we could not see it. They will be angry with you."

Brad had tried to get the Gammans to come and view the excavation. Most of them had refused, although a few—including Lnng, of course—had come and stared uneasily, fearfully. Brad thought that they were awed by the big digging machines.

Brad tried to reassure Mnnx. "There's nothing to fear. The Sky Masters have gone far from here." If they ever truly existed, he added silently.

"They see us," Mnnx replied stubbornly. "They will punish us."

"So what do we have?" Kosoff asked.

Brad stood at the head of the table, beside the professor. The display screens on the walls of the conference room showed views of the newly excavated city.

After six weeks of careful digging, a good part of the long-buried city had been cleared, and Kosoff had summoned Brad back to the starship for a meeting of the department heads.

"It's a city," Brad said, pointing to an aerial view of the dig. "You can see the foundations of buildings, and the rectilinear outlines of streets."

Olav Pedersen asked, "Have you recovered any artifacts from the city?"

Brad knew the Scandinavian's question was strictly pro forma. He had provided that information in the reports he'd submitted.

"Unfortunately, no. All that exists are the remains of the building's foundations. The buildings themselves were smashed flat."

"By the annual floods from the rivers that deposited all that silt, I should think," said Quentin Abbott.

"No," Brad said. "From the analysis that Emcee's done, it looks as if the buildings were destroyed before the river's flooding started burying them."

"Destroyed by what?"

Brad glanced at Kosoff, who seemed to be holding his breath, waiting for his reply.

"According to the Gammans' history, they were destroyed by the so-called Sky Masters."

"That's poppycock," said Pedersen. "Pure mythology."

"Is it?" Brad challenged. "Their *mythology* showed us where to find the city. And predicted that it would be flattened." Before anyone could respond, he added, "Incidentally, there are some indications that the course of the river was altered, so that its annual flood would inundate the remains of the city."

Elizabeth Chang said mildly, "Extraordinary claims require extraordinary evidence."

Pointing at the displays on the walls, Brad countered, "Isn't that extraordinary enough for you? The city was destroyed, its inhabitants wiped out, and the nearby river diverted to drown the remains."

Kosoff said, "You're asking us to believe the aliens' tale of the Sky Masters?"

"I'm asking you to accept the evidence that we've uncovered. A cataclysm took place here some hundred thousand Earth years ago, maybe a bit more. The entire planetary system was disrupted. A whole civilization on planet Gamma was smashed back to the Stone Age, and beasts from planet Beta were created and given the means to travel to Gamma for the purpose of keeping the Gammans from climbing back to civilization."

Kosoff asked, "And you believe this destruction was caused by some sort of conflict, a war with another alien race? An interstellar war?" The disbelief in his voice was palpable.

Before Brad could reply, Abbott suggested, "The Sky Masters may be an invention of the Gammans, an explanation they created to make sense of their history."

Littlejohn spoke up. "Brad, do you actually believe that this planetary system was almost destroyed in an interstellar war?"

"That's a huge conclusion to swallow," Kosoff said, shaking his head.

With a touch of his thumb on the projector control

unit he held, Brad put up a view of the nanodevices built into the eggshell spacecraft from Beta. "Somebody built those craft. Somebody created those nano-machine controls. Somebody created those six-legged cats and set them on the Gammans every time the two planets approached each other. Somebody with a technology significantly beyond our own."

Silence along the length of the conference table. Not even Kosoff had anything to say.

"All the available facts point to that conclusion," Brad insisted. "We're not dealing with mythology here."

bOOk FiVE

A man said to the universe:
"sir, I exist!"
"However," replied the universe,
"The fact has not created in me
A sense of obligation."

—stephen crane

Brad walked through the new village, empty buildings waiting for the birth of the new generation of Gammans growing beneath the ground in the farm fields.

Mnnx walked beside him, looking slightly ludicrous in one of the stiff cloth coveralls that the Gammans were weaving for themselves. It hung past his knees, and Mnnx also wore a Gamman version of a ski mask, with his two bulbous eyes bulging out on either side of his head. His hooflike feet were still bare, although 3-D printers aboard the starship were already turning out boots for the Gammans.

The sky above was gray, leaden. A light snow was drifting down from the clouds.

"Winter is coming," said Mnnx unnecessarily.

Brad nodded. He wore a light parka, no hat.

"Yes," he agreed. "But you'll be ready for it. You'll live through the winter and welcome the new Folk when they rise from the ground."

"If the Sky Masters permit us."

Brad turned and started back toward the original village. Mnnx kept pace beside him.

"Are the Sky Masters real?" Brad asked.

"You saw the city," Mnnx replied. "You saw how it was destroyed."

"Yes, I know, but if they wanted to wipe you out, why

didn't they destroy your village too, and the other villages? Why did they let you live?"

"They send the monsters from Beta to kill us."

"But not the new generation growing in the ground. Not the Rememberers in each village. Why let them live?"

"No one knows. Perhaps they will return one day and reveal their purposes to us."

"Perhaps not."

Mnnx fell silent as they walked along the empty street. At last he said, "Brrd, I think that perhaps you have been sent to save us from the Sky Masters."

"I want you to live," Brad said. "I want you to get through the winter and begin to build new lives for yourselves."

Casting an uneasy eye at the gray sky above them, Mnnx said, "That will surely bring the Sky Masters to punish us for disobeying their wishes."

"No," Brad contradicted. "You will live, and grow, and prosper. And we will help you. My people are producing food for you so you can live through the winter, and—"

"But one day you will leave us."

Reluctantly, Brad admitted, "Yes."

"Before the winter fully sets in."

"Yes."

"After you go, the Sky Masters will return and kill us all. They will leave none of us alive, because we disobeyed them."

Brad stared at this alien creature whom he had come to regard as his friend. He's terrified, Brad thought. He does what we tell him to, but he's terrified that once we leave they'll all be killed by the so-called Sky Masters.

"More of my kind will arrive here after we have gone," Brad said. Then he stretched the truth by adding, "They will protect you against the Sky Masters."

Mnnx said nothing.

* * *

Lnng obviously wasn't as frightened as Mnnx. "I believe Brrd," he said that evening as the Gammans gathered inside their homes for their evening meal.

Brad sat among a half-dozen of the aliens, between Mnnx and Lnng, staring into the warming blaze in the fireplace that the humans had shown the Gammans how to build. The flickering flames were hypnotic, Brad felt. There's an ancient bond, he thought, between humans and their fires. A link that allowed us to survive the Ice Age, back on Earth. It's bred into our genes: fire, the energy source that ensured our survival in the time of cold. The energy source that started our climb to the stars.

Lnng's thoughts were much more practical. Pointing at the fireplace, he said, "The food you have given us will allow us to live through the winter. We can welcome the new Folk when they rise from the ground, teach them, help them to become like us."

Mnnx's head drooped despondently. "If the Sky Masters allow it."

"The Sky Masters have gone away," Lnng said. "Why should they return here?"

"To punish us."

"No," said Lnng. "I think they have sent Brrd and his friends to help us. I think the Sky Masters want us to live, not die."

Brad marveled at his optimism. Where Mnnx sees death, Lnng sees life, he thought.

"Tell us the truth, Brrd," Lnng urged. "The Sky Masters have sent you, haven't they?"

With a shake of his head, Brad replied, "No, we came here to help you. We knew nothing of the Sky Masters until you told us of them."

Lnng stared at Brad for a silent moment, then jumped to his feet and shouted, "Sky Masters! Wherever you are!

We live and we will keep on living, thanks to Brrd and his people's help. If you have sent them, thanks be to you. If you have not, then we can live without you."

Mnnx and the other Gammans sat in stunned silence. Even Brad was taken aback by Lnng's declaration. He's committing blasphemy, Brad thought. Then he realized that blasphemy is often the first step up from ignorance.

Instead of outrage, Mnnx merely said, "Sit down, Lnng, and eat your dinner. The Sky Masters will answer you in their own time."

Brad let out a breath. A very gentle response to blasphemy, he told himself. But then, the Gammans are a very gentle people.

He sat in silence and tried not to show the shiver of revulsion he felt as the Gammans shoveled their food into the mouths in their abdomens. At last he slowly climbed to his feet, surprised that he really didn't want to go.

I think of them as my friends, he realized. Despite our differences, I really care about them.

"I must return to my own village now," he said to Mnnx.

The Gamman got up beside him. "You will come back tomorrow?"

"Yes, of course."

Brad got as far as the door before Lnng called, "If you meet any Sky Masters out in the night, tell them we would like to see them."

Gamman faces are not built to express emotions, but Brad thought he *felt* resentment and something close to anger radiating from Mnnx.

Brad and Felicia returned to the starship in orbit around Gamma at Kosoff's insistence.

"Another damned meeting," Brad grumbled as they stepped through the shuttle's air lock hatch and into the starship's receiving bay.

Compared to their quarters down on the planet, even *Odysseus*'s receiving bay was posh. Carpeted floor, floor-to-ceiling display screens, automated sensor arches that swiftly checked their physical conditions as they passed through them. Quiet luxury, Brad thought, every step of the way.

"You are cleared for entry," said Emcee's warm voice, emanating from the speaker grille built into the sensor arch. "Welcome back."

Brad thought this trip to the starship was going to be pretty much a waste of time, but he answered with, "It's good to be back, Emcee."

Felicia did the same.

"The reason for this meeting," Kosoff said, "is to make a final decision about the octopods of planet Alpha."

Brad, Felicia, Olav Pedersen, and Ursula Steiner sat in Kosoff's office, in the comfortable faux leather chairs arranged before his desk. Emcee's seated image filled the holographic display on the office's side wall.

Pedersen said, "It's quite clear: Alpha is orbiting so

close to Mithra that its ocean will boil away eventually—unless we provide some protection for the planet."

"And how long is eventually?" Kosoff asked.

Brad knew the professor's question was strictly for the recording being made of the meeting.

As expected, Pedersen answered, "On the order of a million years, perhaps a bit less." With a slight shake of his head he added, "A long time by human standards, of course, but an eyeblink in the course of a planet's lifetime."

Kosoff nodded. "The energy screen generators that will shield the planet from the death wave can also protect it from Mithra's heat."

Emcee nodded in acknowledgment. "The energy screen can be tuned to absorb some of the star's incoming radiation."

"Like a sun shield," Kosoff said.

Emcee replied, "A partial sun shield."

Kosoff turned to Felicia. "I was a bit surprised to find that you are the leading expert on the octopods, Dr. Portman."

With a self-effacing dip of her chin, Felicia replied, "That's because all the other biologists have been busy working on the Gammans and their planetary biosphere."

Brad noticed that Pedersen looked uncomfortable with the idea that Felicia was almost on an equal rank with himself. Steiner, cool as usual, said nothing. But her knowing little smile told Brad that she found the situation amusing.

Kosoff asked Felicia, "So how would the octopods react to our sinking a half-dozen generators into their ocean?"

With a tiny shrug, she replied, "They probably wouldn't react at all. The problem with the octopods is that they are intelligent enough to realize that their habitat is shrinking—their ocean is warming noticeably—but they have no way of changing things. They are accepting their fate because they can't do anything to change it."

"They have no technology."

"None."

Steiner spoke up. "They seemed quite curious about the sensor pods when we first put them into the sea to study them. But when the pods didn't react to their questions, or even to their touching them with their tentacles, they just ignored the pods and went about their business as if they weren't there."

Unconsciously stroking his beard, Kosoff said, "They decided that the pods were neither food nor danger, so they could be safely ignored."

"That's about the size of it," Steiner replied.

Straightening up in his chair, Kosoff said in a louder, firmer voice, "So we can drop the generators into their ocean without harming them."

"I believe so," said Steiner.

Focusing on Felicia, Kosoff asked, "Do you agree?"

She hesitated a heartbeat, then answered, "The only question in my mind is whether the energy that the generators emit might harm them in any way."

"Impossible," Kosoff said flatly. "The generators have been thoroughly tested on Earth. They produce no harmful biological effects."

"On human cells," Felicia pointed out. "We don't really know that much about the octopods' biology."

"I wanted to obtain a few specimens for study," Steiner pointed out. "For dissection and thorough examination."

"And we decided against it," said Kosoff. "Maybe we should review that decision."

"Wait," Brad objected. "Why do we have to sink the generators into Alpha's ocean? Why not put them in orbit around the planet? Then there's no question of biological interactions."

Kosoff's brows knit, but he said, "I suppose that's a possibility."

"It would be safer," Felicia said.

"And there'd be no question of the ocean absorbing some of the generators' energy output," Brad pointed out.

Steiner protested, "But we would miss the chance to study how the energy generators affect the alien biology."

Pedersen started to speak, thought better of it, and clamped his lips shut.

"I agree with you, Ursula," said Kosoff. "It seems a shame to waste such an opportunity."

Brad disagreed. "Look. Are we here to do some esoteric biology experiments or to save an alien species from extinction?"

"If you put it that way . . . "

"That's the way it is," Brad insisted. "We're dealing with a life-or-death situation for those octopods. They may not have the means to save themselves from extinction but we do! We have a responsibility to protect them as well as we can."

"Shall we vote on it?" Kosoff asked.

"No," said Brad. "Let's review the mission protocols first."

Kosoff gaped at him. "The mission protocols? *You* want to refer to the mission protocols?"

With a tight grin, Brad said, "Yes."

Kosoff let out a theatrical sigh. "All right. Emcee, what do the protocols have to say about this?"

Without a nanosecond's hesitation, the master computer's avatar replied, "Species survival is this mission's number-one priority. All other goals are secondary, including scientific investigations of alien biology." Its image looking very humanly apologetic, Emcee added, "Sorry, Dr. Steiner."

Steiner's brows knit, but she said with something approaching good grace, "We must follow the protocols, of course."

Kosoff glared across his desk at Brad. "The devil can quote scripture when it suits his purpose."

Very seriously, Brad replied, "When it suits the mission protocols."

thinking the meeting was over, Brad started to get up from his chair.

"Wait," said Kosoff, motioning for Brad to sit down again. "There's something else I want to discuss."

Brad dropped back into the chair, thinking, More talk. More time wasted.

"What is it?" Pedersen asked.

"Those cats on Beta. How can we prevent them from attacking the Gammans the next time the two planets approach each other?"

Brad immediately replied, "We send a team to Beta and wipe out the monsters, once and for all."

"You can't do that!" Steiner objected. "They're an alien life form, just as much as the octopods and the Gammans. We can't destroy them."

"Why not?" Brad demanded. "The only reason they exist is to kill the Gammans. Get rid of them. Now, while they're hibernating."

"They are not hibernating," Steiner said. "From what the surveillance satellites report, the few cats still alive on Beta are breeding, laying their eggs."

"So that they can kill the Gammans when the two planets come close again."

A little less certainly, Steiner replied, "Yes, I suppose so."

Felicia said, "We really don't know much about their life cycle."

"We should study them more closely," said Steiner.

Kosoff nodded agreement. "We have two years remaining before we have to return to Earth. How much can we learn in that time?"

"More than we know now," Felicia said.

"If we could get a couple of specimens to dissect," Steiner mused, "we could learn a lot about their biology."

"You're missing the point," said Brad. "Those monsters were created to kill the Gammans, to keep the Gammans in their Stone Age stage of development, to prevent them from advancing back to their former level of civilization."

Kosoff waved a dismissive hand. "That's the Gammans' mythology. There's no evidence that it's based on fact."

"No evidence?" Brad snapped. "What about those spacecraft the cats use to travel from Beta to Gamma? Completely automated, nanotechnology that we haven't achieved yet. The cats didn't create those devices, someone else did."

"The so-called Sky Masters," Pedersen said, almost sneering.

"Mythology," said Kosoff. "Figments of the Gammans' imagination."

Felicia added, "The cats seem to be programmed to die after a few days on Gamma."

"After they've finished killing the Gammans," said Brad. "There's a *purpose* to their existence. If we want the Gammans to survive, we've got to put an end to those beasts."

Pedersen suggested, "Perhaps we can find a way to prevent them from traveling from Beta to Gamma."

"How?" Brad demanded.

The planetologist shrugged. "I'm not an engineer . . . "

Kosoff turned to the holotank. "Emcee, is there a way to prevent the cats from getting to Gamma?"

The master computer's avatar sat there smiling amiably

for several heartbeats—an eternity for the femtosecond reactions of the computer. At last Emcee said, "That is a question that should be forwarded to the World Council, on Earth."

"Kill them all," Brad insisted. "Now, while we have the chance. They only exist to kill the Gammans. They're instruments of genocide."

Kosoff rumbled, "An eye for an eye, is that what you want?"

Steiner almost smiled. "Who's quoting scripture now?"

Felicia corrected, "That's not from scripture. It's from Hammurabi's code of laws for the Babylonians."

"I don't care if it's from the Magna Carta," Kosoff snapped. "We are *not* here to destroy alien species."

Brad asked, "So what do we do about the cats?"

Kosoff stroked his beard once, twice. Then, "Let me talk to the World Council about this."

Brad thought, A bureaucrat's reaction. When in doubt, buck the question upstairs.

Kosoff focused his piercing blue eyes on Brad. "I have another quotation for you, MacDaniels. When you fight monsters, be careful that you don't become a monster yourself."

"Friedrich Nietzsche," Felicia said.

Brad said nothing. He merely smiled tightly at Kosoff. But he was thinking, How can we protect the Gammans from the monsters?

As they headed back to Gamma, sitting side by side in the shuttle's cramped seats, Brad grumbled, "That was a waste of time."

Felicia countered, "Not really. We decided to put the generators in orbit around Alpha. We've saved the octopods."

He made a reluctant grin. "Steiner isn't happy about it. She wants to experiment on the creatures."

"She's a biologist, Brad. She's got all sorts of new and different species all around her, and she hasn't been allowed to study them."

"You mean she hasn't been allowed to chop them up and poke around their innards."

"Don't be cruel," Felicia said. "How would you like it if you weren't allowed to talk with your Gammans?"

Leaning closer to her, Brad asked, "Fil, how can we save the Gammans from those damned cats? They'll be slaughtered all over again the next time the two planets approach each other."

"The first thing to do," she replied, "is to learn all we can about the cats. Their biology, their life spans, how they breed—"

"Maybe we should arm the Gammans," Brad muttered.

"Arm them?"

"Give them lasers so they can protect themselves."

"Kosoff would never agree to that."

"Maybe I should shoot him first."

"Be serious, Brad!"

He shook his head wearily. "Anyway, the Gammans are too passive. They'd probably hold the lasers in their hands while the cats chewed on them."

Emcee's emotionless voice emanated from the overhead speakers, "Landing in two minutes."

Brad looked out the oval window and saw the base camp flash past. It was growing: more buildings, more vehicles. In two years their encampment had turned into a miniature city.

A city that the Gammans avoid as if it were haunted, he told himself. Even Lnng is nervous, edgy when I bring him out to see what we're doing.

Glancing at Felicia to make sure her shoulder harness was secure, he tightened his own straps and leaned his head against the chair's back.

"I guess you're right," he said. "The first thing we have to do is learn all we can about the cats. And their spacecraft."

The villagers had grown accustomed to having humans among them. Brad tried to keep the contacts to a minimum; all visits to the village were for necessary reasons, no idle sightseeing. Still, men and women from Earth had quickly become commonplace among the Gammans.

It helped, Brad thought, that the aliens were so passive. Even Lnng accepted the presence of humans in the village with little more than an acquiescent shrug of his shoulders.

Very different from how we would react if a crowd of aliens suddenly descended on Earth. Then he realized, Here on Gamma, we're the aliens.

Felicia spent most of her time in the encampment's spare, utilitarian biology lab, analyzing the imagery coming in from the satellites orbiting Beta.

Brad went into the village every day, trying to find some way of getting the Gammans to protect themselves.

He was standing in the village's central square. Funny, he thought, even though this open space is circular I still think of it as a square. The afternoon was warm and sunny, although Brad could see that the distant mountaintops were dusted with snow. Don't let this lovely afternoon fool you, he told himself. Winter is on its way.

As usual, he had driven one of the camp's buggies into the village and parked it in front of the longhouse. Beats walking back and forth, Brad told himself. The Gammans had been curious about the vehicle the first time they saw it. Brad had done his best to explain the "horseless carriage" to them; he had even lifted up its hood to reveal the tiny nuclear-powered electric motor.

Lnng had asked if he could drive the buggy and Brad had allowed him to tool it around the village's central square—slowly. Sitting beside the Gamman, Brad had kept the buggy's remote controller in his lap, ready to take over the controls if he had to.

Once the drive was finished, Lnng stepped out of the buggy with obvious reluctance. "I could travel a long way in this," he said. "All the way to the mountains, I think."

"And farther," said Brad, making a mental note to leave a couple of the buggies in the village when he departed for Earth.

That evening, as the setting Mithra cast purple shadows across the hollow, Brad joined Mnnx, Lnng, and a half-dozen other Gammans as they went into the home they shared for their evening meal. A sharp wind was whistling down from the snowcapped mountains; the weather was turning cold, raw.

But inside the house, the fireplace glowed warm and cheerfully. The Gammans sat in a semicircle on the dirt floor as their stew pot bubbled. Brad thought the stew smelled harsh, unappetizing, but the Gammans seemed delighted with the aroma.

Sitting between Mnnx and Lnng, as usual, Brad saw through the house's only window that it was fully night outside, dark and cold.

"I'll have to leave you soon," he said.

"Leave?" Mnnx echoed.

"I'll come back tomorrow."

"Oh." With obvious relief.

Lnng said, "But one day you will leave for good and return to your own village in the sky."

"Yes, that is true," said Brad.

Lnng clutched Brad's knee with one of his ropy hands, making Brad twitch with alarm. The Gamman asked, "Brrd, why can't you stay here, with us? When the monsters come again you could protect us."

Brad shook his head. "I wish I could."

Mnnx said, "Brrd must return to his own village, far away in the sky."

"But why?" Lnng asked, almost pleading.

Mnnx answered, "It is the wish of the Sky Masters."

"No," said Brad. "The Sky Masters do not control me or my people."

"You think not," argued Mnnx, "but the Sky Masters are very powerful, very wise. They are controlling you even though you do not know it."

"Can that really be true?" one of the other Gammans asked.

"It is true," Mnnx said. "The Sky Masters are all-powerful. They are watching us now."

"No," said Brad. "They have gone far away."

"Even from far away they can see us."

Lnng challenged, "Then why did they let Brrd protect us from the monsters?"

"To test us," Mnnx replied without a moment's hesitation. "To see if we would accept their judgment over us, or give in to the temptation to live, even though that is against their command to us."

Brad asked, "The Sky Masters want you to die?"

"Yes. So that there will be room for the new Folk when they rise from the ground."

"But we've built a new village for them," Brad said.

Lnng added, "We can build many new villages, all across the land."

"And the Sky Masters will return and smash all the villages to dust. They will kill us all for disobeying their commands."

Lnng leaned forward as he sat and reached across Brad to tap Mnnx on the chest. "So the punishment for not allowing the monsters to kill us is for the Sky Masters to kill us."

"Yes."

"Then what difference does it make?" Lnng shouted. "We die either way."

Mnnx was silent for several heartbeats. At last he replied, "We have disobeyed the Sky Masters. They will return and punish us."

"But until they do," said Lnng, "let us live and enjoy living. Let us live today and not worry about tomorrow."

"No," said Brad. "Let us live today and prepare for tomorrow."

All through the drive back to the encampment Brad thought about what he had to do. If there's no way to prevent the cats from crossing to Gamma the next time the two planets come close, then I'm going to have to give the Gammans weapons to defend themselves.

Mnnx is a fatalist, but Lnng wants to live. He's the one who should be leader in the village. He's the one who'll fight.

But how many others will follow his lead? Brad

wondered. How many of them will stand there like dumb animals and allow the cats to tear them apart, the way Drrm did?

Once he got to his quarters, Brad began to tell Felicia what he was planning.

"Give them weapons?" She looked shocked. "Brad, you can't do that. You don't know where it might lead."

"It will lead to their survival," he said flatly.

"It could wreck their culture," she replied, almost pleadingly. "It could destroy them more completely than the cats from Beta."

Brad started to shake his head, but Felicia insisted, "Surely as an anthropologist you can see that, can't you? It would be like giving guns to children."

"Children who are in the grip of an ancient mythology, of superstition and ignorance."

"But you can't force them to change."

"Can't I?"

Almost desperately, Felicia said, "Kosoff won't allow it."

Brad knew she was right. But he said tightly, "We'll see."

"It's fascinating," said Felicia as she stared at the holographic image of planet Beta's bleak landscape.

Felicia and Ursula Steiner were sitting side by side on a pair of the cramped laboratory's padded stools as they intently watched the 3-D imagery of one of the cats limping across the bare, stony ground.

"It looks emaciated," Steiner said.

"It's dying," said Felicia.

"Starving," Steiner murmured.

"They're all dying," said Felicia. "All across the planet."

"It *is* fascinating," said Steiner, staring at the dying cat limping across the barren landscape. "The cats that went to Gamma all died within a few days of landing there, while the few who remained on Beta have survived all this time."

"But now they're dying," Felicia pointed out.

Steiner called, "Emcee, how many of the cats are still active?"

"Sixteen," replied the master computer's voice.

"Across the entire planet?"

Emcee answered flatly, "The satellite sensors have detected sixteen of the animals still active. They all appear to be dying."

"Starving to death," said Felicia.

Clenching her fists, Steiner insisted, "We must acquire

a few of those carcasses for examination, before they completely decompose."

"Will Professor Kosoff allow a flight to Beta?" Felicia asked.

"He must! He's got to!"

Kosoff wasn't surprised by Steiner's request.

"Pick up a few of the dead cats?" he asked as he sat behind his desk.

Steiner and Felicia were still in the bio lab on Gamma's surface.

"Yes!" Steiner replied eagerly. "We've got to examine them before they completely decompose."

Drumming his fingers on his desktop, Kosoff said, "Ursula, a mission to Beta won't be as easy as hopping down from orbit up here to Gamma. Beta's receding from our location, moving away farther each day."

Felicia asked, "But it's still within reach of a shuttle-craft, isn't it?"

Kosoff asked, "Emcee, can one of our shuttles reach Beta?"

"Yes," replied the computer's voice, "although it will only be able to carry a fraction of its usual payload of cargo."

"All we need is two or three of the dead cats," Steiner urged.

Kosoff nodded. "Let me get approval from Earth."

"We mustn't lose any time!" Steiner pleaded. "Their dead bodies are decomposing rapidly!"

"I'll order a shuttle outfitted for the mission. My call to Earth will be strictly pro forma."

"But what if they say no?"

"They won't. Trust me."

* * *

Three weeks later, Brad returned from the Gammans' village to find that Felicia was not at their quarters. Again. It was late, fully night, and he had been looking forward to a quiet supper with his wife.

She's spending more time in her lab with Steiner than she is with me, he thought sourly. Then he immediately felt guilty. She's busy examining the cats that have been brought back from Beta. She's excited about her work. I guess I would be, too, if I were a biologist.

Still, he didn't know if he should break out a prepackaged dinner and eat alone or wait for Felicia to return from her lab.

Neither, he decided. He left their quarters and walked through the darkness to the biology lab.

No one was in the lab. The main room was brightly lit, workbenches and equipment lining the floor. But Felicia wasn't anywhere in sight. Then Brad saw there was a door on the far side of the room. She must be in there, he reasoned as he crossed the room.

A handwritten sign stuck to the door read, NO ADMITTANCE. DISSECTION IN PROGRESS.

That can't mean me, Brad told himself as he opened the door.

The stench made his knees buckle. The reek of rotting flesh. Trying to keep from gagging, Brad saw that Felicia and Steiner were bent over the body of one of the cats, stretched out on the dissection table. Both women were in protective bio suits, wearing breathing masks and goggles.

Felicia looked up as Brad staggered into the lab, holding a hand over his face.

"Can't you read?" Steiner snarled, without turning to see who had entered the room.

Felicia pointed to the closet on the far wall and said, "Get into a breathing mask and bio suit if you intend to remain in here!"

Steiner glanced over her shoulder at him, clearly annoyed.

Brad crossed the laboratory and pulled on a breathing mask. The oxygen felt cold and good. Then he struggled into one of the protective suits hanging in the closet. It was a bit small for him, sleeves and leggings ending several centimeters short. It felt snug as Brad slapped its fasteners over his chest.

"Goggles too," Felicia called, still standing at the dissection table.

"And sterile gloves," Steiner added.

At last Brad was adequately protected, although he knew that any alien pathogens would hardly attack human tissue. But rules are rules, he said to himself as he walked to the table where the two women were bent over their grisly work.

"Making progress?" he asked.

"Yes," Steiner replied tersely.

Felicia looked up at him. "You're right, Brad. These animals are nothing more than killing machines. They're designed to breed, to attack the Gammans, and then to die."

"After they produce a new generation," Steiner added.

"And all aimed at killing the Gammans," said Brad.

Steiner nodded. "It appears that way."

For once, Brad didn't mind attending one of Kosoff's meetings.

The starship's main auditorium was packed for Steiner's presentation. The entire biology staff was there, of course, together with all the department heads and much of each of the other departments' staffs. Captain Desai and a handful of the ship's officers were there as well, sitting with Kosoff in the front row.

Brad sat alongside Felicia, in the midst of the biology team. Littlejohn and the other anthropologists were in the row behind them.

The buzz of anticipatory conversations stopped as Steiner climbed the three steps to the stage. Behind her, the wall-to-wall 3-D display showed a still image of one of the six-legged cats from Beta; huge, powerful, snarling.

Steiner wore a severe white pants suit, with jewelry sparkling at her throat, wrists, and earlobes. Her golden hair was pinned up atop her head, making her look even taller than usual, more regal.

"I am here," she began, "to report on our examination of the catlike creatures from planet Beta."

The audience sat stock-still, taut, expectant.

"What we have found is truly extraordinary," Steiner went on. "I haven't seen anything like this in all my days as a biologist.

"These cats are nothing less than killing machines.

They are built to kill; evolved—or perhaps deliberately *designed*—to slaughter the intelligent bipeds of planet Gamma, and then themselves to die off."

The holographic image behind her changed to show a detailed image of one of the cats' innards. "This was one of the cats that we found on Gamma."

Turning slightly to aim a laser pointer at the imagery, Steiner said, "As you can see, the creature has only a rudimentary digestive system. It can drink water and ingest little else. Its active life span is measured in days. It emerges from its egg, after flying from Beta to Gamma, hunts down all the Gammans it can find, and then dies."

She hesitated a moment, then went on, "It is noteworthy to realize that its digestive system cannot handle anything we would think of as food: meat or vegetables. It kills its prey but does not eat it. It dies of starvation."

From the front row, Kosoff asked, "How could such an animal evolve? How does it procreate itself?"

Looking almost distressed, Steiner replied, "There appear to be three separate types of animal: the males—which are breeders; the females—which lay the eggs for the next generation. They both live for several Earth years before their digestive systems shut down, which kills them. They produce the next generation of beasts sexually, then die off."

"You said there were three types?"

Nodding tightly, Steiner replied, "The steriles, which seem to be little more than killing machines. They are incubated in the eggs that fly to Gamma, hatch from those eggs, and hunt down the Gammans. Within a few days they die—of starvation."

A woman's voice from the audience asked again, "How could such creatures evolve?"

"Frankly," Steiner replied, "I am at a loss to understand how such a creature could evolve naturally. As I said a few moments ago, it looks to me as if they were designed, purposely, by some other species. It is a biological analog to the robots that we design and use."

That caused a stir among the audience.

"Designed? By whom?" someone from a back row shouted.

"We don't know," said Steiner.

"Designed for what purpose?" asked another.

"To slaughter the Gammans. That's the only discernible reason for their existence."

The questions came faster then, and some members of the audience began arguing with others.

Typical, thought Brad. Each scientist wants to solve the riddle with his or her own brilliant ideas.

Steiner went through the cats' life cycle. "They reproduce sexually. The males and females produce the eggs that reproduce themselves, and also the eggs that bear the steriles—which fly to Gamma when the two planets are nearest to one another. Once on Gamma they hatch and slaughter the Gammans, then die within a few days."

"What kills them?"

"Starvation. As I showed you, their digestive systems shut down."

"The females lay their eggs, and then what?"

"Ah yes, those eggs," Steiner said. "They sit on the ground, drawing nourishment from sunlight and elements in the air and soil."

"Like photosynthesis!"

"Very much like photosynthesis. The eggs grow and reach maturity at the time when Beta comes to its closest approach to Gamma."

Steiner pointed to Pedersen, sitting three rows back in the auditorium. "Dr. Pedersen, you understand the mechanics of those eggs better than I. Perhaps you could explain?"

Pedersen rose to his feet. "I wish I could explain. The eggs are laced with nano-sized control systems that we have not yet been able to fully understand. The eggs themselves are a rudimentary sort of spacecraft, it seems."

Kosoff turned in his seat. "They are actively guided to Gamma?"

Shaking his head, the planetologist answered, "Apparently not. The tremendous atmospheric disturbances caused by the two planets' near collision cause cyclonic winds that lift the eggs off the ground on Beta and hurl them across the gap to land on Gamma."

"They land without breaking?"

"Most of them do. Even those that do break hatch out full-grown cats."

Steiner resumed her narrative. "Once the eggs arrive on Gamma, the sterile cats break out of them, fully adult, and begin to track down and kill the Gammans."

The 3-D image behind her showed footage of the mangled bodies of Gammans sprawled on the ground in their own blood.

"Incredible!"

"But true," said Steiner.

"Wait a moment," said Quentin Abbott. Rising to his feet, the astronomer confessed, "I'm a bit confused here. You say the beasts mate and lay eggs. I presume that happens before the conjunction of the two planets."

"Yes. Only a relative few of the animals break out of their eggs before the planets' closest approach. They do the mating and lay the eggs that eventually become the next generation."

"Lucky critters," someone said, in a stage whisper.

"The early bird gets the worm."

"So to speak."

Chuckles and outright laughter swept through the audience. Breaking the tension, thought Brad.

Still on his feet, Abbott said, "So that means the eggs for the next generation of beasts have already been laid."

"Yes," said Steiner. "Our observation satellites have

spotted nearly a hundred caches of eggs on the ground. They will apparently stay there, growing and maturing, until the planet nears Gamma once again."

"They survive their winter, then," said one of the planetologists.

"Evidently so."

"And hatch after they fly off Beta and land on Gamma," Abbott said.

Nodding, Steiner confirmed, "That is our conclusion, yes."

The auditorium hummed with voices. Steiner broke through the chatter with, "Now I'd like to ask Dr. Mac-Daniels to tell you about the Gammans' response to the invasion and slaughter."

Surprised, Brad got to his feet.

"Up here, Dr. MacDaniels," Steiner urged, motioning for Brad to join her on the stage. "Here, where everyone can see you."

Trying to put his thoughts in order, Brad slid past Felicia and the others sitting in the row, then climbed the steps to the stage.

Littlejohn was watching him like a proud father; Kosoff looked warier.

"Thank you, Dr. Steiner," Brad began. "The Gammans have a mythology—or maybe it's more of a philosophy—of passivity and acceptance. They believe that in the distant past their ancestors built cities and created a civilization that spanned the whole planet. Based on their history or mythology or whatever you want to call it, we have found the remains of a city and are excavating it."

Littlejohn called out, "The city was destroyed, wasn't it?"

"Smashed flat," Brad acknowledged. "Nothing left but the foundations of the original buildings."

Kosoff said, "And they believe it was deliberately destroyed."

Nodding, Brad replied, "Destroyed by some force which they call the Sky Masters. The Gammans believe the Sky Masters—whatever they are—crushed their ancient civilization and send those cats from Beta to kill them every time the two planets approach each other."

"You mean there was a war?" an incredulous voice from the audience asked. "An interstellar war?"

"That's one possible explanation," Brad answered. "Whatever the Sky Masters are, or were, they apparently are intent on preventing the Gammans from rebuilding their civilization."

Steiner added, "The biology of the cats from Beta fits in with that interpretation."

Pedersen said, "This must have happened on the order of a hundred thousand years ago—when this planetary system was disrupted."

Dead silence fell over the auditorium. Brad understood what they were all thinking: A war, interstellar invaders destroyed the Gammans' civilization, using technology far in advance of our own.

"It's a fantastic story," said Pedersen. "But it just might be true."

"If it is," Kosoff said, his voice heavy with apprehension, "by helping the Gammans we've made ourselves enemies of the Sky Masters—whoever or whatever they may be."

OCCAM'S RAZOR

Adrian Kosoff stood on the cracked stone floor of the ancient building's foundation, with Brad and Littlejohn on either side of him. Off in the distance the remotely controlled digging machines were patiently enlarging the excavation, uncovering more and more of the remains of the city.

Kosoff had picked a frosty day for his first visit to Gamma. He had decided to come down and see the evidence of the ancient cataclysm for himself. He wore a fur-trimmed arctic jacket and a fur hat jammed down over his ears. Its brim nearly covered the professor's bushy eyebrows.

He was peering at the inscription chiseled neatly into the remains of the stone wall.

"It must be writing of some sort," he said, more to himself than the others. "Has to be."

Bundled into a thick windbreaker, Brad said, "None of the Gammans understand it. They have no writing of their own."

Only a handful of the Gammans had worked up the courage to come and look at the city. Even Lnng had shuffled his feet nervously on the few occasions when he'd visited. Superstitious dread was the villagers' common reaction, together with awe and outright fear of the heavy earth-moving equipment that was methodically uncovering the ancient city.

It didn't help, Brad thought, that Mnnx dolefully

repeated to them every evening that he expected the Sky Masters to reappear and punish them all for surviving the attack of the monsters from Beta.

Raising his voice over the clatter of the digging machines and the keening wind, Brad said, "They smashed this city and everything in it, then diverted the river to bury the remains in silt."

"They?" Kosoff asked. "You mean these so-called Sky Masters?"

Littlejohn, also swaddled in winter gear, said, "Mythology isn't merely stories made up out of whole cloth, you know. Most myths are based on a kernel of truth."

Kosoff nodded curtly. His gaze sweeping the crumbling stones, he muttered, "Pretty big kernel here."

"So what will your report back to Earth say?" Brad asked.

Putting out a hand to touch the stub of stone standing erect before him, Kosoff said slowly, "Abbott's astronomers have searched with their best telescopes for a star that might have disrupted this planetary system. There's nothing in the area that might fit the bill."

"Then whatever perturbed the orbits of the planets here was not a passing star," said Littlejohn.

"Whatever smashed this city flat and then buried it was not a natural cataclysm," Brad added.

Kosoff glowered at them. "There must be a natural explanation for this. There's got to be! You can't believe that some interstellar war took place here a hundred thousand years ago. It's too fantastic."

"Is it?" Littlejohn asked mildly.

"Perhaps a passing mini black hole disrupted this planetary system," Kosoff mused.

"And created the cats on Beta?" Brad challenged.

Kosoff had no answer.

"Occam's Razor, Professor," said Brad. "Fantastic as

it may seem, an interstellar invader fits all the observed facts, including the biology of the cats from Beta." Before Kosoff could reply, Brad went on, "And it fits the Gammans' mythology."

With a single brisk nod, Littlejohn agreed, "Perhaps it isn't mythology, after all. Perhaps it's history."

Kosoff muttered, "Perhaps. Perhaps. I wish we could stay here longer, dig up more evidence."

"We've got about eighteen months before we head back to Earth," Littlejohn said.

"Too soon," said Kosoff. "We need more time here."

"The follow-on mission is already on its way," said Littlejohn.

"Yes. They'll get all the glory, after we've done the groundbreaking work."

Brad interrupted Kosoff's brooding. "In the meantime, we've got to decide what we should do about the cats. We can't let them invade this planet again and slaughter the Gammans."

"The follow-on mission won't be here in time to stop that," said Kosoff.

"We've saved the Gammans once, but we won't be here to save them the next time."

"That can't be helped. We don't have the resources to remain here until the follow-on mission arrives," Kosoff said. "Even if we did, I doubt that the World Council would approve our staying."

Brad started, "They don't understand—"

"No, *you* don't understand," Kosoff interrupted. "We're under the World Council's control, whether you like it or not."

That night, as he lay in bed with Felicia, Brad blurted, "Fil, I've got to stay here."

He felt her body tense. "What do you mean?"

In the darkened room he couldn't make out the expression on her face. But he heard the stress in her voice.

"I've got to stay here through the winter. I've got to help Mnnx and Lnng and the others when the cats from Beta come back."

She turned toward him. "Brad, you can't! You can't stay here alone. How will you survive? You won't have enough food—"

"I've been working through the numbers," he said, keeping his voice soft, not giving in to his own doubts, his own fears. "There's enough food in the backup reserves to feed the two of us until the follow-on mission arrives."

"The two of us?"

"You'll stay with me, won't you?"

A long silence. Brad could feel his pulse thudding in his ears.

At last Felicia said, "If I don't stay, what will you do?"

"You won't stay?"

"If I don't, will you stay here or come back home with me?"

"Fil, don't ask me that. Don't make me choose."

"You've got to choose, Brad. It's one or the other."

"You'd leave me?"

Another long silence. Brad felt as if he were being torn apart.

"You'd leave me," Felicia said softly, sadly.

"But I have to—"

"You'd be killing both of us," Felicia said.

"You'd stay?"

"I shouldn't. I should go back. I should let Kosoff court me all the way home."

"Don't joke. This is serious."

"Brad, I want a normal life. I want to have children, your children."

"But you'd stay."

"I don't want to."

"But you'd stay. You'd really stay with me."

In the darkness, she sighed. "There's got to be some other way. Brad, you've got to find another option."

"There isn't any other option. Either we stay and help the Gammans protect themselves, or we go back to Earth and leave them to face the cats by themselves. Leave them to be butchered."

"You've got to find another way," Felicia insisted. "Otherwise you'll be killing us both."

Brad didn't reply. But he felt a wall separating him from his wife now, even though they lay side by side.

The next morning brought snow. The cheerless weather outside their quarters matched the atmosphere inside. Felicia was up and busy in their minuscule kitchen when Brad awoke, blurry and disturbed by his dreams.

They were a combination of the old nightmare about Tithonium Chasma, plus a new sense of impending doom. Felicia was in his dreams, Brad recalled, but he couldn't quite grasp what she had been doing. He knew that he had felt helpless once again, torn between his guilt and his sense of duty.

Feeling tired, drained, he slipped into the lavatory, then once freshened and dressed, stepped into the kitchen area.

"Good morning," he said to Felicia, as brightly as he could.

She was wearing a simple gray coverall, standing before the microwave as it ticked off its final seconds.

"Morning, Brad." She did not turn to offer him even a perfunctory kiss.

"Uh . . . did you sleep well?"

"Not very," said Felicia. Her face was serious, her luminous gray eyes unsmiling. "You were moaning in your sleep again."

"Oh. Sorry."

"The nightmare again?"

He nodded. "With some new twists."

Her stern expression softened. "I've put you under a lot of stress, haven't I?"

He reached for her, pulled her close. "No, it's my own fault. I wish . . . "

"You wish what, Brad?"

Feeling nearly desperate, he answered, "I wish there was some way I could leave here and go back to Earth. Bring you back to Earth."

Felicia smiled gently at him. "Then you'll just have to find a way, won't you?"

As he drove one of the buggies toward the village, through the thickly falling snow, Brad wondered what he should do. The buggy's energy screen protected him from the snow and the biting wind that was sweeping down from the mountains. Bundled inside his hooded parka, Brad felt warm enough. Yet inside, he was bleak.

Winter, he thought. In another few months Mnnx and the rest of them will have to face the depth of winter. Can they do it on their own? They've gathered in their crops and they have the food supplies we made for them; will it be enough to feed them through the long winter? Or am I killing them just as the cats do, only slower, more painfully?

And over on Beta, Brad knew, the eggs holding the embryos of the cats will hibernate through the time of cold. In the spring the two planets will come close enough to each other so that those eggs will fly to Gamma and they'll hatch and the cats will come out and start killing.

Brad had suggested to Mnnx and the others that they should defend themselves against the cats.

"We don't have your death beam," Lnng replied, sounding almost envious.

"It is wrong for us to disobey the will of the Sky Masters," Mnnx intoned.

"You could make spears," Brad had told them. "We could show you how to make bows and arrows, train you how to kill the cats."

"Even if we could," Mnnx had answered, "the Sky Masters would return and punish us."

Lnng disagreed. "Better to face their punishment than to allow the cats to kill us."

"Do you think you could kill one of the monsters?" Mnnx challenged.

"Yes! If I had to."

Sounding sorrowful, Mnnx said, "No, my sibling. Brrd can kill the monsters. He is not one of us. But we are bound by the commands of the Sky Masters. Without Brrd to protect us, we will be killed by the monsters."

Great, Brad thought as he recalled their discussions. They'll be happy to let me stay and protect them. Otherwise they'll let the cats kill them all. And argue about it until they're all dead.

He heard Felicia's voice in his mind, "Then you'll just have to find a way, won't you?"

Easier said than done, Brad told himself. Easier said than done.

The buggy reached the crest of the low hills that surrounded the village. No, Brad corrected mentally: villages. There's two of them now, one empty.

He stopped and looked down at the villages. A layer of snow covered everything. Looks like an old-fashioned Christmas card, Brad thought. Two hundred light-years from home. Merry Christmas. He didn't feel a holiday mood.

What month is it, anyway? he wondered.

Aloud, he asked, "Emcee, what season is it back on Earth?"

"Spring, in the northern hemisphere," came Emcee's instant answer, from the buggy's control panel.

Spring, thought Brad. It won't be spring here for another thirty-some Earth years.

I can't ask Felicia to stay here, he realized. Not through the long winter. Not alone, just the two of us, wondering if the food will hold out.

Maybe we should try hibernating! Brad suddenly thought.

We could take a couple of cryosleep capsules from the ship and install them in the camp. Then we could sleep through the winter and wake up in the spring, when it starts to thaw.

Immediately, Brad saw the flaws in that approach. The deep freeze of cryosleep damaged the brain's neural networks. Cryosleepers downloaded their minds into the ship's master computer and, once they began to be revived, the neural connections were uploaded back into the sleeper's brain.

We'd have to duplicate all the computer equipment and set it up down here on Gamma, Brad realized. We'd have to duplicate Emcee here in the camp, for god's sake.

Shaking his head as he sat in the buggy amidst the swirling snowfall, Brad knew that duplicating the entire cryosleep system was too big a job for the ship's crew, even if Kosoff would allow it.

No, he told himself, cryosleep isn't the answer. As he put the buggy in gear and started down the hillside, he also comprehended that the Gammans wouldn't be able to understand that Brad and Felicia were merely sleeping in their cryocapsule. Mnnx and Lnng and the others would think we've died, most likely. Committed suicide and left them to face the cats on their own.

Either we stay awake and alert with the Gammans through the whole long winter, or we go home, Brad knew. Either we help the Gammans face the cats next spring or we leave them to defend themselves—or more likely, leave them to be slaughtered.

There's got to be a third way, he shouted silently to himself. There's got to be!

But if there is, he admitted, I don't know what it might be.

That evening Brad returned to the encampment, as usual. The snowstorm had died away, leaving the region covered in white. Brad followed the tracks of his own buggy through the crystal-cold night, still wondering what to do. What to do?

Felicia greeted him with an emotionless kiss as he entered their quarters, then turned her attention to the microwave cooker.

"Do you want some wine before dinner?" she asked.

Brad shrugged. "How about you?"

"I will if you will."

Leadership, Brad thought as he went to the minifridge and pulled out a half-empty bottle of white wine.

"How's everything in the village?" Felicia asked.

"Okay, I guess," Brad said as he poured two glasses. "They're getting more and more nervous about the weather."

"They've never seen snow before, I suppose."

"Guess not. By this time they'd all be dead, usually."

Felicia started to say something but the microwave pinged and she turned her attention to it.

Brad sat at the fold-down kitchen table and watched her set two steaming plates on it. Then she sat opposite him and picked up her stemmed wineglass.

They clinked their glasses.

"The chemistry lab's best brew," Brad joked weakly.

"It's fine," said Felicia. She took a sip, then she put the glass down and turned her attention to her meal.

"What's going on at the bio lab?" he asked, trying to make a conversation.

Without looking up at him, Felicia replied with a weary sigh, "We're doing microanalyses of the cats' cells now. Molecular biology. Ursula wants us to have their complete genetic map before we have to start packing up for leaving."

"Fil."

She looked up.

"I'll find a way," Brad said.

For the first time that evening Felicia smiled at him. "I know you will."

strangely, Brad's dreams that night were almost pleasant. He was a young boy again, climbing the cliffs of Tithonium Chasma with his classmates, laughing that the light gravity of Mars allowed them to climb like superhuman athletes, even in their protective suits.

And then it was Christmas, with his parents and his younger brother David sitting on the floor of their living room in front of the tree that his father had made out of odd lengths of piping and scraps of aluminum foil. It looked kind of sad and droopy, young Brad thought, but it was as good as any tree in the settlement.

Both Brad's parents were scientists, and Christmas held no religious meaning for them. But it meant a tree, no matter how threadbare or lopsided. And presents.

Young Brad tore open the wrapping on the box his mother handed him, while Davie did the same with his present. Dad was smiling at them while Mom gathered up the scraps of wrapping paper and stuffed them into the disposal chute, behind the tree.

He stared at his present. It was an egg: not a real egg, there weren't any of those anywhere on Mars. This was an egg-shaped thing of metal and crystal, beautifully crafted, glinting in the light from the ceiling panels.

This can't be my Christmas present, Brad thought. Davie was marveling at the beautifully detailed spacecraft model he had pulled from his box. But I get an egg? Like an Easter gift?

This is no fun, Brad thought, staring at the glittering egg. It's not a toy, it's a decoration. It's not something to play with; Mom will want to put it on a shelf where visitors will see it.

A lousy egg. That's not a real Christmas present. It's not—

Suddenly he realized that it *was* a present. It just wasn't a present for him.

"Dig them up?" Littlejohn looked startled, almost alarmed. "You want to dig up all the eggs on Beta?"

"And bring them back to Earth," said Brad.

The two men were in Littlejohn's office, in the encampment. The chief of the anthropology team was seated on the small couch set against the side wall, Brad was pacing energetically across the small room: four strides in one direction, then four more in the other.

The Australian craned his head to look up at Brad. "We can't do that. We haven't the tools or the time."

"Yes, we do," Brad countered eagerly. "We can use the digging equipment we've been using to excavate the city—"

"Transport those earth movers all the way to Beta?"

"Yes! Dig up all the eggs on Beta, bring them to the ship, and preserve them cryogenically all the way back to Earth."

Littlejohn slowly shook his head. Brad thought he looked almost like a child sitting on the couch, his feet barely touching the floor.

"Think of what a sensation it'll make back on Earth," Brad urged. "The world's best biologists will be able to study an entire alien species!"

"And push Steiner aside," Littlejohn muttered.

"No, she'll be in charge of the study. It'll be her triumph! The World Council will honor her!"

"Beta's moving farther away every day."

"Then use the starship to transport the digging equipment."

"And leave us here in the encampment?"

"It'll only be for a few weeks. We can survive perfectly well."

"If an emergency comes up . . . "

Perching himself on the edge of Littlejohn's desk, Brad ticked off on his fingers, "We know where the eggs are buried, the satellites have mapped the whole planet; we have the earthmoving equipment to dig them up; and we have plenty of empty storage space aboard the ship."

"And if we dig up the eggs and take them back to Earth with us—"

"The cats won't be around to attack the Gammans the next time the two planets meet," Brad finished his superior's thought. "We'll have saved the villagers!"

A hesitant smile crept across Littlejohn's dark face. "You don't think small, do you?"

"It'll work," Brad enthused. "It'll save the Gammans and show Mnnx that they have nothing to fear. It'll please the world's biologists. It's a win-win situation."

Nodding slowly, Littlejohn pointed out, "If Kosoff okays the idea."

Brad hurried from Littlejohn's office to the bio lab, startling people in the hallway as he sprinted along.

He banged through the laboratory's door and saw Felicia and Steiner seated at the neutrino microscope's display screen, intently staring at a scan of a cell's nucleus.

Ursula Steiner looked up angrily at Brad's intrusion.

"Must I put a lock on the door?" she snapped.

But Brad had eyes only for Felicia. "We can do it!" he shouted as he rushed to her.

"Do what?" she asked.

"Dig up all the egg nests on Beta and take them back to Earth!"

"Dig up . . . ?" Felicia sank back on the stool she was sitting upon. Her face lit up as she realized what Brad was telling her. "Is that why you bolted out of our quarters this morning?"

"Yes! To tell Littlejohn. He agrees with me."

Steiner's expression had morphed from annoyed to curious. "You want to bring all the eggs back to Earth?"

"You can study them to your heart's content," Brad said. "Get the world's best nanotechs to examine the shells."

"That's . . . that's incredible. Daring."

Felicia broke the bubble. "Only if Kosoff agrees to it," she warned.

Steiner nodded. "And the World Council."

"They will," Brad insisted. "They'll have to!"

As usual, Kosoff sat behind his massive desk while Brad explained his plan. Littlejohn had taken one of the padded chairs in front of the desk. Too excited to sit, Brad paced eagerly across the office as he explained his idea.

And as usual, Kosoff's bearded face looked dour, skeptical, unconvinced.

"Dig up all the egg nests on Beta?" he asked.

"And store them on the ship. We have plenty of room: storage areas that have been emptied out, spare hangar space—"

"I don't want those eggs inside this ship!" Kosoff growled. "That's an unnecessary risk. Suppose they start to hatch?"

"Put them in the empty storage compartments outside the hull," Brad countered. "They'll be in cryogenic temperature outside, yet protected from interstellar radiation, just like the foodstuffs the lockers were originally used to store."

Kosoff's grim expression didn't change, but he began to drum his fingers on his desktop.

He uses that desk like a fortress, Brad thought. He thinks it protects him. For a crazy moment, Brad wondered what Kosoff would do if he leaped across the desk and sat in the professor's lap.

Looking at Littlejohn, Kosoff said, "This wild scheme will mean you'll have to end your excavation of the city. We don't have enough heavy equipment for both jobs."

With a dramatic sigh, Littlejohn said, "I know. I'm willing to stop the excavation. We're just uncovering more of the same things: cracked foundations, broken walls. We haven't found any artifacts, not even shards of pottery."

"They've all been taken away by the Sky Masters," Brad said. "Before they destroyed the city they looted it."

Kosoff frowned. "You're spouting Gamman mythology again."

"The evidence is there," Brad retorted. "Or, rather, the lack of evidence."

Kosoff went back to drumming his fingers.

Littlejohn asked Brad, "Are you sure that the surveillance satellites have located *all* the egg nests on Beta?"

Nodding, Brad replied, "Emcee has checked and double-checked the data. Beta is pretty barren, not much forest or dense foliage to interfere with deep radar probes. And the nests aren't that deeply underground. Emcee says we've located them all, with a better than ninety-five percent probability."

Turning to Kosoff, Littlejohn said, "I think we should go ahead with this."

A rare smile crept across Kosoff's bearded face. "So do I," he agreed.

"You do?" Brad blurted.

"Yes. Now all I have to do is convince the World Council."

"I'll give you all the data you need."

"H'mm. Yes." Turning to Littlejohn once more, Kosoff said, "You'd better halt your excavation work and get the earthmoving equipment ready to return here, to the ship."

Brad gushed, "Thank you, Professor Kosoff. Thank you!"

"Don't thank me. This is your idea, not mine. I'm simply going along with you—and the facts of the matter."

It was snowing again, but this time the snowfall was gentle, almost pleasant, the white flakes sifting down from the leaden sky.

Fingering the translating computer in the pocket of his thick parka, Brad stood between Mnnx and Lnng on the crest of the hill overlooking the villages down in the hollow. The buggy he had driven to this final meeting with the aliens stood waiting a few meters downslope, its energy screen keeping it clear of snow.

"You are leaving us?" Mnnx asked, for the fifth time in the past hour. He looked slightly ridiculous in the padded garment that covered him from his sloping shoulders to his booted feet.

Brad nodded inside his parka's hood. "Tomorrow morning, after the snow stops."

"Will you come back, Brrd?" asked Lnng.

Pulling in a breath of the cold air, Brad replied, "I can't come back. Our village is so far away that it would take hundreds of years for me to return. But others from my world are already on their way here. They will help you. They will reach you."

"Will they protect us from the Sky Masters?" asked Mnnx.

Brad hesitated a heartbeat, then stretched the truth. "If the Sky Masters return, they will protect you."

"You said the monsters from Beta will never return," Lnng reminded him.

"That's right. You have nothing to fear. The monsters will never bother you again."

"You did this for us?" asked Mnnx. "Why?"

"To help you to live. To start a new life for you and all the new Folk who will come up from the ground and live in the new village."

"For us."

"For all of you. That is my mission, to help all of you to live, to learn, to grow strong once again."

"You are strong," Lnng said. "Stronger than the Sky Masters."

Mnnx started to speak, but stopped himself.

Maybe I've convinced Mnnx that he doesn't have to be afraid anymore, Brad thought. Maybe.

He found that there was a lump in his throat. Suddenly he realized that he would never see these aliens again, that he would not play any further role in their lives. He was surprised at how sad he felt.

Forcing himself to keep his voice from breaking, Brad said, "I must go back to my encampment now."

The two Gammans stood there, silent, numb. Brad stared at them, tongue-tied, knowing that he had run out of words. Despite the shiver of aversion that he felt at the thought of touching the aliens, Brad wrapped his arms around Lnng, then turned and embraced Mnnx. "Good-bye, my friends," he choked out.

Then he turned and walked swiftly through the snow to the waiting buggy. He blinked tears from his eyes.

The next morning Brad and Felicia stood at a display screen in the starship's main auditorium, their arms around each other's waists. Planet Gamma, below them, was covered in gray clouds.

Dozens of other people were drifting into the auditorium, gathering at the display screens.

"Not much to see," Felicia murmured.

Brad called out to Emcee, "Can we see the village through the clouds?"

Emcee replied, "Switching to infrared imagery."

And there was the village, a tiny dot nestled in the hills.

"Going to maximum enlargement," Emcee's smoothly unemotional voice said.

Brad gasped. The whole population of the village was standing out in the central square, gazing up at the clouds.

"They're trying to catch a glimpse of us before we depart," Felicia said.

Brad did not reply. He couldn't. It took all his willpower to keep from crying.

"Breaking orbit in five minutes," said Emcee.

"You've saved them, Brad," Felicia whispered.

"I hope so."

Professor Kosoff and Dr. Littlejohn sat at a table on the balcony that circled the auditorium, watching the growing crowd on the floor below.

They heard Emcee's announcement, "Breaking orbit in five minutes."

"Going home," said Littlejohn, a crooked smile on his dark face.

"Home," Kosoff murmured.

"You look rather somber."

With a shrug of his heavy shoulders, the professor said, "There's so much we've left undone."

"Oh, I don't know," Littlejohn said. "We've put energy screen generators in orbit around both Alpha and Gamma. We've accomplished what we came here to do. Both planets are now shielded against the death wave."

"Yes, but . . ." Kosoff hesitated.

"The follow-on mission is on its way here. They'll help the Gammans get through their winter."

"Do you believe the Gamman tale about the Sky Masters?" Kosoff asked.

It was Littlejohn's turn to hesitate. At last he replied, "There must be something behind their mythology."

"The cats on Beta," Kosoff muttered. "The nano-technology in their eggs. The disruption of this whole planetary system."

"That's not our problem any longer," said Littlejohn.

"Isn't it? There was a cataclysm here, and it wasn't a natural disaster. Someone made it happen."

"The Sky Masters."

"Someone. And we've interfered with their handi-work."

Littlejohn shook his head. "It all happened a hundred thousand years ago. Whoever did this is long gone."

Kosoff let out a sigh that was almost a moan. "I hope so. I really hope so. If not, we're going to have a tremendous confrontation on our hands."

Littlejohn's voice went hollow. "An interstellar war?"

"Sounds melodramatic, doesn't it?" said Kosoff. "Yet the evidence is there."

For a long moment Littlejohn was silent. Then, "The one I worry about is MacDaniels. Returning to Earth is going to be very hard on him."

Kosoff said, "It's going to be very hard on all of us, returning to a world that's four hundred years different from the one we left."

"Yes, but it's going to hit Brad harder than most of us." Motioning to himself and Kosoff, the Aussie went on, "You and I will have university sinecures waiting for us. We'll be honored and feted. Brad's going to be just another peon returning from the field, a worker with nothing to do. It's going to be hard for him."

Kosoff snorted. "For ten minutes, maybe. Brad's a

born leader. He'll find a place for himself. I wouldn't be surprised if he returns to Gamma. Or maybe runs for a seat on the World Council."

Littlejohn almost smiled. "Do you think . . . ?"

With some heat, Kosoff said, "Don't worry about Brad MacDaniels. Just try to stay out of his way. If we're going to have an interstellar war, he might be just the man we need to lead us."

"Breaking orbit," Emcee announced. The display screens all around the auditorium showed gray-clouded Gamma slide off to one side, then begin to dwindle noticeably.

"We're on our way home," Felicia said.

Brad nodded, but his eyes were still on the screen and the shriveling globe that was planet Gamma.

I'll come back, he promised silently. No matter how long it takes, I'll come back to them.

That night Brad dreamed again. He was at Tithonium Chasma once more, but this time Felicia was standing beside him, out in the open, and the cliffs did not crumble. This time his father and mother and little brother were outside with him, alive, happy, smiling. This time Mnnx and Lnng and the other Gammans stood there too.

And this time Brad held a pink-faced infant squirming and gurgling in his arms.

Turning to Felicia, he said, "We've got a lot to do."

"Yes," she said, smiling delightedly. "Together."

Read on for a preview of

SURVIVAL

BEN BOVA

Available in December 2017 from
Tom Doherty Associates

TOR   A TOR HARDCOVER

"It's obvious!" said Vartan Gregorian, standing imperiously before the two others seated on the couch. "I'm the best damned pilot in the history of the human race!"

Planting his fists on his hips, he struck a pose that was nothing less than preening.

Half buried in the lounge's plush curved couch, Alexander Ignatiev bit back an impulse to laugh in the Armenian's face. But Nikki Deneuve, sitting next to him, gazed up at Gregorian with shining eyes.

Breaking into a broad grin, Gregorian went on, "This bucket is moving faster than any ship ever built, no? We've flown farther from Earth than anybody ever has, true?"

Nikki nodded eagerly as she responded, "Twenty percent of light speed and approaching six light-years."

"So, I'm the pilot of the fastest, highest-flying ship of all time!" Gregorian exclaimed. "That makes me the best flier in the history of the human race. QED!"

Ignatiev shook his head at the conceited oaf. But he saw that Nikki was captivated by his posturing. Then it struck him. She loves him! And Gregorian is showing off for her.

The ship's lounge was as relaxing and comfortable as human designers back on Earth could make it. It was arranged in a circular grouping of sumptuously appointed niches, each holding high, curved banquettes that could seat up to half a dozen close friends in reasonable privacy.

Ignatiev had left his quarters after suffering still another defeat at the hands of the computerized chess program and snuck down to the lounge in midafternoon, hoping to find it empty. He needed a hideaway while the housekeeping robots cleaned his suite. Their busy, buzzing thoroughness drove him to distraction; it was impossible to concentrate on chess or anything else while the machines were dusting, laundering, straightening his rooms, restocking his autokitchen and his bar, making the bed with crisply fresh linens.

So he sought refuge in the lounge, only to find Gregorian and Deneuve already there, in a niche beneath a display screen that showed the star fields outside. Once, the sight of those stars scattered across the infinite void would have stirred Ignatiev's heart. But not anymore, not since Sonya died.

Sipping at the vodka that the serving robot had poured for him the instant he had stepped into the lounge, thanks to its face-recognition program, Ignatiev couldn't help grousing, "And who says you are the pilot, Vartan? I didn't see any designation for pilot in the mission's assignment roster."

Gregorian was moderately handsome and rather tall, quite slim, with thick dark hair and laugh crinkles at the corners of his deep brown eyes. Ignatiev tended to think of people in terms of chess pieces, and he counted Gregorian as a prancing horse, all style and little substance.

"I am flight systems engineer, no?" Gregorian countered. "My assignment is to monitor the flight control program. That makes me the pilot."

Nikki, still beaming at him, said, "If you're the pilot, Vartan, then I must be the navigator."

"Astrogator," Ignatiev corrected bluntly.

The daughter of a Quebecoise mother and French

Moroccan father, Nicolette Deneuve had unfortunately inherited her father's stocky physique and her mother's sharp nose. Ignatiev thought her unlovely—and yet there was a charm to her, a gamine-like wide-eyed innocence that beguiled Ignatiev's crusty old heart. She was a physicist, bright and conscientious, not an engineering monkey like the braggart Gregorian. Thus it was a tragedy that she had been selected for this star mission.

She finally turned away from Gregorian to say to Ignatiev, "It's good to see you, Professor Ignatiev. You've become something of a hermit these past few months."

He coughed and muttered, "I've been busy on my research." The truth was he couldn't bear to be among these youngsters, couldn't stand the truth that they would one day return to Earth while he would be long dead.

Alexander Alexandrovich Ignatiev, by far the oldest man among the starship's crew, thought that Nikki could have been the daughter he'd never had. Daughter? he snapped at himself silently. Granddaughter, he corrected. Great-granddaughter, even. He was a dour astrophysicist approaching his hundred and fortieth birthday, his short-cropped hair and neatly trimmed beard iron gray but his mind and body still reasonably vigorous and active thanks to rejuvenation therapies. Yet he felt cheated by the way the world worked, bitter about being exiled to this one-way flight to a distant star.

Technically, he was the senior executive of this mission, an honor that he found almost entirely empty. To him, it was like being the principal of a school for very bright, totally wayward children. Each one of them must have been president of their school's student body, he thought: accustomed to getting their own way and total strangers to discipline. Besides, the actual commander of the ship was the artificial intelligence program run by the ship's central computer.

If Gregorian is a chessboard knight, Ignatiev mused to himself, then what is Nikki? Not the queen; she's too young, too uncertain of herself for that. Her assignment to monitor the navigation program was something of a joke: the ship followed a ballistic trajectory, like an arrow shot from Earth. Nothing for a navigator to do except check the ship's position each day.

Maybe she's a bishop, Ignatiev mused, now that a woman can be made a bishop: quiet, self-effacing, possessing hidden depths. And reliable, trustworthy, always staying to the color of the square she started on. She'll cling to Gregorian, unless he hurts her terribly. That possibility made Ignatiev's blood simmer.

And me? he asked himself. A pawn, nothing more. But then he thought, Maybe I'm a rook, stuck off in a corner of the board, barely noticed by anybody.

"Professor Ignatiev is correct," said Gregorian, trying to regain control of the conversation. "The proper term is astrogator."

"Whatever," said Nikki, her eyes returning to Gregorian's handsome young face.

Young was a relative term. Gregorian was approaching sixty, although he still had the vigor, the attitudes and demeanor of an obstreperous teenager. Ignatiev thought it would be appropriate if the Armenian's face were blotched with acne. Youth is wasted on the young, Ignatiev thought. Thanks to life-elongation therapies, average life expectancy among the starship crew was well above two hundred. It had to be.

The scoopship was named *Sagan*, after some minor twentieth-century astronomer. It was heading for Gliese 581, a red dwarf star slightly more than twenty light-years from Earth. For Ignatiev, it was a one-way journey. Even with all the life-extension therapies, he was sure that he would never survive the eighty-year round trip. Gregorian would, of course, and so would Nikki.

Ignatiev brooded over the unfairness of it. By the time the ship returned to Earth, the two of them would be grandparents and Ignatiev would be long dead.

Unfair, he thought as he pushed himself up from the plush banquette and left the lounge without a word to either one of them. The universe is unfair. I don't deserve this: to die alone, unloved, unrecognized, my life's work forgotten, all my hopes crushed to dust.

As he reached the lounge's hatch, he turned his head to see what the two of them were up to. Chatting, smiling, holding hands, all the subverbal signals that lovers send to each other. They had eyes only for each other, and paid absolutely no attention to him.

Just like the rest of the goddamned world, Ignatiev thought.

He had labored all his life in the groves of academe, and what had it gotten him? A membership in the International Academy of Sciences, along with seventeen thousand other anonymous workers. A pension that barely covered his living expenses. Three marriages: two wrecked by divorce and the third—the only one that really mattered—destroyed by that inevitable thief, death.

He hardly remembered how enthusiastic he had been as a young postdoc, all those years ago, his astrophysics degree in hand, burning with ambition. He was going to unlock the secrets of the universe! The pulsars, those enigmatic cinders, the remains of ancient supernova explosions: Ignatiev was going to discover what made them tick.

But the universe was far subtler than he had thought. Soon enough he learned that a career in science can be a study in anonymous drudgery. The pulsars kept their secrets, no matter how assiduously Ignatiev nibbled around the edges of their mystery.

And now the honor of being the senior executive on

the human race's first interstellar mission. Some honor, Ignatiev thought sourly. They needed someone competent but expendable. Send old Ignatiev, let him go out in a fizzle of glory.

Shaking his head as he trudged along the thickly carpeted passageway to his quarters, Ignatiev muttered to himself, "If only there were something I could accomplish, something I could discover, something to put some *meaning* to my life."

He had lived long enough to realize that his life would be no more remembered than the life of a worker ant. He wanted more than that. He wanted to be remembered. He wanted his name to be revered. He wanted students in the far future to know that he had existed, that he had made a glowing contribution to humankind's store of knowledge and understanding. He wanted Nikki Deneuve to gaze at him with adoring eyes.

"It will never be," Ignatiev told himself as he slid open the door to his quarters. With a wry shrug, he reminded himself of a line from some old English poet: "Ah, that a man's reach should exceed his grasp, or what's a heaven for?"

Alexander Ignatiev did not believe in heaven. But he thought he knew what hell was like.

As he entered his quarters he saw that at least the cleaning robots had finished and left; the sitting room looked almost tidy. And he was alone.

The expedition to Gliese 581 had left Earth with tremendous fanfare. The first human mission to another star! Gliese 581 was a very ordinary star in most respects: a dim red dwarf, barely one-third of the Sun's mass. The galaxy is studded with such stars. But Gliese 581 was unusual in one supremely interesting way: it possessed an entourage of half a dozen planets. Most of them were gas giants, bloated conglomerates of hydrogen and helium. But a couple of them were rocky worlds, somewhat like Earth. And one of those—Gliese 581c—orbited at just the right "Goldilocks" distance from its parent star to be able to have liquid water on its surface.

Liquid water meant life. In the solar system, wherever liquid water existed, life existed. In the permafrost beneath the frozen rust-red surface of Mars, in the ice-covered seas of the moons of Jupiter and Saturn, in massive Jupiter's planet-girdling ocean: wherever liquid water had been found, life was found with it.

Half a dozen robotic probes confirmed that liquid water actually did exist on the surface of Gliese 581c, but they found no evidence for life. Not an amoeba, not even a bacterium. But that didn't deter the scientific hierarchy. Robots are terribly limited, they proclaimed. We must send human scientists to Gliese 581c to search for life there, scientists of all types, men and women who will sacrifice half their lives to the search for life beyond the solar system.

Ignatiev was picked to sacrifice the last half of his life. He knew he would never see Earth again, and he told himself that he didn't care. There was nothing on Earth that interested him anymore, not since Sonya's death. But he wanted to find something, to make an impact, to keep his name alive after he was gone.

Most of the two hundred scientists, engineers, and technicians aboard *Sagan* were sleeping away the decades of the flight in cryonic suspension. They would be revived once the scoopship arrived at Gliese 581's vicinity. Only a dozen were awake during the flight, assigned to monitor the ship's systems, ready to make corrections or repairs if necessary.

The ship was highly automated, of course. The human crew was a backup, a concession to human vanity unwilling to hand the operation of the ship completely to electronic and mechanical devices. Human egos feared fully autonomous machines. Thus a dozen human lives were sacrificed to spend four decades waiting for the machines to fail.

They hadn't failed so far. From the fusion power-plant deep in the ship's core to the tenuous magnetic scoop stretching a thousand kilometers in front of the ship, all the systems worked perfectly well. When a minor malfunction arose, the ship's machines repaired themselves, under the watchful direction of the master AI program. Even the AI system's computer program ran flawlessly, to Ignatiev's utter frustration. It beat him at chess with depressing regularity.

In addition to the meaningless title of senior executive, Alexander Ignatiev had a specific technical task aboard the starship. His assignment was to monitor the electromagnetic funnel that scooped in hydrogen from the thin interstellar medium to feed the ship's nuclear fusion engine. Every day he faithfully checked the gauges and display screens in the ship's command center, reminding himself each time that the practice of physics always comes down to reading a goddamned dial.

The funnel operated flawlessly. A huge gossamer web of hair-thin superconducting wires, it created an invisible magnetic field that spread out before the starship like a thousand-kilometer-wide scoop, gathering in the hydrogen atoms floating between the stars and ionizing them as they were sucked into the ship's innards, like a huge baleen whale scooping up the tiny creatures of the sea that it fed upon.

Deep in the starship's bowels the fusion generator forced the hydrogen ions to fuse together into helium ions, in the process giving up energy to run the ship. Like the Sun and the stars themselves, the starship lived on hydrogen fusion.

Ignatiev slid the door of his quarters shut. The suite of rooms allotted to him was small, but far more luxurious than any home he had lived in back on Earth. The psychotechnicians among the mission's planners, worried about the crew's morale during the decades-long flight, had insisted on every creature comfort they could think of: everything from body-temperature waterbeds that adjusted to one's weight and size to digitally controlled décor that could change its color scheme at the call of one's voice; from an automated kitchen that could prepare a world-spanning variety of cuisines to virtual reality entertainment systems.

Ignatiev ignored all the splendor; or rather, he took it for granted. Creature comforts were fine, but he had spent the first months of the mission converting his beautifully wrought sitting room into an astrophysics laboratory. The sleek Scandinavian desk of teak inlaid with meteoric silver now held a conglomeration of computers and sensor readouts. The fake fireplace was hidden behind a junk pile of discarded spectrometers, magnetometers, and other gadgetry that Ignatiev had used and abandoned. He could see a faint ring of dust on the floor around the mess; he had given the cleaning robots strict orders not to touch it.

Above the obstructed fireplace was a framed digital screen programmed to show high-definition images of the world's great artworks—when it wasn't being used as a three-dimensional entertainment screen. Ignatiev had connected it to the ship's main optical telescope, so that it showed the stars spangled against the blackness of space. Usually the telescope was pointed forward, with the tiny red dot of Gliese 581 centered in its field of view. Now and then, at the command of the ship's AI system, it looked back toward the diminishing yellow speck of the Sun.

Being an astrophysicist, Ignatiev had started the flight

by spending most of his waking hours examining this interstellar Siberia in which he was exiled. It was an excuse to stay away from the chattering young monkeys of the crew. He had studied the planet-sized chunks of ice and rock in the Oort cloud that surrounded the outermost reaches of the solar system. Once the ship was past that region, he turned his interest back to the enigmatic, frustrating pulsars. Each one throbbed at a precise frequency, more accurate than an atomic clock. Why? What determined their frequency? Why did some supernova explosions produce pulsars while others didn't?

Ignatiev batted his head against those questions in vain. More and more, as the months of the mission stretched into years, he spent his days playing chess against the AI system. And losing consistently.

"Alexander Alexandrovich."

He looked up from the chessboard he had set up on his desktop screen, turned in his chair, and directed his gaze across the room to the display screen above the fireplace. The lovely, smiling face of the artificial intelligence system's avatar filled the screen.

The psychotechnicians among the mission planners had decided that the human crew would work more effectively with the AI program if it showed a human face. For each human crew member, the face was slightly different: the psychotechs had tried to create a personal relationship for each of the crew. The deceit annoyed Ignatiev. The program treated him like a child. Worse, the face it displayed for him reminded him too much of his late wife.

"I'm busy," he growled.

Unperturbed, the avatar's smiling face said, "Yesterday you requested use of the main communications antenna."

"I want to use it as a radio telescope, to map out the interstellar hydrogen we're moving through."

"The twenty-one-centimeter radiation," said the avatar knowingly.

"Yes."

"You are no longer studying the pulsars?"

He bit back an angry reply. "I have given up on the pulsars," he admitted. "The interstellar medium interests me more. I have decided to map the hydrogen in detail."

Besides, he admitted to himself, that will be a lot easier than the pulsars.

The AI avatar said calmly, "Mission protocol requires the main antenna be available to receive communications from mission control."

"The secondary antenna can do that," he said. Before the AI system could reply, he added, "Besides, any communications from Earth will be six years old. We're not going to get any urgent messages that must be acted upon immediately."

"Still," said the avatar, "mission protocol cannot be dismissed lightly."

"It won't hurt anything to let me use the main antenna for a few hours each day," he insisted.

The avatar remained silent for several seconds: an enormous span of time for the computer program.

At last, the avatar conceded, "Perhaps so. You may use the main antenna, provisionally."

"I am eternally grateful," Ignatiev said. His sarcasm was wasted on the AI system.

As the weeks lengthened into months he found himself increasingly fascinated by the thin interstellar hydrogen gas and discovered, to only his mild surprise, that it was not evenly distributed in space.

Of course, astrophysicists had known for centuries that there are regions in space where the interstellar gas clumped so thickly and was so highly ionized that it glowed. Gaseous emission nebulae were common throughout the galaxy, although Ignatiev mentally corrected the misnomer: those nebulae actually consisted not of gas, but of plasma—gases that are highly ionized.

But here in the placid emptiness on the way to Gliese 581 Ignatiev found himself slowly becoming engrossed with the way that even the thin, bland neutral interstellar gas was not evenly distributed. Not at all. The hydrogen was thicker in some regions than in others.

This was hardly a new discovery, but from the viewpoint of the starship, inside the billowing interstellar clouds, the fine structure of the hydrogen became almost a thing of beauty in Ignatiev's ice-blue eyes. The interstellar gas didn't merely hang there passively between the stars, it flowed: slowly, almost imperceptibly, but it drifted on currents shaped by the gravitational pull of the stars.

"That old writer was correct," he muttered to himself as he studied the stream of interstellar hydrogen that the ship was cutting through. "There are currents in space."

He tried to think of the writer's name, but couldn't come up with it. A Russian name, he recalled. But nothing more specific.

The more he studied the interstellar gas, the more captivated he became. He went days without playing a single game of chess. Weeks. The interstellar hydrogen gas wasn't static, not at all. It was like a beautiful intricate lacework that flowed, fluttered, shifted in a stately silent pavane among the stars.

The clouds of hydrogen were like a tide of bubbling champagne, he saw, frothing slowly in rhythm to the heartbeats of the stars.

The astronomers back on Earth had no inkling of this. They looked at the general features of the interstellar gas, scanning at ranges of kiloparsecs and more; they were interested in mapping the great sweep of the galaxy's spiral arms. But here, traveling inside the wafting, drifting clouds, Ignatiev measured the detailed configuration of the interstellar hydrogen and found it beautiful.

He slumped back in his form-fitting desk chair, stunned at the splendor of it all. He thought of the magnificent panoramas he had seen of the cosmic span of the galaxies: loops and whorls of bright shining galaxies, each one containing billions of stars, extending for megaparsecs, out to infinity, long strings of glowing lights surrounding vast bubbles of emptiness. The interstellar gas showed the same delicate complexity, in miniature: loops and whorls, streams and bubbles. It was truly, cosmically beautiful.

"Fractal," he muttered to himself. "The universe is one enormous fractal pattern."

Then the artificial intelligence program intruded on his privacy. "Alexander Alexandrovich, the weekly staff meeting begins in ten minutes."

Weekly staff meeting, Ignatiev grumbled inwardly as he hauled himself up from his desk chair. More like the weekly group therapy session for a gaggle of self-important juvenile delinquents.

He made his way grudgingly through the ship's central passageway to the conference room, located next to the command center. Several other crew members were also heading along the gleaming brushed chrome walls and colorful carpeting of the passageway. They gave Ignatiev cheery, smiling greetings; he nodded or grunted at them.

As chief executive of the crew, Ignatiev took the chair at the head of the polished conference table. The others sauntered in leisurely. Nikki and Gregorian came in almost last and took seats at the end of the table, next to each other, close enough to hold hands.

These meetings were a pure waste of time, Ignatiev thought. Their ostensible purpose was to report on the ship's performance, which any idiot could determine by casting half an eye at the digital readouts available on any display screen in the ship. The screens gave up-to-the-nanosecond details of every component of the ship's equipment.

But no, mission protocol required that all twelve crew members must meet face-to-face once each week. Good psychology, the mission planners believed. An opportunity for human interchange, personal communications. A chance for whining and displays of overblown egos, Ignatiev thought. A chance for these sixty-year-old children to complain about each other.

Of the twelve of them, only Ignatiev and Nikki were physicists. Four of the others were engineers of various stripes, three were biologists, two psychotechnicians, and one stocky, sour-faced woman a medical doctor.

So he was quite surprised when the redheaded young electrical engineer in charge of the ship's power system started the meeting by reporting:

"I don't know if any of you have noticed it yet, but the ship's reduced our internal electrical power consumption by ten percent."

Mild perplexity.

"Ten percent?"

"Why?"

"I haven't noticed any reduction."

The redhead waved his hands vaguely as he replied, "It's mostly in peripheral areas. Your microwave ovens, for example. They've been powered down ten percent. Lights in unoccupied areas. Things like that."

Curious, Ignatiev asked, "Why the reduction?"

His squarish face frowning slightly, the engineer replied, "From what Alice tells me, the density of the gas being scooped in for the generator has decreased slightly. Alice says it's only a temporary condition. Nothing to worry about."

Alice was the nickname these youngsters had given to the artificial intelligence program that actually ran the ship. Artificial Intelligence. AI. Alice Intellectual. Some even called the AI system Alice Imperatress. Ignatiev thought it childish nonsense.

"How long will this go on?" asked one of the biologists. "I'm incubating a batch of genetically engineered alga for an experiment."

"It shouldn't be a problem," the engineer said. Ignatiev thought he looked just the tiniest bit worried.

Surprisingly, Gregorian piped up. "A few of the uncrewed probes that went ahead of us also encountered power anomalies. They were temporary. No big problem."

Ignatiev nodded but made a mental note to check on the situation. Nearly six light-years out from Earth, he thought, meant that every problem was a big one.

One of the psychotechs cleared her throat for attention, then announced, "Several of the crew members have failed to fill out their monthly performance evaluations. I know that some of you regard these evaluations as if they were school exams, but mission protocol—"

Ignatiev tuned her out, knowing that they would bicker over this drivel for half an hour, at least. He was too optimistic. The discussion became quite heated and lasted more than an hour.